"Satan wants your daughter!"

"You must not dismiss this as nonsense, Mrs. Spender," the medium said. "I am not a novice. I have on more than one occasion helped in police investigations. This is different. What I am about to say may sound ridiculous, but it is there in that attic: devil worship, demoniac possession, ritual slaughter and suicide. An elemental is still there, evil and unappeased. Hungering for new victims."

She smoked, frowning, for several seconds. Then, in a more composed manner she went on. "Evil came into this house, innocently invited by a young girl, an artist. It affected what I gather was a hitherto happy family. It destroyed her. It could destroy again. That is why I say, Mrs. Spender, that *your daughter should not come home...*"

Fawcett Crest Books
by Norah Lofts:

BRIDE OF MOAT HOUSE

THE BRITTLE GLASS

THE CONCUBINE

CROWN OF ALOES

ELEANOR THE QUEEN

THE GOLDEN FLEECE

HAUNTINGS

HEAVEN IN YOUR HAND

THE HOMECOMING

THE HOUSE AT OLD VINE

HOW FAR TO BETHLEHEM?

JASSY

THE KING'S PLEASURE

KNIGHT'S ACRE

THE LONELY FURROW

THE LUTE PLAYER

THE LITTLE WAX DOLL

LOVERS ALL UNTRUE

NETHERGATE

OUT OF THE DARK

A ROSE FOR VIRTUE

SCENT OF CLOVES

TO SEE A FINE LADY

THE TOWN HOUSE

WINTER HARVEST

The
Haunting
of
Gad's Hall

Norah Lofts

FAWCETT CREST • NEW YORK

THE HAUNTING OF GAD'S HALL

THIS BOOK CONTAINS THE COMPLETE TEXT OF THE
ORIGINAL HARDCOVER EDITION.

Published by Fawcett Crest Books, a unit of CBS Publications, the
Consumer Publishing Division of CBS Inc., by arrangement with
Doubleday and Company, Inc.

ISBN: 0-449-24272-2

Printed in the United States of America

First Fawcett Crest Printing: March 1980

10 9 8 7 6 5 4 3 2 1

Cast of Major Characters

Mrs Thorley   *Mistress of Gad's Hall*
Mr van Haagen   *A business associate of Mrs Thorley*
Diana Spicer   *Mrs Thorley's daughter*
Everard Spicer   *Diana's husband, a lawyer*
George Thorley   *Mrs Thorley's son*
Deborah Bridges   *Mrs Thorley's stepdaughter*
Tim Bridges   *Deborah's husband*
Sam Bridges   *Their son*
Caroline Taylor   *Mrs Thorley's stepdaughter*
Doctor Edward Taylor   *Caroline's husband*
Freddy Ingram   *Caroline's former beau*
Susan Walford Ingram   *Freddy's wife*
Jenny   *Housekeeper/Cook at Gad's Hall*

Bob Spender   *Present owner of Gad's Hall*
Ella Spender   *His mother*
Jill Spender   *His wife*
John Spender
Tony Spender   *Their children*
Alice Spender

Part
1

Mr van Haagen glanced about the table at Gad's and said benevolently, meaning well,

"It is not often that one has the happiness of seeing so many old faces after so few years."

What he meant was plain; it was only two years since his last visit, and he had not then seen the family together, with so many friends gathered round. Caroline, at the far end of the table, and seated next to Freddy, pulled her mobile, monkeyish face into a mask of extreme age and said, "So now we know!" He laughed; he could always be trusted to see the point. He said, "I'm ordering a wheelchair tomorrow." If she had made the same remark to Edward, her husband for five years—five centuries—he would have looked blank and then said that Mr van Haagen meant well. Nonetheless, it had been a mistake to sit next to Freddy; the mere brush of his sleeve against her arm set all the old hungers flaring. She'd never got over him. Never would.

Mrs Thorley cast a look, doting, but with something dubious, some slight reserve, at her son, in his rightful place at the head of the table. He'd always been a precocious child and physical maturity had come to him with swiftness and ease. At fifteen he was a man. He had inherited his father's height, but he'd never had a gangly, awkward stage, too sinewy for that; and he was handsome; his father's craggy good looks mitigated by her own delicately arched nose and clarity of jaw. A born charmer—and well aware of it. Too well aware of it? Sometimes she wondered had she been wrong not to insist upon his going to school, as once arranged. School was said to knock off the rough edges—but then George had never had any rough edges.

She said, "It was George's idea. When Gad's Glory scored that supreme triumph. George said we must celebrate. And since Diana," with a jerk within a jerk of her head, Mrs Thorley indicated her daughter, "was already here, it seemed a good opportunity."

"Yes, indeed. And for me most fortunate."

He was anxious to please her. Their business association had been most successful. The cross between *her* Durham Shorthorns and *his* Frisians had been a sensation in the cattle world. He had once done her a singular favour—made the rough winter crossing between Holland and Bywater and made wildly extravagant bids for some of her beasts at auction. That was the year when she had done no showing and had therefore dropped back a little. The record price he had paid—or appeared to have paid, put her back in the top class. And she repaid him fourfold. She offered to reimburse him with money, but he had, very sensibly, decided to take stock instead. Since then she had always offered him the first refusal of her best. And now lively young calves of mixed blood were established in Holland, in Germany, in France.

Mr van Haagen allowed himself a tiny, secret sigh. There had been a time, six, seven years ago, when he had seriously contemplated asking Mrs Thorley to marry him. He'd admired her greatly. She was not young, even then, but his first marriage had given him the son every man needed, so he wanted no more children. A good steady woman with a head for business, a trim figure and still pretty face, and the capacity for running a house on oiled wheels would have been just right. But of course no man of any sensitivity would propose, too soon, to a widow. So he had waited and when the time was right, she—to put it bluntly—was not. He'd been shocked when he came over to do her that favour; hair quite white, head jerking, hands tremulous. Aged by twenty years. She had, of course, suffered another bereavement; the loss of a daughter that girl for whom in his half-serious, half-playful fotune-telling in the cards he had seen such disaster, but had only been able to say— Beware of the dark. Actually, in the fumbling uncertain way of the fortune-teller, he had been right. The girl had gone to India, and died, either on the journey or soon after arrival. And her mother's hair had whitened and she'd been taken by a kind of palsy. Nothing much, a jerk of the head, a tremor of the hands; but Mr van Haagen had known then—five years ago— that marriage was out of the question. For one day his nerves, so much more vulnerable than his stolid exterior would suggest, might break down and he would lean across the table and say—*Will you keep your head still!* No longer desirable as partner in bed and board, she was still astute, with him, at least, dead-honest, and still a wonderful provider, with no fuss.

Mrs Thorley had no need to fuss. Jenny was still in the kitchen—her legs, and what ailed them had always been a mystery, obligingly allowing her to do anything she wanted to do, and then drawing a line. They allowed her to cook—and she still did it superbly, but for anything other than cooking help must be enlisted from the village. And no difficulty about *that*. Jenny was related to almost everyone in Stonham St Paul's, and quite a number of people in the next village, Stonham St Peter's. She belonged to a family so intermarried, interrelated, tough, resilient, wide-branched that she could probably have produced, in a crisis, some cousin's cousin or niece from as far away as Nettleton, or Intake, or Muchanger. Two were in action this evening; Violet—not as pretty as her name—who was regular and came up from the village each morning and went back to sleep, and Ruth, older, very pretty who just happened to be home, unemployed at the moment, glad enough to earn two shillings. Recommending her, Jenny had said that Ruth knew all about waiting at table; she'd worked once at the *Hawk in Hand* in Baildon. And certainly this evening the service was going with exceptional smoothness and speed, though, to be honest, Mrs Thorley hadn't taken to Ruth at first sight; there was something pert, something bouncy, more suitable to an inn's public dining room than to a sedate little dinner party in a private house.

Mr van Haagen looked about him again and then turning to his hostess asked anxiously, "Did I say right to say old? Should I be saying well-remembered?"

"That was understood," Mrs Thorley said. "And of course, it must be at least six years since you saw all the girls together. In fact I don't think you have seen Deborah or Caroline since they were married. Diana comes every year and her husband—Everard, you may remember him—usually manages a few days. Unfortunately, this year business took him to Scotland. And Deborah's husband, I don't think you ever met him, he has a very large farm and breeds horses. He finds it difficult to get away."

And wouldn't come if he had all the time in the world! Mrs Thorley had never liked him, virtuous and worthy as he undoubtedly was; Methodist; teetotaler, drinking lemonade at his own wedding! Deborah, that good, capable, most precious girl could well have been overwhelmed, reduced, tamed. But the baby had saved her. Just at the time when one act of defiance—rushing back to Gad's to help succor and sustain, had made Tim Bridges decide that the time had come to tighten the curb, Deborah was pregnant. And Tim knew enough about breeding animals; a gravid female must not be upset; nor a female suckling. And then, just as he was ready to assert himself again, the child weaned, one of his heavy horses had trodden on his foot and broken four bones. So he had been laid up, nursed, cared for most tenderly by Deborah, but the situation which he had once, for a moment visualised, had come about. Deborah had dealt with everything, farm, stables, disabled

12

man in her competent, capable way. He was not much missed.

Mrs Thorley, of course, could not know that Timothy Bridges' God had failed him and that he was taking refuge in a sour disillusionism. She only knew that Deborah now made regular visits, driving a rather-too-frisky horse in the high, yellow-wheeled gig. Bringing the child, a sturdy boy, saying once, in her offhand way, "Of course Tim wanted some Biblical name like Ebenezer. But I stuck out. I agreed on Samuel, it can be Sam and shouldn't cause him any embarrassment."

No doubt about it, Deb had emerged triumphant, but happy?

There were old faces, or faces well- or ill-remembered, missing from this table. Mrs Spicer, the Rector's wife, Everard's Aunt Amelia, and one of Mrs Thorley's oldest friends in this district. She'd gone plodding round, doing her duty, as always, and caught a cold which settled on her chest. Nothing that a boiled onion wouldn't remedy. Even her husband had bestirred himself for once, harried the tatterdemalion maid. Prayed. To no avail. She'd died as quietly as she had lived, and but for the efforts of a few of his parishioners, Mr Spicer could well have followed her to the grave. He was here this evening simply because it had seemed wrong not to invite him, with a good meal ready to be served. . . .

Also missing, and more missed, was Mr Walford. After years of being shackled to the bedside of a vaguely-ailing wife, he was freed by her rather sudden death, and set about making up for lost time, burning the candle at both ends. He still gave his Brewery meticulous attention for Freddy, his son-in-law, knew almost nothing of the technique, though he was splendid on the sales side. Evenings which had been so quiet and so long in the big old house, where the invalid could not bear the slightest noise, now became riotous and all too short; all-male parties often did not break up until one o'clock, two o'clock, with too much

13

eating and drinking. A genial and generous host, a happy and appreciative guest, Mr Walford romped through his last years and was then felled by a fatal stroke.

Perhaps Mr and Mrs Gordon and their son James should not have been present at this festive board, for Gordon and Son had treated Everard abominably, using him—so much better qualified in law than either of them, as a kind of office boy, never increasing his salary or offering the partnership on which he had set his heart; so he'd gone to London in disgust. But to make a feud of it would have been awkward for Mr Gordon was still Mrs Thorley's lawyer and had, on occasion, been helpful to her, sometimes actively and once at least through inertia. And on one of her earliest annual visits home, Diana had said she did not in the least mind meeting the Gordons; she would enjoy showing them how their miserable behaviour to Everard, so far from keeping him down, had set him up. It was both true, and untrue. Everard had joined a big firm, in the City, Upton, Binder and Smith, but a partnership still eluded him and although he earned more, living in London was unbelievably expensive. Diana would scrimp and save all the year in order to appear at Gad's in stylish new dresses; then she had a baby to show, a most exquisite little girl, and Diana knew how ardently Mrs Gordon longed for James to settle down and give her grandchildren. This year, also she had a triumph to report. No, Everard would not be coming to Gad's this year, he'd gone to Scotland on *most* important business; something to do with the administration of the Lumsley estate. He was, at this minute, staying in Lumsleydale Castle. A shrewd knock that, for when the Gordons had sent Everard on errands which involved an overnight stay he'd only had second-class hotel accommodation. Mr Gordon looked suitably impressed. But at the back of his mind something stirred; Lumsley? Lumsley? Ah, yes, a rather shady business, illegitimacy somehow involved. Nothing he'd wish to handle.

There was a new face at the table. Doctor Raven, pleasant, young, shy. Not so long ago, Mrs Thorley could remember, there'd only been old Doctor Taylor and then presently, his son, Edward. But the Hospital had grown, so that by the time Caroline married Edward—and old Doctor Taylor retired—it could afford a resident doctor. And then, thanks to Caroline's innovations, a roundabout and coconut shies and competitions, instead of the usual fund-raising methods, the Hospital could afford half another doctor. Residents came and went, but Doctor Raven seemed permanent. Half his time was his own and he had a little surgery at the upper end of Scurvy Lane. Edward was invariably kind to the newcomers, partly because he was fundamentally kind, and partly because he had himself been so lucky; he'd never had to take a paid post, or set up on his own, he'd just slipped into his father's practice. Caroline was kind to them, too. One might almost say motherly—a strange thing to say of Caroline, the least motherly of creatures. But the truth was that Caroline could assume almost any role as the fancy took her. She'd been such a flirt. And then so infatuated, so positively ill-behaved with Freddy Ingram. But he'd married Susan Walford, and after some days of crying—and a little good advice from Mrs Thorley, she'd married Edward, settled down, and never since put a foot wrong. But no child yet!

Mr van Haagen, eating ruminatively, not unlike one of his own placid animals, vaguely remembered an evening in this house when, because he could neither play the piano nor sing, and a guest should do something in return for hospitality, he had offered to read the cards for the ladies. He had exercised his art scores of times since and naturally could not remember much detail, but now, confronted with four of the five girls whose fortunes he had told that evening, certain things came back. He'd seen Miss Diana living in a big city—and she was now resident in London. Horses had loomed large in Miss Deborah's future, and behold, she had married a famous breeder of horses. For Miss Caroline he had foreseen floods and floods of tears and then a multitude of good works. His eye lingered on her as he wondered whether the tears had been shed and forgotten, or whether they were still to come. She looked merry enough now. Of them all, he thought, marriage had changed her least, and of them all she was now the most stylish, her hair looked positively French, drawn up to the top of her head and then cascading in curls to the nape of her neck—a fashion said to have been introduced by the Empress Eugénie. The shift of the curls lent something coquettish as she turned her head, speaking now to Mr Ingram, now the poor old parson who seemed to be taking his widowhood more heavily than Mr van Haagen had taken his. Diana and Deborah had stuck to the demure style which had prevailed when they first put their hair up, parted in the middle, looped smoothly over the ears and then gathered into a kind of bun. The only difference was that Diana's was smooth, carved in ebony, and Deborah's was red and unruly, a curl kept breaking away to be pushed back impatiently.

Upon the fourth girl, Miss Walford then, now Mrs Ingram, Mr van Haagen's eye lingered for a moment. Not in approbation. Six or was it seven years ago . . . such a dull, quiet, dim . . . And yet the cards had said a courtship of the whirlwind. And that was true, too. In fact the cards never lied, and reading the future in them was not magic or psychic, or any of the other things which gushing ladies said; properly handled, as his grandmother had taught him, it was an exact science.

But it was not because Susan Walford had made the whirlwind marriage, as predicted, that his eye lingered. An expert, used-to-dealing-with-animals eye. Possibly those who saw her often didn't notice, but to Mr van Haagen she looked very ill. The hair on a human, like the hide of an animal, was the surest sign of health, or ill health. And Mrs Ingram's hair looked scanty, dry, without lustre. Any animal with such a stary coat . . .

Susan—once she had been Poor Susan because she also was shackled to her mother, and then she had been regarded as fortunate, marrying Freddy, so handsome and popular, sat there and asked herself—Shall I be able to see

16

this through? So lovely, Di and Deb and Caro and I all together, I must. I must.

She could not remember when the pain first started, a silly little, niggling little, something-to-be-ignored stitch in her side. She couldn't even place it; now it was behind her ribs, and the next minute lower down. She was determined, absolutely determined not to mention it, not to be like her mother, always ailing, always demanding attention and company, a nuisance to everybody. Not me! I will not repeat that deadly pattern.

Hadn't there been a boy, somewhere far away and in a time long ago who had stood up and smiled with a fox, or was it a wolf? gnawing his vitals away? In Sparta? Very well, she would be Spartan. But sensible, too. One day, saying nothing to Papa, then alive and happy, or to Freddy, she'd driven herself into Baildon and consulted Edward, Caroline's husband. All terribly embarrassing. And futile. Edward had prodded; Does this hurt? Now if I press, do you feel anything? Or here? Here? Susan could truthfully say, No, because the pain was not to be located—and because Edward often sat at Mr Walford's overladen table, he surmised that it could be indigestion. (Susan had not then begun to look ill; in fact looked better than she had ever done in his knowledge of her.) He gave her some sound advice about diet, about tight lacing and about taking exercise—though not immediately after a meal. He made her up a bottle of bismuth mixture. He then suggested that she should go through and see Caroline. Before their respective marriages the two girls had been great friends, gay Caroline and Poor Susan. One of the things Edward admired about Caroline was that she was so tender-hearted.

"Thank you, Edward," Susan said, "but I don't want anyone to know about this," she pressed her hand to her side. "In fact you are the only person I've ever said a word to." It would have been disloyal to Mamma to explain why.

Next time Edward saw her—it was at a dance—she looked, and felt, thinner. Overdoing it? Women had no sense of proportion! Tell them not to overeat and they'd

17

go on a starvation diet; suggest reasonable exercise and they'd walk ten miles. It was perhaps not etiquette to mix professional with social activities, but he mentioned her loss of weight and said he hoped she wasn't cutting down too drastically. She said: Oh no. Twice during that evening Edward caught sight of her, left hand pressing her side, and he made an opportunity to ask about the pain.

"Oh, better, thank you. It just comes and goes."

Edward was troubled.

The resident doctor at the Hospital at that moment was regarded as a brilliant young man, far too good for the post really, just marking time in Baildon until his father's partner retired—a crusty, pig-headed old man, impossible to work with. And of course the young man was only just qualified; Edward was conscious of the fact that his own finals were now eleven years' distant. Carefully concealing the patient's identity, Edward asked Doctor Watts' opinion. The young man was both flattered and embarrassed, for he admired Edward profoundly and knew how very thorough he was.

"It is very difficult to say without seeing her, and even then, if *you* found nothing wrong . . ."

"Nothing; heart, lungs, sound as a bell, stomach, bowels, uterus."

"An unlocated, intermittent pain. Of course," the young man said, advancing a pretty revolutionary theory, "it could be of nervous origin. Nervous headaches are now recognised."

Roughly, nervous meant nothing wrong functionally; in fact largely a thing of the imagination. But in that area Edward was very sensitive; he and his father had differed over Mrs Walford, the older man cossetting and sympathetic, Edward brisk, saying that if she abandoned bed and sofa and the role of invalid and lived a normal life she'd be all right. And then, quite unaccountably, Mrs Walford had just died. Such a thing made one a bit extra careful.

"Would you examine her?"

"Most willingly."

Nothing detectable; and the woman did not strike Doctor Watts as being the *maladie imaginaire* type; not self-asser-

18

tive, not melancholic. A sensible, apparently happy young woman and inclined to make light of the pain. Still, another opinion might be desirable. Doctor Watts knew of a man, in Wimpole Street. A wonderful reputation. . . .

Getting Susan to London was less difficult than Edward had imagined. Both her father and Freddy were indulgent and thought that a day's shopping would do her good. And she would not be obliged to make the now-possible day trip by train alone because she had chosen a day when Edward Taylor had business in London.

Nothing; no explanation, no help, even from Wimpole Street.

The pain did not exist, except for her, its host, its victim.

Then her father died with dreadful suddenness and that was enough to explain further loss of weight, and pallor, and anyway everybody looked horrible in dead mourning.

Susan had a brother, Richard. Between them had been the link of shared adversity—the invalid mother who could not be left, even with the most reliable of hirelings. Richard had been more fortunate than Susan, he had gone away to school, and he spent some time getting experience in a big brewery in Burton-on-Trent. Then he'd come home and fallen in love with Diana, who had fallen in love with Everard Spicer. Richard had made some excuse to go back to Burton-on-Trent and there settled, but not married.

Could there perhaps ultimately be no heir to the Brewery; to the big, comfortable old house?

I shall have no child; nothing could live with this pain. I'm beginning to doubt if I can, myself, much longer. Give up; ask Edward for some opiate drops and swallow the whole lot in one go. . . . What, then, of Freddy? Oh he'd be all right. He'd do the decent thing and wait a year, then remarry. Not Caroline, for she was married. There had been a time when Susan had been dismally sure that Freddy would marry Caroline; they'd got themselves talked about. Susan had been the most surprised, most dizzily delighted girl in the world when Freddy had chosen her instead. Caroline had showed no sign of minding. In no time at all she'd been engaged to Edward, and ever after the life and

19

soul, the centre of gaiety at every gathering at which she was present.

Surely this was the longest dinner party in history. How much longer could it go on? Nothing cured the pain, but sometimes a change of position mitigated it a little. Please, Mrs Thorley, dear Mrs Thorley, rise, lead the movement towards the drawing room. And please, Di, please Deb, don't suggest that we should just steal up and peep at the children, three of them now, Di's two—a most beautiful little girl, rightly called Belle, three years old; a boy not quite so engaging yet, named Melville, and best, most enviable of all, Deborah's boy, Sam; four years old and by all accounts very naughty. . . .

Once, coming downstairs after a dutiful inspection, only two of them then, Sam and Belle, angelic in Sleep, Susan had said to Caroline, "Don't you sometimes wish . . .?" And Caroline had said vehemently,

"No I do not! I see quite enough of children, what with the Hospital and the Ragged School and the various treats. And between you and me, that Sam is a devil. He'll lead poor Deb a pretty dance before he's done."

Caroline's refusal to be wistful, sentimental, yearning, had been slight comfort to Susan just then. A part explanation, too, of her charm. All things to all men; look at her now, turning one face to Freddy and quite another to Mr Spicer. It was a gift. Caroline was quite hollow, like a bell, responding to every pull of the rope. Less popular with women. Women seemed to see a little further; and if, presently they all went up to look at the children, three now, mothers, she'd say: Oh, how lucky you are. Or: How I envy you.

Mrs Thorley's thoughts centred now and again about the three grandchildren, small occupants of a great deal of space. It did indeed seem ridiculous that a house so spacious—comparatively spacious, as Gad's should suddenly seem so congested.

"Oh, for God's sake, Mamma, let's have *somebody*

young," George said when the party was under discussion. A reasonable request. "Whom would you like?"

"The Faulkner twins," George said with revealing promptitude.

Consternation struck Mrs Thorley from varying tangents. Calf love. Part of growing up, and quite usual in boys far less mature than George; she was prepared to be tolerant of it; but she didn't want George to invite a snub. The Faulkners were very definitely County and Mrs Thorley was extremely class-conscious. County herself to begin with in Westmorland; married to a man of her own class, but a wastrel, a gambler who'd squandered her quite considerable dowry and dragged her down to the lowest depths. After he shot himself, positively the only alternative to gaol for debt, she'd known that worst kind of poverty— genteel; lost in Leicester, too proud to seek further help either from her own family or her husband's, making a very precarious living for herself and Diana and Lavinia. Then she had married George Thorley of Gad's Hall in Suffolk and become a member of another class—middle, solid respectable. All splendid chaps, as her father often said; acceptable in the hunting field—it was often their land that was ridden over; acceptable in Local Yeomanry units—they invariably had good horses. *But one did not invite them to dinner*. The real hallmark of social acceptance. Mrs Thorley, in all her years in Suffolk, had been careful, from a kind of inverted pride, had never once referred to her origins, or those of her first husband. She was a widow, with two little girls, who'd married George Thorley, with his two little girls, Deborah and Caroline, and once she had edged out the more bucolic of George's friends and captured what might be called the professional class—still middle, but better-educated, she was content. Then, in a way, when having paid her debt to George Thorley for rescuing her from Leicester by bearing George, and was widowed again, she had broken the rigid mould by going to business—a woman on her own and a match for any man.

In George, son of a late marriage and so much indulged

that behind his wish to please, his capacity to be charming, a boundless self-confidence lay. A trap to the unwary, Mrs Thorley said,

"I doubt whether Lady Faulkner would allow Chloe to come to an evening party with no other chaperone than her brother."

I never did. I was always most careful. Lenient; young men were always welcome here. But I spoke very strictly to Caroline about riding, unaccompanied, in Freddy Ingram's gig. We have our standards too!

"She would. If I asked," George said. "Lady Faulkner likes me, so does Sir John. And so they should. I saved Jonathan's life, don't forget."

It was true. On George's first day out with the South Suffolk. Hounds in full cry; everybody else too much absorbed in the chase to realise that the Faulkner boy had come to grief at a hedge with a deep ditch on the other side. George, a novice, but coached by Deborah, who had hunted for four years and who said: Don't go for the broken-down hedge, it always means heavy going on the far side. Choose your own place. I always do, and I more than make up lost time. George, choosing his own bit of the hedge, his own unslippery landing beyond, had spotted Jonathan—somebody not known to him then, just somebody who looked young at the Meet, and therefore seemed to justify George's presence. Now, face down in a narrow but deep ditch, he looked very dead indeed. George, having dismounted and hauled the boy out, hoped somebody would notice, come to his aid, know what to do. Nobody did. The hunt swept by. Well, get the water out of him. If he could. Whack, whack, whack! And if he's hurt, not merely half drowned, I'm making things worse. The water came out in spurts, followed by the remains of the boy's breakfast. And air went in, little gasps.

"Are you all right?"

"All in one piece, anyway. That bloody nag!"

"Those bloody people!"

They grinned at one another; conspirators against a world where neither horses nor people were quite up to the mark.

"What you need now is a good dose of brandy. I wonder . . ." George looked about him. Not a house in sight, and to him pretty unknown territory; the wrong side of Layer Wood. Just then a lumbering old man on a lumbering old horse, bringing up the rear, lumbered through the damaged fence and landed safely. Geroge ran forward. Urgent, but mannerly,

"Sir. Do you happen to have a flask about you?"

"Somebody taken a toss?" the old man asked, gladly reining in. His hunting days were over; he only turned out these days just to give countenance and to indulge Old Charlie, once the best leaper in the county and still an addict, inclined to run up and down his meadow and make woeful noises if he heard the hounds.

"Never move without it." Lord Norton produced a silver-topped flask. "Serious?" God send it might not be, for if it were serious he would be compelled to get down, and these days it took a good strong heave from a good strong man to get him into the saddle at all.

"No," George said, "he's all in one piece. Thank you."

Sign of the times, Lord Norton thought, with the petulance of the old; they come out younger and younger! We shall end with babies in basket saddles! But he was not averse to a pause, an interruption, a cast-iron excuse for not being in at the kill. And Old Charlie, after a first spirited start, was feeling his years, too. Thinking of what he would say—I had to stop to succour the wounded—he wheeled Old Charlie round, saw one boy ministering to the other. Recognised the other, one of his many grandnephews. Or godsons. He muddled them a bit these days.

"Good God! Johnny Faulkner?"

"Yes, sir."

And nothing to be proud of, distant as the relationship might be. Soaked, muddied and green-gilled. And the other boy—older of course, but nevertheless very young, so neat, competent and in control, screwing back the silver top of the flask.

"And who're you?"

"George Thorley."

23

"Gad's?"

"Yes."

"Remarkable woman, your mother."

"Yes, sir, she is."

Two boys and only one horse. The one standing there, waiting, meek as a lamb, was obviously a Thoroughgood, from Nettleton. It was said that the family of Thoroughgood had been breeding horses there since the Middle Ages, starting with a couple of Arabs somebody brought back from the Crusades. This one was perhaps not a prime specimen, but even so its price would be more than John Faulkner could afford. Ergo it must be young Thorley's. Well, well, well! That's where the money was, these days. Business! Venting an unacknowledged flash of discontent upon an innocent victim, his lordship looked sternly at Johnny and said, "Where's *your* horse?"

"I don't know, sir. It ran off."

"Shocking! Did nobody ever tell you? First rule after a fall. Catch your horse. Horse without a rider, danger to everybody."

"But, sir, Uncle Roger, I was in the ditch, face down."

Unplacated, the old man said, "No excuse. No excuse at all."

"Excuse me, sir, it is. He was unconscious. He'd have died if I . . ."

Lord Norton muttered something that sounded very much like: Pity you bothered! "I'll have my flask back, if you've *quite* finished."

"I see what you mean about bloody people. And he's about the bloodiest. And I'll bet you a sovereign that as soon as he's within earshot of anybody, he'll say he saved my life. Well, I shall tell them different."

"You ought to get into some dry clothes. D'you know where we are?"

"I'm a bit off beat myself. But we did cross a road back there. I'll get a lift. Look here, I've spoiled your day quite enough. You go on."

"And end up behind your uncle! No, thanks! I tell you what. You take my horse and I'll get a lift. You'll be home

24

and dry quicker that way. Come on, Goldie. That's his name. He's very tender-mouthed, you won't jag him, will you?" One couldn't have implicit faith in a boy who'd come a cropper at such a simple fence. "Where do you live?"

"Stratton Strawless."

Not very near; never mind. "I'll drive over tomorrow and fetch him. D'you know, he doesn't even have to be tied. He'll follow a gig, like a dog."

"You're a lucky chap. I'll tell you what. Come to lunch tomorrow.

Lady Faulkner's reaction when she heard of the misadventure was very different from that of her uncle. Jonathan was her only son. Three girls and hope almost abandoned. Even of the twins Chloe was born first. Four! The name Jonathan meant *God-given*, and so he was. She never called him anything else, though to most people he was Johnny. She was delighted that George Thorley had been asked to lunch, so that she could thank him personally and perhaps make him a small present.

Sir John said: "Any boy who owns a Thoroughgood at his age doesn't need anything *you* could give him, my poor dear."

"It's the spirit of the thing that counts," Lady Faulkner said vaguely.

And of course, to one prepared for a farm boy—splendid, kind and thoughtful though he might be—George Thorley with his poise and beautiful manners was a complete surprise.

So had begun a resilient if interrupted friendship between the two boys. Johnny was at Eton and had other friends, and many relatives with whom he spent part of the holidays, but whenever he was at home he and George met, and George had been invited to two parties; one at Christmas, one to celebrate the twins' sixteenth birthday. It was, Lady Faulkner reflected with sorrow, about the only debut poor Chloe would make—unless some wealthy relative came to the rescue. But who? Of Lord Norton one naturally expected nothing.

It was at the birthday dance that George Thorley fell in

love with Chloe, whom Nature had endowed with every quality to make her suitable for a first love. Her flaxen hair fell in curls, rather like a spaniel's ears on either side of a heart-shaped face, her eyes were smoky blue and set too wide apart, her mouth had the pursed, petulant shape known as rosebud. She also had the desirable trait of being completely stupid. No Faulkner was overweighted with intelligence, but as was commonly understood to be the case with twins, the wits of a normal child had been divided between the two, Jonathan getting the lion's share. Chloe's mental blankness gave her the approved innocent look, and given half a chance she should have made a good match. But unless her father decided—as he was highly unlikely to do—to sell some land, Chloe would have no chance, she'd probably marry the young Stanton boy and join all the other land-rich, money-poor, family-proud people of whom there were too many in Suffolk.

When George suggested inviting the Faulkner twins and Mrs Thorley had made her protest about the unlikelihood of Chloe being allowed to come, and been answered, she said,

"And if Chloe came, my dear, it would raise a problem. Mr van Haagen is always a little vague about dates, but suppose his visit did coincide with the party. We have only the one guest room."

That would of course be for Chloe Faulkner. Deborah would stay the night; she and Di would share the room they had always shared; the room once shared by Caroline and Lavinia would be given over to the children. What was known as the Little Room, perfect for one guest, had long been occupied by Jenny and it would be impossible to usurp her now, even for the one or two nights.

"We'll take that fence when we come to it," George said. "Just write and invite them. *Both*."

Quite a long time ago Deborah's husband, Timothy Bridges, had seen in George the spoilt only son, an incipient dictator. Once when George had been under his roof at

Foxton, he had done his conscientious best to correct, reprove, admonish, reduce, but what could a man do in a mere ten days?

Mrs Thorley wrote; well aware of the difference between letting a boy come for a day's shooting, or to stay for a night before, or after a Hunt on this side of Layer Wood, and letting a daughter attend an evening party, stay a night. Mrs Thorley knew her world; she knew what the answer would be; glad acceptance on Johnny's part, civil regret, a previous engagement would prevent Chloe. That would be all right. Johnny could share George's room; the guest room would be free for Mr van Haagen.

She was reckoning without something which the Faulkner twins had shared more equally than they had shared their wits—a complete—and eventually ruinous—devotion to one another, and a deadly sullen obstinacy. Jonathan could not, or would not see why Chloe should miss a party. Chloe could not or would not see why she should miss one hour of Jonathan's company. Jonathan said stormily,

"You may have forgotten; I haven't. But for George I should have died in that ditch and never gone to a party again. Except, of course my funeral!"

Chloe shed a few tears and said she couldn't see why if Johnny could go to Gad's, she couldn't.

Lady Faulkner thought of the accident, of George Thorley's prompt and effective action. Suppose, just suppose, George had looked down and thought: He is not a farmer; one of us; let him drown. . . . Class was important, but there were times . . .

"They're both coming."

"What did I tell you? And I have been thinking. If Mr van Haagen should happen to arrive just then, he could go upstairs. In the other attic. Or of course he could share my bed with Johnny, and I'd go up. But I think he'd prefer a room to himself, don't you. He's a bit old, and Johnny snores like the devil. I did think," George said, in his curiously mature way, "about Johnny and me going up, but it's such a small bed and we couldn't get a bigger one round that bend. And I think the attic could be made quite comfortable."

No real reason why is should not be. The window which Deborah had, in a desperate moment, most ingeniously knocked out had been replaced long ago. The narrow bed was comfortable—Mrs Thorley had always treated her servants well.

"Leave it to me," George said.

Like every house of its period and above poverty level, Gad's was overfurnished and had things in reserve. No provident housewife waited until a lamp, for instance, was broken and an emergency created; she had one in store. George went about like a light-hearted magpie, taking from this room and that everything he considered necessary to make the attic so comfortable that it would make up to Mr van Haagen for having to climb an extra flight of stairs, steep and twisted. The room that yielded most was the one in which the children slept. It couldn't possibly matter to Sam, aged four, Belle aged three and a half, or Melville, still in a cot, whether their washstand was mahogany, furnished with flower-painted crockery, or deal with plain white such as had served Jenny when the attic was hers. Helped by Violet—only too glad to get away from Jenny's sharp eye and strict tongue, George converted the attic into a very snug and cosy room with only its sloping roof and dormer window to show that it was, in fact, an attic. Unconsciously, George was exercising his innate ability to set a scene, and having done so he wished it to be admired. He invited Mamma to do so.

It was five years but for a month since Mrs Thorley had set foot even on the attic stairs and now she said with what George considered a regrettable lack of interest;

"I haven't time now, dear. I'm sure you have made it very nice."

He invited Diana, who at least accepted, and made nothing of the stairs. In London she lived in a horrid, most inconvenient house, built narrow and high, three floors and a basement. She looked round, observant, not very appreciative. So that's where the proper washstand went! And the quilted bed-cover. But she said, "Yes, very nice. Actually, though, the other attic is much larger."

"Didn't you know? Mamma and I agreed to keep that one locked. Always. A kind of memorial to Lavinia."

Diana's memory of that terrible, shocking, disgusting time had blurred, been silted over by her own problems. . . .

"I see," she said, and backed on to the landing and looked at the padlocked door, and was, for some unknown reason, filled with a sense of desolation. She still loved Everard; in that more fortunate than Caroline, who loved Edward so little that she had found her honeymoon boring, and unlike Deborah, who had loved Timothy, gone all Methodist, worn a print dress, worked, lived like a servant—and then suddenly rebelled. Diana loved Everard, but here on the attic landing she was conscious of a loss of faith in him. Not in him. She corrected herself quickly. In the world, where rewards were so unfair, so absolutely unpredictable. And at the same time Diana suffered a pang of self-distrust, completely alien to her; Everard might have done better if he had not married me; he could have chosen a girl with money, or influence in the right quarters. . . .

She was not prone to entertaining self-derogatory thoughts and quickly dismissed this one.

It was as well that a place was prepared for Mr van Haagen, for on the very morning of the party, there was the letter. Unless delayed by wind and weather, the cross Channel boat should be in Bywater at eight o'clock in the morning, and—since there was now a railway link between Baildon and the port, he would be in Bywater at eleven. "We must have much discussion, Madam."

Mrs Thorley said, "I think I'd better meet him. I'll pick up the fish, meet the train, and then take him to lunch at the *Hawk in Hand*. That will relieve Jenny, she has enough to do making ready for this evening. And we can have our much discussions over lunch. Diana, dear, will you see to the flowers? Deborah said she'd be here at about four."

Once upon a time—and in years actually not so long ago—the *Hawk in Hand*, like the Corn Exchange and the

Cattle Market, had been all-male territory, one of those citadels which Mrs Thorley had stormed. The inn made, had always made, some provision for women—they travelled too, by coach at one time, more lately by train, but they ate in semi-private rooms. There was also, at the back, overlooking the yard and stables a place where women could await their husbands on market days. They could even drink tea while they waited. But the dining room, overlooking the Market Place, had been strictly a man's place until one drowsy, rather short-staffed midday. The inn was always inadequately staffed in mid-summer. There was so much alternative employment; casual, and overpaid; pea- and fruit-picking, helping with the harvest on family farms, rushing down to Bywater to man the bathing machines, the new hostelry which called itself a hotel. Mrs Thorley, still in her widow's black then, had arrived with three men and somebody with more taste than tact had suggested segregation. The two-shilling ordinary was about to be served in the big dining room . . . perhaps the gentlemen would like to go there and talk business and perhaps the lady would like to come this way.

Deceptively ladylike, in voice, in manner, Mrs Thorley said, "But it is *my* business we propose to talk about. Ah, that corner table; just right for four."

When, years later, Lord Norton had said to George by that muddy ditch, "Remarkable woman, your mother," he had not been exaggerating. She was remarkable; she had taken what for her husband had been an expensive hobby and turned it into a profitable business. The herd, at one time subsidised by the ordinary farm, was now the subsidiser. Ordinary agriculture was in rather a poor way.

Mrs Thorley was so well-known now, so accepted in the man's world that nobody thought about it any more. She would meet Mr van Haagen, take him to lunch at the *Hawk in Hand,* pay the bill and not cause an eyelid to flicker. There had never been the slightest smear upon her reputation; devoting herself to a business as she had done— except for a little time which those with good memories recalled, when she seemed to be beaten, hadn't entered a beast for any show, or been seen herself for a time—she had married all her girls well. And when you came to think of it, it was proof of her good management that all four girls—her two, George Thorley's two—had been treated so equitably that nobody could distinguish between them. Not even her enemies, and she had some, had even found a harsher term than "unwomanly" to throw at her; she was known as a hard bargainer, but known also for her absolute integrity.

Diana derived a bitter-sweet pleasure from seeing to the flowers. Nothing grew in the narrow, sunless strip of garden behind the dismal London house, and bought flowers had very short lives. Here there was plenitude, she could be lavish.

George cut flowers, too, but furtively. A bowlful of pink roses just in the best, half-open stage, to liven up the guest room where Chloe would sleep tonight. Trying it, in this position and that—on the dressing-table, the top of the chest of drawers, the bedside table, he was temporarily in the grip of a passion—recognised by his mother as calf love—which was capable of overruling all the elements, lurking, incipient, in his nature. He was conceited, self-assured, egoistic, exhibitionist, arrogant, cynical, ruthless: but, prowling about the guest room, he was just a simple boy, bringing an offering to the shrine of a goddess.

Sex as sex—and he knew all about it—had nothing to do with his feeling for Chloe Faulkner. It would have been unthinkable, revolting. All he wanted was to adore—and to please, to pay tribute.

Presently Deborah arrived, with Sam, and she and Diana, who had not met for a year, immediately started, over tea, child-talk, comparing ages, weight, teeth and of course Deborah must spend some time admiring the new baby. It was quite a while before George could decently say, "Deb, come and see what I have made of the attic."

Deborah seemed to start. *"What attic?"*

"The one I have made ready for Mr van Haagen. Next

to the locked one. You remember?"

I remember and nothing, nothing, wild horses would not induce me to go near that place again.

"I didn't know," Deb said, "that Mr van Haagen was expected. . . . Should I not have said I'd stay overnight? I don't mind driving in the dark and Sam is quite good when he's asleep."

Di said, "That wouldn't help much. Mr van Haagen couldn't very well share a bed with me, could he?"

George, watching and listening, had an odd thought: Now if Caro had said that it would have had a different flavour. A joke, with a kind of challenge in it. Said by Diana it was a plain statement.

"Dear George," Deborah said, "I don't suppose that the attic needs my approval. Sam stop it! I will not have you be so rough."

It was a pity, but it was a fact that almost since the two children—called cousins though they had no blood kinship, Deborah being a Thorley and Diana an Osborne—could crawl, there'd been a kind of antagonism. Deb's Sam was older and bigger, but Di's Belle was vicious; she bit. And because of something which had happened in the past, seeing one human being, however young, biting another, however aggressive, made Deborah feel just slightly sick.

Almost as soon as the two children had been separated, Mrs Thorley and Mr van Haagen arrived. They'd spent the afternoon down at Park Farm, where the herd was housed. And they had perfected their next move in the five-year-game of tit-for-tat. Her idea; you couldn't really call it dishonest, just a little tricky, but extremely profitable.

Coming in with her fellow-conspirator, Mrs Thorley said, "Deb, my dear," with some feeling. No amount of time could blur her awareness of what she owed to her stepdaughter. Then she felt the teapot, poured a cup for Mr van Haagen, and one for herself, cast an unmaternal glance upon Sam who was a ruffian, and upon Belle who was a vixen, cooed over Melville, noting that the week he had already spent in the country had improved his colour. Mr van Haagen, who had eaten a hearty lunch and knew that a good dinner awaited him, made a substantial tea, saying as he took his second slice of Victorian sponge,

"I am too much eating, is it not? I am gross." He eyed his paunch with a mixture of concern and complacency. Deborah, with her lopsided smile, said,

"Shakespeare believed that well-fleshed men were the most trustworthy."

"Indeed so? The great Shakespeare?" Of formal education Mr van Haagen had none but he had somehow picked up a working knowledge of what and whom it was correct to admire. Obligingly, Deborah gave him the full quotation and he said, with delight, that he slept well, too.

The children resumed their running battle and were removed, a romp in the garden to tire them a bit, a good wash and into their sleeping attire, and the ruffian and the vixen would lie down peacefully together in the big bed, looking like angels.

"I'll leave you, George, to show Mr van Haagen to his room."

She slipped away to lie down on her bed; she had never fully recovered the energy and resilience which had been hers before the catastrophe, and the involuntary jerks, the tremors were tiring.

Carrying Mr van Haagen's bag, George led the way, past the guest room which on former visits he had occupied and on to the foot of the attic stairs. Treating the matter as lightly as he hoped Mr van Haagen would do, he explained the position. Without apologising for it. Apologies were all very well in their place, but when uncalled for were apt to give the wrong impression.

"To me," Mr van Haagen said, "where I sleep is of no importance. I can sleep anywhere. On a cattle boat. In a cowshed." He'd had a hard youth, quite unlike that of the boy now with him, privileged from the first and with a thriving business awaiting him.

"It is only the stairs," George said, "I'm afraid, sir, you'll find them a trifle steep."

"To me also steep is not an impediment." To prove it he

took the stairs rather too nimbly and arrived on the attic landing slightly out of breath. I am too gross, he thought to himself; after this evening I must eat less. "Ah," he said, entering the room which George had aimed to make not only comfortable, but pleasing to the eye. "Very nice."

"And the view is wonderful. From up here you can see five church towers."

George went to the window and cast a look which he did not know was fond and yearning, to the West; towards Stratton Strawless. Somewhere, on a road between the trees, screened from him by the great sprawling mass of Layer Wood, Chloe—and Johnny, of course—would be making their way. He gave a sigh of sheer bliss.

Bliss was intensified when, some time later, Chloe appeared in the drawing room with one of his roses, cut short and pinned to the bodice of her white muslin frock. He thought it a high compliment and could not be expected to know that Chloe had added the rose because she hated the white muslin so much; it was a school-girl's dress. She had a better one, the blue taffeta she had worn at her birthday party, much lower at the neck, much fuller in the skirt, but Lady Faulkner had decreed that it was altogether unsuitable—as well as being very difficult to pack. "You are not going to a ball, my dear. It would be in the worst of taste to appear overdressed."

George could not, of course, have Chloe seated, as he would have have wished, beside him at the table. All must be correct, and married women took precedence. Still his time would come. Afterwards there would be dancing. All that was needed to bring that about was a word to Caro: Let's dance; a word to Deb: Play a merry tune. For so small a company the hall was big enough and its black and white floor perfect. The old people could play cards or just sit.

That happy dream, Chloe's hand in his , reared up, rose-coloured, and then crashed in grey ruin.

Mamma rose and made for the door. George opened it, and as she passed she murmured, "*One* glass, darling, for you and Johnny," meaning the port wine. A quite unnecessary warning for George grudged the time it would take him to drink one, and sit, being amiable while his elders drank two. But this little pause in the evening was essential; it gave the ladies time to do what was known as titivate. Gentlemen, having drunk their port, drifted out, if they wanted to, to a convenient bush. The decanter had barely completed its first circuit when the door opened and there was Caroline, white-faced.

"Edward, will you come?"

Edward, calm, schooled to face emergencies, rose, quickly, but without haste, and as he walked to the door asked, "What is it?"

"Susan," Caroline said. She burst into tears, ran to Freddy, who was in the act of rising, and clutched at him. "Oh, Freddy . . . It's Susan. She's . . . she's . . . It's dreadful." Freddy steadied her. Arm around waist, drawing her to the doorway, saying something about a faint. Doctor Raven was on his feet too, professional and cool, well aware that where Edward Taylor was, he was of only secondary importance; thinking about the silly way women had of tight-lacing—in which case just cutting the stay-laces sufficed; thinking of other things, too, such as heart attacks.

"I'll go," he said, briskly authoritative, "but the fewer people crowding round the better."

"I am thinking from the first," Mr van Haagen said, "that she is an ill woman."

Very soon, Poor Susan was not only ill, but dead. Whatever it was that had gnawed at her had reached this evening some vital spot. She had collapsed in pain, too searing and violent to be concealed any longer, but she died in peace, in a morphia-induced coma; fortunate, insofar as one could use the word, in having two doctors in attendance.

Chloe Faulkner went—quite understandably—into a kind of hysteria. "Like a trap," she said, again and again. "She was just beside me and she fell over and screamed, just like something in a trap. Johnny, Johnny, you don't know how terrible it was. Like a trap. She was just beside me and . . ."

It was to her brother that she turned and he tried to explain, to excuse, saying that Chloe was very sensitive, poor darling, she'd never seen anything like this, the best thing to do was to get her to bed. He did not say, and to give him his due, he did not even think that such things did not happen in well-regulated households. But the implication hung in the air.

Mr van Haagen said, "For me, I am blaming the husband. With any sense of his head he should have known. The skeleton at the feast. Is that correct? She did not die in one evening, poor woman. By degrees rather and he should know. If not, who? I am saying of what I know. I have for some, many years, a wife not in good health. Of her I am very careful. Always."

Having delivered himself of this fair judgment, Mr van Haagen took himself to bed, and for what happened next he could not blame anything or anybody. And he certainly was not drunk. Before dinner two small glasses of sherry, two glasses of wine at table, one glass of port wine, interrupted. To a man of his size and experience in hard drinking, nothing at all. Nor could he claim to have suffered a shock. It was sad, of course, that death should come, so suddenly, to one so young, but the poor woman was marked for death. Years ago, he remembered, in the cards; in the cards. For Miss Walford a whirlwind courtship, marriage soon, and then nothing. No children. Her destiny was written and he had read it; but he still blamed her husband. No amount of care and precaution could have kept the poor woman alive, but she could have died, privately, in her own home, her own bed. Thus thinking, Mr van Haagen brushed his teeth, undressed, wound his watch and got into bed. To a man who led a busy life, an early night was always welcome.

The guests had all departed, practically silent. Caroline had suggested that Freddy might like to stay at Gad's, he could rest on the settle in the living room. Or he could spend the night with her and Edward in Baildon, and if necessary Edward would give him a sedative. Freddy refused both offers, though he looked shaken and stunned.

It was very kind, he said, but he must get back home; he'd have a lot of things to do in the morning. Everybody knew what things. . . .

Mrs Thorley, Di and Deb huddled together in the living room and drank tea. In all innocence Deb had suggested whisky to Mamma, who looked very upset, though she had not shed a tear. Mrs Thorley replied that tea would do though she craved whisky. It was strange how, after all this time, five years, whenever she was tired, or worried she thought of whisky and how it had sustained her—and almost ruined her.

"Susan was my oldest friend," Diana said, ready to cry again.

"I know," Deb said. She had cried too. Poor Susan had not been her best friend, but she'd liked her. And to die like that made everybody seem so vulnerable. In fact one of Deborah's first actions had been to run upstairs and assure herself that Sam—and the other children, of course— were all right. Once Death got a foot in the door. What rubbish!

They talked of when they had last seen Susan.

"Not more than a fortnight ago," Mrs Thorley said. "Just before you came, Di. It was at Caro's. She seemed to be perfectly all right then. And in fact, Caro, who has been more with her lately, said this evening that Susan had never said a word about feeling unwell. Of course Mrs Walford died very suddenly."

"But she'd been ailing for years. As a matter of fact, I haven't seen Susan very lately. I did think she looked a bit thin," Deb said. And her hair looked a bit dry and brittle; the result of something she used to brighten it. She'd begun to use it—yes—at that party, that doomed party, when Mr Walford broke away and left Mrs Walford with a nurse and Mrs Walford died. And Lavinia met that horrible man whom I disliked, distrusted, loathed on sight. . . .

"People don't just die of being thin," Diana said.

George, restless and discontented, said,

"I'll just pop up and see if Johnny wants anything."

Johnny had taken Chloe to bed. He seemed to be well-acquainted with his sister's hysterical turns. "What she needs is a night's sleep. She'll be right as rain in the morning."

Attention shifted, refocussed itself.

"At school, Miss Hardwicke always said that the best cure for hysteria was a smart slap across the face."

"I am inclined to agree." Mrs Thorley's comment was dry.

"I can't ever remember you slapping one of us, Mamma."

"I can't remember one of you being hysterical." Certainly when Caroline heard that Freddy Ingram was to marry Susan Walford, Caroline had gone all to pieces, but a few *verbal* slaps had sufficed.

"I once read . . ." Deborah was the great reader, "that behaviour like that comes from a wish to draw attention. She's a very pretty child, with nothing to say for herself. I mean compared with Caro. . . . So if she felt a bit neglected and then this happened . . . I rather like the boy. Sound about horses, and crazy on hunting, and he never had a proper mount. In fact I told him that if he'd like a day out with the South Norfolk, I'd lend him my Dragon."

"So you have two now," Diana said, trying, and failing to keep sour envy out of her voice. Two hunters, what opulence. And only five years ago Deborah was so downtrodden; wearing a print dress, working like a servant.

"Two of my own," Deborah said, as casually as though she were speaking of handkerchiefs, "but plenty of others handy. I school them, you see. For other people. . . . So many people don't have the patience, or the knowledge, or what you might call the knack of it. I charge, of course."

(I could make a living anywhere, any day of the year. And Tim knows it. He also knows that it would be very difficult to divorce me simply because I'm good with horses and pay regular visits to my stepmother, and very occasionally spend a night at Gad's. Go ahead, she had said, during one of their quiet but corrosive quarrels: Make a fool of yourself before the world.)

In the guest room Chloe lay in bed; Johnny sat beside her holding her hand. The white muslin dress lay on a

38

chair, the pink rose beginning to die.

"A hot-water-bottle, if that is not too much trouble," Johnny said in answer to George's query if there was anything he could do, fetch.

"I'll get it. Shan't be a minute."

Jonathan Faulkner sat by the bed and thought what Hell being a twin was. A life-long three-legged race. And that was no flight of fancy. That he and Chloe had both suffered mumps at the same time was understandable; they'd both been at home then. But well on into his second half at Eton, when he hadn't seen Chloe for weeks, he had measles, and far away, at Stratton Strawless, Chloe went down with the same complaint, and on the same day! How explain that? Not much alike to look at, but sex explained that; tied together by something far stronger than physical resemblance, or mental ability. In nature they differed, too. He could take the sudden death of somebody known as Mrs Walford, in the middle of a party without being upset. It was a pity, and of course very sad for her husband. It had flung Chloe into one of her states, and he had done the best he could to deal with it. Now and then, when he thought about it, the future bothered him a bit. He wanted not to stay in England and always be poor, and at the same time rather grand. He dreamed of going to India. Fortunes could still be made there. He dreamed of coming home rich, say after ten years, mending not only the decrepit leaking roof of Stratton Strawless Manor, but every tenant farmer's roof; building cowsheds, draining that low-lying land called Rainwater Meadows, perhaps bringing under the cultivation that utterly opposite part of the estate, the Common, dry, sandy, riddled with rabbit holes.

It was a good dream, and not an impossible one. But whenever he thought about it, up came the question: What of Chloe? Despite what some people said, India was not very healthy or very comfortable for English women; so he couldn't very well take her. Leave her? Then his parents would marry her off to somebody like Peter Stanton, a good enough fellow in his way but quite unsuitable as a husband for somebody so delicate, so sensitive, so much in need of understanding as Chloe was.

The kitchen was still active, for successful party or ruined one, the clearing up afterwards was just the same. Jenny, her duty done, was taking her ease, drinking tea, her much-tried legs propped up on a stool. Violet was washing up at the sink and Ruth was drying.

Jenny said, "Violet, if I've told you once, I've told you a thousand times. Glasses first. Then the silver, and in a jug of hot water. They dry better. As for you, Ruth, I'd athought you'd aknown."

George said, "I want a hot-water-bottle." Curious request on such a sultry evening. The kitchen was indeed hot despite an open window, an open door, for the fire in the range had been kept in so that there should be hot water in the boiler for all this washing up.

"Somebody else took poorly, Master George?" Jenny asked with genuine concern. It could happen. She did not remember the occasion, but she'd heard tell of it; a summer fever that had wiped out half the village. That had been a hot summer, too. Inside her shrivelled skin Jenny's brittle bones shuddered.

"No, just for comfort."

"You see to it, Ruth. The kettle's only just off the boil and the bottles are there, under the dresser, right-hand side."

Jenny was old enough to remember the time before hot-water-bottles. A time when comfort was derived from bags of salt, heated in the oven, or bricks.

Ruth, gladly abandoning the dull job of wiping dishes, busied herself. George looked, a bit dismally, at the long dresser upon which some remains of the feast had been deposited, awaiting removal to the larder, awaiting, finally, Jenny's thrifty verdict; fish-pie; shepherd's pie or into the pig-pail. For one dismal moment these left-overs symbol-ised the whole party so carefully planned, so eagerly an-ticipated. He felt the need to assert himself, get back into his own skin. He said,

"You girls are late. I'll just see if there's anything I can do, and if not, I'll drive you home."

There was nothing he could do. Johnny took the bottle and tucked it in.

"Thanks. She'll be all right now, but I think . . ." He took stock of the room. "Yes, if it's all the same with you, old boy, I'll doss down in that chair. Just in case. . . ."

"Violet gets down here, don't you, Violet? I'm a bit further on, if you don't mind. Good night, Violet. See you soon. Sunday, if I don't go to Bywater. Now, Master George. Sharp left by the church and then a bit. After that it's Shanks' Pony, walk through the wood. A bit skeery, this time of night."

"Are you going to Bywater?"

"If I get a job. There ain't much around here, is there?"

"I suppose not."

With Violet sharing the seat it had been necessary to sit close, now, with Violet gone, Ruth did not move away; if anything she snuggled closer. She was, as the landlady of the *Hawk in Hand* had said, a thoroughly loose girl; not necessarily a disadvantage if a girl knew her place, but with the son of the house, and him with less sense than a cuckoo, it was instant dismissal and out you go! She was not designing or mercenary, on the contrary, inclined to be choosy. Nature had endowed her with a gift she enjoyed using—with the right person, and George Thorley was right to her eye. Like everybody else she thought him a good deal older than he was.

Initiation being bound to come sooner or later, George could have done much worse; might have spent himself and his money on some indifferent, custom-hardened hireling. As it was, the new and delirious experience healed a wound which, all unknowing Chloe Faulkner had inflicted when she turned to her brother, not to him, for comfort and support in her distress. At that moment George had felt himself rejected, a new and most uncomfortable sensation. Now, without consciously connecting the two things, and certainly not the two girls, he was restored. He had still a long way to go before reaching the certainty that every man wanted two differing female elements in his life, a bad girl to tumble, a good girl to adore, but this evening, wrecked and then salvaged, set him on his way.

Mr van Haagen woke as though someone had shaken him by the shoulder. Ha! A child crying. There were children in the house. No! Not a child crying, at least, not now; a low voice murmuring. The matter, no doubt, comforting. Strange that sounds should carry so far. He turned, prepared to sleep again, and then was aware of a horrible smell. God in Heaven! He knew what that was, what he had done. Left his cigar to smoulder instead of stubbing it out properly. It might, indeed, have been left balanced on the edge of the ash-tray and tipped over, burning the lace mat, even scarring the bedside table. He could not imagine how he could have been so careless, except that that poor girl's death had upset him, as it had upset everybody. Hastily he lit his candle. There was the end of his cigar, properly stubbed out. There was his watch, showing the time to be a few minutes after twelve. And now that he was properly awake he realised that it was not the smell of burning, it was . . . it was . . . In none of his languages, native or acquired, could he find a word. Except evil. Similar to, different from, worse than something he remembered very vividly; a time when a dyke broke and the sea came in, and everybody was so busy mending the dyke against tomorrow's tide, and tomorrow's, that even human bodies had been left to rot, and dead cattle had been left to the crows.

Why here? In this pleasant room?

And why did he feel fear? No, more than that, terror? A paralysis that made his body rigid, and creeping inwards seemed to check his breathing, stop his heart. Death. No, because he could still see and hear . . . even speak.

Those who dabbled in such matters—Mr van Haagen never had—would have recognised his state as that of genuine trance and Mr van Haagen as a true medium between two states of being. They were few, charlatans and impostors were many . . .

When it was over—and how long it lasted he never knew, for he did not think of looking at his watch, Mr van Haagen knew more than anybody, more than Mrs Thorley, more than Deborah about what had happened to the girl whom he had warned to beware of the dark. Who had, so they said, gone to India—a dark subcontinent—and died.

42

Deb was first down in the morning. Five years at Foxton had inculcated the habit of early rising and there she could refute Tim, by being first down, taking old Emma a cup of tea. Here at Gad's on her rare overnight visits, she did the same thing, giving Jenny a little surprise.

There, behind the closed door of the drawing room, Poor Susan lay, decently covered by one of the last of Deborah's mother's fine linen sheets. Poor Susan. And it was such a lovely morning. Oh dear!

Deb went into the kitchen, got the range going, put on the kettle. Remembered that there were three guests in the house. The Faulkner girl would probably expect breakfast on a tray, and China, not Indian tea. Deb went into the living room to fetch the tea-caddy. It was not until she had flung back the curtains that she saw Mr van Haagen on the settle.

It gave her a jolt. She said, "Oh!" and he woke, rubbing his eyes. But, as was his habit, instantly alert and aware. Ready with his story.

"I am unable to sleep," he said, glad that his nightshirt was long and not rucked up. "So I come down, walk a little, give myself a drink and am then overcome. You will please excuse me."

She gave him a funny look. What had happened to him last night was as clear, and in a way as real, as anything that had ever happened to him in his life. She, Deborah Thorley, Mrs Bridges, had played no small part in what he had seen—No! lived through. And just for a moment he felt that she knew that he knew. But she only said,

"You'll like a cup of tea? Mr van Haagen, there is no need to be embarrassed. I'm married. I have seen a man in his nightshirt."

Just so he had lived with her; practical, helpful, sensible, taking evil, even the ultimate evil in her stride; burying the dead, comforting the living and then going back to the horses.

After living with himself for fifty-two years, Mr van Haagen knew that he was not a man given to fancies. He was not even a religious man. Asked to describe his faith he would have said—Lutheran. His forebears had fought Catholicism, the religion of Spain, the enemy and the oppressor, for more than three hundred years; just as they had fought the sea and made the polder land. So why did he now feel a wish, recognised, suppressed, bobbing up again, to tell Mrs Thorley that her attic floor was haunted, that it needed a priest, with bell, book and candle, to perform the rite of exorcism? One reason for not doing so was pity. She had lived through something so horrible—no wonder her hair was white and her head jerky. And now, this morning, more trouble to face, a dead woman in her drawing room and presently the undertakers. . . . No, he could not possibly add to her bothers. But he did reflect, in a rather vague way, that life bore hard on the strong. Almost as though if one blow didn't floor you, there'd be another and another. She'd survived her first husband's death, and then that of her second; she'd inherited a failing business and made it prosperous; she'd lived through what he had lived through—but not in his flesh—all that took place in that locked attic. He knew it, down to the last sordid detail. But better say nothing. Go away dumb and on his next visit make some excuse for not staying in this house again.

"We were supposed to be on a kind of round trip, George. Your party last night, and then on the Stantons'. But I doubt if she's up to it. I mean it was a shock, that poor woman falling down, screaming, practically on Chloe's feet. I think I'd better take her home and skip Muchanger. I must say, old boy, until . . . what happened . . . it was a damned good party. And that sister of yours, Mrs Bridges, is it? We got on like a house afire."

The Lumsley affair of which Everard had been sent to make a preliminary investigation was very unpleasant indeed. The first two firms approached by Lady Lumsley refused to touch it, phrasing the refusal tactfully, of course, saying that as they saw little chance of such a lawsuit being

44

successful they could not in good conscience advise her ladyship to proceed. Upton, Binder and Smith had no such scruples; all was grist to their mill, and it was a reputation for being able to wash dirty linen in public and render it snow-white that had prompted Lady Lumsley to seek their services—after the two snubs which she recognised as such.

She was unprepared for Everard, so unmistakably a gentleman. It made things easier in a way, and at the same time more difficult. Easier because since he must be housed in the Castle and was therefore to some extent her guest, it was better that he should be presentable and at ease; more difficult because the unpleasant aspects of the case would, she felt, shock him more than they would have done an older man of coarser grain. After all, an address in Great King William Street had promised little in the way of gentility and Mr Spicer had been assigned a bedroom in the East wing; not quite servants' accommodation, but only one step above. (That of course was easily corrected. One order and Mr Spicer's luggage was transferred.)

She had, with the same thought in mind, ordered a very simple dinner, no need to confuse the poor man with too many courses. Too late to rectify *that* now, but she ordered up better wine.

They were four at table in what was called the small dining room—rather larger than a whole floor at Everard's London house. There was Lady Lumsley's aunt, Lady Cowdray, a lady of incredible age and stone-deaf, but with bright lively eyes, and his late lordship's agent, Mr MacFarlane. Both knew more than they were prepared to reveal, until they saw which way the cat jumped.

Light, dinner table conversation.

"Is this your first visit to Scotland, Mr Spicer?"

"No. When I was young, my godfather came up regularly, salmon-fishing in the Spring and for the grouse in August."

It was like excavating a ruin, Everard thought. Happy days about which it did not do to think too much. And come to think of it, there was in his own life, not quite a parallel, rather say the obverse face of the situation here.

Lady Cowdray's eyes had for some years been obliged to serve as her ears as well and she thought: Alison is clever! She'll have this young fellow eating out of her hand and breaking his neck to serve her. Mr MacFarlane brushed aside Everard's reference to past grandeur; summer visitors! and just hoped that Everard was a better lawyer than he looked.

"I understand, Mr Spicer, that talking to one's lawyer is rather like the confessional. I mean, if I'd committed murder and told you so, you'd still be obliged brief Counsel to defend me."

"That is oversimplification. It would certainly be my duty to ascertain, so far as was possible, that when you made such an admission you were sober, in your right mind, not trying to protect another person, acting under threat—things of that kind. It would not be for me to judge."

"And then?"

"I should brief Counsel. *He* could judge, to a limited extent, insofar as it would be for him to judge whether or not to accept the brief. Having done so it would be his duty to prepare the best possible case for your defence. Am I making myself clear?"

"Even if I had admitted . . . ?"

"The question is hypothetical, Lady Lumsley. I cannot recall a case where a client approached his solicitor with such an admission and then asked help in his defence. It would not be reasonable. Unless, of course, he intended by such action to show himself insane within the meaning of the act."

"I see."

Actually the opening gambit had been hypothetical. Start with murder and then when one was forced to say the word *adultery* and the word *impotent* the shock was less.

She looked very young; but the boy whose future was concerned was six, so she must have been married for close on seven years. Married, perhaps at sixteen. To a man of sixty-nine. Everard had briefed himself as well as he could, and Lord Lumsley had a two-inch obituary in *The Times*. His widow was one of those women who looked well in black. She had fox-coloured hair and amber eyes, but neither the dead-white, or rough-red complexion which as a rule went with such hair, nor the sandy eyelashes. Her skin was—well, it was a cliché—just the colour of cream, a whiteness delicately stained as though the colour of her hair had faintly drifted down. Her neck was very long and very slender, seemingly too slight to support the wealth of hair, pinned with tortoiseshell prongs, not ordinary hairpins. And her hands were beautiful, very long, very narrow, and that same cream colour.

"I have nothing to admit, Mr Spicer. Neither murder nor . . . adultery." There she had said it.

"Your letter to Mr Upton said very little. It would be of help to me, if you would . . . give me details. Please bear in mind that I am a married man, with two children of my own." Everard was not given to leaps into imaginative understanding, but he made that one. Because he knew vaguely what she was about to be forced to say, and she looked so young and so frail. Mr Upton would have recognised and dismissed her—lecherous as a tom cat; Mr Binder would have recognised and dismissed her—mercenary as Shylock; Mr Smith *had* recognised what he called a stink and given a stink and some titles, and a very shaky case, hit or miss, a lot of publicity anyway; leave it alone. He'd been overruled.

"I will begin at the beginning. . . ."

Unlike most women she was lucid and concise.

The late Lord Lumsley had married years ago, begotten a son and a daughter. His daughter married and had a son. The heir to Lumsleydale had fought in the Crimea, survived, failed to settle down, gone to Africa, been killed in some nameless squabble.

"He died," Lady Lumsley said, "without issue. I think that is the phrase. So then my late husband married me. Wanting an heir, you see. And after two years Alastair was born. Publicly, of course, his father accepted him—no man wishes to put horns on his own head. But to me his behaviour was abominable: it had been from the moment that I told him I was pregnant. He denied, absolutely, that the child was his. He gave as his reason that he was impotent. He was *then*, but not *before*, if you understand me." Her amber eyes filled with tears. "Mr Spicer, I cannot describe what Hell my life has been for the past seven years. We went nowhere, never entertained. His age was the excuse for that and I could have borne it, but he was so unkind to Alastair. . . ." A few tears brimmed. "I was often obliged to interpose myself to prevent violence. And he put a woman of unspeakable severity in charge." Lady Lumsley's eyes dried, her voice steadied. "I dismissed her within ten minutes of hearing of his death!" There was a quiet triumph about that statement.

The lawyer in Everard stood back and said drily: A very sad story but no grounds for contesting a will.

Yet without doubt it was a strange will for a man of the world, a man of great wealth to have made. Everard had seen a copy. A single sentence. I, Alexander St Barbe Sinclair, fourth Earl of Lumsley, of Lumsleydale Castle in Inverness hereby bequeath to my daughter, Lady Dorothea Morton, everything, not in entail, of which I die possessed. It was signed and the signature had been witnessed; Ian Ross; Hector Alston.

Any lawyer would have taken the precaution of revoking former wills. Any half-literate farmer writing his own last testament would have been more specific about the extent of his possessions. Any man in his right mind would surely have appointed at least one executor.

"Have you the original, Lady Lumsley?"

An ornate, yet unformed, feminine hand; signature very shaky; witnesses obviously men who could just write their names and no more.

The lady waited for some comment and when none came—one of the first things a lawyer learned was not to be hasty—said,

"*She* wrote it, of course. He went to visit, a fortnight before his death, and had a summer cold. He came home after two days. . . . I know, Mr Spicer, that this is not a legal argument, but it supports my conviction. He was passionately attached to this place. Sinclairs have lived here since the Flood. . . . I know, I *know* that he hated me, and Alastair; he would have died happy to think we must beg our bread, but we would never have left Lumsley Castle to certain ruin, with only eight hundred acres of moorland to prop it up. Which is what this will means. . . . He *knew*. Before he took this idea into his head and ceased to talk to me, he often spoke about the little crofts that were once here. Not profitable, but self-supporting. . . . Then his grandfather made a fortune, coal I think and could afford to evict the crofters. He spoke with regret about that. But he also said once that it took half the income from one coalmine to keep this place watertight and he wouldn't mind if it took the whole. *And* all the rents of the properties in London. I am convinced that if this were his real will, he would have made some provision for the Castle. Imposed some condition upon Lady Dorothea, or set up a trust fund. Isn't that logical?"

"Yes. But logic is not law. Had he made former wills?"

"Mr MacFarlane says he did. When we were married. Mr MacFarlane made it for him."

"Mr MacFarlane?"

"Yes. You would hardly have guessed, Angus is such a silent man, but he is a fully trained lawyer. His father was agent here—before my time of course, and my husband then employed, when necessary, a firm of lawyers in Edinburgh. In some way they displeased him, and—this is Angus' story—my husband said to old Mr MacFarlane, "We have a bright boy here; we'll have him taught monkey tricks; the homegrown article is always best . . . That, the first will, was perfectly fair. Lady Dorothea was to have a street in London—the Mortons are not well-to-do."

On the far side of the room old Lady Cowdray looked at her watch and folded her knitting. She knew just when to be present and when to absent herself. Knowledge invaluable in a chaperone. By applying it skilfully, she had been able to live here, in great luxury, instead of eking out her wretched pittance in genteel poverty. In the loud, toneless voice of the very deaf she said, "Good night, Alison dear. Good night, Mr Spicer. Don't sit up too late; you've had a long journey."

Mr MacFarlane lived in great comfort in what had been built as the Dower House. Edward spared an envious glance around the big, handsome room, half living room, half office. Heavy silver inkstand on the carved, leather-topped desk, deep comfortable leather chairs, a side-table well furnished with decanters and glasses. The scent of stocks and lavender came through the open French windows. If the agent felt this his pleasant way of life was threatened, he gave no sign. He was not a talkative man, but what he said was to the point.

"Aye. His lordship came home and took to his bed. He had not a strong chest and he'd had his three-score-ten but we didna think he was dying. He gave me that thing that calls itself a will. Sealed and addressed to her ladyship, and he said, 'Keep it safe and give it to her the minute I'm dead.' God forgive me, I thought it was a letter. So thin."

"And why should God forgive you for obeying an order, Mr MacFarlane?"

A very curious expression crossed the healthy, honest-looking face.

"I would have done it differently. The least I could do would see that she was sitting down, and alone. As it was the shock felled her. With Lady Dorothea watching—she'd been the house the last two days."

If I had known, I would have done *very* differently. Put the damned thing in the fire!

"Was he in his right mind?"

"Difficult, Mr Spicer. I don't know how much her ladyship told you." The man was cautious. So was Everard.

"Enough to explain a possible motive."

"Aye. Well, in that regard his mind was not sound. Idée fixe. Apart from that, in itself an affliction, he was sound enough, except when he had laudanum in him."

"Laudanum?"

"Crude. He could not bear pain. He could not bear a

50

night with a cough. A twinge of toothache, his teeth were bad, and must be expected, or a pain in the chest and he took to the laudanum as a sensible man takes to the whisky. He carried a bottle with him, and having a drink taken, he was like putty. I know." Mr MacFarlane knew. Dozens of times, dealing with the obstinate old man, he had waited for the right moment. And in his mind he was as sure as he was of his own name that Lord Lumsley had gone to his daughter's house, the cold already on him, had resorted to the black bottle with its bright label, saying "Poison," and then been putty in *her* hands. But such a surety was no agrument in law.

Mr. MacFarlane eyed Everard distrustfully. A Saasenach, a Londoner and a lawyer. Sent up here to tell the silly creature that she had a chance. They'd drag her name in the mud, keep up the pretence until she was penniless. And that wouldn't be long; all she owned were the jewels his lordship had given her at and soon after her marriage. And there was even an argument to be put up, in good legal terms, against her continued possession of them. What a woman owned, even what she earned, was, legally speaking, her husband's property. And that ill-made, iniquitous will was very sweeping: everything, not in entail, of which I die possessed.

"I told her ladyship then, that very morning, when she said she would fight it, that she stood no chance. Granted it's not a will he would have made in his right mind, condemning as it does the one thing he loved better than himself to certain ruin. It is the Castle I mean. The care he took, making his real will. But that is no argument. No more so than the laudanum."

"No. I am afraid the laudanum must be ruled out of court . . . I suppose you don't have the earlier will."

"I have it. It is not worth the good paper it is written on."

"I'd like to see it," Everard said.

"Darling, I can't. We know now that it *is* smallpox. Raven and I must work our heads off. Of course I should wish to

51

pay my last respects to Poor Susan; and I'm sorrier than I can say for Freddy. But I can't spare the time. And you won't be alone *there*. Your mother . . . I really am most terribly sorry, but my duty is to the living. If you get a chance to speak to Freddy, please apologise and explain."

"I will," Caroline said. "And the wreath was from us both. He'll understand. Don't worry."

So you went, wearing black, to the funeral of your best friend; the girl at whose engagement party you had been gayest of all, whose bridesmaid you had been, whose husband you had loved—and still did.

In fact Caroline had loved Freddy enough to make excuses for his choosing Poor Susan instead of herself. He'd been nothing more than a travelling salesman; a very good one, and he appeared to enjoy his job. But it offered no real security, and although he contrived to let it interfere with his social life as little as possible, there were times when he had been obliged to miss some joyous occasion. He had expensive tastes and enjoyed comfort. Caroline's dowry was a mere five hundred pounds. Marriage to Susan gave him a great deal of independence, a comfortable home, a share in—and after Mr Walford's death complete control of, a flourishing brewery. No happiness, though, no more than Caroline's face-saving marriage to Edward had brought her. She knew that every time they really looked into one another's eyes. He might seem to be laughing his head off, but the look was there.

It was there this afternoon.

"Edward asked me to tell you how deeply he sympathised, Freddy. He intended to be present but something they hoped was chicken pox turned out to be smallpox."

"I fully understand. Tell Edward that I shall be everlastingly grateful to him for making certain that she did not die in pain."

Freddy meant that, sincerely. He'd married Susan for strictly mercenary reasons, but no man with any feeling at all could live for five years with a woman so amiable, undemanding, self-effacing, grateful for any small attention without becoming fond of her and glad that she did not die in agony.

It was a conversation which anybody could have overheard. Several did. A few—Mrs Thorley among them—remembered a time when Freddy Ingram and Caroline Thorley had got themselves talked about. Both had settled down admirably. About the extent to which Caroline had settled down, Mrs Thorley had entertained a doubt or two. She had understood Caroline's infatuation, her despair when the engagement was announced; she had, in fact, pointed out to Caroline the face-saving action. And both Freddy and Caroline had behaved impeccably. Still . . . Caroline had never, in five years, given a party of any size without including the Ingrams. Anything she organised—and Caroline was now a great organiser—Susan and therefore Freddy must take part. Even the modest party at Gad's Hall . . . the party at which Poor Susan had died. . . . "Oh, Mamma, do ask Susan and Freddy. All of us and Susan, together for once. It will seem like old times."

There flitted though Mrs Thorley's mind a hope that Caro would not do something silly. Silly was really the worst word that could be applied to anything Caro had done in regard to Freddy—dancing four times in succession, driving alone with him. She was just capable of being silly again; widowers were as useful as bachelors as escorts to women whose husbands were very busy.

"I made a special point of giving Freddy your message, Edward. He quite understood and he said such a nice thing about you. He said he would be everalstingly grateful to you for making certain that she did not die in pain."

In his flat way, Edward said, "I just happened to be there." The poor girl was dead now, so he saw no harm in saying, "Actually I was not even surprised. She had been in pain for quite a long time."

"Oh! Why?"

"That nobody knew. She couldn't even define the site of it, and nobody could find any cause. She was exception-

53

ally brave about it; anxious that nobody should know."

"Poor Susan! What with one thing and another, she didn't have much of a life, did she?" Caroline took a few breaths, a bite or two, a sip of the wine which Edward had thoughtfully brought up to cheer her after the ordeal of a funeral. Then she said, "I'm afraid Freddy will be lonely now. Richard came down for the funeral, but he was catching the evening train."

"Well, we'll do our best for Freddy, darling, once I've got this plague off my hands. Ask him to dinner or something. . . . Caro, would you mind . . . I feel I should just look in at that isolation shed. It is such a shambles. You know, I still regret Diana's going away. When she was there in Friars' Lane, you only had to slip through the gate in the wall and be sure of company."

It was four years since Diana had left the elegant little house in the cul-de-sac, so fortunately situated just to the rear of the house in which Edward and Caroline lived. And nobody regretted, or to an extent, resented the move, more than Diana did.

Everard, after his successful interview with Upton, Binder and Smith, had gone house-hunting. As he had feared when contemplating, backing away from and then contemplating again this critical move, rents were extortionate and his field of choice was limited since he must be within easy reach—that meant twenty, thirty minutes on a horse omnibus—of the City. He considered himself singularly fortunate to hit upon St Anne's Crescent. Some fifty years earlier a speculative builder had bought the garden of a big derelict house and there erected six most desirable residences with gas and piped water laid on and with an aspect; for, roughly completing the circle of which the Crescent formed the northernmost sector, there were some trees and shrubs, the last outpost of what had once been a lovely garden.

Diana, with her capacity for forgetting or ignoring the unpleasant, did not remember the house in Leicester where Mamma had made a precarious living for herself and her two daughters by drawing designs for dresses and pottery and giving piano lessons, on a hired instrument. Had she done so Number 4, St Anne's Crescent would, despite its inconveniences, have seemed pleasant. When she made a comparison it was with Gad's, which she secretly thought of as home, or with Friars' Lane, upon which she looked, even after a year of marriage, as a kind of toy in which she played at keeping house.

St Anne's Crescent appalled her and she reflected that it had been a mistake to let Everard do the house-hunting; but she was in the early stages of pregnancy and disinclined to travel unnecessarily. Mustering her courage on arrival, she told herself that perhaps her condition was responsible for her feeling of gloom and her apprehension about the number of steps; eight up to the front door from the pavement; eight down to the back door in the area. Impossible for perambulators. Never mind, perhaps before *that* happened, the inevitable messy outcome of the messy side of marriage, she would have found something more suitable. It would not be for want of trying.

Resolutely—she was, after all, Mrs Thorley's daughter—she set about making the best of things and it was typical of her that the first room to be quite in order was the drawing room, very small when stark-empty and now overcrowded. In Diana's little Suffolk world people called upon newcomers, exercising discrimination, of course. She expected calls from her neighbours. And she was right.

Mrs Appleyard called.

So far as a group of six, mean-faced, rather pretentious little houses could be said to comprise a social unit, centring about a leader, Mrs Appleyard was that leader; the one who lived here longest, and whose husband had his own business, a double-fronted shop in the High Street, just around the corner; on one side he sold fish, on the other vegetables. She was—and rightly—conscious of having come up in the world, for Alf had started his career with a barrow, hawking fish and vegetables about the street. She had helped him to heave himself up in the world by continuing—making nothing of three pregnancies—her work in a pickle factory.

And when the great moment had come and the shop in the High Street was his, she had refused to live in the room above it; so they had moved into St Anne's Crescent and been proud.

Unfair to say that Mrs Appleyard and Diana disliked one another at sight. There was no reason. Mrs Appleyard was doing the right thing, visiting a new neighbour; Diana was lonely, torn up by the roots.

But the Tower of Babel was built high, an affront to God, it was said, and when the builders were scattered, doomed to speak different languages, there were within those differing tongues, other divisions, almost as dangerous. Mrs Appleyard thought Diana's voice and accent namby-pamby; Diana thought Mrs Appleyard's very coarse.

"You're not a Londoner, are you?"

"No. My home is in Suffolk. That is a picture of it."

Years ago when Lavinia could paint what she saw, but even then with a strange twist, she had painted Gad's hall and contrived by a trick of perspective, cunning use of light and shade, to make it look like a mansion. That was before Lavinia's pictures had always had something more wrong with them than mere exaggeration, and Gad's Hall, more impressive in paint than in actuality, had hung just to the right of the grandfather clock on the half landing, for years, passed a dozen times a day unnoticed. But, on the verge of exile, Diana had said she would like it, something of Gad's to take away with her.

"Very nice," Mrs Appleyard said, mentally discarding Diana as a neighbour. Snobbery could cut two ways. There was the namby-pamby voice, the white hands that looked as though they had never done a stroke of work, the high nose and the husband who was a solicitor.

Perversely, nobody in St Anne's Crescent felt elevated by the coming, to Number 4, of a professional man and his dainty-mannered wife. Mrs Appleyard, the greatest snob within at least a mile's radius, said that Mrs Spicer was a snob, and for the wives of men who had done marvellously; in the Post Office, on the Railway, in the Insurance business and in a printing works, that was enough.

All the silly little houses had been built on the assumption that each would have a maid of imperturbable disposition and the constitution of a donkey. Such, if they had ever existed, were now extinct; only Mrs Appleyard had a resident maid; everyone else managed with a daily woman and even they were not easily found in this area, women preferred to clean offices, early morning, late afternoon work; and they could clatter their pails in company. Diana, alone, literally alone in London and completely out of her depth, had asked Mrs Appleyard's advice about how to set about getting a maid. In Baildon, in the first year of their married life, Everard, in the grip of one of his bouts of economy fever, had been against employing permanent help who must be housed and fed as well as paid, but here, with Diana pregnant and a house with so many stairs—both conditions for which he felt, in an obscure way, responsible, a proper servant was necessary.

When Diana, innocent of having given offence, asked Mrs Appleyard's advice, that lady shot a glance at the hands which Diana had taken such pains to keep nice and thought—It'd do you no harm to do a bit of work, my fine lady! She said she would ask around, but she had not the slightest intention of doing so. Then she shot another glance at the picture which had put an end to neighbourliness and said,

"Of course you had plenty of servants *there*."

Skipping, as was her habit, the time when Katie had left and not been replaced, and her own year of managing with Mrs Wedgewood's desultory assistance, Diana said,

"We always had a cook, and it was easy to get girls from the village." She thought of the coalshed down in the area here and added, with unconscious wistfulness, "And there was a boy for coal and wood and cleaning knives—that kind of thing."

She had no intention of sounding grand or of making a false impression. That kind of behaviour was practically unknown in the society in which she had grown up, a place where one's origins and circumstances were known to everyone, where like mixed with like and knew exactly

57

where he stood. If there was an inaccuracy in her statement it was in referring to Willy as a boy when he was a grown man, married and a father; but he had been the boy about the place for as long as Diana chose to remember.

"Maidservants and men servants, and cooks," Mrs Appleyard told the neighbours. "And if you ask me she've come down in world."

Curiously nobody wanted to rub shoulders with those who for some reason had come down in the world, superior as they might appear to be. Coming down, like going up, was contagious.

Diana was doomed to loneliness; she, who in her little, much-lamented pony carriage had driven about making visits, been recognised and welcomed everywhere within a limited range.

Everard's business associates offered little in the way of social life. Mr Upton, a bachelor and a misogynist, lived very comfrotably in his club; Mr Binder, a widower with four children, had set up house, wisely he thought at the time, with a widowed sister, mother of three, in a pleasant, spacious house at Mortlake. The sister said, with truth, that she had no time for entertaining. Mr Smith led a normal—and very enviable life—he had married well—in Theobald Road, which had retained something of a country atmosphere, front gardens and trees. Diana thoroughly enjoyed the one dinner party there—experimental on the Smiths' part. The two women had got on well together, despite a slight difference in age. Both were pregnant, Mrs Smith the fourth time, having suffered three miscarriages. She suffered a fourth within two hours of the Spicers' departure and held them to blame—at least not *them*, Diana, so likeable, so potentially companionable, interested in needlework. Inadvisably Mrs Smith had taken Diana upstairs to show her the beautiful work she had done for the benefit of the unborn, and the drawer had stuck, needed a strong tug, and that did the damage. Florence Smith never wanted to see, or hear of Diana Spicer again, a feeling of rejection which was exacerbated when in due time she heard that Diana had given birth to a little girl.

Long before that happened the question of help in the house had been solved—by Everard. Diana had done her best; one by one she had accosted the four women who worked in the Crescent and asked did they know of anyone in need of a job, whole time, part time, even two hours a day. One of them did; at least she said she thought Maggie might be able to fit it in, she'd try, poor soul, an extra shilling or two mattered to Maggie, married as she was to a terrible drinker.

Maggie—Mrs Carr—arrived and at the first sight of her Diana's hopeful heart sank; she was such a poor little thread of a woman, bone-thin, she looked as though she had never had a square meal in her life, and would be utterly incapable of heaving a scuttle of coal from the shed in the area to the drawing room. It was Diana's first encounter with Cockney toughness. For all her frail looks Mrs Carr, scuttling about like a timid hunted animal, managed in the one hour that she fit in, to do all the rough. She worked in a kind of frenzy, for this hour's job had literally been fitted in between others.

It was far from satisfactory, but at least it took care of the front steps.

Eight of them. Eight to every front door, and somebody—probably Mrs Appleyard—had decreed that they should not be merely scrubbed, but whitened, at least once, preferably twice a week. Diana was enough of a conformist to wish hers to match the rest. Deborah, who was given to such thoughts—as Diana was not—would have seen in those white steps a protest against the general grime. Diana only thought that London—at least this part of it—was filthy. Dust seeped in; lace curtains were grey and rough to the touch within a fortnight. And not clean dust either. In the High Street, in Skelton Road, almost as busy, with the Crescent making a link between the two, horses dropped their dung, which dried and was pulverised by later traffic.

Everybody else took the filth for granted. Mr Apple-yard's fish and vegetables, the butcher's wares opposite, were exposed. Diana washed everything from both shops. Half an hour's shopping in the High Street made the very flounce of her petticoat grimy, and Everard, in order to keep up appearance, needed a clean shirt every day.

They'd been far better off in Baildon, but that was a thing which Diana never said. She still loved Everard. She'd chosen him, and she had had plenty of choice. One aspect of marriage, the bed part, she had never liked much, its outcome she dreaded but Everard, with his good looks, his beautiful voice, his beautiful manners had not changed. He was hers and she was his until death did them part. He'd done his best, taking a job with more promise; she'd do her best. And things, being so bad, must improve. There must be some change.

Change came; for the worse. Tap, tap on the back door. The daily woman from Number 6 who had produced Maggie.

"Thought I'd better tell you, ma'am. Maggie can't come. She's in the 'orspital. 'E always did knock her about something shameful; last night he went a bit too far. Laid her out for dead. They reckon she'll die. And a blessed deliverance."

It was Diana's first—No, strictly speaking her second encounter with the seamy side of life. Everything to do with Lavinia had been squalid, for five months, but Mamma and Deb had borne the brunt and the whole thing was best forgotten. But this was here and now. Horror!

"How shocking!"

"No more than could be expected. Bound to happen, we all said it."

Behind the shock Diana's strong self-preservative instinct sprang up.

"I suppose, Mrs . . . er . . . er Butler, you don't know anyone else?"

'Eartless bitch! Getting her name wrong, too. It wasn't Butler, it was Buckler.

"No, I don't."

Everard was very good. He carried up the coal and took down the ashes. About the front steps he did nothing, could not be expected to. They worried Diana. Everything here was so grey. Even the trees and shrubs in the little bit of garden had been so laden with dust before summer ended that their change of colour when autumn came was hardly noticeable. The only spot of colour now in the whole place was the white of the steps. In which, after four or five days, those of Number 4 made an exception, neglected; grey stone against grey stucco.

Something of Mrs Thorley, her mother, rose up in Diana. She had sense enough to know that in her condition she should not lift anything heavy; half a bucket of water would do. A pair of old gloves would not protect her hands from water, but they should save her nails from the hearth-stone. So early in the morning that the grey December dawn had scarcely broken, the dainty, fastidious Miss Osborne of Gad's Hall whitened her own steps.

Even Everard noticed the gleaming whitensss. He had not shared Diana's concern about them; he said: Let them go. It's a silly habit, whitening steps that look dirty again once they're walked on. All the same, if the dear girl minded so much, and in her condition, too, something must be done. He consulted with one of the women who cleaned the office and she said that she did know a girl who was looking for a living-in place.

"That is exactly what we need."

"She ain't much to look at, but she'd be willing."

Bessie Simpson was nothing to look at; in build she was much like Mrs Carr, but whereas behind Mrs Carr's har-assed, hunted expression there was a hint of starveling prettiness, Bessie's face was a disaster; she was violently cross-eyed, had prominent teeth and no chin. A great dis-appointment to her mother who had three quite bonny girls, who sold flowers by day and other wares by night. Mrs Simpson considered that she had made her contribution to the family good when, very early in the morning, she took a light barrow round to Covent Garden and used her experience in the selection of flowers. Ninety per cent of those who bought flowers from street vendors were men, and they looked first at the seller, then at what she had for sale; and as Mrs Simpson said, with cruel truth, set Bess down in Piccadilly Circus, offering red roses at a penny a dozen and nobody would buy. So Bess had remained at home, a slave to her tyrannical mother and her hardly less demanding sisters. She was thirteen and rebellion was stirring in her, she'd be better off in a living-in job with only one mistress. Seemingly tireless, endlessly willing, and showing towards Diana that pathetic devotion which ugliness can give to prettiness—provided the prettiness is accompanied by civility, she was to be Diana's strength and stay. Quite apart from the work she did she actually saved money, spurning the shops in the High Street. "Twice the price and half as fresh," she said of what Mr Appleyard and his fellows had to offer. Turning out of the other end of the Crescent, trotting along Skelton Street, she searched for a market. There must be one. She did not think in square miles, she thought in terms of streets and their character. Behind Skelton Street there was a warren of little streets, lined with little houses, far humbler than the Crescent, which Bessie considered grand. The women in them must shop somewhere. They did in a jumbled noisy open space, called The Maypole, or simply The Market. It had seen Maypoles in its day, and some ancient, but still honoured law had prevented it from being built over, so the street traders had moved in with their incredibly varied wares. Once Diana broke one of her best tea-cups. Bessie said,

"Don't you worry about that, ma'am. I'll take one along and match it." She came back with a cup absolutely indistinguishable from the others.

Bessie could cook, nothing fancy of course, but considerably better than Diana who had come to art late and unwillingly whereas Bessie had started at the age of eight, with no praise for a successful attempt and a clout for a failure. Not, perhaps, the ideal way of tuition, but extremely effective.

The baby was due in April. Diana, doing everything

correctly had consulted the doctor in the High Street who had recommended a highly efficient midwife, trained and experienced; she had served for fifteen years in the lying-in ward of St Bartholomew's Hospital. The interview had emphasised to Diana the difference between life as it had been and life as it was. In Suffolk old Doctor Taylor had been a friend, Edward was her brother-in-law; there she would have been fussed over. Here she was one of many; just another pregnant woman. She had put out a wavering signal for help, or rather assurance, saying, "I rather dread it." And the doctor had said there was nothing to dread; natural process; she was young and healthy, in Mrs Mitchell's hands she would be quite all right, but of course, if something did arise, he was only just around the corner.

Mamma?

Her presence would at least have helped to establish Diana's identity in this alien and faintly hostile place. But neither Everard nor Diana wholeheartedly wished for her presence. She'd been rather against the move, counselling patience, saying that Mr Gordon could not live forever, saying, in effect—Stick to what you have, that pleasant little house, access to Edward's stables and garden, and all that Gad's can supply. In a way they had defied her and in her letters home Diana had made the Crescent sound rather better than it was. One glance and Mamma's bright eyes— the only thing about her that had not changed—would reveal the truth; they were worse off now than they had been in Baildon in the house she had chosen for them; Everard within easy walking distance of his office, Caroline practically next door; friends all around.

Nevertheless Diana craved the feeling of security that Mamma would bring with her and was actually writing a letter asking her to come, when the need to go to the water closet—one of the real amenities of the gimcrack house, made itself felt.

The doctor in the High Street, casual and indifferent as he was, had been absolutely right when he said that there was nothing to dread. No worse than the colic, the result of eating green gooseberries. . . .

"You was lucky," Bessie said. "Girls is always easier than boys and better early than late. And I was here to do for you. That was lucky too."

Everard was relieved that his first-born was a girl. For his son he would be satisfied with no education inferior to his own and would have already been worrying about school fees. Girls were comparatively cheap to rear and educate. He hoped for a boy, of course, one day, when the financial outlook was brighter. How and when such an improvement would come about he had no clear notion; in fact there in London with a big and busy firm, he seemed to have run into much the same blind alley as he had in Baildon; he was clever—all the partners admitted that, here, as in Baildon; Better have a word with Spicer was the rule; he was industrious, punctilious almost to a fault, and getting nowhere.

He was always most conscious of his lack of status—and money—when he boarded the horse-bus each morning and evening. There was never enough places, people pushed and shoved and Everard must push and shove, too. Once, looking round at his fellow passengers, he thought: *Eyeless in Gaza at a mill with slaves*. All his fellow slaves, exhausted by a day's work, sank back into apathy, glad to have obtained a seat, glad of the respite. They'd known nothing else, bred to it, as he had not been.

The baby, another link in the chain, dismiss that unworthy thought! was enchanting. The star-fish of a hand, reaching out like a tendril, had caught Everard's cautious finger and hung on. When her smoky-blue eyes focussed there seemed to be recognition in them.

Illusion, self-deception, Everard told himself in his saner moments; baby apes would clutch and hold onto a twig. Any human baby's eyes would look in just that way at a shape that promised something, a lift, a jog, food.

They had discussed her name, amicably. Everard's mother, the dimmest of dim memories, had been called Belinda; Mrs Thorley was Isabell. Compromise; call the baby Belle, which meant beautiful, which she was, almost from the first. As Bessie said, "I seen early ones afore this, all the wrong colour, green, yeller, purple and none of 'em thrived. This little beauty, she'll do."

So it seemed, through April, through May, into June. Very hot this year and terribly dusty, except in the strip of back garden, facing North and shielded from the morning and afternoon sun by the high walls designed to protect neighbour from neighbour. There the dust, the filth of London, went almost slimy.

"Would you mind, Everard, if I took Belle to Gad's? I think a short stay, in the country . . . And Bessie could look after you. Until your holiday. Then you can come too. Wouldn't that be nice?"

That was the first of the annual holidays; seeing Deborah with her Sam, Caro with no child, Susan Walford the same, Pheobe Mayhew not even married. Click, click, click, a bit like shaking a kaleidoscope, the same colours and shapes, but taking a different pattern.

Except to say that London was hot in summer, dirty and overcrowded at all times, Diana did not complain. Her house sounded pleasant, she had found help of the most satisfactory kind; she always appeared to be well-dressed. When Everard came down, usually in the final week so that he could escort his family home, there seemed to be no lessening of affection between them. Yet the vertical lines on Diana's forehead were deeper every year and sometimes, caught off-guard, her face wore a look of discontent. There had been a time when Mrs Thorley had been secretly concerned about Diana's apparent friendlessness, but since Belle's birth this seemed to have improved and Diana often referred to going out to tea or entertaining in a modest way, in her own home. As a matter of act the circle of acquaintances, centring about St Anne's Church, was of the utmost dullness. Nobody young at all; nobody under thirty except one poor down-trodden girl who in the presence of her domineering old mother dared hardly open her mouth.

Diana had never been as frivolously gay as Caro, but she had enjoyed parties, the company of her contemporaries, most of whom had admired her, consulted her about fashions, what to do with greasy or frizzy hair, or freckles. She had never been such an outright flirt as Caro, but young men as well as young women had admired her.

Outside this stuffy circle there was entertainment to be bought, theatres, concerts even balls in aid of this good cause or that. But the West End, where such delights were to be had, was a long way away. Neither Everard nor Diana would have dreamed of attending a theatre or concert, leave alone a ball, without wearing the proper clothing—conspicuous and somehow rather silly on a horse-bus. Hired cabs were expensive, and so, of course, were tickets. There was, in the vicinity of the market which Bessie had discovered, a music hall called The Maypole; but neither Diana nor Everard would have been seen dead in such a low place.

Everard could read, or work on papers he had brought home. Diana, never a serious reader, flipped over the pages of a magazine, paying most attention to articles about clothes, beauty aids and changing styles in house-furnishing. A hardly recognised boredom possessed her and she was always glad to go to bed. Glad, too, when Everard said, "I'll be along presently. Good night, darling." Then she could be asleep or pretend to be when he retired. So *that* could be avoided. She wanted another baby—a boy—but not too soon. Later, when things got better, when Belle needed less attention. Belle had passed her third birthday when Diana became pregnant again, and was almost four when Melville was born. This time there was hardly any need to discuss the name. Everard's mother had been a Miss Melville before her marriage, so it was a family name, it went well with Spicer and had a kind of dignity about it. When his hair began to grow after the birthfluff had rubbed off, it had a reddish tinge. Strange, since Everard was fair and Diana dark.

"Gracious," Diana said, "I hope he isn't going to be like Deb's Sam."

Sam Bridges, conceived in ecstasy, but gestated in another mood, was a very odd child indeed. He was that rarity, a nine-stone baby. Deborah had laboured from Sunday morning, through the night, through Monday and Monday night, until Tuesday at daybreak to bring him into the world. The baby clothes she had prepared were too small from the first moment. As soon as he could walk and needed shoes they were the shoes of a two-year-old. He walked sturdily at a year, talked fluently at about the same time, and was, as soon as he was mobile, so venturesome as to be almost suicidal. In his parents' bedroom there was a tallboy, eight drawers high. That, for some reason which nobody could define, offered him a challenge. He pulled out all the drawers and climbed them, as though mounting steps; when he reached the top one, his weight and the weight of the open drawers below him tipped the balance and the whole thing came crashing down with him under it. Any ordinary child would have been killed or seriously injured. Sam emerged without a bruise or a scratch. He went into the loose-box where Tim's most famous, but worst-tempered stallion stood and emerged unscathed. "Nice horse," he said. He fell into the well in the stableyard, leaning too far over to see what was in it and why he had been told, most strictly, not to go near it. But he fell into the bucket and was pulled up, soaked, very happy. It had been an adventure and he was one who, from the first, welcomed any adventure, and if no adventure offered itself, made one. He was, unless provoked, of sunny disposition, but if angered was almost frightening to see. Such temper, his father said, not unreasonably, must be curbed. A good smack on the bottom.

"He's a baby, Tim!"

"All the more reason. Bring up a child in the way he should go."

"I will not have his spirit broken," Deborah said. "When he is old enough to be reasoned with, I shall reason with him."

"By then it will be too late."

"That remains to be seen."

What Deborah said was now law at Foxton. To the struggle for supremacy in what might have seemed an unequal battle she had brought weapons of her own, superior intelligence, a glibness with words, a rocky intransigence. Something cold and deadly.

"I know that you disapprove of hunting. I am not particularly fond of chapel, prayer meetings, camp meetings, temperance meetings. Suppose I expressed my dislike by refusing to attend. Could you drag me, by the hair, screaming? Imagine it."

Timothy Bridges imagined it and shrank away from the reality. His temper had been curbed when he was young; he never shouted; Deborah had fallen, just at the right age, into Mamma's keeping; so she did not shout either. Their disputes were never noisy. Once Tim said, again not unreasonably, that it was in *his* stable, on *his* pasture that Deborah proposed to keep her hunter.

"Not necessarily, if you object so much. Mr Craig, I am sure, would house my horse, or my horses, at a very reasonable charge."

Which of course she could pay; her father had left her five hundred pounds. She never referred to her legacy in actual words; she had no need to say as Diana had been forced to do, wanting this or that which Everard said they could not afford, "But, darling, I will pay out of my money." Neverthless Timothy Bridges was aware of that five hundred pounds.

And once, after a quiet dispute, he had thought things could be made right in bed. Deborah made no protest until almost the crucial moment and then she had said a terrible thing. "If you wish to commit rape, go ahead." Could any woman have chosen words more daunting?

Out of the quiet disputes a truce emerged, guarded on both sides, but workable. There had been love once, and where had it gone? Take a little ball of quick-silver, press on it, half a dozen little bright fragments scattering off in all directions, try to recapture one of them and it also broke away.

But outwardly a good marriage. It took a mother's, no, a stepmother's eye to see that though Deborah now did what she wished, went where she wished, loved her child, naughty as he was, she was not as completely happy as she deserved to be. For one thing her very smile had changed; it had once been entrancing, a bit crooked, making one dimple in her left cheek. Somewhere along the road it had vanished.

Intermittently, and—as she would have been the first to admit—without any definite reason, Mrs Thorley worried about her girls. That Diana was not truly happy in London was proved by the way in which she counted, like beads, the remaining days of her holiday: Oh dear, only four days, three days, two days left. Deborah, acquiring not a discontented look, like Diana's, but stern, and thin; it was the paring away of flesh from her strong-boned face that had made the dimple disappear. Of them all Caro gave the greatest impression of being happy, but Caro could don a mask at will and once Mrs Thorley had clapped one on her face, saying that if Caro did not get up, dance at Poor Susan's engagement party, accept the invitation to be Susan's chief bridesmaid, everybody would say she had been jilted by Freddy Ingram. But she certainly had not said: Marry Edward Taylor. In fact she had given all her girls an exceptional freedom of choice. Even Lavinia had been free to take her own fatal way. But that had all been dealt with and should be forgotten. And what good did worrying about the others do? Just an excuse for insomnia; the waking, as though somebody had shaken her by the shoulder, just as the tall clock on the landing struck three. Conduct with yourself the endless argument, ignore the anodyne of whisky; think—We all have our troubles; think, well, at least Diana took away as much as she could carry, freshly killed fowls, two dozen eggs; and Deborah who needed nothing in the material sense had gone off jauntily letting Sam hold one rein and think he was doing the driving.

So what of Caroline?

Nothing untoward, it seemed. Caroline and Edward were not the only people who felt that Freddy would be lonely. He had always been popular and now he was extremely eligible. For at least six months the hospitality proffered him was of the most sedate kind, an invitation to dinner, or to spend a quiet week-end. Mourning must be observed. Christmas eased things a little. In the week preceding it the Theatre at Baildon put on SHE STOOPS TO CONQUER, and the Saturday night's takings—cheap seat prices doubled and those of the more expensive ones trebled, were to go to some kind of charity—a fund for helping old actors and actresses. It was, as Mrs Fallowfield said, A Good Cause; so she would take a party. But even a theatre party, in a good cause, looked better with a man or two in it. Barbara, Diana's contemporary, was married, but there were three younger girls. Why not invite Mr Ingram? Freddy's presence was noticed by other mothers of daughters, and the Hospital Ball, organised by the Friends of the Hospital, was looming up. If a young widower could attend a theatre, why should he not dance—in moderation of course.

It was at the Hospital Ball that Caroline showed her first, and perhaps her only flash of discretion. Freddy still had a violent, almost a hypnotic attraction for her. It had never weakened; never would. In the past, when they were both unmarried, she had got herself talked about, but that didn't matter, because she was positive that Freddy would marry her. Instead he had married Susan and she had married Edward. She'd understood, after the first terrible days of heartbreak, and forgiven him; and for five years and some months, though their eyes occasionally communicated, and on the occasions when they danced together their bodies had acknowledged the truth that their behaviour denied, Susan had stood there, a bulwark between Caroline and the ultimate folly. Now there was nothing, except marriage vows to Edward, and Caroline knew how all too easily she would ignore them and plunge headlong.

"Thank you for asking me; but I am not dancing this evening."

"Why not?"

"You forget. I am a member of the Committee." Still the youngest, in some ways the most powerful because she represented the younger generation and her purely flippant idea of adding swings and roundabouts and coconut shies to the stereotyped Garden Fete had raised a great deal of money. At the same time, because she was young and light on her feet anything demanding much physical effort could be left to her.

"There is such a crowd," Caroline said, "that there will be three sittings for supper, and I am in charge. Unless I keep a sharp lookout the third sitting will get nothing but blancmang. . . . Who're you with, Freddy?"

"The Garrards."

"Steam-rollers! Look out for your toes!" Caroline said, and whisked away.

But they both knew that there would be another time.

Cruel fate arranged that it should be under Edward's roof. It was in February, so far an exceptionally mild and pleasant month. It was Edward himself who had suggested a little dinner party, a gesture of welcome to the latest young resident doctor at the Hospital. It was Edward who had suggested inviting Freddy, using a valid argument. Everybody else who must be invited was a bit elderly; the newcomer was young, only just qualified, he'd be a bit overawed, feel a bit out of place.

"That is something he must learn to live with, I suppose," Caroline said. She had.

"I don't want to depress him from the start. How about Freddy?"

"He could hardly be called young, dear. He's at least three older than I am."

"I know. But he can keep conversation going. He's like you in that. And we haven't seen much of him lately."

"Very well," Caroline said.

Who could have reckoned with Edward being called out? Who could have reckoned on the fog coming on and everybody—except Freddy—making for home before it grew worse?

Turned to jelly, breathless, half-swooning with desire—but she had known it before, riding, as she should not have done, alone with Freddy in his gig and risking another scolding from mamma. Then there had been virginity to be guarded, and Freddy had understood. Now Caroline could only gasp, "Not here! Not in Edward's house."

"Where, then? When?"

Caroline, coming to it a bit late for a country girl, had learned to drive after Diana went to London, leaving behind the little pony carriage and the pony, growing fat from lack of exercise. Caroline did not know, nobody knew, or remembered, or understood why she should be timid where horses were concerned. Her own mother, the first Mrs Thorley, had been a rational, practical woman; her husband had bought a new horse, satisfactory in every respect except that he was terrified of perambulators. So Caroline's mother had had one of her practical ideas and taken the perambulator—with Caroline in it—into the stable, just to show the horse that there was nothing to fear. Confined to the limits of his stall, faced with the dreaded thing, the horse had gone temporarily mad, kicking and rearing. Caroline's mother had backed away, thinking in her practical fashion that she should have pushed in an empty perambulator. But for the child in the baby carriage the damage was done; for her the horse was always a potentially dangerous animal. She had never wanted to ride one, as Deborah had from the start, and she had never driven until Diana went to London. Then she had braced herself, in order to be mobile and moderately independent. She was now fully capable of driving to Sudbury.

She had always known that what with Edward was a meaningless, dead business would be different with Freddy; and she had been right. Caroline wept from sheer joy. For as long as she lived she would remember that day; the heady, tremulous anticipation as she drove through the winter countryside, with Spring just waiting in a few swelling buds, and openly proclaiming itself in scatters of crocuses along the drive to what was generally known as the Brewery House.

She had, on that day, a perfectly legitimate, unquestionable errand; helping Freddy to sort out Poor Susan's clothes.

Wearing the falsest of all her false faces, Caroline had explained that Freddy couldn't be expected to do it.

"And it isn't something to be left to servants. They couldn't distinguish between what was good jumble and what should be given to the poor. The things have been there since last summer and should be put to some use."

"It's a wretched job for you, darling."

"Yes. But since what you told me . . . about Poor Susan being ill for so long before she . . . Well, you know, Edward."

Edward knew. He said,

"Don't stay too long. Get back in the light. I'd come with you and drive you, but I really have a full day."

"I know."

There was never any time. And never actually the right time. What they needed was a night—a thousand nights together. There was a six-year-old thirst to be slaked. And excuses were running out. It was perfectly true to say that there was not merely Poor Susan's wardrobe to be sorted, but her mother's as well, perfectly true to say that Freddy found himself suddenly obliged to entertain some potential customers and needed somebody who could see that the luncheon table was properly set. But it was all hurried and furtive; absolutely satisfactory in itself, a gulp of water in the desert, enough to make one crave more. More. More.

"Couldn't you get to London?"

"I suppose so. But what good would that do? If I say I must visit Diana, I must visit Diana. She is the last person in the world to connive."

"One night with Diana. One with me. I know the perfect place."

There was one heart-stopping moment. Edward remembered how Poor Susan had made the excuse of shopping to go up to London and see a doctor, supposedly more knowledgeable than he was. He said,

"Caro, darling, you're not hiding anything from me, are you?"

"Hiding? What should I have to hide?"

"I just had the idea . . . Well, darling, it's almost six years and no child. . . . *I* don't worry. I've known plenty of babies born after ten, eleven years. I thought you might . . . Believe me, darling, there's nothing to be done—and anybody who says there is is a dangerous quack."

Caroline spared a thought: What on earth has happened to me? Everybody said I was so *soft*. I even used to take chocolate to Lavinia, and flowers. Now I am harder than nails.

"I wouldn't dream of doing anything of that kind, without consulting you, Edward. All I proposed to do was to go and stay with Di, a night, or two, and do a bit of shopping. I've never even seen Di's house."

Di's house!

One of six squashed into so small a space. Grey. Di's maid, too sinister-looking to be believed. Di's guest room, if it could be so called. And Di had always made it sound rather grand. Did Di deceive herself? Am I deceiving myself? Do we all do it? In different ways.

Aware of the discrepancy between Number 4, St Anne's Crescent as she had described it and the reality, Di was inclined to enlarge upon the social success which she and Everard were enjoying.

"You remember last summer Everard couldn't come to Gad's because he had to go to Scotland? Apparently he did something very clever. He never talks about business, of course, but Lady Lumsley herself told me that she owed Everard more than she could ever hope to repay. She admires him very much." Dinner at Lumsley House in Piccadilly had been a most dazzling event.

"Expensive, though," Diana said ruefully. "Even Everard agreed that I must have a new dress, and we were obliged to hire a conveyance, of course."

Apparently whatever financial reward Everard's singular service had merited had gone to the firm; Everard was to be paid in social recognition. Not quite as empty as it sounded though, for a fellow guest that evening, "He was Charlie Somerton, he's Lord Westward now," had remembered Everard from Eton, greeted him with pleasure, sympathised with his circumstances. "You poor chap! Until my grandfather died—and it looked as though he'd last forever—I was a wage slave, too. Stock Exchange! Frankly, I got so downhearted, I couldn't make up my mind between jumping into the Thames or emigrating." His lordship had been Everard's fag and remembered him as one who had not made inordinate demands or been as free with punishment as most were, and when later in the evening he asked Everard where he lived and Everard had described the district in general and Number 4, St Anne's Crescent with sour truth, had said, "Damn it all, we can do better than that, surely. I'll bring the mind to bear on this."

With his natural pessimism Everard said that nothing would come of it, Diana must not count any chickens. But he wronged his ex-fag in thinking that he would promptly forget. Within a few days came the news that a lease of a house in Somerton Road ended on the last day of June and if Everard liked, the house was his.

"And at *such* a low rent," Diana said. "I honestly believe that Lord Westward would have offered it rent-free but feared to hurt Everard's feeling. A bare ten pounds a year more than this. And it's huge. . . . Of course," she said, "the rates will be considerably higher in such a nice neighbourhood, and Everard will have further to travel every day. But for the children's sake alone . . ."

She had, on this occasion, the wrong audience. She could have said that Everard had done the Queen herself a service, gained entrée to Buckingham Palace and been offered a house in Carlton Terrace and Caro would have said—as she said now—"How *lovely* for you. Oh, Di, I *am* glad." But her mind was elsewhere, thinking: This time tomorrow . . .

Tomorrow started with the shopping expedition which was the excuse for this visit. They went to Hawksley's, one of the earliest and certainly the best-known of the departmental stores. Its boast was that it could supply anything from a pin to an elephant and its founder had recognised the fact that most shoppers were women who enjoyed a cup of coffee in the middle of the morning, a light lunch, a cup of afternoon tea.

Caroline had plenty of money, but her shopping seemed to Diana a bit aimless, not as Diana's shopping had been since her marriage, direct and purposeful. They wandered about, staring, fingering fabrics, admiring displays. Caroline was being wildly generous—but then she always had been. "Look, Di, when you move you'll have a proper nursery with room for a rocking horse." Order the rocking horse for Melville, a doll's house for Belle, a Paisley shawl for Mamma, light as air, warm as fur. A pipe for Everard, and one for Edward. For herself and Diana something so pretty, so new-fashioned, so altogether delectable, feather boas.

At that Diana protested. "Caro, you have already spent so much. . . ."

"But for you I should have been obliged to stay in a hotel, Di." (But for you I should not have an excuse for staying one night, leave alone two. You'll never know it, my dear, prim and proper Di, but you have opened the gate of Heaven to me. And I hope to God that by the time you next come to Gad's you'll have forgotten that I stayed with you only the one night.)

A whole line of cabs waiting outside Hawksley's.

"Of course you must ride back in comfort. I dragged you out, Di. And thanks for everything." They exchanged sisterly kisses and embraces.

"Albertino's. It is in Gerrard Street."

"I know," the driver said. None of his business, but she looked young and very respectable and he had a Puritan streak in him. He couldn't help feeling a bit sorry, having two daughters of his own.

76

It was in Albertino's establishment, specifically designed to cater for illicit affairs that the word divorce was first mentioned.

It was feasible; a man whose wife had committed adultery could cast her off, after a somewhat tedious legal process, shaming to both.

"Edward *might,*" Caroline said, her voice slow and dubious. "But it would hurt him—and he has been so kind to me. It would hurt us, too. I should be ostracised."

"Not in France, darling. I have contacts there. I've sold wine in England, surely to God I could sell it in France. I could sell my half of the brewery. Richard would be only too glad to buy me out and come home and take charge. . . . Let's do it. Let's elope."

Behind this frivolous all-for-love-and-the-world-well-lost-Caroline there were generations of sturdy people, yeomen farmers and women of the same stock; accepting what life gave, looking out, sniffing the air: There will be frost tonight, better see to the lambs! Studying the sky: No sign of rain, the corn in Top Field will hardly be worth scything. Stolid, law-abiding. Their blood in her veins could not prevent her being tempted, but it gave enough ballast to prevent a too hasty acceptance.

"That needs some thinking about."

She had always been an emotional rather than a rational creature and there seemed to her a vast difference between a clandestine affair—all right, call it adultery if you liked—which nobody knew about and which therefore hurt nobody and doing something which would hurt Edward so much, which might even deal him a mortal blow, hurt and shock Mamma, and Di and Deb, shock, if it did not hurt the little community in which she had spent her whole life. I'm bad; I know I'm bad; I'm being bad at this moment, but there *is* a difference. Divorce is an ugly word. . . .

And was there, at the very back of her mind, a tiny distrust of Freddy? Of the very quality which made him so attractive, his light-hearted attitude towards life, his disregard for convention? Give him his due, he had been, at least outwardly, a good steady husband to Poor Susan; but she had been ill and he appeared not to have noticed; and, let the fact be faced, all the time he was married he had been conducting a very secret kind of flirtation with Caroline.

As I with him. Pots shouldn't call kettles black! But look forward.

One day you will age and lose what looks you have. Women live longer, but men age better. Could you count upon Freddy, ten, fifteen years from now?

It did indeed need thinking about. And once you began to think you rather took against Albertino's. No reason. So far as one could see it was clean. Luxurious too, but somehow it smelt wrong. Caroline had sufficient imagination to make her kind—to Lavinia, locked away in the attic, to the children at the Ragged School, the patients in the Hospital; now it turned about and demanded: Who slept in this bed last night? Who will occupy it tomorrow?

There were no public rooms at Albertino's, but room service was prompt and efficient, softly moving waiters, quietly moving trolleys which opened out into tables, food piping-hot brought along in dishes with double bottoms, filled with boiling water.

The Caroline who had always been ready with the quip said,

"This is all a bit too professional for me. I'm only an *amateur* prostitute!" That made Freddy laugh.

Hours later, she thought to herself: Not even that! For, waking very early in the morning, she lay and felt that her craving for Freddy had at last been stilled. It had smouldered like a bonfire all these years, alternately stirred a little, and then damped down. None of their comings together had been completely satisfactory until last night. Now she seriously believed that the thing had burned itself out. She was cured! She told herself that she was not only a bitch, but a fickle bitch into the bargain.

Freddy, when he woke, was surprised to find Caroline up and dressed and ready to go. In him also desire was stilled, but he had more self-knowledge, and more experience than Caroline possessed and knew that this condition was only temporary.

"Hullo, darling. What's the hurry? We're not at the Brewery House now."

"I just want to get out of this place."

"Why? What's wrong with it? It's a very nice place. And it will now proceed to provide us with a very nice breakfast."

"I don't want any."

"Are you all right?" He thought, with a mixture of complacency and tolerance, that last night had been enough to exhaust anyone. A more sensible woman would have stayed in bed till lunch time.

"I'm all right." But the glass on the ornate dressing-table had showed her a pale face, its always monkeyish look emphasised, and dark smudges under the eyes. "I must catch the nine o'clock train from Liverpool Street."

"Why? There's another at eleven."

"I know. But I absolutely promised Edward I'd be back for lunch."

Now I am lying to Freddy, too.

With a quite audible sigh, Freddy prepared to pull himself from the bed.

"Don't come," Caroline said hastily. "By the time you're dressed and have the bill paid, I shall have missed the train."

Outside Albertino's unobtrusive doorway, the porter blew a shrill whistle and a cab appeared immediately. There was nothing noticeable about early and unaccompanied departures. There were people who in the ordinary way smashed about in their own carriages—some with crests on their doors, who used anonymous hackneys when visiting Albertino's.

The train pulled in at Baildon at a quarter to twelve and Caroline was surprised, and frightened, to see Edward on the platform, scanning each carriage. Mamma! Mamma taken ill, a message sent to Di's house. Di thinking Caroline already home. And Edward, *kind* Edward, come to meet her, support her, break the news gently.

But at the sight of her, Edward hurried forward, smiling, taking her in one arm, her dressing case, and the one light parcel in the other.

"I'm such an ass," he said. "You told me Thursday, but for the life of me I couldn't remember which train. So I thought I'd better meet them all."

"Then what a good thing I came early. You would have had a wasted day."

"You look thoroughly exhausted, darling."

Exhausted how and where? Push that thought away!

"London is tiring. In Hawksley's alone I think Di and I must have walked five miles."

"You didn't buy much."

"I spent a lot. Some on things to be delivered. My dear, I have so much to tell you. . . ."

And that, at least, *was* true. Di's horrible house, Di's prospect of moving, Di's new friends, all that she had seen in the shops, all that she had bought. The rocking horse and the doll gave Edward a pang. He accepted his present graciously though it was not exactly the pipe he would have bought for himself. He admired the feather boa and the shawl meant for Mrs Thorley. Generous girl, most of what she had spent had been spent on others. All she had bought for herself was a bit of frippery.

Mrs Thorley was pleased with her gift, so pretty, so light and so warm. She was glad to hear that Diana, at the end of June, was to move from what Caroline described as a rabbit hutch of a house, for a better one in a better district. But, acutely class-conscious, as life had taught her to be, she could not avoid worrying a little about Diana's association with people of title and substance. It was an exposure to risk. No doubt Lady Lumsley, grateful to Everard, who by some legal sleight-of-hand had served her well, was grateful, and no doubt Lort Westward, offering Everard the lease of a rather grand house, was being friendly to an old school fellow. But without money, without obvious family connections, above all, without land, the way of the social climber was hard. Not that Diana was likely to be silly, not that she and Everard were not fit to mix in any society, but . . . Mrs Thorley knew the world thoroughly; in the house where she had been born, neither the family solicitor nor the family doctor would have dreamed of entering by the front door: and then, after many vicissitudes, she had almost ended in Leicester, with only one door which she was almost ashamed to open because to do so was to reveal the poor furnishing of her front room. From such indigence George Thorley had rescued her and she had settled comfortably into one section of what was called the middle class, married her three remaining daughters into it. And she knew, or thought she knew, what would one day happen to Diana. Somebody would say: Oh, from Suffolk? Then you probably know my great-uncle, Lord Norton. And to that what could Diana say except: Just by sight.

Still, let's not take too gloomy a view. Perhaps doing something clever for a titled client would advance Everard in his profession. And certainly, if Diana's house was anything like Caroline's description of it, the move could only benefit the children.

Violet opened the door.

"Ma'am, it's Ruth. Asking to see you, special."

"Oh dear. Is she *still* out of work?"

Because she had once herself been a seeker for employment, Mrs Thorley's sympathy was ordinarily on the side of those who were out of work through no fault of their own. But Ruth Marsh did seem to be singularly unfortunate where jobs were concerned. Since that party, last summer, when Poor Susan died, Mrs Thorley had employed her twice; once at Christmas, and then to help with the spring-cleaning.

"Out *again*," Violet said in a tone which neither Mrs Thorley nor Caroline noticed, except that it implied that Ruth had been fairly recently employed.

Had Caroline not been there, Mrs Thorley would have gone out into the kitchen, prepared to tell Ruth that she had no work to offer and that really two references were as much as, rather more than, any responsible woman could provide for so casual a labourer. As it was she said, "I'll see her. No, Caro dear, don't go. I haven't heard half about your visit."

Last July, leaving for some reason the *Hawk in Hand* at Baildon and glad to earn a shilling or two, helping Jenny and Violet, waiting expertly at table, and again at Christmas, the girl had seemed to Mrs Thorley to be, or at least to look, rather pert and bouncy, but in fact her look belied her. Neither then nor at Christmas, nor during the spring-cleaning had she said a cheeky word, or refused the most distasteful job. It was the fact that she had turned up, offering to clear the drawing room after the undertaker's men had finished, that had made Mrs Thorley give her a reference, employ her over Christmas, give her another, employ her again for the spring-cleaning.

Why she had lost her most recent job was all too apparent. Pregnant. Well, nobody, however kindly, could be asked to supply a reference for a girl in that state. There flashed through Mrs Thorley's mind the horrible thought that this girl was just about as advanced on this road which had only one ending as Lavinia had been on that March morning, six years ago. But that was different. Lavinia had been sheltered, even her insanity hidden from the world. This poor girl . . .

"It's Mr George's," the poor girl said. "We went together last summer and we're being going together, off and on ever since. It's his, I swear."

Caroline had never seen Mamma, her placid, managing, unfailing stepmother, in a rage before. In fact it had been Mamma who had imposed gentle manners, self-control. . . . But now Mamma rose up in wrath, and said, "How *dare* you? Accuse a boy, only just sixteen. You've been whoring about for years, and dare to come here, brazen-faced with such a lie. Get out of my sight. Get out of my house. And I warn you. . . . You go spreading this lie about and I'll have you run out of the village. On a hurdle, and to the sound of rough music."

She had never seen that particular treatment applied to an errant woman; it must be one of the things George

Thorley had told her; he'd been a great repository of old stories, sayings, customs. The rough music was the noise made by the banging on kettles and saucepans and buckets which mixed with the hoots and the jeers. Ruth was familiar with the term and blenched slightly but she stood her ground.

"I ain't a liar, Mrs Thorley, ma'am. It's God's truth I'm telling you. If you don't believe me, ask *him*."

Thank God George had gone to meet Johnny Faulkner in Baildon. They'd lunch at the *Hawk in Hand* and spend the afternoon at the theatre. Not that Mrs Thorley wouldn't have something to say to *him*. Later on.

"I should prefer to ask why you were dismissed from the *Hawk in Hand*; and from the two situations I helped you to find."

That shot went home. Ruth began to cry.

"I ain't asking much. I ain't whored about as you call it. *They* get paid. I never took a penny. A present or two now and then is all. And I wouldn't be asking now, but what else can I do? I can't get a job, like *this*, can I?" Tears and mucus smeared her face. She appeared to have no handkerchief. In silence, Caroline handed over her own. Ruth used it vigorously. "I gotta sister down at Bywater, but she ain't got a penny to rub against a key. Four shillings a week, till I'm over this. . . . Me father ain't noticed yet, when he do he'll take his belt to me."

Just then it was not so much Caroline's sense of being fellow-sinner as pure pity for anyone in such a plight that made her lean over and whisper to Mamma, "I'd help with it." Mamma's return whisper was positively a hiss. "To give her one penny would admit obligation." Aloud, and in the most unkind way, Mrs Thorley said,

"If that is all you need possibly all the men with whom you have been intimate could contribute it between them."

Caroline was shocked. Who could imagine Mamma being so cruel. Mamma, always so kind, even to Lavinia, who, after all, but for her family would have been in exactly Ruth's position. Caroline did not realise then what an only son could mean to his mother. Mrs Thorley seldom made

83

much display of her feelings. She had managed to treat her own two daughters and her stepdaughters with such impartiality that everybody was astounded. And if in a moment of terrible crisis she had said, "I want Deb," that was completely understandable, Deb was so practical. Mamma had been fond and just, calling them all her girls. But her relationship with George was something completely different. He was her son, and the son of his father to whom Mrs Thorley owed so much. His birth had justified George Thorley's choice of second wife, past her youth. For these things alone his mother would have loved him, but George, from the first, had possessed such charm. To say that he was the apple of his mother's eye would be a profound understatement, and to have this common, loose-living, blubbering girl . . .

The little pony carriage overtook Ruth just before the lane which led only to Gad's joined the road which ran one way to the village, one way towards Baildon. Caroline stopped and said, "Get in. I want to talk to you."

In the face of Mamma's hiss that to offer a penny was to admit an obligation, Caroline dared not offer money, but she could offer something; beginning with being a Friend of the Hospital, Caroline had, over six years, become involved in other good works. She was able to say, "I am sure I could find you work in the laundry, either at the Hospital or the Workhouse; and then . . . then, when you were . . . er . . . brought to bed a place in the lying-in place. There, I can assure you, you would have every care. My husband devotes a lot of time to the women there."

It was the only thing Caroline could think of, taking hasty leave of Mamma and hurrying the pony along in order to overtake the poor girl and offer the best solution possible.

"It's good for you to bother," Ruth said. She did not sound particularly grateful. "But then what? My name smirched forever and another bastard brat in the Workhouse. I know your mother didn't believe me but what I said was true. I've fooled about a bit, but it's his, your brother's. You always know."

Caroline imagined George's child among the Workhouse Children. Things had improved a good deal since OLIVER TWIST—compulsory reading at school, and a book which had evoked many of Caroline's facile tears—and the Baildon Board of Guardians were on the whole liberal-minded; the Workhouse Children were soundly, if dully fed, and adequately if hideously clothed, but even at the Ragged School which some of them attended, they were distinguishable by their dull look and subdued behaviour as well as their uniform. To and from school, to and from church, on the occasional walk, they walked in couples, supervised by an under matron who wore a nurse's uniform to which she was not entitled, and whose only contact with them seemed to be orders to keep in step, to close up there. In the interest of hygiene both boys and girls had their hair cropped very short. They looked like what they were—Nobody's Children, and they seemed to be aware of their unwanted state. Imagine a miniature George . . .

About the sternest thing that Edward had ever said to Caroline was that she acted without thinking. She did so now.

"Do you *want* this baby?"

"Want it? Would *you?* I mean if you was me. Even if I got the money and went to my sister. She got five of her own. To get a job I'd hev to leave it there, and what sorta life would it hev?" What indeed? Edward, though he would get up in the middle of the night to help a woman in Scurvy Lane with a difficult delivery, had often said that one of the main causes of poverty was that people had more children than they could feed. And on at least two occasions which Caroline could remember Edward had . . .

"Don't think I didn't try," Ruth said. "I was earning when this started. I could afford two shillings for female irregularities, advertised in the paper. No more use to me than old Mother Carey's brews. And they say heaving things . . . One week I got a job, sacking and heaving potatoes out of a clamp. I worked alongside men till I dropped. All no use."

"Could you walk to Baildon?"

"Of course I could. I ain't that far gone yet."

Tomorrow was Sunday, a difficult day.

"On Monday," Caroline said. "Say twelve o'clock. You know the Gateway to the Abbey ruins, those niches where statues used to stand? If you're there just at twelve, on the left-hand side one there'll be a package for you."

"That'll end it? My God? If it'll work, I'll say a prayer for you every morning and night that I live."

"And never say a word." A bit late to be cautious now.

"I swear Almighty God."

Everard never discussed business with Diana, the dear girl simply wouldn't have understood. Edward, though he could maintain professional secrecy, as he had done about Poor Susan while she was alive, was more inclined to talk to Caroline, especially when his mind was troubled. As it had been about ending a pregnancy. He'd done it twice to Caroline's knowledge; both times in very pitiable cases; one a typical Scurvy Lane case; a woman, not old, completely worn out, ten children all crowded into nine years; so anaemic, so undernourished that another pregnancy would certainly kill her. The other a woman, in better circumstances, but with a deformity which prevented her giving birth in the natural way. Two Caesarean births. Pregnant for a third time.

In both cases Edward had doubted, changed his mind, balancing the strictly ethical view against realism. Asking himself questions, and talking to Caroline, whose mind was at least lively and receptive. Miss Hardwicke, who had taught all the Gad's Hall girls, and who had thought highly of Deborah, dismissed Diana as Young Madam, despaired of Lavinia, had once thought that if Caroline would only *give her mind* to her lessons, and not be such a magpie picking up this bit of information here and another there, she might be regarded as educated. That had not happened, but the magpie mind, sharpened since marriage, by boredom, had made Caroline very knowledgeable.

Once before she had stolen from the dispensary which adjoined the room where Edward held his surgery. And

that had been something to relieve pain, Lavinia's child-
birth pains, up there in the attic at Gad's. Now she stole,
well, why? To rid Ruth of her unwanted burden. To end
Mamma's worry. To save some unborn child from bastardy
and penury.

It took a bit of managing; the parcel in brown paper
placed in the niche and then to be watched over, pretending
all the while to be watching the planting out of geraniums
in the beds flanking the grim old gateway. Ruth was punctual and adept, snatching the package up. Pray God it
works.

Mrs. Thorley had been a tigress in defending George,
and she was a tigress in rebuking him.

"I always knew you were stupid—all boys are—but that
you should be so stupid never once occurred to me. I know
you think of yourself as a man, and God help us, you're big
enough." A hard thing to say, for she had always been so
proud of his size, his precocity. "But to go about seducing
village girls . . . I'm thoroughly ashamed."

If, at that moment George had spoken the truth, looked
ashamed, said that he had been the seduced rather than
the seducer, the future might have been different, with
Mamma scolding, but granting a kind of absolution; a very
bad thing to do; and never do it again. But George said,
"Silly bitch! Why did she come whining to you. What were
you supposed to do about it?"

"Provide her with money until the child was born. And
presumably make provision for the child afterwards." Mrs
Thorley spoke very sharply. "Do you not realise the gravity
of your offence? Did it not occur to you that a child might
result? A child born out of wedlock."

"Frankly, I don't see why it should be pinned on me. I
wasn't the first—she said so. And there've been others
since." He appeared to be utterly unrepentant. "I don't say
I might not help her a bit."

"Oh. With what?"

"I could sell something. My watch. Things like that."
George spoke amiably, smiling even.

"All your father's," Mrs Thorley said, her irritation increasing. His father's watch, cuff-links, studs, all of the best quality.

Unperturbed, George said, "Well, why not? After the girls had their whack it was all to be mine, wasn't it?" No disputing that. What was more George Thorley, when making his will, though still feeling that he had many years ahead of him, had suffered the intimation of morality which strikes on such an occasion, and he had looked ahead, thinking: If anything should happen to me . . . He trusted his wife completely, had taken the unusual step of appointing her sole executor, but he had wanted her burdensome stewardship to be as short as possible, so had willed that George should inherit at eighteen. With a start, Mrs Thorley realised that in just two years George could sell not something, but everything if he so wished. A sobering thought indeed.

George's inborn distaste for any unpleasantness asserted itself.

"Oh, come on, Mamma, surely you and I aren't going to quarrel about a silly little thing like this. Probably all a lie anyway." He put his arm around her and dropped a light kiss on the top of her piled-up hair. And with the gesture authority quietly passed from her to him. She had always been indulgent, overindulgent, and he could wheedle almost anything out of her, but she had, in the last resort, been Mamma, the head of the family. It was no longer so.

It was curious, she thought, that two of her children, Lavinia the daughter of a bad man, George the son of a good one, should be alike in indulging in illicit sexual relationships, and alike in showing absolutely no awareness of guilt. Lavinia had never once said: I'm sorry, for all the trouble she had caused. George had shown no sign of repentance in a situation which would have made most boys of his age blush and stammer.

It must be something in *me*. But what? My first marriage was anything but satisfactory, Stephen was far from faithful,

88

we often moved in a raffish circle, I had opportunities. I never put a foot wrong, neither then, nor when I was widowed. I had looks then, I knew a lot of people. I could have found an easier way of making a living for myself, Diana and Lavinia than by drawing designs, teaching ham-fisted children to play the piano, and finally letting the spare bedroom. I lived like a nun. And widowed a second time, I was not, in that way, completely shelved. Given the slightest encouragement, several men, including Mr van Haagen . . .

At the thought of him her eyes went involuntarily to the pretty little desk in the window embrasure.

Yes; I have a hard conscience, too! The only difference is that it operates financially, not amorously.

The thought of Mr van Haagen put an idea into her head. Over supper that evening she said, carefully casual, to George,

"My dear. I have been thinking. Would you like to go abroad? As you know, Mr van Haagen and I do a good deal of business, and of that side you at present know nothing. Mr van Haagen travels extensively. It would be almost the equivalent of the Grand Tour—except that it would not include Italy. But you would see Holland and France and Germany, and even Denmark. It would at least be experience for you."

"That would suit me well," George said. "It wouldn't interfere with the season." He meant the hunting season and the shooting of partridges and pheasants. It meant leaving Gad's, but only for a short time; it meant leaving Goldie, but Johnny Faulkner would be only too glad to exercise the horse for him.

"Yes," George said, "I'd like that."

Caroline's invaluable Mrs Humberstone said, "There's a young person asking for you, ma'am. Ruth, she said, and you'd know her."

"Yes. I do. Show her in."

What now? If the stuff hadn't worked and even Edward

said nothing in this world could be one hundred per cent certain, what was Caroline to do? Give money, which Mamma had forbidden?

But Ruth came in smiling. She carried in one hand the rush basket in which servants transported their few belongings and in the other a bunch of the pale, very sweet-scented wild-flowers known as oxslips, a relative of the cowslip which would grow anywhere. Oxslips were more selective and therefore rare. They grew in profusion in one part of Layer Wood but not in others; and they refused to be transplanted. Years and years ago, when Deborah and Caroline had been motherless children, running wild as people said, one of their games had been making gardens, bringing things in from the wood. No transplanted oxslip had ever survived.

Ruth was—thank God—her own shape again; indeed rather less curved, and rather pale.

"Are you all right, Ruth?" Hadn't she said something about heaving sacks of potatoes? Now she dropped the light rush basket as though it weighed heavy.

"Yes. And all thanks to you. I can't tell you . . . I thought you might like these. Nothing else I could think of to bring you." Ruth held out the bunch, wilting already, oxslips resented being picked as well as being transplanted, but, dying, they gave off their peculiar fragrance and Caroline remembered, on two different levels, like a layer cake, romping about the woods with Deborah, and years later turning aside, in one of those gig rides with Freddy, one of those tantalising, inconclusive . . . Oh God!

Caroline said, "Do sit down," for the girl looked as though she might drop. She had walked from Stonham St Paul's.

"I can't stop," Ruth said. "I got a job in London. Thanks to you again."

"You don't look . . . very hearty, yet. Was it bad?"

"It was quick. And it's over," Ruth said. She mustered a ghost of a smile. "I gotta catch this train. Goodbye, I'll never forget you."

Well, perhaps she had behaved in what Edward would

90

call an unethical way, but at least she'd helped somebody. So why sit down beside the flowers and cry? Because life was so hard—not only on poor girls like Ruth, but on fortunate ones, like herself.

"I missed Caroline by a hairsbreadth last Thursday," Mrs Bostworth said, when Edward had assured her that her ankle was not broken, merely badly sprained, and had strapped it up for her. "In fact I incurred this injury hurrying down the stairs at Hawksley's. Marble looks well, but it can be very treacherous. Such a pity. She was just saying goodbye to Diana—with whom I should have liked to exchange a word. Caroline and I could have shared a cab to the station."

A man less busy, or of more suspicious nature, might have spotted a discrepancy, but Edward simply said, "Keep it bandaged, Mrs Bosworth, and rest it as much as you can."

Mrs Bosworth was beginning to feel that the world was changing. She was old enough to remember Edward's father, dear old Doctor Taylor, never in a hurry; never brusque. *He* would have made much of a sprained ankle, chided her for hurrying, agreed that marble steps were treacherous, and then over a glass of sherry regaled her with a little gossip, discreet, of course, as befitted his profession, but often by omissions or ellipses, very enlightening. There was none of that easy-going comfort from a visit by Edward. On this occasion he had not given Mrs Bosworth a chance to make her next remark—that it was curious that she had not seen Caroline on the five o'clock train, nor at Baildon station.

The true gossip has a nose as sensitive as a truffle hound's. Forced by her sprain into inactivity, Mrs Bosworth indulged in speculation; visited, in her affliction, by Mrs Catchpole and Mrs Garrard, she mentioned, idly, what had struck her as curious. "Lame as I was, I was obliged to hobble almost the full length of the train in order to obtain a seat and there was no sign of her. And when I mentioned having seen her outside Hawksley's, it occurred to me that Doctor Taylor was very abrupt."

"He could hardly be more abrupt than usual," Mrs Garrard said. "I much prefer Doctor Raven. We were forced to call upon him when James broke his collar bone and Doctor Taylor was too busy, for some reason, to come immediately."

Mrs Catchpole said, apropos of nothing tangible—merely the vague idea that Caroline's behaviour had been curious,

"She always was extremely flighty. I must say I endured agonies when my Simon showed a distinct partiality for her. Truly I thanked God when she turned her attention to Mr Ingram."

Mrs Garrard, who had not relinquished all hope of Freddy proposing to . . . well, Monica, or Rosa, when the year of decent mourning was expired, said,

"That came to nothing. It was probably all talk."

Mr van Haagen wrote—his English so much better when written than spoken, that he would be enchanted to have George for the summer and he assured Mrs Thorley that for George it should not be all work and no play. There would be a visit to Paris, not that pedigree stock was ever seen there, but buyers were. George would be most welcome and he should have a good time.

"God, you were born lucky," Johnny Faulkner said, when George told him what his immediate future held. Johnny, having reached the age of seventeen without showing any pronounced academic promise, had left Eton at the end of the summer half and was destined to act, for as long as his father lived, as a kind of foreman—which meant that he took all the blame, and a kind of agent, which meant that he took all the responsibility, for an estate which hadn't really shown much profit for many years.

George was aware of having advantages; two compact farms, Park with its herd and its meadows, Gad's with cornfields, very different from what Johnny would eventually inherit. But there was another difference, too. Ancestry, family connections; roots in the past. It was true that a Sir John Faulkner, a knight of some repute, had been killed in Crécy, his body brought home and laid under an impressive stone memorial in the church at Stratton Strawless. A Thorley had been there too, with his long bow, and his family, stretching their resources, had brought him home to lie with his fathers in the churchyard at Stonham St Paul's.

BUT ... There was a difference which George had partially overcome and meant, one day, to overcome absolutely. But age—about that there was nothing to be done. Johnny and Chloe, twins, were seventeen when George was sixteen, and Chloe had, without benefit of a London season, found a husband. Prayers were sometimes answered, Lady Faulkner thought.

Of the two boys who had loved Chloe, Johnny gave more evidence of distress. No Thorley ever wore his heart on his sleeve—at least after one rebuff and George had suffered that one rebuff earlier in the year, at the Hospital Ball, a charitable affair, where various levels of society met but did not mingle. No uninformed person, looking in, could have told the sheep from the goats, but invisible lines were drawn and defended.

Fifty years later George Thorley was able to say, with proper pride, that the evening dress made for him on that occasion was still in use. At sixteen he was as tall as he would ever be, and the years neither fattened nor shrivelled him. Wearing his new outfit and extremely well-shaved ... But not allowed to dance with Chloe Faulkner. Lady Faulkner, always so grateful because George had saved Johnny's life, always so nice to him, had taken on another aspect, had intervened, had said, while Chloe stood dumb, "Chloe's programme is full."

Warned off!

Over Chloe's engagement, marriage, presentation at Court, George Thorley bothered himself far less than Johnny did, trying to explain what being a twin meant. Saying,

"Oh, I know she'll be all right. Damned great house in Lincolnshire, damned great house in London, bagsful of the needful. But ... well I know they say girls age earlier.

I always looked on Chloe as years younger than me, to be honest, a bit dim-witted, in a nice way, needing to be looked after. I don't mind telling *you*, you're an understanding chap. I feel as though I'd had an arm lopped off."

In the first week of July, Diana and Everard moved into Somerton Road, and if only, if only they'd had a little more money, everything would have been perfect. There'd been no shortage of land, nor of labour a hundred and fifty years earlier when the present Lord Westward's great grandfather had decided that ten decent houses let to decent tenants might pay better than the strawberry field which was part of his inheritance and nothing but a nuisance. The field, within spitting distance of Hyde Park, was rented out in patches for minuscule rents, most of them never paid; the weather had been too wet, and all the strawberries had got the mildew, or it had been too dry and the strawberries had withered. Or they had been stolen. Always some excuse.

Ten houses, built in the new way, a terrace. But not pinched. Decent houses, in which, Lord Westward reflected complacently, he would have been willing to live himself if things got worse. No through traffic, Somerton Road led nowhere; like Friars' Lane in Baildon, it was a cul-de-sac. The decent people whom that long-dead Lord Westward had visualised as living in his fine new houses were City men, riding or driving to their places of business each morning, or men retired from the Army or the Navy without having made much of a fortune. Naturally all such people would keep horses, probably a carriage. So behind all the houses and given access from one end or the other past the houses, there were stables, and above them living accommodation for grooms or coachmen. Between the houses and the Mews as such subsidiary buildings were called, there were gardens. Here, as in St Anne's Crescent, each to his own, but with a difference. Here the boundary walls were set well apart, letting the sunshine in, and to a large degree the stark boundaries were screened by ornamental trees or shrubs.

It was paradise to a young woman who regarded herself as country-bred; who had gone, taking Belle, taking Melville, taking herself, out of dusty, dirty London to breathe the fresh air at Gad's. This year there would be no reason— no excuse?—for such an excursion. She would miss seeing Mamma, and Deborah and Caro and her friends—one of whom, the former Barbara Catchpole, had had a baby recently. But staying in London would save at least one new dress—the garment she had bought specially for dinner at Lady Lumsley's was not suitable for wear at Gad's, and it would save the fare. Everard, always worried about expenses, should be pleased.

Everard was not; he wanted Diana to go to Suffolk because he had received an invitation to stay in Scotland. Diana had not been included. This omission Everard explained to himself by the fact that in part his visit had to do with business; also to be considered was that lady Lumsley had borne in mind that a woman with two small children—and no proper nurse—would find it difficult to absent herself for a fortnight. The real reason was, of course— and Everard knew it—that Diana had not quite slipped into the new milieu as he himself had done. It was not through any gaucheness of manner. Diana's manners were perfect and she had poise—of a rather static kind. It was not that she was less intelligent than those of the set in which Lady Lumsley moved, the level of intelligence there was not high. It was just, well, poor darling, she was out of her depth; she had neither the background nor the adaptability. Everard had the astonishing thought that both Caroline and Deborah would have done better, thus transplanted. Caroline, set down between two strange men at dinner, would soon have had them laughing; Deborah would have talked about horses and hunting. Diana, with her correct little answers, prim little questions was at a loss. Provincial!

Everard himself had slid back effortlessly; he could say of his humble—comparatively humble occupation, "Oh, like Old Father William, I took to the law. . . ." He could refer, caustically, to himself as a wage slave. The years he had enjoyed with his godfather, his years of luxury and privilege, calamitously ended, had left him with something indestructible and recognisable. At that first memorable dinner at Lumsley House, Diana's neighbour, for lack of anything else to say to a woman he had never seen before, asked whether she had enjoyed the latest opera at Covent Garden and Diana could only say, "I'm afraid I haven't seen it." Asked the same question by *his* neighbour, Everard said, "No. The last opera I saw was in Paris, a long time ago. Nowadays, having thrashed my way on to a horse-bus and off again, at the end of the day—I work in the City—I've had enough of people and of noise by the end of the day." Diana's answer had been correct, and sterile. Everard's different in tone.

So, when Diana said that this year there was no need to go to Gad's, Everard, to her surprise, had insisted that she should. She needed a rest after the move. He'd be in Scotland; and wouldn't her Mamma miss her now that George had gone to Holland?

Certainly the move had been exhausting, not because Diana had been obliged to lift and carry, but because there was so much contrivance to be done, all at the least possible cost. Curtains had been especially troublesome. Diana had been through this hoop before; none of her Friar's Lane curtains had fitted the mean little house in St Anne's Crescent; but shortening was easy, lengthening practically impossible. New curtains were an absolute necessity, and by the time they and a few other things had been bought her dowry would be exhausted.

They were not yet actually in the state which Everard had feared and talked about at the beginning of their marriage; they were not in debt, but the future was daunting. His fare had trebled and he had joined a club. He proposed to compensate for this extravagance by economising on luncheons at his usual chophouse and sustaining himself by taking a cup of coffee—peculiarly greenish in colour and of sinister flavour, and a sandwich. Anxious not to be seen by any member of the firm, or any clerk from the office in the act of frequenting such low places, he sometimes walked half a mile. And he was always very hungry when he returned in the evening.

Bessie worried about prices and mourned the old Maypole Market. This did not seem to be an area promising anything in the way of a market; and there was a notice at the mouth of Somerton Road, and several others, warning off street vendors. Still, she did not give up hope and scuttled about until she found Soho, cheaper and even more varied than the old Market. It was a good old trudge, especially coming back with a load, but well worth it.

Soho, as Bessie told Diana, was full of foreigners, but they understood English all right, though some would short-change you if you didn't look out. Trust me to look out.

One day on a foraging expedition, Bessie passed a young woman. They had never seen each other before, might never meet again; yet they were linked. Bessie, looking at Ruth, thought: Dressed-up tart! And Ruth, looking at Bessie, thought: That could be me! That was all.

The foreigners had brought their own religion with them and Ruth was on her way to light a candle for Caroline as she had done every week since coming to London. Lighting a candle seemed somehow more of a gesture than just saying a prayer. Ruth was not a Catholic, knew nothing of the ritual, but in her first week in London she had shared a room with a red-haired Irishwoman of dubious morals but extreme piety. The church was St Anthony's and therefore his shrine was nearest the door, and the biggest and brightest. The candles varied in size and price. One day Ruth was going to light a great fat shilling one on Caroline's behalf.

She did not know that one of the legendary qualities attributed to St Anthony was the finding of things that were lost.

Mrs Thorley said to Caroline, "Diana is coming, after all. I had rather gathered from her last letter that she would not come this year. I'm glad."

"Yes, you must miss George, Mamma."

"I miss him, naturally. I have missed you all. . . . But George is enjoying himself tremendously."

And *this* year Caroline would not go and look at Diana's children, and Deborah's one with the I-don't-care look, which really said I-care-very-much.

Caroline was going to have a baby of her own.

What had that wretched girl said? "It's his. You always know."

Caroline knew.

There had been some days of agonising indecision. Go to Freddy and say: All right. I'll come away with you; or stay here, pretend and pretend? Deceive Edward but in doing so make him happy. And, teetering on the knife edge of decision, Caroline thought: God's teeth! I don't even *know* myself, I've slept with them both. It's imagination. It's because I feel guilty. Avoid, just for once, the hasty, impulsive action. Even the most level-headed of women didn't go rushing about saying: I'm pregnant! just because they'd missed a few days, a week, a month.

The desire for Freddy which had seemed quenched forever that morning at Albertino's had recovered, and that made the decision harder. So did the fact that if she told Edward the truth *now* sheer anger might lessen the hurt. Now and again she imagined life with Freddy, in France, which she only knew from his descriptions of it—all very lyrical. An old château on the outskirts of a whitewalled, red-roofed village, vineyards on terraced hillsides, all in hot sunshine. Married to, living with, loving Freddy, openly with no furtiveness, no guilt. Nonsense, you silly girl; you'd always feel guilty! And always just that tiny bit insecure. Pregnancy isn't a very pretty condition. . . . Once you wondered what age with Freddy would be like, think what his attitude might be when you're bulging and blotchy and useless in bed. Oh dear!

It was Edward who precipitated the decision; that and her tendency to speak before she thought.

"Darling," he said one day at breakfast, "are you all right? Is there anything on your mind?"

Irresistible! "I wouldn't say on my *mind*, exactly!"

Edward had expected the revelation of some trivial bother—so far as he knew all Caro's bothers were trivial—gaped, understood. He got up and came around the table, knelt, burrowed his face into her lap and mumbled something about this being all that was needed to make life perfect. When he lifted his head she saw the tears in his eyes, on his lower eyelids. But, typically Edward, he was himself again almost immediately, assuring her that there was nothing to be worried about; she shouldn't even feel pain, beyond a pang or two. There was this marvellous chap called Simpson who advocated an anesthetic for women in the last stages of labour. It had been resisted at first, but the Queen herself had taken advantage of it when her last child was born.

So the choice was made, and Caroline's common sense assured her that it was the right one. Sometimes she fingered, rather hesitantly, the notion that even her apparently disgraceful behaviour had been right. After all she had been married to Edward for more than five years and nothing had come of it. Perhaps, in a way, Edward's joy and pride owed something to Freddy.

Now and again bits of—well, what? You couldn't call it knowledge. Superstition; folklore, drifted back into her mind. One was reassuring; babies with two fathers, it was said, were always boys. Nobody knew or could even guess why, but in fact a glance into the history of the Workhouse Children gave some indication. By far the greater majority of the boys were illegitimate, the offspring of loose-living women. (Like me!) All but a few of the girls were the product of genuine marriages, ended by death or some other calamity.

"Naturally," the Head Matron said, "records are incomplete. We have some children who were simply abandoned." Why Mrs Taylor should be interested in the origins of the children who had fallen into the Poor Law Guardians' hands was a bit puzzling, but not to be questioned.

So the chances were that Caroline's baby would be a boy; and curiously, Edward seemed to think so too, though now and again he caught himself up in the planning of the unborn's medical training, taking over, carrying on, and said, "But of course, darling, it could be a girl. And if she's anything like her mother, she'll be adorable."

Less comfortable was an idea, no more, about inherited colouring, especially of the eyes. Somebody, who, when and where, Caroline in her light-hearted way had forgotten, had said that two light-eyed parents never produced a dark-eyed child, or vice versa. Her own eyes were greyish-bluish-greenish; Edward's clear steely grey; Freddy's brown. A brown-eyed child . . . but, thank God, Edward was unlikely to have heard this rural theory, or, if he had, paid any attention to it.

By late July, when Diana came, Caroline seemed settled, happy, the flighty quality in her outgrown. There had always been something about her young stepdaughter which Mrs Thorley had faintly distrusted, something wild, too outspoken, careless, too easily moved to tears or laughter. All that was needed now. A bit belatedly, but better late than never, Caroline had conformed.

It was about Diana, whose behavior, speech, everything had always been so impeccable, that Mrs Thorley worried now; not because of anything Diana said or did, but the way she looked. Drawn, anxious, and—are my eyes now deluding me?—with a white hair or two. Diana! Always, in the old days, the one inclined to squander money on cosmetic preparations, the one whom other girls had consulted. And now—well, Mrs Thorley had never deceived herself, Diana wore the look—ten years too soon—which she herself had worn in Leicester.

Poor diet? That was what she had told herself, facing that face, morning after morning, angling to see, in a cracked glass, whether her hair was tidy.

Rescued by George Thorley, lifted from the weak tea and bread level, Mrs Thorley had improved in looks, plumped out, not too much, just enough, so that for a time she had defied the years—until Lavinia . . .

Mrs Thorley applied herself to the process of trying to fatten Diana a little, but ten days of good feeding did not lift the drawn look, and if it stemmed from a secret worry, plainly Diana intended to keep it secret. She deftly evaded all the openings which might have led to confidences. Quite right, too; a decent reticence was one of the bedrocks of good behaviour. But Mrs Thorley could not forget Caroline's description of Diana's first London home and the pretence which Diana had kept up. Was her new home any better? Or, horrible thought! even worse? Or, possibly so much better as to be outrageously expensive? Unlikely, Mrs Thorley thought, for Everard was the reverse of spendthrift, in fact if anything he erred on the other side. Very cautious. Indeed he would have deferred his wedding if Mrs Thorley, anxious to meet Timothy Bridges' impatience and her own, perhaps stupidly old-fashioned wish not to have Deborah married first, and not to have Deborah married in chapel, had not intervened by hiring the little house in Friars' Lane and thus speeding things along.

Deborah made two visits during Diana's stay; once for the day, and once staying overnight. Last year—was it only last year?—when Deborah's Sam was five and Diana's Belle was four they had squabbled and fought and everybody expected trouble to break out again as soon as they met this year. But a twelve-month interval had worked wonders in Sam; in him the Thorley precocity was at work, as it had been in George, and in Deborah, whom everyone who didn't know had always taken for the eldest of the Gad's Hall girls. Sam at six was as big as most boys at ten and his attitude to Belle, who had changed very little except to become prettier, was now kindly, quite amusingly patronising. He said, "If you are a good girl, you shall have a ride on my new pony. *When* I get it." He shot a glance, half-assured, half-questioning, at his mother.

"You'll get it," Deborah said. "In fact, I've been writing to Mr Thoroughgood and we may collect it next week." Deborah gave her son a smile, not the one of the old days, entrancingly lopsided because it produced a dimple in one cheek, not in the other. "Now get along with you. Play ball with Belle, and don't throw too hard. Remember, she's only a girl." Holding Belle by the hand, and followed by Melville, just steady on his feet but resolutely determined not to be left out of anything, Sam went off, and Deborah thought: What a daft thing to say! Only a girl. When she'd proved, and went on proving almost every day of her life, that she—only a girl—was as good as most men, and better than many.

Most of the disputes between her and Tim had been quiet ones, wordy battles, most of which she had won by cool argument. But they had had one physical confrontation—apart from the bed thing. Both on their feet, fully dressed, and in the open; in fact in the chapel yard. Deborah and Tim had reached quite a comfortable compromise about chapel going and hunting, and Sam had been taken to chapel, as a good little born Methodist should, from an early age. But there came the Sunday morning when the preacher was the man whom George had mimicked so well, after his one miserable, curtailed visit to Foxton; the man who said er after every other word. Sam, too young to be critical but now old enough to be bored, had begun to wriggle and shuffle and then to kick the back of the pitch-pine pew just in front of him. Father on one side, Mother on the other had quelled that outlet of nervous energy, and Sam had taken refuge in saying er, loudly and distinctly, every time the preaching man said it. Worse than kicking, which could be controlled by a hand on each active young knee. And far more embarrassing, for the poor man with the impediment which he resolutely ignored in his effort to serve his God by preaching, halted, looked confused.

Tim took his naughty boy by the arm and dragged him out and within a minute the service was disturbed again by the sound of two good hard smacks and the roar of a child affronted rather than hurt. Everybody within the claustrophobic little building—except Deborah—heard the smacks with a kind of satisfaction. Naughty children should be spanked; they had been spanked in their time, had spanked, or were prepared to spank any child of theirs. But Mrs

Bridges rose, swiftly, and silently, and went out. No other sound disturbed the preacher, but he had lost the thread of his discourse and jumped from fourthly-er to finally-er.

Outside, near the tree under which Sam's paternal grandparents lay in their eternal rest, an unseemly scuffle was going on. Tim still had his hold on his son's arm and on Sam's face the marks of a heavy hard hand, back and front, were already reddening; but Sam was kicking.

"You *louts!*" Deborah said, getting between them and pushing, Tim with her left arm, Sam with her right. "I'm ashamed of you both." Released, Sam dodged behind the tree and from its shelter glared at his father, his father glared at his mother. Deborah glared at them both, seeming to divide her displeasure impartially. The first notes of the final hymn began to sound.

"Come along," Deborah said, "we don't want people staring at us." Straightening her hat, she set off at a brisk pace. Tim, like most Methodists, kept the third commandment very literally and Foxton was only a mile and a half from chapel, so they walked. For the same reason the Sunday dinner was always cold.

"I can't eat. My mouth hurts," Sam said.

"Come here and let me see."

Tim Bridges was anything but a violent or cruel man, but his hands were hard and heavy and into the two blows had gone years of frustration. The boy was already thoroughly spoiled; Deborah had seemed, from the first, to set herself against any form of correction; Sam was too young to know right from wrong; Sam's spirit must not be broken, and so forth. It had been, all unknown to himself, his wife's face, rather than his son's, which Tim had slapped that morning.

The inside of Sam's face on one side was cut and one tooth was hanging askew. It was a superficial injury and the tooth was one of the baby ones, due to fall any day. Still that did not excuse . . .

"I'll make you some bread and milk," Deborah said. Servants were supposed to do the minimum of work on Sunday; Emma, too infirm now to get to chapel, spent most of the day resting and reading, not without difficulty, what she called the Good Book. Eva, the girl brought in to help when Deborah rebelled against acting as kitchen maid, went to chapel and then spent the rest of the day with her family.

Placing the steaming bowl before Sam, Deborah said, "Take it as hot as you can, and hold it against the cut."

More spoiling! In a properly run household Sam would have had no dinner at all, possibly no supper either.

Presently Sam produced the tooth and said, "It's out."

Something was wrong. On every former occasion when he had lost a baby tooth, he'd been told to put it under his pillow and see what it had changed into by the morning. It had changed into sixpence. For the first time or two it had seemed like magic to Sam, but he soon saw through it. It was Mother! And he was beginning to suspect that it was Mother who filled the sock he hung up each Christmas Eve.

No mention of pillows or magic today. He really had offended Mother. Father he bothered less about, Father was often angry with him, though he'd never hit him before. Anyhow, I kicked back.

"I'm sorry I was naughty in chapel."

"So am I. But you're going to be sorrier, my boy. You won't have a ride on your pony for a week."

"A week!" Sam's face, slightly swollen on the more injured side, took on an almost ludicrous look of dismay. At his age a week and a year were hardly distinguishable.

"A week," Deborah said. "You were naughty to start kicking the pew and it was even worse to make fun of Mr Sturgiss."

Sharp young wits noted that no mention was made of kicking Father.

"By the time he's ten he'll be ruined for life," Tim said. "You give way to every whim and fancy. You never correct him. You interfere when I attempt to."

"You are mistaken. He is being punished for his behaviour this morning. I have banned his pony rides for a week."

That was, of course, part of the trouble. Somehow or other she always managed to be in the right, even when she was in the wrong.

Timothy Bridges was a simple, God-fearing man, little given to analysing his own motives, but he knew that married to a tractable, meek, God-fearing woman, he'd have been happy, and kindly disposed to her. Going to Gad's Hall that day and falling in love with the girl who shared his love of, feeling for, horses, had been the worst day's work he ever did. And the maddening thing was that everything had promised so well. Deborah had given every sign of being meek and tractable, and if not actually God-fearing, capable of becoming so. Then, it seemed to him, she had, by a single act of defiance, rushing off back to Gad's, against his wishes, simply because her half sister had died somewhere at the other end of the earth and Mamma needed her, radically changed.

He was a man of markedly humane nature, particularly where horses were concerned. To the proper woman he would have been kind, even slightly indulgent; he would have taken pride in his son's size and fearlessness. As it was, all had gone wrong. Love and loving-kindness had suddenly vanished and into the emptiness it had left something as sour as bile had seeped.

Listen to her now!

"Perhaps I was over severe, for I must admit that Mr Sturgiss' sermons affect me in much the same way."

"He cannot help his affliction."

"He could avoid exposing it and driving everybody mad with boredom. *I* can't embroider, but I don't insist upon doing it and expect everybody to admire my efforts."

Unanswerable.

Sam quickly solved the problem of no pony rides. Mother had said pony, not horse. And there were plenty of horses at Foxton; the great amber-coloured Punches which Father bred, the heavy horses; lighter ones for riding and driving, and a few old broken-down ones which Father

105

said he had rescued. Sam went to the gate of the pasture where the big ones were, made enticing noises and soon had several to choose from. He chose the biggest, climbed the gate and scrambled on. Funny! The horse, well-fed, weighing a ton, seemed to have a very sharp backbone. And also seemed to be quite unaware of the fact that Sam, in choosing it, had done it a favour. It kept trying to brush him off as though he were a fly. Sam clung on to its mane. The horse tried to knock him off by lumbering near a tree, bruising Sam's knee and ankle, but Sam stuck on and finally steered back to the gate, where by this time an anxious little crowd had gathered.

"Now do you see about not breaking his spirit," Deborah said.

"It was downright disobedience."

"No. I said no pony."

"It was dangerous. A stallion, running with mares. He could have been killed, do you realise?"

"But he wasn't." He'd been well-bruised, and Deborah having ascertained that no bones were broken had said, "And serve you right!" But she had been at the gate, her heart in her mouth as the silly saying went; Sam so very small, the great horse, never ridden, not bred for riding.

"All right, he wasn't. God was good. But surely even you must see that this kind of thing can't go on. He's defiant, and reckless, and in the end he'll be uncontrollable. Then where shall we be?"

After a little silence, Deborah said, coolly, calculatingly,

"If you wish, not here. I think the time has come . . . Let's face it, Tim. We aren't suited; we made the mistake of thinking that because we both had a feeling for horses . . . We deluded ourselves. On no other subject do we think alike, not even over the boy. We just make each other miserable. So why go on? We have only one life, you know. Why spend it in misery that can be avoided?"

"We're married. For better or worse."

"I know. But there is such a thing as divorce."

"Do you realise what you are saying?"

"I have given the matter some thought. You can't accuse

106

me of adultery, which would simplify matters for you. But I am quite willing to desert you."

"You must be off your head." Surely only insanity could account for an apparently decent woman using the word adultery in such a way. It was one of the words just acceptable when in the Bible, not elsewhere. As for the suggestion, it was infamous!

"No. I'm sane. And I'm serious. Think it over."

He did so and with naïve astonishment saw that the infamous suggestion was not entirely unattractive. A man should be master in his own house and here he was not, never had been after those first few happy weeks. Talk about a square peg in a round hole—the square peg could be whittled down and rounded, made to fit, but nobody yet had found a way of making a round peg fit a square hole. She'd as good as blackmailed him—I'll do all your chapel things in return for being allowed to hunt, and from that bargain she'd gone on encroaching all the time; giddy worldly tunes on the piano, regular visits to Gad's, sly little digs at nonconformity, teetotalism—all the things by which his life had been governed for as long as he could remember. Awkward about bed, too. . . . Yes, there was a good deal to be said in favour of a clean break. No shame about it. In the eyes of his fellow men, and of the law, fully in the right.

But . . . Well, visualising eventually another marriage, comfortable as an old slipper, no conflict, no arguments, Tim thought of age. He had waited to marry, being a bit choosy, and he was now older, seven years wasted, except for Sam. He could not be sure of breeding another boy like Sam who would be well-nigh perfect, once brought under control. It could be done in a fortnight, without interference from Deborah.

"All right. But I keep the boy."

"Am I likely to leave him with you? He still has bruises on his face. But for me you'd probably have knocked *all* his teeth out. Oh no, if I go, Sam comes with me. And you'll never find us."

She was capable of making that kind of escape.

"It beats me what this is all about. Haven't you got a comfortable home? Have I ever looked at another woman? Have I ever grudged you anything? Thwarted you in any way?"

"It is this everlasting atmosphere of disapproval," Deborah said. "The constant friction. You're always right, with God on your side. God is always on the side of the big battalions. I'm always wrong. I can't live in this air."

It had all begun long ago. Deborah and Caroline, motherless, running wild, picking up coarse expressions and swear words. And suddenly the introduction of a new mother—to be called Mamma—and her two perfectly behaved children. To please Mamma, to win a look or a word of approval, Deborah would have jumped into the moat. And it was the same at school; to please Miss Hardwicke, anything, anything. The desire to please, not inbred, but inculcated early, had governed her life. But there was a limit to it. Especially when one had learned that in practically every situation one knew best, or did best.

"You may know what you're talking about—being so clever; but I'm blowed if I do. Anyway, let's drop it."

The uneasy peace continued. Perhaps Tim grumbled less, was a little less openly critical of Deborah's handling of Sam, and of Sam's behaviour. Indeed, with regard to the boy he reversed his tactics and began to woo his favour. "Like to come to market with me today, son?" Making indulgences, allowing the boy to hold the reins on the homeward journey when friskiness had worn off, buying him bags of good wholesome sweets, none of your bright-coloured rubbish; and once, on a warm day, an ice cream.

"Mother, there's a new shop in Thetford. It's called a tea-shop. Father had tea, but I had ice cream, on a glass plate. It was wonderful. And the people were foreigners; not black like on the missionary box, but not quite white either. And they talked in a funny way." Here Sam became a little cautious—he'd got into trouble for imitating Mr Sturgiss, and "you wisha one-a vanilla," did faintly resemble that preacher.

Privately Sam believed that Father was trying to make

up for hitting him so hard. Cheap at the price, really; the tooth was bound to fall out sooner or later, and the bruises hadn't hurt long. They'd also served as a good excuse for not washing his face. Anyway, a boy with so many new experiences behind him, a new pony in the offing—and a Thoroughgood at that—was far too old to quarrel with a girl cousin.

At the mention of Sam's having a Thoroughgood the little vertical lines between Diana's eyebrows and the little down-curving ones at each side of her mouth deepened slightly. Really life was grossly unfair. Caroline in Hawksley's, spending money like a drunken sailor, Deborah able to buy a thoroughbred pony for Sam while she and Everard were so pinched, and likely to be more so. She had urged Everard, when the move was being discussed to ask for a rise and he had replied, a trifle wearily, that he'd had it, in April; ten pounds, as agreed. Against steadily rising prices the increase went nowhere but stark economic facts remained, Upton, Binder and Smith could easily fill his place with a man, not so good, of course, but quite adequate and cheaper. He had repeated what he said many times before; without money enough to set up on your own, or some influence behind you, you were doomed from the start. But surely, Diana argued, the wonderful job he'd done on the Lumsley estate business should count for something. At that Everard looked displeased and said that there was nothing particularly clever—in the legal sense—about finding a paper which had been overlooked, put in fact into a used envelope by a man who was quite prepared to say: "Aye, I had drink taken at the time, as well as being upset in my emotions, he being like a father to me and me watching by his deathbed day and night." Little finesse was needed there; more was called for in persuading Lady Morton that she would be very unwise to contest a will, plainly dated ten days later than the one which left everything to her. Everard had—suspicious from the first—asked could he see the two men who had witnessed the will, made in *her* writing and in her house. Both had gone to Canada.

Which was, as Everard said, a singular coincidence. That had made her think.

It was not an exploit of which Everard was proud and financially he had not gained a penny. Socially, he had. Apart from being so empty of pocket, he was back where he had been when his godfather had been alive. He was even about to shoot grouse again. He'd had something, a true instinct, or a layer of self-assurance, which had made him able to round the difficult corner of having no gun, no country clothes. Given the right tone of voice, the right light touch, it was perfectly acceptable to say, "I had a pair once, rather nice, Baxters, but you can't eat a gun. I can't remember now whether I sold them or pawned them in Cambridge. Anyway, since I was never in position to bail them out it comes to the same thing."

Lady Lumsley said that there must be about fifty guns in the gun room at the Castle and Everard could take his pick.

"That is all very well—and thank you. But any decent ghillie would shoot me on sight. In town clothes. . . ."

Charlie Somerton, Lord Westward now, said pop along, dear boy; order a tweed suit, better still, two, weather being what it was, and put it on his bill. God bless you, what difference did it make. "I only pay him about once in four years and I *know* he charges interest. You might as well benefit."

Diana's annual visit usually lasted a fortnight, and during it Deborarh—her right to do so now unquestioned—usually came over twice. She did so this year, on the second visit staying the night because of collecting the pony.

Diana, no longer able to feel superior to Deborah, whose rough, ill-behaved little boy seemed to have reformed; nor to Caroline, so long childless, but now due to have a baby at about Christmas time, was feeling depressed; only two days left of her holiday where meals which she had not planned, of which she had not counted the cost, appeared with regularity, and where common justice did not demand, as it did in London, that she should pull her share of the load. Bessie was a blessing, a true gift from God, but Bessie could not do everything, and when she went marketing down in Soho . . . Oh, cheaper, much cheaper—but how much nicer to be able to leave the children and the house in Bessie's reliable hands and saunter out to Hawksley's oneself, place an order, have things delivered. As everybody else in Somerton Road, in the whole neighbourhood did.

Looking at the glossy pony—Sam had demanded that everybody should come and view his new acquisition—Diana said,

"Really, Deb, I sometimes wonder if you realise how lucky you are."

Me, lucky? How little you know!

There'd been one of those quiet disputes about replacing the pony which Sam had first ridden at the age of three, but it had not developed into anything much. Tim had said, "All right. Have it your own way. You always do." But all the time he'd been planning a sly trick. During the argument she had said, "I'm prepared to pay for it. The best is always cheapest in the end." And just as she was preparing to hand over the shining sovereigns, Sam had forestalled her.

"Father said he would pay. He gave me this." Sam produced what was not to him money, just a bit of paper. A cheque, signed by Timothy Bridges, good anywhere.

All the same it was an underhand trick. It made her feel silly in her own eyes. Not in those of Tom Thoroughgood, or of Sam, neither of whom cared much, or even noticed who paid, or in what form the payment was made. But not to have told her; quite possibly telling Sam to say nothing; going behind her back.

She'd always been a sensible girl and had grown into a sensible woman, and now her own sense told her that she was taking a stupid view not only of this small issue but of her whole relationship with her husband. To begin with she'd been a blind fool to marry him; she should have seen how entirely unsuited they were. When you made salad dressing you shook the oil and vinegar together and they mixed, temporarily, but in no time at all, and under no

111

outside influence, they separated again, not through any fault in either of them, simply a law of nature. In the second place she had deceived Tim, pretending to be other than she was. He'd made no secret of his Methodism or his teetotalism, of his distaste for display. *She* had been the false one; drinking lemonade even at her own wedding!

In this self-accusatory mood she did not blame—as she often did at other times—Tim's rocky unyieldingness, his unctuousness, his lack of considerateness for her youth, her different background, even her ignorance of what kind of hat to wear in chapel. She blamed only herself.

So, out in the sunshine, surveying the pony, when Di said about being lucky, Deborah said, after a scarcely perceptible pause,

"Yes, I suppose I am." She remembered what Caroline had reported about Di's horrid little house, and Di spending a whole day shopping without buying anything. Di had kept up a brave front—but then we all do; Mamma's training perhaps. Nobody would guess how Tim and I quarrel, nobody ever guessed how much Caroline felt not having a child. . . .

And now Deb noticed—she was not so fashion-minded as Di, though she liked to be reasonably well-dressed— that this was the same dress as Di had brought to Gad's last year.

"I don't mean to insult you, Di, but I'm sure a house move must be very expensive. If fifty pounds would be any good to you, you're welcome. I've no use for it. I brought it with me to pay for the pony, Tim forestalled me and gave Sam a cheque."

Diana's eyes widened. "Are you *sure?* It's a great deal of money, Deb."

Deborah then said something that Diana was to remember. She missed, of course, half its significance, the half implied when Deborah said, "And it's not Tim's money." She noticed, and remembered the next words. "I earned it."

Not always easily, especially when a potentially good horse had been mishandled and one had to start again; but

112

it was work she enjoyed and she was making a name for herself. Tim of course had been opposed to that, and so it had seemed unfair to use his stable, his fodder and his pasture; so, as she had once suggested, Deborah had moved the whole thing out to Mr Craig's, and Mr Craig was a man of whom no man could be jealous in *that* way; a good breeder and a good trainer in his day, he had fallen victim to what old-fashioned country people still called the joint evil, really a form of rheumatism that encroached inexorably.One stick, two sticks, presently a wheelchair.

"Well, if you are sure you can spare it. It would be a great help. If you would regard it as a loan, Deb. In Everard's profession it takes a little time to get established. . . . And of course the move *was* rather unexpected. It just happened that Lord Westward—he was Everard's fag at Eton and apparently remembered him kindly, had this house. . . ."

Sam, faithful to his word, for Belle had been good and never once resorted to biting, heaved her into the saddle and said, "Just pretend you're sitting in a chair."

Diana asked was it safe, and assured that it was, said, "He's very like George, don't you think?"

"I suppose there's a family resemblance." Deborah's mind shifted again; once Tim had said of Sam that he bid fair to be a spitting image of George. And that implied disapproval. And after all what was so wrong with George?

Mr van Haagen had no fault to find with his own son, Pieter, now thirty years old, happily married, the father of three girls. Pieter fitted well and performed conscientiously in that corner of the business which had been assigned to him. But Mr van Haagen had never derived anything approaching as much pleasure from his son's company as he did from George Thorley's.

To George everything was new and everything was wonderful, his capacity for enjoyment, for picking up just enough of any language to get along with, seemed to be infinite. And everybody seemed to like him.

Everybody had always liked George; he'd had one little

setback, his not being able to woo his first love, but though he would remember her, with sentiment, forever, he'd soon recovered; after all, he was only sixteen and she was a year older—in addition to being what was called County. It had been what was known as a non-starter from the first. Within a week of his arrival in Amsterdam he had temporarily forgotten Chloe Faulkner, who was not to be wooed, and also the girl Ruth, all too easily wooed, and was prepared to fling himself wholeheartedly into a new life. In that he could hardly have found a better guide and mentor than Mr van Haagen.

Mr van Haagen was acutely aware of the responsibility laid upon him, and of the trust which that good woman, Mrs Thorley, had reposed in him. He must not, definitely not, allow himself to be misled by the boy's size and apparent maturity. A widow's only son. Not ignorant, no country-bred boy could be that, but innocent. I must talk to him like a father, Mr van Haagen reflected; and curiously it was easier to have such conversations with this boy than it had been with his own son. George was both quicker in understanding and less resentful of advice.

It was all, in a sense, good advice, though not particularly moral in tone. George must beware of this, beware of that, and the talks covered a wide range of subjects, starting, correctly, with alcohol. Drinking on an empty stomach was very bad; mixing too many drinks was very bad; drinking too much at any time was bad, but particularly so when talking business or playing cards. "So, fortunes have been lost," Mr van Haagen said. He was not against the frequenting of brothels, occasionally; too often was unadvisable at any time but especially for the young, and naturally one must exercise discrimination. George knew, through his association with the more sophisticated Johnny Faulkner, the definition of a brothel but he had never seen one. Such a thing did not exist—officially—in Baildon, though George's brother-in-law Edward could have named certain houses which were very little better than brothels. Discrimination must be exercised because of diseases. Like every good patriot of every country, Mr van Haagen attributed the diseases to a foreign origin; and for a Dutchman the culprit was not far to seek—it was the East Indies. "That is why," Mr van Haagen explained, "never, never a place that is cheap, and never near docks."

George was getting an extension of the liberal education begun in the Rectory at Stonham St Paul's, and enjoying himself immensely.

"Really, he is good to write so often," Mrs Thorley said, and then, looking up, realised that the letter which had arrived by the same post for Diana—Everard's writing— had given the poor girl a shock. It was . . . It reminded Mrs Thorley of the first moment after Caroline had opened Poor Susan's letter announcing her engagement . . . Except that Diana was not crying. But then she never had cried as easily as Caroline did.

"Is he . . . ill?"

Diana seemed to have difficulty in speaking; she swallowed on nothing, lifted her cup and drank. That gave Deborah time to think of the children. "Sam, go and see if your new pony likes toast. Take Belle with you."

Diana said, "Not ill. Mad."

Neither Mrs Thorley nor Deborah took the word very seriously. For one thing they had both had close contact with Lavinia when she was truly mad; for another the word was lightly used.

"He had the fortnight's holiday to which he was entitled," Diana said. "Then somebody issued a further invitation— deer stalking this time. And he wrote asking further leave. And was refused. So he wrote and gave in his notice. He says . . ." She stared at the letter with unseeing eyes, "that he is going to set up on his own."

Neither Mamma nor Deborah could really share her horror. They hadn't lived in cut-throat London, completely dependent upon one man's earnings. Inadequate, but at least sure.

"It may not be a bad thing," Deborah said.

"My dear, I often *thought* and you sometimes *said* that Everard was wasting his talent, working for other people."

115

"I know. I know. But if he's said it to me once he's said it a thousand times—without enough money to buy a partnership or start upon your own, or without influence, it's hopeless. And now he's done that very thing. It'll be the ruin of us all."

Mrs Thorley had always had—as her second husband had recognised—a good business head. When she was widowed and left in sole charge she had set herself a fixed goal; to so improve the prosperity of the farm and of the herd that she could pay the girls the modest dowries left them in their father's will, and hand over to George, when he was eighteen, the business in a flourishing state. She had worked hard and taken some risks. She had slipped back a little, unable to spare time or attention, during the months of Lavinia's madness, but to recoup the loss she hit upon her plot with Mr van Haagen, and that had been extremely lucrative.

She could afford to help Everard over the difficult starting period—say two years; always assuming that he would be in a position to repay the money, if only in instalments.

Had she the right to do it? It was, after all, Thorley money, even if she had earned much of it. She couldn't have built the business from nothing. And—such a strange thing to think after all these years—Diana was not a Thorley. She had tried so hard to make no distinction between the girls, but she saw one now. Also she must ask herself, was Everard ever likely to be very successful? He had many things in his favour, good looks, a beautiful voice, beautiful manners, a good education, excellent qualifications. Why hadn't they taken him further? Was he merely unlucky? Did he lack something that was essential to success? Some defect of personality? No sense of humor.

She could remember her first sight of him, in Gad's barn at the Christmas party for the workpeople. She'd liked him well enough, he'd been most civil and helpful, but she hadn't entirely liked him; something prim and mean about his mouth; but then, that should be no drawback in his profession. But the whole thing needed more thought.

It had not taken long to think all those things. She

reached over and touched Di's shoulder.

"Don't take too glum a view, my dear. It might be a turning point. And it is possible that among his—new friends, there is somebody with influence."

"Oh," Di said bitterly, "I have no doubt of that! And I know who! Alison Lumsley. I can just hear her. Promising to send him twenty clients a day because she would tell them how wonderful he is. And telling him that if he worked for himself he could take free time just when he liked. And he fool enough to believe her. By Christmas she'll have forgotten his name."

When a façade breaks there is rubble; and the better and more elaborate the façade the more rubble. Diana began to cry, and crying, she was far more pitiable than Caroline.

Deborah began to think. Of her five-hundred-pound dowry she had spent only a hundred on a half-trained and to the casual eye not very promising hunter, bought from Mr Craig. It had seemed unfair to spend Tim's money on something of which he so strongly disapproved. It had partly been her success with that animal that had started the training business.

She'd let Di have the remainder; not to help Everard to set up on his own—whatever that might entail—but to ease things for her. Over the first few fences, so to speak.

Deborah was rather given to semi-philosophical thoughts, and she thought now—Curious that Caroline who spoke without thinking should have summed Everard up on that first night and called him greedy. Later Everard had proved to be greedy and a bit idle. All the time when they'd been getting the little house in Friars' Lane ready and Deborah had been painting and whitewashing and doing a bit of impromptu cooking, he'd always turned up to eat, never to tackle a down-to-earth job. . . . Curious too, that of the three of them, Di, Caro and herself, two had made love marriages. Caro had, Deb was sure, married on what was called the rebound. Caro had been quite obviously crazy about Freddy Ingram, but at his engagement party she'd practically got herself engaged to Edward. And unless Caroline was as secretive as Di had been, as Deb was still, her marriage had really turned out best. Life was the very devil.

The Devil! Instantly Deborah thought of Lavinia, and then by transference of the shrubs which she had planted, with some help from Willy, under the walnut tree at the very end of the garden. There, under a mass of green things, shrubs and bushes which in due season flowered and were beautiful, Lavinia and her baby lay. Lavinia had killed the baby and then herself. How deep did the roots reach by this time?

"Di, don't cry about something that hasn't happened yet. We'll think up something. Mamma, I just want a word with Willy before I go."

"Good morning, Willy."

"Morning, Miss Deb, Mrs Bridges, ma'am. Anything I can do?"

"Yes. Those shrubs that we planted. Do you remember?"

I remember everything, my dearie, back to when you was, well maybe twelve and me about eighteen. Bloody silly and I always knew it. But I swear to God, if things had been a bit different, you'd look happier like than you do. More cherished.

"They need a thorough good pruning, Willy. I walked round the garden last evening and I thought they looked very overgrown."

"Maybe. Tell you the truth I ain't had all that much time on my hands. And autumn is right for pruning."

Tell you the truth I don't much fancy that end of the garden much. Tell you the truth I didn't mind that day when we worked together and you held the blasted things and I stamped them in. That was all right, that was. And for your sake I did a bit of watering, so they grew. Done a bit of pruning from time to time, too, all for *your* sake. But alone, down that end, I don't feel easy. Never have. Always felt as though I was being watched, and that ain't a nice feeling. And once . . . well, if he'd ever mentioned *that*, he'd have been a laughing stock for the rest of his life. It was one of them big foreign flowers with a fancy

118

name. . . . It'd looked like a face, a pale face, watching.

"For most things," Deborah said, "but I read some-where, or somebody told me, that some shrubs should be pruned as soon as they finish flowering."

"Tell you what; if you can spare the time. It'd be best if you come and show me. That'd be best."

"All right. Get me a pair of shears, too, Willy. I might as well help as stand and watch you."

One more little memory to store away. The two of them working together; the way it might have been for life if only he'd had five acres and a cow, and she hadn't been Master's daughter.

"So you see, if the going gets rough, Di, I can let you have a hundred a year for four years and never miss it. And by that time I shall have some more saved. But it is for you and the children—not for propping up a business or any-thing like that."

"What you gave me last night will be the greatest help, Deb dear. And I won't ask for more unless I am really driven. . . . It really is so mortifying. Seven years married and worse off, really, than at the beginning."

"It may be just the jumping-off space that Everard needs."

"I wish I dared think so. And I wish that I could earn a little. The only thing I ever did better than anybody else was embroidery."

The idea didn't drop into her mind like a seed and ger-minate; it sprang up, complete but for one vital detail—an outlet for such talent, but surely, in the whole of London there must be many places. One only had to look. At the thought of seeking buyers for her skill, Diana felt a little sick. That would be mortifying, too. But nobody need know. If there was anything at all to be said for London, it was there one could, if one wished, be anonymous.

Hawksley's had little trouble with the shoplifters who were a pest in many of the cheaper stores; on the whole their floorwalkers were there to help, not to guard.

"Can I help you, Madam?" Sometimes, because of the

layout of the various departments, customers, especially new ones, needed a little guidance. The display case was not always in close proximity to the counter where the things were actually sold.

"No, thank you," Diana said, and went on studying the three blouses exposed in all their beauty. They—or some like them—had attracted her eye on that shopping expedition with Caro in March. Having found them, she had thought: Thank God they are still in fashion. But they were bound to be, they were so very pretty, and though extremely modest, almost, well, almost seductive. They were actually double; the inner, closer-fitting bodice made of silk or satin, and embroidered, the outer, looser blouse of sheer gauze, so that the embroidery was veiled as though by a light morning mist.

Narrowing her eyes, Diana studied the three closely. The embroidery was good enough, but she could do better. It was with a positive feeling of being in her right element again that she turned away and went down to the basement, where stuff was sold by the yard and embroidery silks were ranged like rainbows. Two of Deb's golden sovereigns were spent, happily, and Diana hoped, profitably.

One advantage of this far-too-big house was that one room could be a workroom where work did not have to be tidied away, every snippet of thread picked up as soon as it fell. One advantage of Everard's being away was that Bessie spent less time on shopping and cooking and could give more attention to the children. In three days of happy—but although she did not know it, frenzied—work, Diana had produced a blouse better than any in Hawksley's show case. White satin bodice, embroidered with wild roses and forget-me-nots, the motif repreated in the modest collar where satin and gauze met, and on the cuffs of the voluminous sleeves. It really was so beautiful that she didn't want to part with it. Some imp at the back of her mind whispered: Keep it yourself. Common sense told her that for two pounds she had bought what was necessary for the making of a pretty thing which Hawksley's could sell for ten guineas, which left, even by her simple arithmetic, eight pounds to be divided between herself and Mr Hawksley.

This time she did need direction. "Can I help you, Madam?"

"Yes. I wish to see whoever buys for this department."

"You wish to make a complaint, Madam?" It did sometimes happen, especially with things bought ready-made. As more and more things were nowadays.

"No. I wish to see whoever buys for this department." Diana wore her haughty look, which even her headmistress had acknowledged, and dubbed her Young Madam.

"If you will come this way, Madam."

Suddenly there was no thick mole-coloured carpet. Bare stone stairs. Abandoned, for the floorwalker, having said, "The first door on the right, Madam," had done his duty, Diana climbed the stairs and was in a different world.

It was not a large room. Its one uncurtained window looked out upon a blank wall which, because it was made of white tiles, reflected a harsh, rather eerie light. Near the door two women, both elderly, both wearing black sateen overalls, were sorting things at a trestle table. Near the window two men stood, the bigger one with both his shoulders and one extended arm draped with strips of fur which the other, thinner, older was studying with every evidence of disgust. There was a desk set slantwise at the end of it another woman, seated, pencil in hand, a notebook before her. She was a hunchback.

As Diana took stock of the room, the thin man said, both tone and voice unpleasant:

"Come here, Flo. What'll look all right on you ull look right on anybody." The little hunchback stood up and went to the window and the man who had spoken snatched two pieces of fur and placed one on each of her misshapen shoulders. Regarding them with no mitigation of disgust, he said, "They'll do." The move brought Diana within his line of vision and his expression changed. She looked like a customer—but customers never entered this part of the building; more likely a buyer of surplus stock. For no matter how shrewdly one estimated the market, no matter how carefully one bought, no matter what reduction of prices was made at the end of each season, or each fashion, something was bound to be left over and must be disposed of to humbler, less-up-to-the-minute establishments.

"'Keep you a minute," he said with as near an approach of civility as he could attain. The further civility of offering a seat could not be managed; there were only two chairs in the bleak room; one was his own, his throne, the seat of power, the other was now again occupied by the hunchback, who was writing with extreme rapidity what was being dictated to her. The man who had been exhibiting the furs was folding them with extreme care and placing them in a kind of leather sack; and saying, Thank you, Mr Burton, sir; and: Yes, August 31st; had they ever failed to keep a delivery date?

Mr Burton said, "The day you do, out!"

It was all so different from what Diana had imagined. Hawksley's was so extremely dignified that she had imagined even a department buyer to be, and the room in which he operated to have some dignity, too. And she had expected such an interview to be private, at least.

At last the fur-seller moved away, touching as he did so that lump on the hunchback and saying, "Just for luck, dearie. You don't mind?"

The woman said in the dead voice of complete resignation, "People do it all the time. Even in the street."

Mr Burton then looked at Diana and made a curious sound. Not quite Yes, in the questioning way of what do you want, what can I do for you. It was more like, Yah! A recognition of her presence, a resignation to his next job.

"Mr Burton. I have something to show you." She lovingly unfolded the paper and revealed her masterpiece. "I made it," she said, "in three days. It is better than those on sale downstairs."

That this was true did nothing very little to assuage Mr Burton's never-far-absent irritation.

"Six months out of date," he said. Abruptly, he began to punish Diana—despite her errand, by her dress and her voice one of the customer class—for his undying grudge against all customers. "It was a *fad,*" he said, mouthing the word as though it were an obscenity. "Somebody had one, then everybody wanted one, I was at my wit's end. . . . Now dead as pork." That was the knife edge between demand and supply which a buyer for a place like Hawksley's constantly bestrode. A fad caught on, blazed itself out. The uncertainty of his working life accounted for Mr Burton's insomnia, his indigestion, his constantly irritable temper.

Utterly deflated, Diana folded the blouse, wrapped it in paper. She thought: Nothing I do ever prospers. And yet behind it all she saw the point. If she, if anyone with a bit of skill with the needle, could make, in three days, for two pounds something that Hawksley's sold for ten guineas . . .

She said, "Good morning, Mr Burton," and walked towards the door. One of the women, sorting, packing, unpacking at the trestle table, looked up and said out of the corner of her mouth, "Try Preston's. Oxford Street." Before Diana could say Thank you, Mr Burton called in his querulous voice, "Wait!" Something in Diana impelled her to go on, to ignore such rudeness. In the whole of her life nobody had spoken to her like that. Not even Miss Hardwicke, at school. On the other hand . . . Diana hesitated just long enough for Mr Burton's next words to reach her and he said, "You have a good hand with the needle. Could you embroider a kimono?"

"I could embroider anything, Mr Burton, if I knew what it was. What exactly is a kimono?"

"The latest fad." Mr Burton sounded more disgusted than ever. "Connie, show . . . Miss . . . Mrs . . ."

"Osborne," Diana said.

"Osborne, a kimono," Mr Burton said.

The woman who had been kind enough to suggest Preston's in Oxford Street fumbled about and produced something so beautiful as to take one's breath away. A kind of dressing-gown or wrapper. Blue silk, embroidered on the back, on the fold-over fronts and on the wide sleeves with sprays of white flowers, a pink tinge here and there; cherry blossom? and strange, long-legged birds.

Forgetting her role, Diana said, "How beautiful."

"Pretty enough," Mr Burton agreed. Any enthusiasm he had once felt for the goods he bought was long since exhausted; saleability was the only criterion. And although the kimonos were fantastically cheap, they were rare. In the shop they would *not* be cheap.

"Could you make that kind of thing, Mrs Osborne?"

"There is far less actual needlework than in this blouse. A great deal more embroidery. Of exceptional quality, too." Diana narrowed her eyes as she had done when studying the blouses. Unexpectedly humbled in the sphere at which she had always excelled, she asked with a kind of awe, "Who did such fine work?"

"Those we have are imported from Japan. But nobody can guarantee a supply, or a date of delivery; which makes it very difficult. Well, can you or can't you?"

"Yes. But it would take me a week. What would you pay me?"

"A pound each."

By Mr Burton's standards very high pay indeed. But while the craze lasted—each one different, each one made to order, each one very special, and a week to wait . . . probably twenty-five or thirty guineas each. Selling—except of surplus stock—was not Mr Burton's job. He bought. And although he knew and employed indirectly a great many women who lived by plying their needles, he had not yet seen any work so nearly Oriental in standard as that on the blouse which he had rejected.

"I'll see what I can do," Diana said, and went away, leaving everybody in the bleak room astonished, partly by the munificent offer—even Mr Burton himself felt that he had been slightly carried away—but even more by her casual air. She had not asked who would provide the materials upon which she would see what she could do.

Preston's in Oxford Street was far less imposing than Hawksley's though it did its best. Its front, though narrow, was glassed and polished, it had a doorman, just as attentive to a customer who came in a hired cab, or on foot. Preston's had not been able to expand as Hawksley's had done because on each side of it small, independent businesses were still surviving. But its day would come.

"The buyer. Oh, you mean Mrs Preston. She does the buying."

Mrs Preston, though tightly corsetted, bulged here and there in a comfortable-looking way; her room too was far more like a well-used sitting room than an office. Her voice was singularly akin to Bessie's, and her eyes, bright and shrewd, were not unkindly. She was drinking tea and without hesitation she told Diana to sit down and have a cup. Then she said,

"Watcha selling, dearie?"

Once again Diana unfolded the paper and displayed her handiwork.

"Far too good," Mrs Preston said. "Musta taken you a week."

"Three days."

"Once they took on . . . We had women running them up, two a day sometimes. Nothing like this, of course. Coarse and quick, while the rage lasts. You gotta catch the tide in this trade." The vagaries of fashion bore almost as hard on Mrs Preston as on Mr Burton, with a difference; she was responsible to nobody but herself.

"I ain't saying this ain't something special. Very nice indeed, but no call for such work down here."

Out of date at Hawksley's, too good for Preston's. A dead loss.

On impulse Diana said, "Mrs Preston, did you ever hear about a thing called a kimono?"

Mrs Preston drained her cup and set it down; both actions she performed noisily and would by Mamma, or Miss Hardwicke, have been rebuked.

"I heard," Mrs Preston said cautiously. It was not for her to tell anyone, let alone a complete stranger, that she had her spies in other shops, and in workrooms. "Sorta dressing-gown, ain't they? Somebody brought a few in for presents;

then everybody wanted one. I b'lieve Hawksley's had a few. Never on show though. . . . And they're hard to come by. Dear as fire, too."

Almost forgetful of her disappointment over the blouse, Diana said,

"But so beautiful." She described the one she had seen. Then with a deepening of the little frown lines above her nose, she said, "And I don't see why they should be so expensive. They need not be silk. Any firm, fine cotton cloth would do. Embroidered, as you said, with coarse thread and quick stitches. I could make one in three days." She had told Mr Burton a week, but then he had not been asking for quick coarse work.

"Could you reelly?" She sounded, and was, a trifle absentminded, for she was thinking of the women she knew who were only too glad to sew in their own homes. Preston's, unlike Hawksley's, did not make clothes to order, and so had no workroom, just a woman and an apprentice who would make minor alterations. But when something like the double blouses caught on, there were plenty of willing hands. Hands was what they were; they could copy anything, but they could not make something they had never seen. A sorta dressing-gown would mean nothing to them.

"Could you make me a model? In three days?"

"Oh yes."

"And what would you charge?"

" A pound," Diana said, daringly.

It was a lot for three days' work, but not too much for a model.

"Let's go down and pick the stuff," Mrs Preston said.

Only then did it strike Diana to wonder what Mr Burton had expected her to work with, should she accept his offer. To give Mr Burton his due it had not occurred to him to wonder, either, for he had no experience with casual, outside labour; it was just that these damned kimonos were driving him crazy.

Mrs Preston never had the slightest hestitation in supplying her outside workers with what she called stuff. She knew and they knew that if it were not brought back, absolutely clean, beautifully sewn, and on time they'd get no pay, and no further work. The taking of names and addresses was really mere formality.

"Osborne. Mrs Osborne," Diana said; and asked her address, looked at Mrs Preston with that haughty look to which her high-bridged nose was so eminently suited, and said, "Does that really matter?" And Mrs Preston immediately jumped to two erroneous conclusions; this Mrs Osborne was obviously a lady, a bit come down in the world and ashamed of her address; or she was a woman who had left her husband and did not want to be traced. Mrs Preston, whose own married life had been very unhappy—but fortunately brief—quite understood that.

In the workroom the two pieces of work went on, unevenly matched, rather like a horse and a donkey pulling the same cart, but making progress. It was relief to turn from the very fine work on real silk—bought with Deborah's money, to the coarser easier work on the sateen, a cotton fabric with a deceptively shiny surface. And then, after a spell at the coarse, quick work, it was a relief to turn to the other, slower work. On the real silk there was not one of what were called lazy Daisies; and on the sateen there was not one petal or bird's wing of what was called raised satin stitch. And yet . . .

It was August now and the evenings were darkening, so she was working by gaslight; at the end of the third day, Mrs Preston's model ready, and Mr Burton's half completed, if you looked at the backs of both kimonos, and did not look too closely, you could hardly tell the difference. In this light—and nobody would wear a kimono in full daylight, the sateen looked like the silk and the Lazy Daisy flowers almost as pretty, certainly as effective as the raised satin stitch ones.

Mrs Preston was delighted with her model, cheap fake though it was. She said she'd never seen anything quite so pretty; but she did not order another. Why should she, when there were dozens of women who, once shown what to do and provided with the materials, would do the work for ten shillings or less.

Diana's connection with Mr Burton, superficially less agreeable, was to last longer. He inspected the work with his usual expression of dissatisfaction; he fingered the blue silk. Not quite Hawksley's quality, but then the silly woman—all women were silly, hadn't given him time to tell her how to go about things.

But obviously, he approved.

"And you can make one like this in a week?"

"Oh yes." After all she made this and the other inferior article within the week; and although next week Everard would be home, so that Bessie had more shopping to do, and more cooking in the evening, so that she would have less time to devote to the children, Everard—if he stuck to his intention of setting up on his own, would be much preoccupied; and he would probably wish to dine at his Club—or with Lady Lumsley and all his other fine friends.

That was how she thought of them. In fact she had liked them as little as they, apparently, had liked her. She had not enjoyed herself at all at that first dinner party at Lumsley House; it had all been very grand, but exceptionally dull. The meal itself had lasted for at least two hours and her companion on the left seemed to think that conversation should consist of questions: Have you seen . . . ? What did you think of . . . ? Have you read . . . ? The only answer was, No; or, I'm afraid not. And that made her sound dull, too. The man on her left, older and bearing a singular resemblance to the Duke of Wellington, appeared to be rather deaf. Indeed he admitted it. Gone a bit hard of hearing, he said; 'fraid I didn't catch your name. Alison, like all the young, did tend to mumble.

"Spicer."

He cupped his ear. "Spicer," Diana repeated, a little more loudly. "Mrs Everard Spicer."

"Ah yes." The ancient, modelled-on-the-Duke man said, masticating and ruminating at the same time, "'Fraid I never knew a Spicer; but Everard . . . Yes." Possibly he took it for a hyphened name. "Came out of India; very rich; most hospitable chap."

"I think he may been my husband's godfather."

"Ah yes." It was not a thing one could say to a pretty young woman, but godfatherdom, like charity, covered a multitude of sins. Funny how fashions—even in manners— changed; such a remark would have been perfectly acceptable, regarded as humourous, anywhere, in his youth, and even now, at this very table, there were women who would have laughed and retorted that fortunately the same could not be said of godmotherhood. But he sensed something prim and prudish about this young woman and refrained. He blamed all the changes on that dull, pompous, pious German fellow whom the Queen had chosen to marry. And really Alison should have given him a more lively dinner companion; somebody who knew that he was deaf and had something to say. He fell back on an old standby and asked her what part of the country she came from. At the mention of Suffolk he brightened.

"Ah, then you'll know my old friend John Faulkner. Used to have the best shooting in the county; but running down, like everything else. And what can you expect? Taxes and wages going up all the time. How is he?"

He plainly expected her to know the state of Sir John's health; and all she could say was, "I don't know." It was with relief that he turned to his other neighbour, the owner of a strong penetrating voice. Diana was then left to the asker-of-questions, who had decided that a young woman who hadn't seen, hadn't heard, hadn't read, might have sporting proclivities, so he asked if she enjoyed attending race meetings.

Later with all the ladies in the drawing room, it was worse. They did not deliberately exclude her—though nobody made any definite effort to include her. It was just that they had friends, acquaintances, and experiences in common. Somebody called Veronica had just had a fourth baby, another girl. Absolutely disastrous, because if Algie inherited Mortmain he'd gamble it away within a year.

Somebody said, "It must be Hell for Veronica."

Perhaps Mrs Thorley, by the time she went to Gad's, was slightly old-fashioned about language; Deborah and Caroline, running wild, had picked up some very unsuitable words and expressions; gently but firmly eradicated. It gave Diana a mild shock to hear a lady, Mrs Murry-Miles, wearing satin and diamonds, use the word Hell like that. And the next remark shocked her even more. "Frankly, in Veronica's place, I should have felt inclined to do a swop. There're plenty of boy babies about."

"Sylvia!"

"Well, why not? A queen did it. In a warming pan. And Walter was fishing in Scotland at the time."

"Walter, anyway is so foxed, he couldn't tell boy from girl. Up to a point."

"What point? If you ask me he never did make a clear distinction."

Well, Diana thought, I suppose it is all very funny judging by the laughter. She entertained the thought which, unknown to her, Everard had entertained earlier. Either Deborah or Caroline whould have been more at east here. Deborah would have known which queen had, or had not, smuggled a baby—which baby?—in a warming pan. Asked had she seen a play, been to a concert, been to the races, Deborah would have said, God no. I train hunters. And then the talk would have been about hocks and fetlocks and such things. Caroline? What she would have said or done was quite unpredictable except for the certainty that she would not have sat within earshot of a man, however stuffy, or old and deaf without finding something to say, probably something silly or giddy, but something.

Feeling out of place—yet in no way inferior, Diana had endured her first grand dinner party, and presently an end-of-the-season garden party given by Mrs Murray-Miles. That had been a little better and she had been actually glad not to have been included in the invitation to Lumsleydale; and positively happy to go to Gad's and be back in her own sphere, just as Everard was happy to go to Scotland and be back in his. She had not, of course, reckoned that Everard would be so weak-minded as to allow himself to be persuaded to take such a risk.

Curiously—and yet typically—she had never known a second of sexual jealousy. She had always had the capacity for turning a blind eye, for ignoring what she always thought of as the sordid side of life—like scrubbing steps, scouring saucepans. The idea that Everard might be unfaithful to her had never once occurred. Why should he be? She had never much enjoyed what she called the messy side of marriage, nor the even messier and very painful process that resulted from it, but she had always been acquiescent. A good wife! Even when she had been free to gad about before the birth of Belle, had Everard ever come home to an empty house, no fire burning, in cold weather, or open windows in summer; had he ever not been served with some kind of meal, or been met by a wife who whatever *her* day had been, wasn't clean, well-dressed, welcoming? She had recognised Lady Lumsley as a persuader, talking Everard into taking a risk; but as a danger in another way, a temptress, a Delilah, that thought had never once troubled her innocent, naïve, provincial mind.

Nor did it when Everard returned, bringing with him a rather nasty-looking sack containing two brace of grouse and a great lump of meat—a haunch of venison. She was not even suspicious when he, always so careful about money, produced a dress length of beautiful tartan cloth for herself and a Cairngorm brooch for Bessie. What she *did* think, and immediately rebuked herself for thinking, was that such a generous gesture was intended to be placatory, for she had written him a reproachful letter, saying that he was making a leap in the dark and she felt that he should have talked the matter over with her first.

Diana accepted what she took to be a peace-offering in the right spirit; she was genuinely pleased with it. Fashions, even in colours, came and went, but so long as Queen Victoria reigned, anything Scottish would be stylish.

Bessie, equally delighted with the one non-utilitarian thing she had ever owned, tackled grouse foreign to her as a peacock, with good will, and over the meal Everard

131

explained and justified his risky decision.

"I'll tell you two things, darling. One happened in Baildon—and I was hurt at the time. There was an older farmer with some grievance against his landlord. He had no case, and I told him so, using the *simplest* possible language. He was greatly annoyed, called me a la-di-da ass and accused me of being on the landlord's side *because we talked the same*. He demanded to see Mr Gordon, pushed his way through and left the doors open. I will not repeat what he called me to Mr Gordon. Mr Gordon—and James too, when he chose, could suit their manners and their voices to their company. As a matter of fact, old Gordon in a most uncouth way, told the silly man exactly what I had been trying, patiently, to explain. And in reverse, the same thing happned last year when this Lumsley will dispute arose. Upton himself said he was sending me to Scotland to deal with it. He said, 'You talk the same lingo. They'll trust you.'"

"And they did."

"Exactly. I know I have repeatedly said—there was no need to remind me of that, Diana, that without money or influence, but there are exceptions. That evening—the post arrives there late in the afternoon, I said to Charlie, 'Exeat refused. I'm to report back to London on Monday, or else. . . .' So then we all began talking about it, and Charlie said, 'Sack them before they sack you,' and a man you haven't met, I think, Lord Romsey, said he was turning some of his property, just off the Strand, into offices and I could have three rooms on the ground floor at a peppercorn rent, if I put out a brass plate and made the place look respectable. And everybody—there was quit a crowd—said they'd let me handle their legal affairs, and direct other people to me. So you see, it isn't quite the leap in the dark that you think."

"I see. Well, darling, I just hope it will work. I didn't mean to sound as though I doubted your . . . your ability. I was just taken by surprise, and a bit frightened. I was afraid that Lady Lumsley, because you have been so successful with her, had overpersuaded you."

"Alison? She wasn't even there. Of course she promised to help as soon as she knew what was afoot."

The house party at Lumsleydale—the first for seven years—had been a very riotous affair. Lady Lumsley had wasted time to make up. There were far more men than women and so far as Everard could make out only three married couples. Lord Romsey was one of two widowers, Lord Westward one of the three bachelors and the men who had wives elsewhere all had perfectly plausible excuses for their lonely condition; one had a wife who hated Scotland, it was too cold for her even in August; another wife went, with the punctuality of the migration of birds, to Aix-les-Bains to take a cure; a third had to go to Ireland, taking her children, to visit her crotchety old father who unless kept sweet by regular visits might disinherit her, and who hated his son-in-law—always had. Went in fact a dangerous shade of purple at the sight of him. There were two young, moderately pretty girls, vaguely family, a widow who was not only gay but rich, and two very dashing women—one claimed to have shot a tiger in India, and wore two of its claws, mounted in gold, as a brooch—whose husbands occupied positions of great power in unhealthy places. There was also, of course, old Lady Cowdray, who could be trusted to see that the two young girls behaved themselves, and also to know when, and when not, her presence was desirable.

It was perhaps a typical house-party, with the exception of Everard. Indigent young attorneys were not usually found in such gatherings, but after all, he'd been at school with Westward, and he'd saved dear Alison from total beggary. Also, he was a damned good shot; and he had an admirable outspokenness. The after-dinner amusement was gambling, and on the first evening he said that he couldn't afford to play. "Suppose," he said, "I lost my shirt—one of my five!" All the owners of dozens of shirts found that amusing. The lady who had shot a tiger took careful aim at a new target and said she'd take a side bet: if he lost his shirt she'd stand him six.

"And if I win."

"Then we'll play a game of forfeits," she said. And that was not such an outrageous suggestion as it might have seemed; for under all the sophistication there was the childishness of the privileged and the protected. They were still capable of unself-conscious romping. They'd none of them ever been short of money, or ridden on a horse-bus or said "Sir" to any man except as a courtesy. Everard had, but in this congenial, intimate atmosphere, he could slough off all the horrid things which should never have happened to him.

Seduction was easy.

Alison, at the end of a romp, a children's game, Hide-and-Seek, for which a castle, five hundred years old and much built-on-to was most admirably adapted, said to Everard,

"Would you mind? There are a few papers that I can't make head or tail of. If you wouldn't mind. . . . They're in the library. I told them to light a fire there. Good night."

The woman who thought that Scotland was too cold for her, even in August, was not so far wrong. The days were warm, but immediately after sunset a chill came. The library, heavy curtains drawn over its mullioned windows, a pedestal table with a lamp and the papers on it, set close to the hearth, was very snug. Everard sank down into a leather chair and gave a little sigh, half satisfaction, half exhaustion. Except for the man who had once been his fag, he was the youngest man in the party, but he felt—not for the first time—that he was older than anybody else. Older both in mind and body. In body because he was unused to this physical exercise in the open air; ever since his godfather's death he'd been obliged to lead a sedentary life. He'd been obliged to take his work at Cambridge seriously, he had to qualify. In Baildon and in London he had been obliged to earn a living; so his muscles had grown flabby, whereas *they*, and that included old Romsey who was sixty and proud of it, had been riding, shooting, playing tennis, playing polo. In mind he was older too, and almost for the same reasons, he'd been obliged to fight against the world and was mature enough to see that Hide-and-Seek was a childish game, which could, when played in a building so vast, be other than childish.

The papers demanded no real attention at all. How could they? MacFarlane was qualified and shrewd. And still in charge. Asking Everard to look them over was just Alison's nice way of making Everard feel that he was singing for his supper, as the phrase went. But all done so tactfully, so sweetly, as things should be done in civilised circles. It was like her, too, to be sure that during this pretence at work, he should lack nothing. Within arm's reach a box of cigars, two decanters, one full of port wine, one of brandy. Everard helped himself and reached for a book. . . .

Brandy on top of sherry before, red wine during, port after dinner, combined with a day's exercise in the open air and a romp, made him sleepy, and there was no reason to combat the pleasant feeling. No hurry to get to bed because there would be no hurry in the morning. No horse-bus to catch. Here, as in similar establishments, breakfast was a movable feast with every dish one could possibly desire, ranged over hot-plates, in silver-covered dishes on the vast side-board; fresh toast, coffee, or tea arrived at the touch of a bell.

Until the eighteenth century there had been no library at Lumsleydale Castle, but then it had become fashionable to instal one; and a fad which accompanied the fashion was to have one door at least made to look like a section of the book-lined shelves. Everard had not inspected this room and did not know of the door's existence. When it opened and showed a shape blocked in against a background of the palest possible golden light, Everard was not absolutely certain that he was not dreaming. It was a woman—and his dream had been mildly lascivious. As she advanced towards the area of mingled lamp and fire light, he knew who it was, and that he was wide awake.

She said, "Poor dear! I did not intend to keep you up all night."

Her gleaming hair was loose, pouring in ripples over her shoulders, and not plaited for the night. She wore a garment

135

unlike any that Everard had ever seen before. (Lady Lumsley had been the fortunate recipient of one of the first kimonos to be sent to England—as gifts.) All women above the poverty line owned a dressing-gown, a modest garment, high at the neck, long in the sleeves, and buttoned or hooked all down the front.

Alison said, quickly, "Don't get up!" and came and sat on the arm of the chair. The kimono, held closed only by the sash, opened and revealed a leg, slender, shapely and white to halfway up the thigh. She made one of those gestures, far more enticing than the exposure, pulling the yellow silk in an apparent effort to conceal, but quite ineffective.

"Don't you think," she said, "that it is time that we went to bed?"

Back in London, face to face with Diana, indisputably a good wife, but never, let the fact be faced, a sharer of that kind of wild rapture, Everard experienced many mixed feelings; a little shame—after all his parents had been ordinary, decent. God-fearing people; a greater sense of deprivation. Like a bell in his mind tolling, Never again. Quoth the raven, "Nevermore." And alongside it all a determination to succeed; to justify himself and to give Diana everything she wanted. He'd never had a fair chance, now he had and he would make the most of it.

That autumn he was at home very little; he was running a strictly one-man business; he could not afford a clerk, cheap though they were, nor an office cleaner. He shared, with the other occupants of 19 Essex Court, a doctor, a dentist, and a publisher, the services of an ancient, bent man who cleaned the front of the building, and the communal entry and polished all the brass plates. That cost four shillings a week. The old man was willing enough to add to his duties and would have cleaned Mr Spicer's office along with the others, but Everard dared not commit himself to any such outlay—yet. Behind the locked door he did with his own hands all that was necessary in the way of cleaning. Then, as often as not, he went to his Club, partly because it pleased him to be there, partly because there, if anywhere, useful contacts should be made. He was not unaware of the irony of it.

Diana had no sense of irony; she just thought that it was a pity that at a time when she had found agreeable neighbours she was obliged to look upon them as stealers of time. She was still trying to make two embroidered kimonos a week for Mr Burton, who was thus able to please two demanding customers a week with something made to order, something very special indeed and worth every penny of the charges which crept up, stealthily week by week. He had tried to cut Diana out altogether by suggesting that the things should be made in Hawksley's own workrooms, but the woman in charge there, a battleship of a woman, a real slave driver, had said: All right, but to produce two such things a week would mean engaging four extra women.

"But this one woman, a Mrs Osborne, makes two in a week, Mrs Sheldrake."

Mrs Sheldrake said, coarsely, "Christ did miracles."

It was funny, Diana sometimes thought, that her embroidery had always been her pride and joy, the one thing she had wanted to do, the one thing at which she wished to excel. She had always liked to be given time to get on with whatever piece of work she had in hand, just as Deb had liked to be left undisturbed with a book. But one could have a surfeit even of a likeable thing. However, being Mrs Thorley's daughter, she stuck to it until just before Christmas, when Preston's window suddenly blazed with kimonos; cotton on cotton, but very pretty, the ideal Christmas present. After that nobody who *was* anybody wanted a kimono.

Time and life had moved on elsewhere. At Foxton, Tim Bridges said, with right on his side, with every justification, that he had not bought and paid for a Thoroughgood pony in order that Sam should go hunting.

"But I keep trying to tell you . . . I shouldn't dream of it yet. George started at fourteen and that was a bit young.

137

I just want Sam to come to the Meet so that he and the pony get used to the people and the hounds."

"With the idea in mind that one day he will hunt?"

"If he takes to it."

"Over my dead body."

"Go ahead," Deborah said. "One cliché deserves another. Say you'd rather see him dead at your feet."

Tim couldn't say it. What father could?

"You blackmailed me," he said, slow and steady. "Time and time again. If I didn't let you hunt you wouldn't go to chapel. I gave in. Then, over some rubbish dispute you spoke of divorce, of all things! And I gave in again. Over this I do not intend to give in."

"Very well."

"And what do you mean by that?"

"What I said. Very well."

Tim imagined that for once he had won; and running his mind backwards over his married life regretted every instance when he had given in. If only he'd taken a stronger line from the beginning things would have been very different. He cherished this illusion until the next Sunday morning, when Deborah came down to breakfast in her riding habit, dark green, the jacket cut like a man's, modest enough—but not chapel wear.

"Aren't you coming to chapel, Mother?"

"Not this morning, my dear."

"And what am I going to say when people inquire after you?" As they would. Deborah had a way of endearing herself to the most unlikely people. Even the fact that she hunted seemed to not to be held against her as it would have been against anybody else, and once when Tim was awkwardly trying to explain and excuse this un-Methodist activity a crusty old man said, "Well, vermin gotta be kept down somehow, Mr Bridges, and you ain't supposed to shoot the creatures. It's different for you. I'm a tenant. 'F my landlord got a notion I'd shot one, I'd be out on my ear come Michaelmas."

"I can't say you are ill," Tim said.

"You can tell them I've become a free-thinker."

"What's that?" Sam asked.

"A person who doesn't go to chapel."

"Then I'd like to be one, too."

Tim reached out and boxed his son's ear. "Don't ever let me hear you say such a wicked thing again."

"And don't ever let me see you box his ear again. Children have been deafened that way. If you must hit somebody hit somebody your own size. Try me!"

"You touch my mother and I'll knock your teeth down your throat," Sam said.

Over the fireplace hung the text whose validity George Thorley had questioned: CHRIST IS THE HEAD OF THIS HOUSE.

Deb said, "That'll do, Sam." She gave him her slightly crooked smile, enchanting still, though the dimple had gone. "In any case, you can't be a free-thinker, or anything else until you are twenty-one. Run along now and wash. You have egg on your chin."

"Now you see what you have done," Tim said with suppressed violence when the boy had gone. "Always, in every way, you pull against me. You'll be the ruin of him."

"I will not see him hit for making an innocent remark. And for *you* to talk about pulling against . . . Haven't you done it to me? From the very start? I've accommodated myself to you, and you've thwarted me at every turn. Even over visiting Mamma."

"I did not consider her a good influence."

"Because you are smug, self-righteous, bigoted. She's the best woman in the world."

"So *you* think!"

"I *know*."

All through the hymns and the prayer and the long sermon. Tim thought of his problem. Sam sat there beside him, or stood beside him and sang. Perhaps less heartily than usual. And his left ear was reddened, slightly swollen. Tim felt ashamed, and then angered because such shame was forced upon him—he, so well-known for his gentle handling of horses, cracking his own son over the ear. For

139

copying his mother. She was the one who should be punished; she was the bad influence. Without her . . .

"I'm not talking about divorce. Whom God hath joined
let no man put asunder; but we could live apart. You could
go back to Gad's and live with your mother and hunt four
times a week if you wanted to. I'd make you an allowance.
Four pounds, five, a week.

"Don't strain yourself. People get hernia that way."

"Will you be serious and listen to me? We can't go on
as we are, tugging the boy between us, like two dogs at a
bone. Better give up while there is something to be saved."

"Sam?"

"Yes. He stays here, he belongs here. He's my son."

"It may surprise you—but he is my son too."

"Will you stop your daft, clever talk and give me a
straight answer?" He wished that it were permissible for
a man of principle, a good Christian, a good Methodist to
clout his wife across the face.

"The answer is, No. How could I leave him to you? I
want him to have an ordinary, happy childhood and not
grow up narrow-minded and twisted."

Tim remembered his wedding day; the three Gad's Hall
girls in yards and yards of white satin, in lace by the lily-
decorated altar. All the worldly people drinking champagne
at Gad's afterwards. Just the sort of ceremony his mother
would most heartily have disapproved, the sort of thing he
had tried to avoid but which had been forced upon him by
Mrs Thorley, that misguided woman.

"You promised to honour and obey," he said flatly.

"And love," Deb reminded him. "I must have been in
love to make such rash promises."

Well, if she wouldn't go and leave the boy with him, he
must exert his authority over the boy. Once before he'd
struck him—blows really aimed at Deb; then he'd been
penitent and tried to regain favour with his son. That hadn't
worked. He'd try a different tack. He didn't believe in
knocking horses about, but if one proved too frisky and
unmanageable, a cut in the corn never failed to work. He'd

140

try sending Sam to bed without supper for a week—that'd teach him who was master here.

Deb countered that by absenting herself from the supper table, and playing the piano, lively tunes; dance tunes! And, since fasting from half-past twelve dinner one day to seven o'clock breakfast the next seemed to bring no response except surliness from Sam, he suspected that Deb was smuggling food. And he was right, he caught her red-handed. Friday was the weekly Prayer Meeting evening; he left for it ostentatiously and then turned back. Deborah and Jessie, Jessie! that sound Methodist who had at first disapproved of her mistress, and then come to admire her, were preparing a supper tray, cold chicken, ham, a mound of bread and butter, cheese!

Decent men didn't quarrel with their wives in front of servants. Besides, he was speechless with rage, so he turned and walked out, went to the Prayer meeting and in the Biblical phrase, "wrestled with God," admitting that he had done wrong in yoking himself to an unbeliever and praying for delivery from an impossible situation.

Some prayers are answered; not always straightforwardly.

George Thorley's stay with Mr van Haagen was nearing its end. He had vastly enjoyed moving about in the wider world, but he was not sorry to be going home. Gad's was in his blood, the heritage of unreckoned generations. Foreign places were fascinating, all the foreigners he had met had been kind—that is, susceptible to his charm, which seemed to be capable of overriding even the barrier of differing language. A ready smile, good looks and a strong desire to be liked went a long way.

A few days before he was due to embark, George said, "Mr van Haagen, you have given me a most wonderful time. I've never enjoyed myself so much." The right thing to say, even if not strictly true; George enjoyed everything which was even moderately enjoyable. "And I would very much like to do something for you. And I would, if you didn't think it too silly."

"It is now two months we have been together, my dear boy, and I have yet to hear you be silly."

"At Zwolle, tomorrow you are selling some stock. Nobody knows me there. I could bid against everybody and jerk the prices up."

Mr van Haagen gave the deep, rumbling belly laugh of a fat man.

"This is your own thought?"

"Yes. It came to me in the night. I was thinking what a good time you had given me and wondering what I could do. To show gratitude. Not to repay. I can never do that."

"You are," Mr van Haagen said portentously, "your mother's son."

George grinned. "Well, so I was always led to believe."

Mr van Haagen laughed again. "No harm to tell you now. Now that you originate. It is a game which your Mamma and I have played, many years. For what she sells, I bid, by person, or agent or letter; what I sell, she does the same. By such contrivance prices go up. Two or three times perhaps, not so. Then we console each other. Not that much consolation is needed. The second bidder is happy to hear that to send the animal he wanted across the sea, with a man to attend, is not so profitable as to sell to him. At the last price he offered. You understand. It is not dishonest. It is just business. Goot business. And your Mamma thought of it. So tomorrow, you understand, to bid against a written offer would be to bid against your Mamma. Against yourself.

"And that would never do, would it?"

"It would be confusion."

"Then all I can do . . . God, it sounds so little after all you have done for me. . . . But I promise you, Mr van Haagen, any time you come to England, the best hospitality I can offer. . . ." George smiled and said, "Never again that attic for you. Though I'd done my best with it."

"So I know." The memory of that terrible night in the attic, next door to the one which was locked and most vilely haunted, wiped all the joviality from the Dutchman's face. That night had taught him something about himself—that he was the possessor of something not quite canny, some mediumistic quality which he had always denied. His ability to see something of the future and something of the past by studying certain cards selected from a pack he regarded as merely a matter of obeying certain rules, taught him by his grandmother; not unlike, he often explained, reading words on a page. Since his experience at Gad's he had been reluctant to indulge in what he had thought of, and called, his one parlour trick.

Yet now that this boy of whom he had become so fond was about to depart, he was moved by curiosity and a kind of protective feeling. Nobody could change what the cards foretold, but their authority was not absolute and there were undefined areas concerning which a warning might be given. He had warned that most unfortunate girl at Gad's to avoid the dark; unfortunately it was too late.

"If you would like, George, I will look in the cards for you. Or do you scorn such things?"

"You mean tell my fortune," George said with his charming smile. "I don't scorn such things. At Fairs or Fetes, if there's a fortune-teller, I make straight for her. One old gypsy hag told me I'd die a pauper. I thought that damned ungrateful. I'd just given her a shilling!"

"That perhaps was why when sixpence would have served." Mr van Haagen had noticed George's extreme open-handedness—and also his extraordinary luck. He seemed to attract money. They'd gone together to a casino in Paris and Mr van Haagen had been very careful and fatherly, providing George with counters to the value that could be lost without harm and telling him to stop once they were lost. George had made a great deal of money that evening—and spent it on presents for everybody.

I must not allow such thoughts to influence me, Mr van Haagen said as George went through the routine of selecting his cards.

Yet money figured prominently, even at first glance.

"You will always have money; sometimes much; sometimes little. You will disperse it, unless you mend your ways. A little more care with money, if you please."

When Mr van Haagen read the cards he treated them as though they were as fragile as dried rose-leaves, moving them into this arrangement and that with one touch of a finger-tip. The gypsy had not been quite right, though not far wrong. A great lack of money was indicated, but Death would intervene. Very sudden death at a good old age.

"You have many years. Perhaps that is why you should be careful with the money so that it lasts you many years. Also you have many friends. So many friends. I do not remember when I am seeing so many years and so many friends for one man. And goot health too. Yes, even when you are old, the same health as now you enjoy." Why then should the indication of *real* happiness be so lacking? Carefully, Mr van Haagen moved the cards again. Ah, in the heart's affairs!

He was still sticking to his grandmother's rules, and one of them was to tell the true but not the unpleasant, to tell the pleasant but not the untrue; and that of all the rules was the most difficult. After a pause, he said, "With you where the heart is and the marriage is, they do not lie side by side. But," Mr van Haagen looked up, an expression of surprise on his wide face, "that you know already, is it not? Yes, a lesson bygone, but with less such confusion. Confusion will be, but take it gently, gently. It will pass. . . . Now, marriage at good age and of children one. A boy."

No particular joy in that relationship either, but there was nothing unusual about that; Mr van Haagen had his Pieter, he respected him for his solid qualities, his business acumen, but outside business they had nothing in common.

"I think that is all."

"Well, thanks, Mr van Haagen. The best I've had yet."

And what more could a man ask, Mr van Haagen asked himself, gathering the cards together, than long life, splendid health, great popularity? So why feel sad? Why feel that this delightful boy deserved more and better?

George was home; so glad to be home that if Mrs Thorley had not had his letters saying how much he was enjoying himself, she could have suspected him of being homesick.

All the way from Baildon station, where she had met him in the gig, he'd kept saying that everything looked the same, rather he had been away twenty years instead of two months.

The table in the living room was littered with things, unwrapped just enough to show their contents. Gifts for everyone.

"And last, but not least, Mamma, *you,*" George said, producing with pride a pair of diamond earrings.

"They're real," he said.

"But how could you possibly afford...?"

"I *knew* you'd ask that! Well, I could. I won a lot of money in a place called a casino; that was in Paris; but I bought those in Amsterdam. Amsterdam is the place for diamonds—something to do with South Africa. Do you like them?"

"Of course. They're lovely. Thank you, George."

"With my love," he said, and bent to give her another kiss. But her head jerked and the kiss landed on her ear.

"Put them on," George said. And her head jerked again and her hands were unsteady. George realised that something had changed.

"Is something worrying you, Mamma?"

"My dear, yes. I didn't want to greet you with miserable news, but it's Deb. She just went away, nobody knows where. She just went away. She sent me a letter, saying she was doing so, but she didn't say where she was going. Then Mr Bridges came storming down, accusing me of harbouring her. Most fortunately I had her letter, and Jenny and Violet and Willy could all swear they had not seen her. But he was *most* unpleasant, indeed very rude. Not that that matters. I never liked him from the first and his opinion of me ... It is Deb. Homeless, out of touch, lost. She was the best of them all. .... George, it's all over and done with but *I* was once cast on my own resources—as Deb must be now. And it was horrible. Honestly, when I think of Deb and Sam adrift in the world, it really is more than I can bear—and I've borne a lot, one way and another."

"We'll find her," George said. "And anywhere Deb went,

she'd be all right. I mean . . . she is so sensible; she wouldn't just have gone off unless she knew where. Did she say why?"

"Nothing specific. Just that life had become intolerable and that she was leaving for Sam's sake. And that she would write."

"I can't say I blame her. He's an impossible man. Had she any money?"

"She had her dowry—five hundred pounds; except for fifty. That she gave to Diana. But she may not dare to touch it. To transfer money might reveal her whereabouts. I know—nobody better—how sensible Deb is, but, George, she knows nothing of the world. She's never even seen a big city."

"I don't think she would go to a city. She'll be somewhere where there are horses. Did she and Sam take their horses?"

"No. According to Mr Bridges, they all went in the gig to Thetford. Deb had some shopping and Sam was to get his hair cut and they were to meet at four o'clock, at the minister's house. And there was a letter—addressed to Mr Bridges, telling him. Really, if he hadn't been so violent and blamed me for it all I should have felt quite sorry for the man. It must have been a terrible shock. But I'm even more sorry for Deborah; she must have been desperate to do such a thing."

The one earring which Mrs Thorley had managed to hook in twinkled and shimmered, emphasising the shaking of her head.

Not the homecoming which George had anticipated. He felt both uneasy and resentful. He hated to see anybody unhappy and would go to almost any length to relieve their distress, but when there was nothing one could do . . . Then impatience and self-preservation took over.

"They'll be all right, Mamma. You mustn't be upset. I tell you what. Tomorrow I'll ride over and talk to that man—Craig, I think that was the name. Deborah hired a meadow and some stabling from him. He might know something. We'll find her, don't you fret. Now, how about a welcome-home drink? What would you like?"

"Whisky," Mrs Thorley said, giving in. Whisky had served her well in the past, enabling her to endure the unendurable; then for everybody's sake—but mainly George's—she had renounced it, pulled herself up from the crutch that if offered, been sober, attended to business. Now for some reason it seemed to matter less. George was older, he could manage. And the whole business about Deb had been such a blow because in a way it mirrored a part of her own life; a woman alone, anonymous, fighting the world with nothing much to fight with. This was something different from Lavinia's more tragic and dramatic story; never once had Mrs Thorley been able to put herself into Lavinia's place. Into Deborah's she could slip all too easily and Deborah was not so well-equipped; she'd seen nothing of the world. And was so good. Clever, yes; resourceful, yes; dependable, yes; but completely unsophisticated.

"Well, " George said, "at least we know now that Deb didn't act on the spur of the moment. I saw Craig; he knew nothing except that Deb had paid him to the end of the year and said she wouldn't train any more hunters. He thought she was going to have another baby. So she tied that up neatly. Then I went to the bank at Thetford. They were far more cagey but I ferreted out the fact that Mrs Bridges' account there was dead. And that, I may tell you, took a bit of doing. I had to pretend I was French and that Deb owed me ten pounds. It's a curious thing," George said, "but it was the same everywhere Mr van Haagen and I went, foreigners get preferential treatment. If I'd gone in and asked outright, said I was her brother, they'd have chucked me out. As it was—and believe me, Mamma, I was *very* French—I finally got what I wanted to know. Deb took her money. So she didn't go unprepared, and she isn't starving—yet."

"That is some comfort. It is very clever of you, George."

"Oh, George, how clever of you. Just what I wanted. Everything about me is getting so ugly now, except my hands." Caroline slipped on the bracelets, smooth oblong plaques of jet linked together, making a white hand look even whiter. "Lovely, how sweet of you. Now sit down and tell me everything. I've been so dull."

Pregnancy, however much coddled, was a loathesome state. Caroline had always known that she wasn't actually pretty, but she had been presentable. Now she was not. Even her face was swollen. As for her ankles . . . She'd tried to joke about it. "What's that new complaint, Edward? Something to do with elephants."

"Elephantiasis."

"That's it. It's happening to me."

"Darling, I think there has been only one case of it known in England. A certain amount of oedema is quite common in pregnancy."

"You say that when I begin to grow a trunk," Caroline said. And that was the last joke she made so far as Edward could remember. She'd just lain back, eschewed all company, obeyed all the rules, and grown fat and full, like a vegetable marrow. There'd been none of the quips and none of the self-will. When the question of engaging a proper nurse arose, Caroline said, "I think Miss Humberstone should pick the person. If we did and chose somebody Miss Humberstone didn't like there'd be trouble. I'll leave it entirely to her. And to you."

The dullness of which she now complained to George was largely self-inflicted. Female company had never pleased Caroline much and now she hated it; all women, young and old, seemed to think that pregnancy was the beginning and end of all things; and they were capable of congratulating her in one breath and in the next launching out into some horrifying tale of what they, or someone known to them, had suffered. As for men, who would want to see a man when one's face was blown up like a balloon? Edward had now achieved his aim of having Caro to himself, except for Mrs Thorley, who paid at least one visit a week, and Doctor Awkwright, who dropped in with fair frequency.

George, to whom superficial gallantry came easily, assured Caro that she didn't look a bit ugly; on the contrary,

148

very pretty. Then he gave a lively account of his visit to Mr van Haagen. He spoke with special enthusiasm about Paris, happily oblivious to the fact that the mention of France lacerated Caro's feelings; for Freddy had adhered to his plan and was now living there. And with a little more ruthlessness, a little more guts, she might have been with him.

"And what do you think about Deb?" George asked. He assumed that Caro knew.

"What about her?"

"Oh God!" Perhaps there were things that women in Caroline's condition should not be told. "I thought Mamma . . ."

"Unless Mamma has business to do, she comes to see me on Sunday. What about Deb? Is she ill? Hurt?"

It was all right then. Mamma had only received Deb's letter last Monday, and would doubtless have shared the information with Caro tomorrow.

"Far from it! She's done what she should have done years ago. Run away from Tim Bridges."

"Deb? Who with?"

Curiously that aspect of the business had not occurred either to Mrs Thorley or to George.

"She took Sam, of course."

"Where did she go?"

"That nobody knows. That is what Mamma is so worried about. But she's all right, I'm sure. She has some money, and before that is gone we'll know where she is and can send her some."

Apparently there were some things that pregnant women should not be told, for Caro was beginning to cry.

"Oh, for God's sake, Caro, don't you start. It's nothing to cry about. Wherever Deb is she's better off—and so is the boy—than living with that horrid man. I stayed there, you know, and I'd have run away the first day except that he'd have blamed Deb."

Caroline was not crying, directly, about Deb; she was crying for herself. Deb had done exactly what she should have done, given a mite more strength of character. Now,

149

through fumbling and indecision, she was stuck here for life.

Edward always knew; he said, "Darling, you have been crying. What about?"

"Only silly little things. First I was touched because George brought me these. Not many boys of his age, on their first trip abroad, would have been so thoughtful. And then he told me something which upset me a little. Deborah has run away."

"To Gad's?" In Edward's experience most women who left their husbands—and many had the soundest of reasons—went home to their parents.

"No. She's just disappeared. Gone away, leaving no trace."

"That is practically impossible," Edward said. In fact, in all his experience, which though limited in scope had great variety, of all the women who had left their husbands, because of a black eye or the man's infidelity, or a mere fit of temper, only one had failed to be traced—until four years later when her body had been found, buried in a field. Tim Bridges had not, Edward thought, blacked Deborah's eye, or been unfaithful, or killed her. He was a very dull dog, but fundamentally a good chap. And Deborah was a good sensible girl; if she'd flung off in a fit of temper, she'd soon realise the impossibility of her position and come back, willing to forgive and to be forgiven.

"You simply must not worry about such a trivial thing," Edward said. "Wherever Deborah is, she's all right. And I bet she'll be home within a week."

"My name is Willoughby; Mrs Willoughby," Deborah said, "and if you wish for a deposit, here it is." For the first time in her life she was free—her own woman—and although Mamma, back at Gad's, had thought of Deborah as unsophisticated because she had never seen London or any other great city, such a thought had underestimated Deborah's reading and the fact that she could read, not only a printed page, but a map. It was, after all, Deborah who

150

when Lavinia was pregnant and mad and needed some cover story to save them all suggested Killapore as a possible destination in India. Deborah, though she had travelled so little, knew more than most people of her kind about the outer world. Some of what she read might be rightly denounced by Tim as rubbish, but even in rubbish there was sometimes a grain of information, and from less rubbishy books, *Rambles South of the Thames, A Visit to Glastonbury, Norman Churches Still Unspoiled,* and works of a similar nature, Deborah's magpie mind had accumulated a number of facts which were of use to her when it came to choosing a destination of her own.

She did not wish to live in a big town; and in a small village any new arrival would be conspicuous. A place about the size of Baildon would be ideal. It must possess, or be within easy reach of a good Grammar School, for Sam must be educated and she would not be able to afford boarding school fees. Preferably it would not be in hunting country, for a certain section of the hunting fraternity had, like County families, interconnections, and she might be recognised.

She needed, she thought, a hiding place for about nine years. Sam, properly schooled and handled, should by the age of sixteen have enough strength of character to stand up to Tim, or anybody else; and he would have had a peaceful childhood, untroubled by parental dissension. She was certain that she had taken the right course and this certainty bore her up through several disappointments in finding a suitable place and the prospect of being poor for a long time— But better a dinner of herbs where love is than a stalled ox and hatred withal. There she had Biblical authority.

Now she had found a small, isolated, self-contained town in a Shropshire valley. It was called Abbey Norton and offered houses for sale or for rent because its population was falling. Some young people had been drawn away to the industrial Midlands, some had emigrated in search of wider, more tractable fields. The house she finally settled upon stood about a mile outside the little town and was cheaply rented for its size because it was delapidated. It had a neglected garden, a piece of small rough pasture, a stable and a pigsty. Sam should have a pony.

Here Deborah set about weaving the kind of story around herself and Sam just as she had once woven a story about Lavinia. She was Mrs Willoughby. Memory threw up the name which had been her own mother's maiden name; she was a widow.

"And you have his birth certificate?" the Headmaster of the Grammar School asked.

"I am afraid not. Sam was born in India. He remembers nothing about it," she added hastily. "We came home when he was a baby. I intended to go back, but then my husband died—suddenly."

Fundamentally, Deborah detested lies, and paradoxically, told them very convincingly because she looked and sounded so honest. "We have lived with various relatives. But I thought the time had come to set up house on our own." Perfectly understandable—the boy was old enough to be company for her now.

"He has had previous schooling?"

"Only such as I could provide. He reads quite fluently, and can do simple arithmetic."

The Headmaster had before this encountered boys brought up—and sometimes taught—by their mothers; they were usually namby-pamby cry babies, spoiled and ignorant.

"We'll have him in, and I'll set him a test or two."

Sam had entered into the whole thing with the enthusiasm of a seven-year-old given a part to play. Life without Father was very enjoyable—though he missed his pony and did not eat so well as he had at Foxton. Mother had explained everything; make one slip and he'd be back at Foxton, with Father, and without her, before he could blink, and that was not a pleasant prospect. Children apparently belonged to their fathers.

Sam was far from namby-pamby; he'd been taught to say "Sir" when addressing an elder man; he read fluently, could

152

add and subtract. Very satisfactory; he could start on Monday.

Deborah whitewashed the kitchen at the Stone House, and thought that there was a strange affinity between herself and whitewash. She had done the whitewashing at Diana's first home in Friars' Lane in Baildon; she had whitewashed the attic at Gad's, blotting out the terrible paintings which Lavinia had done on the walls. Now she was whitewashing for herself and Sam.

She'd bought the minimum of furniture—all secondhand; two people needed only two beds, two chairs and one table; but two people who had absconded without luggage needed clothing for the coming winter; needed crockery, and cooking utensils. She'd paid a year's rent, £26, and term's fees, £10—but that included a midday dinner, in advance. She'd bought a pig, and six fowls, and a pony, a rather sorry little creature, which perked up surprisingly when better fed and required only to jog a mile and back in a day.

All these things cost money, and well before Christmas, Deborah was assessing her capacity to *earn*. It was very limited. In a larger and more flourishing, and more socially ambitious community than the one she had chosen she could have given children a few elementary lessons; she could, as Mrs Thorley had done in her time, have taught some girls to play a few tunes on the piano. Had the need to avoid anything horsy not compelled her to settle in a place where horses were used for use, not for pleasure, she could have used her one inborn gift and schooled hunters. As it was she could not even fall back upon that last resort of a woman without means—needlework. Nobody could deny that she was handy, she could drive a nail straight, plant things, deal with harness; but that small thing, the needle, was defeat from the start.

One evening, late in the year now with everything practical that could be done, over and done with, and Sam doing his homework at the kitchen table, Deborah was struck by a feeling of deprivation. No book. She had always been a

153

prodigious reader, at school where Miss Hardwicke had given her, in the last year, the run of her small library; then at Gad's where books could be obtained from the circulating library in Baildon, or even bought; then at Foxton where books from the Thetford circulating library had been denounced as rubbish. Abbey Norton had no library, no bookshop even; it was in fact a very backward community.

The fire glowed in the range, the lamp cast a good light and Deborah would have been glad to read anything, even one of Tim's dismal books, the *Guide for Local Preachers*, or *St Paul's Steps Retraced*.

Quite suddenly the need to read became, like the making of the chicken house fox-proof and all the other things which had occupied her, something to be done by herself. Make your own book! Tell yourself a story. Deborah said, "Sam, have you an empty writing book?"

Ordinarily it was Mother who ended the evening sessions by making cocoa and saying, "Time for bed." On this evening Sam waited, and waited, and finally said,

"Shall I make the cocoa?"

"That would be kind," Deborah said, without looking up.

Sam made the cocoa and placing the cup on the table, said,

"That's a very long letter."

"It's not exactly a letter. It's something . . . else."

Deborah wrote regularly to Mamma, and there was no need to make her letters sound cheerful; they exuded happiness. She had been very cautious about her new name and her address; she preferred nobody but Mamma to know; if Di or Caro wanted to write to her they could do so through Mamma—not that either of them was much of a letter writer. Mrs Thorley had told George that Deb had found a home, placed Sam in school, and reported every other scrap of news as it came along, and George showed no curiosity. So long as Deb was all right and Mamma not worried he was content. He allowed Mamma to send on Deb's present from Holland, a gold brooch in the form of a fox head, and he occasionally said, "Send her my love," or "Tell her we're solidly behind her if it comes to needing money."

He had positively enjoyed a face-to-face encounter with Tim Bridges in, of all places, the yard behind the *Hawk in Hand*. A planned encounter since places where spiritous liquors were sold were sinks of iniquity in Mr Bridges' eyes.

"I've been waiting for you to come out," Tim said. "George, *where is Deb?*"

"I don't know."

"You must. Look here, George, you're old enough to understand. She's my wife. Sam is my son. I want them back."

Rather gleefully George repeated something which had been said to him in the past when he made some inordinate demand,

"Then I'm afraid want will be your master. I don't know where Deb is. And if I did, I wouldn't tell you."

George stood there, confident, handsome, saucy, elegant, smooth-speaking, the epitome of everything which Gad's represented and Tim distrusted.

"You're a liar."

"No man calls me a liar," George said, still smoothly, but hotly. The high romantic days, when a man whose word was questioned called the questioner out to a duel, were long over, but George squared up and said,

"You take that back."

"You're a liar."

The innyard had seen many fights in the past, and would see others, but the present innkeeper disapproved of people resorting to fisticuffs on his premises. It got a place a bad name, and his usual method with squabblers was rough and ready. Take them both by the scruff of the neck and chuck 'em into the Market Square. He was a huge man, six foot three inches in height and he weighed eighteen stones, all bone and muscle, no flabby flesh. In his day he'd gone twelve rounds against Irish Paddy, the most notable bruiser of the time. He was light and swift on his feet, and before any blow was struck, had interposed his bulk, saying,

155

"Gentlemen!" For the two preparing to hit one another were not drunken drovers. One looked like a Methody minister—and that was shrewd of the landlord, for Timothy Bridges wore his sober chapel-going suit when he went to market; and the other—God help us—was young Mr Thorley, very young Mr Thorley, but already a known customer and generous. But they were not going to be allowed to fight in *his* yard, however respectable they were. So he put himself between and said that if they had a difference of opinion it should be settled privately.

"I take it you don't want to make a raree show for ostlers and drovers."

Neither did, so that was the end of that.

Then Tim tried Mrs Thorley again, and again rebuffed, though she was magnanimous enough to tell him that she had heard from Deb and that she was well and happy, he tried a despicable trick.

"That Mr Bridges," Jenny said, "waylaid me in the yard and said he'd give me a sovereign to do a bit of spying for him. Amongst your letters, ma'am. I told him . . ." Jenny's face turned poppy red. There were expressions one could use to a man who had offered such an insult, but they were not fit for Mrs Thorley's ears. "I said no," Jenny finished on a weaker note.

There were people who said that all new-born babies looked exactly alike; and it was true that one could not tell anything from hair colouring, for if they had hair at birth it rubbed off, and the eyes of the new-born were always a slatey blue, but there was always, just a brief time—which might be outgrown, when the baby, boy or girl, looked like a very old version of its father. Mrs Thorley had noticed it with all her children, and looking at Caroline's little boy for the first time, she thought—Freddy Ingram! The ears particularly, set rather high and pointed, like a faun's.

God send, she thought, that nobody else would notice, or that the resemblance would vanish. Above all, God grant that Edward would never see.

This new anxiety threw her into such a jerky state that

Nurse Rose, who had allowed the child's grandmother to hold it, hastily took it back.

Caroline's baby was born on Christmas Day, and everybody had made sure that there should be as little pain as possible. Nurse Rose rather disapproved of methods she regarded as new-fangled, but she could not argue against *two* doctors. Doctor Awkwright had been involved too. And Nurse Rose, though hired and installed a fortnight before the event, had not come into full power until it occurred.

Miss Humberstone had chosen Nurse Rose as the one, of all the applicants, she could live with; a woman of very similar background, though Nurse Rose, unhampered by family ties, had been able to train for what, if not quite a profession, was a specialised job. Caroline, who partly from tact and partly from lethargy had allowed Miss Humberstone to do the choosing, had taken against Nurse Rose at first sight. Too much like Miss Hardwicke, who had on occasions criticised Caroline severely. But after all, what could one ask of a nurse for one's child except that she should be exceptionally clean, willing and conscientious, and that she should be able to get along with Miss Humberstone, about whom the activities and the splendid organisation of the St Giles' Square house centred?

Caroline came out of the anaesthetic haze to hear Edward saying,

"Darling, we have a little boy. Perfect in every way." Most fathers took for granted that their children would be perfect, but Edward, like every doctor, had seen the freaks which two ordinary parents could produce, and had had some bad moments. To Doctor Awkright, who had once mentioned the sex of the unborn, Edward had said, "What do I care? So long as it has its arms and legs in the right place; and its head, of course."

One glance was enough. Caroline knew what Edward must never know. And though she was not yet fully herself, had, as usual, the word ready.

"How old he looks! Edward, he looks just like your father!"

Edward, who had not considered his son's looks, agreed

157

and made for once a light-hearted remark,

"He'll grow younger every day!"

After an interval devoted to admiration of the baby, Caroline said, "Where is Mamma? I thought she was here."

"She was, darling. . . . Until it was all over. Then she went home."

In one tiny corner of his professional mind, Edward was concerned about his mother-in-law. He liked her and admired her. That jerk of the head—a thing of long-standing, and non-progressive, could be dismissed as nervous tic akin to a twitching cheek or a blinking eye. There was also the pleasant-sounding term, "A benign tremor," but Mrs Thorley's extreme shakiness, after it was all over, after she'd seen the baby sound and safe, smacked more of the irreversible paralysis agitans. He had not seen much of her lately, and when she arrived to be with Caro during the birth, he had been too much agitated himself to notice anyone else's condition. But *after* . . . he had noticed and was a little worried. He soon forgot that though in the joy of presenting Caro with a set of cameo trinkets, brooch, necklace and earrings.

The abrupt cessation of orders from Mr Burton which followed the gay display in Preston's windows early in December dismayed Diana for a short time, but she did not despair. Some other fashion would come along in the New Year, and she had established herself with the irritable little man as a good worker and one who was punctual. In the meantime she had leisure to cultivate the acquaintance of her new neighbours, so much more to her taste than those in St Anne's Crescent, or than Everard's fine friends. Nobody in the cul-de-sac called Somerton Road was very rich, or very grand; and on the whole they were people who had come down in the world, rather than scrambled up. Here poor Lavinia's idealised painting of Gad's Hall and Diana's pointing it out—My old home—roused no rancour at all. It and Diana's nice manners could be matched, or outmatched, often in a nostalgic manner. Almost every woman with any pretension to gentility could draw and paint with fair adequacy, and even some men did not despise the art: This is the bungalow in Simla, where we spent the hot weather; This is Cape Coast Castle, just at sunset; not very polished perhaps, but the sun goes down fast in the tropics; This is my old home, painting by my Aunt Augusta.

Everybody in Somerton Road had a resident maid—a few had two, but even two was a come-down after India, after life aboard ship, or in the Army. Dinner parties were rare, tea-parties frequent. Only two of the houses were occupied by young couples and only one of them, the Cressets, had children. That family employed a proper nurse who proved amenable to her mistress' suggestion that little Belle Spicer should sometimes accompany her charges on walks in the Park. Young Mrs Cresset could not imagine how Diana managed with only Bessie as maid-of-all-work. But she did not despise Diana for her apparent penury, because if her husband's tea-import business failed to pick up, and fairly soon, she might be in the same position. The upper-middle-class solidarity in Somerton Road was as viable as the lower-middle-class solidarity of St Anne's Crescent, and much easier to deal with.

Just before Christmas, Lady Lumsley decided to give a children's party. Not, as she explained, just Hunt the Slipper and similar games, followed by tea and buns. She proposed to hire a conjurer of international repute who would entrance the children and entertain a few dull adults who did not exactly fit in on other occasions. It would slide into another kind of party, sherry for those mothers who had accompanied their children, and for such fathers as came to collect their families. A piece of hospitality aimed mainly at what Lady Lumsley called The Dullies. And into that category Everard's wife, so prim and provincial, slid all too easily.

About Diana as Everard's wife, Alison Lumsley had no conscience pangs at all, and had the woman shown a spark of liveliness, she would have included her, gladly, in the gay round. But Diana had failed the test. So, bringing her daughter, Belle, "and friend," Diana was invited to a party intended to wipe off a lot of Dullies; women who took the business of motherhood seriously, following the Queen's example, a few elderly people who had reverted to the early bedtime and the tastes in amusement of childhood. Belle's only friend in London, in the world, was the elder of the two Cresset boys, so Diana asked him, and Mrs Cresset felt more than rewarded for her kindness over the walks in the Park.

What existed, during that autumn and winter, between Lady Lumsley and Everard could hardly be described as a love affair; there was no fondness in it on either side, merely a mutual attraction which needed physical contact to fan it into appetite. Meetings were easy enough to arrange; they met at her house, in the houses of a few people who liked Everard, but time alone together was difficult to find since Everard was married and must be in his office all day. (Not busy in his office—in fact the lack of business was alarming, but it made it all the more necessary that he should always be there to deal with what little there was to be done.)

Everard's brass plate, like the doctor's, attracted some chance clients, mainly of the humbler kind. He drew up a few wills, did some conveyancing of property, appeared in magistrates courts on behalf of a few people who had a defence to put forward, and money to pay; but it was all small stuff. That euphoric moment in Lumsleydale Castle, when everybody had said that he *must* set up on his own, and everybody promised him *volumes* of support, seemed to have been a bud which died before it flowered. And joining Brinkley's Club had been equally disappointing. No single bit of business had emerged from that pleasant place—so far.

Had he and Diana still been living at St Anne's Crescent, the Club would have served another purpose; he could then have said that business demanded that he sleep in the West End occasionally; but Somerton Road was the West End, practically fifteen minutes' walk away from Brinkley's. Still, after its fashion, the Club served. He could say, "I shan't be in to dinner, darling. Something may be looming, and I'll have a bite at the Club." Then—and such occasions were always arranged beforehand—he and Alison were free to be together.

It was all extremely unsatisfactory; everything was unsatisfactory. At home penny-pinching and a wife who never was much of a one for bed, now definitely feared another pregnancy: Two takes us all our time to provide for; three would be ruin. Until things improve.

It cost Diana a great deal to make such an outright statement; she had always been one to evade real issues. Engaged to be married, she had set about embroidering—not learning to cook. Practicality had been forced upon her and she hated every aspect of it. She hated the penny-pinching, too; worried—not about the rent, she still had some of the money Deb had given her, some of what she had earned—but for the future. Belle's education did not present much of a problem, little schools for girls were plentiful and cheap; but there was Melville. Everard said he must go to Eton—had even put his name on the waiting list; but first he must either have a tutor or go to a preparatory school. It was all very worrying, and life would have been unbearable but for the little round of tea-parties in Somerton Road and the friendliness of her neighbours. And, of course, Bessie, who trudging down to Soho could make sixpence go as far as a shilling. And the hope that some new fad would come in with the New Year and that Mr Burton would employ her again.

But this is not what I wanted, or expected when I fell in love with Everard. This is not as it *should* be. We've all, except Caro, gone wrong. Lavinia—better not think of her, and yet the picture was a reminder—Deb run away, me in this mess.

Miss Hardwicke had never insisted upon what was called copperplate writing, up strokes thin, downstrokes thick. A waste of time, she called it, what she demanded was legible writing, something as easy to read as print. By the end of February, Deborah had filled three notebooks with this easy-as-print writing and the tale that she had set out to write for herself was told. It was a strange mixture, an amalgam of what she knew and what she imagined, and what she had read. She knew, better than most, what was involved in keeping a living body hidden away, a deadly secret, yet needing food and sanitary arrangements, and exercise; what she imagined was a different and far less domestic background, and what she had read had provided her with a background and a motive. France, during the Revolution. . . . The hidden person an aristocrat who had endeared herself to an innkeeper of great determination and resource—Mamma to the life. The story had a tragic ending, most of the stories which Deb had enjoyed reading ended unhappily, and the story of Lavinia, the one story she knew at first hand, had been unhappy in the extreme. The innkeeper had a task even harder than Mamma's had been, for he could not leave his inn to underlings as Mamma had left her herd to Joe Snell; and he had no collaborators, as Mamma had had in Di and Deb and Caro; also he was subject, as Mamma had never been, to searches. Ordinarily the door of the hidden room was concealed by a cupboard, its shelves piled with bed linen. It was mounted on rollers, made by the man himself—given the motive and the tools, Deb could have rigged up a contrivance—but once, in a very tense scene, a search was made when the linen cupboard was out of place and the hidden door in full view. Then the inkeeper had to rely on his wits and said quickly that the revolutionary soldiers who were still searching for La Marquise, opened that door at their peril because behind it there was a man dying of smallpox. That sent them clattering down the stairs!

When she started to write herself a story because she had no new book to read, Deborah had not visualized it as a book, printed and bound, but at the end she read it through and realised that it was a tale that she would have enjoyed reading; it deserved a wider audience. Like most readers she had taken note of titles and of authors, but not of publishers and the only book available to her was the one she bought to enliven her train journey on the day she ran away. That was published by Hammond and Curtis, a firm who had an office in Regent Street. But they—or rather he, for there was not and never had been a Mr Crutis, he was a myth, and existed only as a cover for Mr Hammond when he, a kind man, was forced to be unkind. The firm had moved to 24 Essex Court, just across the hallway from Everard's office. The rent was less and it was better-situated; trades, professions and businesses were inclined to occupy certain areas. The Post Office had been alerted to the change of address of Hammond and Curtis and in due time Deborah's three notebooks, neatly packed, reached Mr Hammond, who, having nothing much to do that morning, began to read with the professional suspicion and scepticism proper to publishers. . . .

Presently he felt a regret that there was no partner, no Mr Curtis to share the excitement of this new discovery—new in exactly the right way; there had been enough of cloying sentiment, tastes were changing. But not yet quite to the point where everything in THE HIDDEN ROOM, by D. Willoughby, would be accepted by the circulating libraries, the foremost consideration in the publishing trade. It would not do to come under the ban of Mr Mudie's circulating library, or of Mr Smith's stalls at railway station; but with just a few adjustments THE HIDDEN ROOM was a protential winner. There had been plenty of books about the French Revolution, but every one had taken a stance, pro, or anti a political situation. THE HIDDEN ROOM avoided such imponderables and told, simply and clearly, the story of two people, involved in one incident.

Mr Hammond went out to lunch, brooding over the title. Did THE HIDDEN ROOM give a little too much away? In his mind he fingered possible alternatives and settled on SECRET. Back in his office, he wrote and his clerk copied—one should have a record of such things—a letter to D. Willoughby, whom Mr Hammond assumed to be a man, partly because the drinking scenes were so explicit—and must, with a few other things, such as the mentioning of the emptying of chamber pots, be cut. Women writers did

163

mention drunken orgies, but none, in Mr Hammond's experience, had ever given an exact description of man being drunk and sick on his own boots.

The Brontes, of course, had all taken pseudonymous, male-sounding names, and so had many other writers, and yet Mr Hammond was surprised when confronted by Deborah who had come, at his invitation, to discuss a few changes in her very promising book. *His* very promising book, as Mr Hammond had thought of it until this moment of meeting. He was shaken; all that stuff about chamber pots, and vomit on boots! How could he possibly discuss, with a woman? And yet it was this woman who had written the little pieces which might offend Mr Mudie and Mr Smith. He fell back on Mr Curtis, his partner, who refused manuscripts with the utmost ruthlessness, and cut pay down to the bone and did all the other things which allowed Mr Hammond to preserve his kindly, genial, sympathetic façade. And so far as Mr Hammond remembered, nobody had ever questioned Mr Curtis' verdict. Until now, when D. Willoughby said,

"He's wrong. I am a reader and it always irks me when quite important things are slurred over. What people live on, for instance. Income, or earned money—that kind of thing."

"You may be the exception, Mrs Willoughby. Most people read to escape from reality."

"Oh." Deborah pondered that for a second. "Even so, Mr Hammond, the escape is more *thorough* if the world into which one escapes is made to *seem* real."

Mr Hammond, having survived the slight shock of finding that D. Willoughby was female, and having sidled around the bits to which Mr Curtis was said to have objected, could now study his new author without embarrassment. Like everybody else he thought her older than she actually was; early thirties. Very well-dressed. Deborah, when she dressed herself on that last morning at Foxton, had donned a dress and basqued jacket of good broadcloth, stuff that would wear and weather well. For working in the house and garden at Abbey Norton she had bought the cheapest, shoddiest clothes. Obviously a lady, Mr Hammond concluded, composed, even slightly authoritative in manner. So how did she know exactly how men behaved when they were drunk? He ventured to ask, in an indirect way.

"That scene," he said, "where everybody, even the landlord, becomes so intoxicated is very real indeed."

"So it should be. It happened, but of course with different people."

For there had been a time which Deborah could remember, before her father married Mamma, when her father and those who were then his friends had drunk themselves silly and some had been sick. From the half landing where the grandfather clock stood, a curious child could see it all.

And possibly those incidents had inculcated her love of horses, waiting patiently, intelligent enough to take a drunken master home.

"Yes," Mr Hammond said, "there is the ring of truth there. And of course . . . on the other matters to which Mr Curtis took objection."

Deborah said, "But when a person is incarcerated he or she must still perform natural functions. That is what I mean about slurring over things. Any reader must know."

"I agree with you," Mr Hammond said. "But Mr Curtis does not." Mr Curtis, that myth, represented Mr Mudie and Mr Smith. "With the slightest adjustment, Mrs Willoughby, this could be a very successful novel indeed. Mr Curtis was so taken with it—on the whole—that he suggested a down payment of fifty pounds, and twenty pounds for each subsequent impression."

Had Deborah been on her own, carefree, foot-free, she would have reverted to the language of her youth and said: To Hell with Mr Curtis. Had she known a little more about the trade upon which she had embarked she would have said: Very well, I'll try a less timorous publisher. As it was she had Sam to think of, and the long years ahead; and she knew no other publisher. And after all, fifty pounds was no negligible sum, just for some words written in these notebooks.

"All right," she said, giving in with ill grace.

"And you will make the . . . the amendments?"

"No. Mr Curtis can do that, since he is so fussy. I still think he's wrong. You may tell him so and ask him to reconsider."

Mr Curtis was going to have a good deal of reconsidering to do for D. Willoughby had impressed Mr Hammond. He had had a good deal to do with she-novelists as they were called; some were very feminine and fluttery, some conceited and arrogant; all rapacious, even those who claimed to be writing for pin money. Whatever he offered—and thirty pounds down was more usual than fifty, they tried to extract a little more, and he invariably said that he would consult Mr Curtis, who as invariably upheld his decision. There was about this young woman something forthright, and unyielding, which he recognised as integrity.

Like everybody who struck what looked like gold, he was anxious to find out how deep was the vein.

"And have you further books in mind, Mrs Willoughby?"

There again she was different. Most she-novelists, given such a lead, would have begun to talk about the absolutely marvellous idea already crystallising in their minds. D. Willoughby looked thoughtful for a moment and then turned upon him one of the most entrancing smiles he had ever seen and said,

"I sincerely hope so. Writing a book is the next best thing to reading one."

Since completing THE HIDDEN ROOM—now to be called SECRET, Deborah had found that the evening hours hung heavily. She would willingly have helped Sam with his homework—but it was mainly in Latin, of which she had no knowledge at all. It was still too early to work in the garden; she mended in her inept but thorough way anything that needed mending. Everything in the sparsely furnished kitchen was as clean as it could be, and between the substantial tea which greeted Sam when he came home and the cup of cocoa just before bedtime there was an aching void. Yes, she would certainly write another story.

She would have liked, on this visit to London, to have visited Diana, but thought it inadvisable. For one thing she felt that she had let Diana down, promising her financial help whenever it was needed and then running away with only a limited amount of money to keep Sam and herself for nine years. Also Diana was married to Everard, who was a lawyer, and the law was all on the side of Tim, a husband wronged indeed.

Better not; better go straight home, close the hen house against the ravages of foxes, which in this unhuntable region were an everlasting menace, feed the pig.

Calling upon Mr Hammond, Deborah had been within a few feet of Everard. She was so single-minded that in looking for Hammond and Curtis on a brass plate she had not noticed Everard Spicer's.

Being, on her return to the station, fifty pounds better off than she had been earlier in the day—and with the promise of more to come, she allowed herself the indulgence of buying two books. Richness indeed! Yet, in the jolting train, there came between her and the printed page a kind of film, shadowy and vague with another story, one of her own making, advancing, retreating and then coming forward again, more clearly. Two main characters, both admirable in their way, but irrevocably divided in opinion. Against what background could they be placed? The answer came, clear as a bell; the Civil War in England; one of the ill-matched pair would be for the King, one for Parliament; each working away like a mole, and a child, Sam, torn between them. By the time that the train reached the end of the line, five miles short of Abbey Norton, Deborah had her story and was ready to begin again. Through the February dusk, lingering, with its promise of Spring and primroses, she walked happily, gulping down the fresh air. London, she realised now that she had time to think about it, was a horrible place, crowded, noisy, smelly and full of decrepit old cab-horses, kept going only by the whip, and donkeys even more pitiable than the one whose load she had once attempted to lighten by buying up a lot of heavy things.

Nothing to be done about it. Nobody was rich enough to save them all.

London was horrible; Caro had found it so, even on her honeymoon; and there was Diana doomed to live in it forever. It just didn't bear thinking about, and things which could not be thought about must be resolutely ignored. She had agreed with Mr Hammond that most people read to escape from reality; now she admitted to herself that some people wrote for the same reason.

Diana had no such escape. Ever since Christmas she had haunted Hawksley's, looking for something in the embroidery line which she could produce, imitate, quickly and cheaply. There was nothing, no fads.

She made a dress for Mrs Cresset, but naturally she could not charge for that because Mrs Cresset's nurse now took both Belle and Melville on little walks. Wearing gloves to protect her hands, she worked in the garden, but she was, for a country-bred girl, singularly ignorant about plants, and it was not until the old sailor, he who had painted Cape Coast Castle at sunset, and had never had an inch of ground to till until he retired to Somerton Road, pointed it out that she knew the difference between the true rose bush and the suckers. She worried perpetually about money. The rent, the rates, the full bill. Everard admitted frankly that self-employment took a long time to show a profit and that he was earning only just enough to keep the office going. In the past he had always been rather haughty about what Diana referred to as *her* money, been against her spending it, warned her that five hundred pounds would not last forever. Now he had changed and when she produced some money did not even ask how she had come by it. He simply said, "Thank God!" and a second later, "I'll make it up to you, darling, one day." Even as he said it he asked himself when that day would be. Security was like the horizon, it receded as one moved towards it.

Sometimes it seemed as though everything he had ever done had been a mistake; moving from Baildon, moving from St Anne's Crescent, setting up on his own. Sometimes he felt like one of those wretched men who tramped about the streets between two boards advertising a new play, a new restaurant, a new shop; but both his boards read FAILURE!

There were brief intermissions, now and again in Alison's bed, now and again at Brinkley's. But such pleasant times became more and more divorced from reality, further and further removed from the bread-and-butter business of ordinary life. The feeling which he had at first enjoyed and revelled in, of being amongst his own kind again, faded. March was a particularly bleak and hostile month. Alison and her gay crowd had gone to the South of France; Brinkley's was being redecorated, given over to men with scaffolding and ladders and paint pots. The East wind blew relentlessly, sometimes with flurries of sleet. The ancient crooked man who had cleaned the hallway and kept the brass plates bright came croaking, came voiceless, did not come at all—he'd died of pneumonia in Bermondsey Hospital—and the younger, but less active man who took his place jerked up the charge; five shillings a week from each tenant now. Imagine, just imagine being in a position where one shilling a week mattered so much.

Everard's mood was sometimes suicidal but his nature was not. He was too self-confident, despite all rebuffs, too self-preservative to do himself any damage. Years ago Caroline had summed him up in one word. Greedy. She'd referred only to the matter of food, but her judgement had not been far wrong; Everard was greedy; he wanted money, security, sexual satisfaction, social recognition, all so far, except for Alison, elusive; things just brushed with the tips of his fingers, never yet grasped. But in a blind, obscure way, even at his most desperate, that little nugget of self-assurance stood steady. One day . . .

Mrs Thorley avoided, so far as she could, any close contact with Caroline. She knew that she was being inconsistent, for she had done her best, stretched every available resource to its limits and beyond in order to protect Lavinia. But the two cases were not comparable. Lavinia had been caught in a web of evil, had practised black magic; and she was mad, been possessed, and if her own last words could be believed, impregnated by the Devil.

This was different. Caroline was not a demented, deluded young girl; she was a grown woman, with a devoted husband whom she had betrayed. Of her three sons-in-law, Edward was the only one of whom Mrs Thorley had fully approved, and the thought that Caroline could have done such a thing to such a good man filled her with disgust.

And sometimes, because she was an extremely rational woman, Mrs Thorley was disgusted by her own disgust. She told herself that Caroline could have had a good reason; a sterile marriage for five years? Perhaps that was the explanation, in which case . . . But somehow she could never fully accept it, and when she saw Edward fawning over the baby, her skin seemed not to fit and the shakiness which she did her best to conceal took over. Mrs Thorley did not think in terms of placard-bearing men, she just thought how sad life was. The four little girls, two her own, two George Thorley's, all always treated as her own; and gone such different ways, all regrettable. Lavinia mad, possessed of the Devil and lying under the walnut tree; Diana poor, in London; Deborah absconded, and Caroline, obviously an adultress. But thank God the baby, filling out, had lost that early resemblance to Freddy Ingram. Only those high-set, rather pointed ears . . .

I notice such things because I breed cattle.

I notice.

But to what end? There would be no point in scolding Caroline now. And in any case what right had she even to think so critically? So far as men were concerned her own record was clean, but some of her business dealings with Mr van Haagen were of dubious probity; and she drank more than she should. All that Spring she visited St Giles' Square as rarely as possible and stayed only briefly. One day Caroline remarked upon this change of habit and Mrs

170

Thorley said, "I don't like the way Edward looks at me—as though I were a patient. When I need a doctor, I'll send for him." The words came out more tartly than she realised. There was truth in them. Lately she had been aware of Edward eyeing her now and again, almost furtively, with speculation and curiosity. Then the tremor and the jerkiness increased. Like most other people she credited doctors with some extra perception and wondered whether he knew what ailed her. She was always almost ostentatiously abstemious in his house. One tiny sherry, please, Edward.

Caroline repeated this scrap of conversation, making, as usual, a joke of it: "Mamma says you look at her cross-eyed or something."

"I am interested," Edward admitted. He had no intention of worrying Caro. He had dismissed the idea of paralysis agitans because that was a permanent state, whereas his mother-in-law's condition was variable; even the jerking of her head followed no regular pattern; he'd run into her once in the Market Place, talking to a man, a cattle dealer by the look of him, but with manners enough to stand aside a little and wait. On that occasion Mrs Thorley had seemed as steady as a rock, and Edward attributed the whisky odour to the man. "I think her tremour is of nervous origin," Edward said. "After all, she is no longer young and she's had a hard life. If you ask me it's time she sat back a bit and let young George pull his weight a bit more."

There had been no need to tell Caro to sit back. Being pregnant, and then feeding the baby for three months, had provided an excellent excuse for shuffling off all the dull aspects of the good works which had accumulated ever since she became engaged to Edward. Nobody wished her to resign from any committee, for although many women didn't like her much, all the men did and everybody acknowledged her talent for raising funds. The Friends of the Hospital Committee had always met in Mrs Bosworth's house—now they met at Caro's because Mrs Taylor could not possibly be expected to exert herself yet; nor could she be expected to visit the Hospital, the Ragged School, or the Workhouse. But her ideas, her knowledge of what would attract people, and money were still invaluable.

Caroline was too soft-hearted to be a bad mother, too careless to be a good one. Not that it mattered. Nurse Rose enjoyed being omniscient in the nursery, just as Miss Humberstone enjoyed being omnipotent in the household. Caroline had traveled through her vale of tears; her shallow nature had betrayed her over Freddy Ingram. Over him she had not been a butterfly, but it was over now; Freddy somewhere in France was very different from Freddy within reach and any guilt Caroline felt over Noel's parentage—born on Christmas Day, the baby's name was forechosen—was easily cancelled out by Edward's joy in the child. Edward said that Noel grew more and more like his mother every day; and it was true that Freddy's colouring had not been transmitted; Noel's eyes were like Caroline's, bluish green, and his hair was fair. Dominant strains, thought Edward, who had read Mendel; Noel like George, like Sam Bridges, was a Thorley.

In that year there was a spell of weather in May quite as hot as August, and in the squalid, overcrowded rookeries of Soho, and other areas of London, there were outbreaks of cholera, but what Bessie couldn't see she did not fear, though in a way she shopped more carefully, avoiding shops and stalls too near an open drain or those which seemed to have changed hands overnight. She always shopped early in the morning, leaving Madam to deal with the breakfast, all prepared, as far as possible, overnight. She was always back in time to do the steps and the brass, and the washing up. Then a resuscitating cup of tea and she was ready to wash, clean, cook, to perform all the duties which in betteroff households took two, even three women. On this morning she came in, sweating and panting partly because of the effect the weather had on herself, but, more urgent, the effect it had on meat. Unless parboiled, or thoroughly doused with vinegar, meat could go off in the course of the day.

Diana, who usually at this hour was upstairs, making beds, doing a little light dusting, was in the kitchen, leaning against the sink and looking like death. The horrible idea that the sickness, so prevalent in what Bessie called the poor parts, had actually encroached into this most respectable neighbourhood and struck the mistress of whom she had the most genuine affection made Bessie's small world rock. She dropped the two heavy baskets just inside the kitchen door and ran forward.

"Oh, ma'am, are you ill?"

Diana just managed to shake her head.

Everard, unable to afford a proper lunch, must have a good breakfast; growing children needed a good breakfast, too. She had *just*, only just, managed.

Something, age-old, very female, took possession of the kitchen, no words needed. Until Bessie said, almost as an accusation,

"You've gone and fallen for another."

"I am afraid so." Really it was an appalling situation. It was difficult enough to manage as it was. That horrible Dutchman, pretending to tell fortunes, had said, three children, life in a city, just enough money. Diana, with her capacity for disregarding the unpleasant, had been curt and disbelieving, had dismissed the whole thing from her mind.

"You want it?"

"No. Not just now. It is extremely . . . inconvenient."

"Well, you don't have to, you know, ma'am. You just say. Where I come from, there's doses; clear you out in a blink. Cost a shilling."

Could squalor, the sordid part of life which Diana had so sedulously avoided, go deeper? To this I am reduced. I could—and curiously this was the first time she had thought of it—I could have married Richard Walford, lived in that big old house, lived in luxury, had a dozen children. It was only a fleeting thought to be sternly dismissed.

"Would it . . . Would it do me any damage, Bessie?"

"Lor' bless you, ma'am, no. No more'n a dose of salts."

Bessie knew; she had lived among prostitutes, would have been one herself had she been a little less positively ugly.

"Very well," Diana said after a pause. "Take a shilling from the jar."

"I'll take fourpence, too. I got fourpence left over from

the shopping. Then I can ride. Be quicker like that. You go and have a lay down and forget all about it."

There was a certain amount of comfort to be derived from Bessie's point-blank, commonsense attitude, but not enough to prevent the rising tide of nausea.

"There're the children," Diana said feebly.

"Miss Belle's big enough and old enough to look after herself and her brother for one morning," Bessie said harshly. Surely to God! Getting on for six! What hadn't Bessie been doing at that age, with the threat of Dad's belt always looming?

What Bessie brought back was essentially the same thing that Caroline had filched from the surgery in order to help Ruth, and in a way, Mamma and George. Diana had some scruples about swallowing it; she was an extremely conventional, orthodox young woman, and apart from conniving with Mamma to keep Lavinia's shame hidden, she had never said or done anything which lessened her self-esteem. She had worked for pay, which was lowering, but not shameful. This was, in a way which she would have found difficult to put into words, but felt very deeply. Something in her was outraged when at last she raised the glass, tilted it, gulped; and when the desired effect was brought about, some virtue, some fortitude seemed to go with the cleansing flow. She'd never been an easy crier—unlike Caroline; she'd been, in her own way, tough. She'd faced scrubbing steps in St Anne's Crescent, embroidering until she was almost blind, living from hand to mouth, being snubbed by Everard's fine friends, and done all this with dignity and self-control. So far as she could order her life, it had been orderly—never once, for instance, had she failed to wash her hair on Friday. Now, helped by Bessie out of what Bessie called a muddle, something within her collapsed. She cried for the slightest reason, or for no reason at all.

Even Everard, preoccupied with his own apparent failure, and knowing nothing of the pregnancy or its termination, was alarmed. She had not been cut out for or by life trained to be the wife of a poor man, but within her limits she had always operated well, always been spruce, tidy, agreeable, a loving wife, a loving mother. Now for some unknown reason, she had changed, and one night she gave him a real fright.

He woke from deep sleep and slowly realised that somebody was moving about in the room; and that Diana was not in bed beside him. He said, "Di!" There was no answer. With some agitation he reached out and lighted the candle. The wavering, strengthening light showed her standing, in a curiously rigid posture, midway between the foot of the bed and the wardrobe.

"Di, what is it? If you want to go across . . ." That was the euphemistic term for the water closet, adjoining the bathroom on the other side of the landing.

Diana said, "I don't know."

"Darling, surely you know better than to go stumbling about in the dark. Here, take this candle."

Diana had never before shown the slightest sign of having been influenced by her schooling; now she turned about and confounded Everard by saying, "'How far that little candle throws his beams! So shines a good deed in a naughty world.' That, my dear, is a quotation. But don't ask me to explain it. I never could, you know. I could never explain anything, even to Deb or to Everard, or Mamma. It's a very lonely life when you come to think of it."

She stood staring into space, talking to herself.

Everard hopped out of bed, took her by the arm, steered her back towards bed. "Di," he said, "wake up. You're dreaming. I'm here. I'm Everard."

Diana said, "Really. I apologise for any seeming discourtesy, but I did not recognise you immediately. I admit that my sight is not what it was. Quite possibly my memory is failing, too."

He got her back to bed and in the morning she remembered nothing of it. He was quite prepared to talk about it. He said,

"You gave me a fine fright last night."

"How?"

175

He was cautious. "Getting up and trying to go across in the dark."

"That I am sure I never did. You must have been dreaming."

It was again the day for Bessie to go marketing, and Diana's day for making breakfast, which by this time she could do quite adequately. But she was short of temper. She said to her beloved son, "If you can't eat your egg properly, I shall take it away from you." Melville thereupon burst into tears and Diana cried too.

In his office Everard held his pen poised; Dear Mrs Thorley, after all these years, sounded rather formal, especially when one was about to ask a favour, but Dear Mamma sounded too familiar. Better be on the safe side.

"I have," Mrs Thorley said, "a letter from Everard. He says that London is unusually hot for the time of year and that Diana seems to be a bit under the weather. He wants me to write and invite her to come now."

"Well, why not?"

"No reason at all," Mrs Thorley said. "I just wanted you to know."

For in tiny ways authority had moved over to George, ever since that evening when she had attempted to scold him over his behaviour with Ruth. His talent for enjoying himself, and making others enjoy themselves, was already well-developed; he would seize on any excuse for a party and he liked to have overnight guests; nobody to whom the fondest mother could possibly take exception, and to George's credit it must be said that he was just as charming and attentive to quite old people as to his near contemporaries. The elderly guests were mostly men connected with the Cattle Shows, the Cattle Sales. "Poor old Bennett," George would say, "he'd be far more comfortable here than at the *Hawk in Hand*, and we ought to provide him with a little company." It grieved and puzzled George that Mr van Haagen never took advantage of Gad's hospitality.

Lady Faulkner, once Chloe was safely married, had allowed the sun of her approval to shine upon George again; and Johnny Faulkner was inclined, Mrs Thorley thought, to exploit George and Gad's. Johnny and *his* friends, who rapidly became George's, too, used Gad's as a base from which to shoot, hunt, attend point-to-point meetings and, finally, the races at Newmarket. The Faulkners' place at Stratton Strawless was a bit off the map, and for all their grandeur the Faulkners were pretty hard up. And as George said, "We can afford to entertain a bit." It was true; business was booming. And although in the past, some well-meaning people had warned Mrs Thorley of the danger of spoiling an only son, it was difficult to find any real fault with his behaviour. She had never seen him the worse for drink, for instance (And if it happened, what could I say?). Johnny Faulkner was a year older than George and some of his friends were older than he was. They did get drunk occasionally. George gambled a bit, but never to any great extent, and he was almost invariably lucky. He was not overattentive to the business, but then, why should he be, when she was there to take care of it? One was only young once; let him make the most of it.

"I just wanted you to know," Mrs Thorley said, "in case you had planned anything."

"I never do. Things just happen to me."

Something had happened to Diana; Mrs Thorley saw that in the moment of meeting the train. Everard had simply said that Diana was a bit under the weather, but the poor girl looked ill, pale and thin. She'd had the best figure of them all; where had the pretty curves gone? And she had always been so fastidious, so well turned out. Last summer, Mrs Thorley remembered, Diana's composure had cracked and she'd cried after reading the letter that told her that Everard had decided—without consulting her—to set up on his own. But she had recovered, and letters had been cheerful; all about her nice new house; her nice new neighbours.

Well, let's hope that there's nothing wrong that a good long holiday in the country can't cure. And here I am, shaking like a leaf. Any little thing upsets me nowadays; and I can't take a drink until I get home.

These days she drank a very peculiar mixture, happened upon by sheer accident. Knowing that she would be cut off from supplies for a whole day because she had to attend the newly founded Cattle Breeders' Association, she had prepared herself and poured some whisky into what she thought was an empty bottle of eau de Cologne which happened not to be quite empty. The brew had been quite effective, and ever since she had carried one of the eau de Cologne bottles, in its half nest of wickerwork with her in the gig, but she must resort to it now.

During the drive from Baildon to Gad's, head jerking, hands unsteady, Mrs Thorley came to the conclusion that she worried too much and too easily, for Diana seemed all right. She expressed interest in Caro and her baby, for whom she had made a garment, beautifully smocked. She talked about Deborah and said she blamed Tim. Anybody who couldn't get on with Deb couldn't get on with anybody, Di said, and Mamma agreed. About her own state of health she was reserved, defensive. "I did not feel too well for a day or two. But I was singularly fortunate; one of neighbours employs a nurse, a very nice, willing woman. She took charge."

Di sounded all right, but she looked all wrong.

The children, Mrs Thorley noticed, were extremely well-behaved. Mrs Cresset's nurse stood no nonsense and had a firm belief in the virtue of a good smack on the bottom.

"And what of Deborah, Mamma? You never did give me her address."

"That was her wish, Diana. But she sounds very well and happy. She seems to have found some way of earning money. She did not say in what manner."

"Something to do with horses, no doubt."

"Possibly."

In fact for all who had the time and the inclination to read, Deb's way of making money was plain and certain.

Mr Hammond, who knew his job, had discarded the title

THE HIDDEN ROOM as being too revealing, too naïve; but the essence of the title, he had used, pictorially; a locked door with Heaven knew what secrets behind it. The picture chimed perfectly with the new title, SECRET, and the book sold as hot cakes were said to do. Mr Mudie wanted it, Mr Smith wanted it, countless people who bought instead of borrowing books wanted it. It was one of the lucky books, people went about saying: You simply *must* read it! When the mythical Mr Curtis had made his cuts, the book passed one of the tests of the times: Would you like your young sister, your daughter, to read this book? The answer was a resounding Yes! With the valuable addition that men could enjoy it too. It was not pious, or too much concerned with domesticity. It also had the appeal of being almost classless. The lady hidden was an aristocrat, the innkeeper was a man of the middle kind, and there were servants and drovers, even rough soldiers, sympathetically treated, not stock figures, real people. Something for everybody, suspense, romance, solid worth. Twenty pounds for each subsequent impression, Mr Hammond had said, but to Deborah the words had been virtually meaningless since she did not know what an impression was. To her a book was a book; but there was twenty pounds at the end of May—forty in June, sixty in July.

In a curious way Deb never regarded the money as real; to her it was akin to the fairy gold which turned into crumpled leaves when handled. She disposed of her pig on the tit-for-tat basis common in this area; a man came and took away the pig, killed it, allowing her a good joint for roasting and some sausages, and presently she was to have from this or another pig a side of bacon and a ham. She bought another pig. In her fowl run she had some home-reared pullets which would lay in November, and the first fowls she bought; they would be eaten one by one. The garden provided her with potatoes and greenstuff. Even with her rent and rates and Sam's fees paid, she was fully solvent without Mr Hammond's payments.

There were many things she could have done with the money: furnished a comfortable sitting room, bought new

179

clothes, but the kitchen was comfortable and she seemed to have lost her taste for finery. She could look back with a wry smile at the resentment she had felt when Tim told her to take the yellow rose wreath off her hat. The one indulgence she allowed herself concerned books; there was a lending library in Shrewsbury which supplied books by post to people who lived in small towns or the country, so she was no longer starved for reading matter; but without being conscious of conceit, she thought her own book, A HOUSE DIVIDED, more entertaining, and wrote in it diligently. It was completed by August, and once again Mr Hammond regretted that he had no one with whom to share his jubilation. D. Willoughby was that rare bird indeed—a writer capable of taking a hint. No cuts were necessary here. And yet, when he had finished reading and rejoicing over what he recognised as saleability, he was left with a faint unease. The dissension between the Puritan husband and the Royalist wife was just a little too well-portrayed. No open quarrel, no shouting, no blows, just the steady divergence of opinion, eroding what had been a good marriage; it bore some resemblance to the situation which existed between Mr Hammond and his own wife, though in their case no such great issue as a Civil War was involved; it was just that after a few halcyon months they seemed not to agree about anything. It was all here, with a good deal of what Mr Hammond called top-dressing, costume stuff, the ebb and flow of war, man and wife intriguing against one another; and a strangely ironic ending: the son of the marriage—loved by both parents, and the real subject of the dispute—being sent off with money and three good horses to join the Parliamentarian forces, and entrusted, at the same time, with his mother's last trinket, to sell for the King; and the boy riding away to join neither party, intending to buy a ship and turn pirate. Old enough to choose for himself.

It has everything, Mr Hammond thought before sitting down to offer D. Willoughby slightly better terms; down payment the same, but twenty-five pounds for each subsequent impression.

At Gad's, Diana seemed to improve in health; her flesh plumped out, her hair regained some of its lustre, but she had what Mrs Thorley called mental lapses. They went to see Caroline and the baby, and Di presented the smocked dress. Caroline thanked her.

"It is such beautiful work, Di. But then you were always so good with a needle."

"It isn't easy, you know. Take a week, it goes nowhere. Wednesday lunch time is the halfway line, so you must be finished and ready to start on the next. It is difficult, by lamplight, to tell a certain blue from purple, so one lays them out in daylight, and then one forgets. Old men forget and we shall be forgot."

Mamma and Caro exchanged a look, concerned, bewildered.

"Yes," Diana said in that same reasonable, amiable way. "I talk too much. It is confusing for you. I apologise.

Just then Miss Humberstone came in with the tea-tray and Diana seemed to recover from whatever it was. She talked with animation and apparent pleasure about her new house, her new neighbours. They were both left with the impression that they had misunderstood, or, looking at Noel and the dress he was to wear, had missed some vital connecting link.

Two, or perhaps three nights later Mrs Thorley was wrenched away from that comforting thought. She had taken her nightly dose and was drifting into sleep when she was aroused by a noise on the landing. George, she thought with as much anger as she could ever bring to bear upon him. He'd said he would be late and she had told him to come in quietly because of the children. And yet, she realised as her mind cleared, that the noise on the landing was not George's kind of noise. When George came in noisily he took two stairs at a time and tended to hum or whistle.

She relit her candle and holding it went to the door and knew a moment of sheer terror. Something in white, fumbling along in the dark and crying. Lavinia? No, of course not; what rubbish. Diana.

She took her daughter by the arm, noting as Everard had done the unyielding rigidity. She steered her into her own room and said, "My dear, what is it?"

"I don't know. It's lost. Why should you interfere and add to my misery?"

"Darling, I'm your mother. You're dreaming; sleep-walking."

"Why should you accost me? I have nothing valuable."

Caroline at her worst had never wept so copiously or so heartbrokenly.

"Diana, you must wake up! Look at me. I'm your mother."

"I suppose that makes a difference, but I have forgotten what it is. I don't see so well and my memory is failing, too. All a very great pity."

"Lie down," Mrs Thorley said. She pushed Di into the warm bed. "And stop crying. You have nothing to cry about. Whatever it is we'll talk about it in the morning. Sleep now. Sleep. That's right. Let everything go, darling. Sleep."

Diana changed from rigidity to flaccidity and slept. Donning her warm winter dressing-gown, and leaving the door open in case one of the children should cry out in the night, Mrs Thorley lay down alongside, outside the bed, but under the eiderdown. An uneasy, troubled night.

In the morning George, who sought popularity, even with mere children, took Belle and Melville to Baildon to savour the delights of ice cream, and that gave Mrs Thorley an opportunity to talk to Diana. She was less easily deceived than Everard had been and far more persistent.

"I am willing to believe that you remember nothing about it. But surely to goodness you must have wondered why you woke up in my bed, not your own."

"Now I come to think of it, of course I should, but Mel was calling me. I went straight to him, still half asleep. Are you quite sure, Mamma, that you didn't dream it all?"

"I am absolutely positive. My dear, something must be troubling you. It would be far better to bring it into the

182

open and talk about it and see what can be done. Is it money?"

"We still have to be careful; almost tiresomely so. But we are not in want. And Everard's business must improve."

"Is your sight worrying you?"

"My eyesight? No, why do you ask that?"

"Because at Caro's the other day you mentioned a difficulty in distinguishing between two colours. And last night you said you did not see so well as you did. Possibly you need spectacles."

Mrs Thorley for no reason except that she was a good mother had always been concerned about eyesight, considering that Diana might overstrain hers with too much very fine work—so different from plain sewing, and doing her best to prevent Deborah from reading in bed, lying down, so that the candlelight barely illuminated the page.

There the forgotten things and everyday memory did interlock briefly. Sometimes, working against time on the kimonos, Diana had, at the end of a long session, been aware of strain on her eyes.

"Oh no," she said. "I see perfectly. I try to avoid too much close work by lamplight."

Baffled on that trail, Mrs Thorley, like a good, indefatigable hound, cast about and tried another.

"When you were sleep-walking . . ." That seemed the best way of putting it, ". . . you seemed to be afraid that you were being accosted."

"Oh that," Diana said, almost brightly, as though relieved by the change of subject. "Everybody fears it, if obliged to go out alone, in certain streets. This you will hardly believe, but quite recently my maid, Bessie, was in a shortcut, called Brewers' Lane, and a little girl, Bessie thought her no more than six, came from an opening and drove one of those iron hoops straight at her, almost knocking her down. And in the resultant confusion the little girl snatched Bessie's reticule." Diana allowed herself a grim smile. "Bessie grew up in a poor part of London and carries her reticule purely for show, stuffed with rubbish. Her

183

purse she carried on a string round her neck."

In her day, during the bad times, Mrs Thorley had lived in areas where such things had been a daily occurrence, so she was not unduly shocked and she was not diverted—if that were Diana's intention. She charged again.

"Last night," she said, "you also talked about your memory failing."

"It was never good. As you know, Mamma. At school we were always set pieces from Shakespeare or *Paradise Lost* to learn. I never could; that is why Miss Hardwicke despised me so much."

A most unsatisfactory conversation. Well, all she could do was ply Diana with the best of food, see that she rested as much as possible, and enjoyed her holiday. That included the offer to drive her about to see old school friends. Barbara Catchpole, for instance, now married with a little girl somewhat older than Melville and a new baby; wouldn't that be a nice thing to do on a sunny June afternoon?

"I don't particularly want to," Diana said. "And to be truthful, mothers with new babies are very boring. Every time I see one I want to cry."

Mrs Thorley missed the significance of that remark. But she was alerted by something that Diana said a few days later.

"Mamma, if it would not cause you any great inconvenience, I would like to stay a little longer. London is still very hot and Bessie looks after Everard quite adequately. Also he has his Club."

"My dear, you know, you are welcome to stay as long as you like. This is your home."

Was the whole thing another wrecked marriage? Was Diana, both in her ordinary, waking state and during her mental lapses, really running away from a partnership which had become unworkable? Mrs Thorley's own first marriage had been, by ordinary standards, quite unworkable, but she had held on to it; like a bull dog. To the end; the bitter end, when Stephen had shot himself, leaving her cut off, alone with two little girls, Diana and Lavinia; cast adrift in an alien, hostile world.

184

I never ran away from any situation, she thought proudly, and then her inner, honest mind said: Except through whisky!

Undeniable, she admitted, with just that slight shrug of the shoulders with which, when on a rare occasion she had been outbidden, she had turned away from a sale.

Somehow the thought of Stephen, dead, buried long ago, stayed with her throughout the day. He'd fathered Lavinia, who had been demented and suicidal; and Diana, who seemed to have taken a melancholy turn which might lead . . . No, the idea must not be entertained; something must be done. Much against her wish Mrs Thorley decided to consult Edward. And that decision put her in a quandary; stay sober and face Edward all of a-twitch? Drink enough to steady herself and go in smelling like a distillery, for though the whisky and the eau de Cologne was a deceptive mixture, the whisky scent lasted longer. Well, what of it? she asked herself half-angrily. She wanted Edward's help about Diana, not his verdict on her own behaviour. She was in no way responsible to him, and she preferred to be thought a whisky drinker than a poor shaky old woman.

In order to make her visit look professional she used the surgery entry, and arriving deliberately late, had not long to wait.

Edward listened with attention and sympathy and a growing sense of hopelessness. Really there was very little to go on; a scrap of slightly disjointed talk in Caroline's drawing room, and what sounded like a bit of sleep-walking and a crying fit in the middle of the night. And even with much clearer evidence of mental disturbance there was so little one could do except prescribe a mild sedative, advise a change of air and scene, and the latter palliative Diana was already having. If there were any specific worry it might be removed, or alleviated.

"Is it just possible," he asked gently, "that you are worrying overmuch?" She was quite steady, but the scent of eau de Cologne had suffered its usual defeat and Edward was reasonably sure that what ailed his mother-in-law, most admirable woman, was not a nervous tic, or a benign tremor, or the dreaded paralysis agitans. She was an alcoholic! There was no condemnation in Edward's conclusion; poor woman, she'd had a hard life, taking on a man's job.

"It may seem so," Mrs Thorley said, speaking with crispness. "But . . . Edward, I have never spoken of this and I am sure that you will regard it as confidential. My first husband, Diana's father, fell into profound melancholy when things went wrong with him, and committed suicide while still in his thirties."

"Oh." He felt even sorrier for her. And then being only human was momentarily glad that Caroline's father had been hearty jovial George Thorley. Contradicting this reflection, he said,

"One must not pay too much attention to such things, you know. At the same time . . . You say when things went wrong with him. Has anything gone wrong with Diana?"

"I can only say that if it has she has not confided in me. Her new house sounds to be a great improvement on her former one and she has nice neighbours, now."

"Do you think she would confide in Caro—if they had a day alone together?"

Mrs Thorley considered and then said, "I think not. All my girls were friendly with one another, but from the first they paired off according to age. If Di was inclined to talk to anyone it would be Deb. And she is out of reach." That was a slightly misleading statement, for Caroline and Lavinia had never been a pair: Lavinia had no real contact with anyone, until she fell in with those wicked people.

"All the same, we'll give Caro a chance, I think. She has a way with her, you know." Mrs Thorley knew—but it was a way that worked much better with men than with women. "And at the same time I will test Di's eyes."

"She denies that there is anything wrong with them."

"We'll make a game of it. I'll pretend I have some new eye-testing process, I'll test Di's and Caro's and then they can test mine. It may be at the root of the trouble. A hidden fear of needing spectacles. Most women regard them as disfiguring. And of course any preoccupation is inclined to affect one's memory in other spheres. . . . I'm sure you have no cause for worry."

By this time the smell of whisky was quite strong in the little surgery and Edward longed to add that whisky never cured anything, but he hardly dared. Still, he realised that his mother-in-law was caught in a vicious circle, she drank to cure the shakes, and drinking provoked more shakiness.

Quite abruptly he changed his plans for Noel's future. From the moment when he knew that he had a son he had visualised him as a doctor, taking over the practice which had been in the family for five generations. Now he decided that a surgeon had an easier life with far fewer problems. A surgeon asked himself one question: to operate or not to operate, and if he operated as skilfully as he could, his job was done; the patient recovered or died. Nobody came to a surgeon seeking advice on nervous conditions and mental states or even social problems. And the status of surgeons was rising steadily. In the time of Edward's great-grand-father surgery was despised, not even regarded as a profession; but times had changed, and with the coming of a proper anaesthetic, like chloroform, the age of painless surgery was beginning, operations, hitherto unimaginable would be possible. Noel should be a surgeon.

If eye tests were anything to go by, Diana had nothing to worry about on that score; her sight was fully as good as Caroline's and rather better—unless the girls had bungled things—than Edward's own; he seemed to be the one who might presently need spectacles for reading. And Caro, though warned in advance to try to find out if anything were worrying Diana, drew a blank.

"Naturally," Diana said, "I am not so well-placed as you are, but then Edward was established when you married him. Everard has his way to make. But I have no doubt he will do it."

Their day together did produce something of significance which neither of them recognised.

"As you know," Caroline said, "I never was much of reader, but people who do like books, like them; so this year, when the question of the White Elephant Stall for Friends of the Hospital was being discussed, I suggested having a few books on it; secondhand but not raggy. At sixpence each they sold very well, but old Miss Riley—do you remember her? She was a great friend of Mrs Spicer, Everard's aunt; definitely senile now and can't tell Easter from Whitsun; she sent this book, a week late. So it was here and one evening, having nothing better to do, I looked into it. It is very odd, in a way it's exactly what we all went through with poor Lavinia."

"You always thought: Poor Lavinia, and used to smuggle her chocolate," Diana said. "I never did. I thought she was a disgrace, and I only undertook to take stuff to the laundry in order to help Mamma."

"The poor man in this book, trying to keep somebody hidden in a secret room, hadn't even that much help," Caro said. "Of course it's all about long ago when things were different. And yet there is a likeness. . . . And it is a good title, don't you think? Secret. That was what it was, for all of us, until she died, wasn't it?"

"I suppose so. And it was horrid. For myself I wouldn't want to read a book that reminded me of it."

As the eldest of the four when they were all girls together, oh, such happy days, the happy, happy days when we were young! Diana had acquired a kind of ascendancy, and a shadow of it remained; nothing to do with position or possessions. (Caro had seen Diana's horrid little house, slept in her cupboard of a spare room. Don't think of that. Bear in mind that Diana would never in a thousand years cuckold Everard, self-absorbed and unsuccessful as he was, as Caroline had cuckolded Edward, quite the best man in the world.)

Yet Caro was aware of the edge of disapproval in Diana's voice and hastily changed the subject.

Diana's holiday, begun in May and extended, with Everard's full approval, into June, just impinged upon the best time for the Newmarket races. By that time George had tired of his role of fond uncle and in his mind applied epithets to the children—little horrors, little beasts—which he was tactful enough not to use in the company of a fond grandmother and a doting mother. Di had never been his favourite of the girls, but by God he felt a bit sorry for her condemned to their company day and night. A day off the chain would, he thought, do her the world of good. Mamma agreed, so he said,

"Di, come with me to the races tomorrow."

"That is very kind of you, George. But, thank you, no."

Too terribly prim and proper, George thought. He disliked having his well-meant gestures rejected.

"Why not? I assure you, Di, a great many ladies attend race meetings nowadays and enjoy themselves very much."

"I shouldn't. Too many people."

George glanced at Mamma, whose head moved, whether in a warning signal or the jerk which came and went he did not know. Since it accorded better with his own inclination he took it as a negation and said no more.

Next day luck was definitely good, in every way; he'd backed two rank outsiders who simply strolled home; and he came back to Gad's by himself, so there was no witness to a most embarrassing and distressing scene.

Gad's though prosperous was not yet one of those places where one simply dismounted and left one's horse to somebody else's care. But Willy always left a full bucket and a full manger, and rubbing down could wait until the morning. So it was still the last of the lingering dusk when George opened the back door and saw something, white, a figure, moving about in the kitchen.

He had the unshakable nerve of somebody who had never been frightened and whose imagination had a limited scope. He did not think, as in a similar situation Mrs Thorley had thought—Lavinia! for he knew nothing about Lavinia except that she had gone to India, years ago, and died there. And that on the attic floor there was a locked room which had been her studio and was her memorial—his own suggestion—because she had no grave in England. So a white-clad figure roused no superstitious feeling in him. He said,

189

"What are you doing, fumbling about in the dark?" At the same time he lit the candle which awaited his entry and could narrow down the inquiry which could have applied to any one of the four women in the house.

"Di! What are you doing, fumbling about in the dark?"

"What right have you to speak to me in that tone of voice? I know you *employ* me, but civility costs nothing. However, since you ask, I will tell you. I have lost something. I no longer see very well and my memory is going and I need help."

George had somewhere heard about people who walked in their sleep and performed incredible feats such as climbing out of windows and scrambling over roofs, things they could not have done while awake. But did sleep-walkers go about with their eyes open? He'd never bothered to ask. Di's eyes were wide open. And although what she said had no meaning, sounded daft, that part of his nature which was kindly and gallant made him say,

"What have you lost, Di? Tell me, and I'll help you look."

"I don't know. I can no longer remember. What I *do* know is that if this goes on much longer I shall not see to thread a needle. Of *course* money is important," she said, as though somebody had said that it was not. "But what is the use of it when you have lost everything else? And can't see? Or remember?" She began to cry. George walked towards her and took her by the upper arm and was conscious as both Everard and Mrs Thorley had been of the rigidity. But he pushed her towards the rocking chair in which Jenny spent her leisure time and said,

"There, have a good cry. I'll make a cup of tea."

By all but country standards it was still early; the kettle at the back of the stove soon boiled. George, moving a bit clumsily about, in familiar surroundings, but with an unfamiliar purpose, got together what was needed, at the same time keeping an eye on Diana, who sat stiffly in the chair, crying and letting the tears run down unstaunched so that the front and the lap of her white nightdress turned grey with the dampness. Hers was not the posture of one having a good cry which would bring relief.

190

He carried the steaming cup towards her and said awkwardly,

"Here, Di. Drink this and try to pull yourself together."

"I daren't. It's poison! Oh, I know all the arguments. It may not damage me physically. What about my mind?"

George knew several lurid tales of husbands who had poisoned their wives, or wives who had poisoned their husbands. Di *had* looked very ill when she arrived at Gad's, and had postponed her return to London. It seemed completely absurd to suspect that stiff, self-righteous Everard of the slightest misdoing; but then, weren't they just the ones who got away with murder? And didn't it look a bit sinister that Everard had not shared Di's holiday either last year, or this? Last year perhaps he couldn't help it, but this year he was his own master.

"It's a cup of tea, Di. I just made it. It'll do you good."

She stopped crying as suddenly as she had begun and reached for the cup and saucer.

"Thank you. It is very kind. As a matter of fact Mr Burton has just informed me that he has no further work for me. I must not allow my dismay to show. I shall walk through Hawksley's as though I owned it."

She drank her tea and George drank his. His good luck had been properly celebrated with champagne, a drink that always left him thirsty.

He was completely bewildered; not even sure if she were asleep or awake. His instincts were kindly, his nature impatient.

"Look here, Di, *I* don't know what you're talking about. Don't go rambling on. Tell me what's the matter and I'll see what I can do."

"I don't know. I lose things. And I forget and I can't see very well."

"What do you mean talking about poison?"

"Oh, it undoubtedly *was*. I was extremely indisposed for several days. That was why . . . But there you are; my memory is not reliable."

The cup of tea having failed, all George could think of was bed.

"Come along, Di. Let's get to bed. You'll feel better in

the morning." He'd feel better, too, when he'd had a talk with Mamma.

In fact he felt rather worse for it was almost impossible to associate Diana calmly supervising her children's breakfast, eating her own, with the distracted, rambling creature of the previous evening.

"Honestly, George, I know little more than you do. Except that Edward has assured me that Diana's sight is perfectly good, and that in a whole day, alone with Caroline, she had mentioned no trouble or problem."

"Last night, just for a moment, she seemed to think that somebody had tried to poison her. Do you think that Everard could possibly . . . ?"

"No, I do not. And for a very simple reason. Men who intend to poison their wives don't—after one abortive attempt—send them home to recuperate. It wouldn't make sense."

George allowed himself to laugh at his own absurdity.

"Mamma, you are my absolutely favourite woman. The only logical woman I know."

"And your experience is so wide?" She said that lightly, but almost instantly reverted to seriousness. "All the same, we cannot blind ourselves to the fact that something— something which she will not admit, even to herself, is wrong with Di. I've tried to talk to her, so has Caro. Nothing useful emerged. Apparently *you* got no sense out of her last night."

"Wait a bit. Of course, I see your reasoning about poison—that was silly of me, but last night she talked about work; about a Mr Burton having no more work for her and walking out of Hawksley's as though she owned it . . . I couldn't make head or tail of it but it was something she felt deeply. Does it make sense to you?"

"Perhaps." In her good days Mrs Thorley had had no need to walk through Hawksley's as though she owned it; she had more than owned it, being a customer with ready money in her hand.

In the good days that she remembered Hawksley's had

192

employed a few sedate women, all in black, all wearing black satin aprons, in some departments, and it had also had dressmaking and millinery rooms. Was it possible that Diana had sought employment there, perhaps overstrained her eyes by too much close work; perhaps lost something, or forgotten something, made a mistake in matching two colours, and been given what was vulgarly called the sack? Diana, so proud, so fastidious, so good with her needle. Mrs Thorley could imagine the shock and humiliation. Quite enough to upset her mind.

"It is possible, my dear, that you were given some kind of clue. I shall think about it. I'm sure she'd be better if whatever it is were brought into the open."

"If it's anything to do with money, we could help her, couldn't we?" In George's simple philosophy the very word work implied penury. He'd never really worked, not even during his lessons with old Mr Spicer, and where the farm and the herd were concerned he did exactly what suited him to do; showing off, being charming, leaving all the real work to Mamma.

"I offered help a year ago, but Deborah had forestalled me . . . But then of course Deborah's own circumstances changed."

It was rather like a mist on an autumn morning, slowly clearing, allowing glimpses of solid shapes to emerge.

"I shouldn't like any sister of mine to be short of money," George said. And despite everything Mrs Thorley felt a small glow of satisfaction. She had made, out of discordant elements, a family. And in a way held it together.

Knowing how secretive Diana could be, Mrs Thorley made a direct attack, but speaking as casually as though mentioning the weather.

"What work exactly did you do for Mr Burton at Hawksley's, my dear?"

For a second or two Mrs Thorley felt that she had made yet another wrong step. Diana looked as though someone had struck her a heavy blow—from behind. Then she said violently,

"Who told you? I never told anyone. I never even used my own name. Even Everard didn't know. Sometimes I had to work late and he'd ask what I was doing. Not really interested. And I'd say making something for the children, or embroidering a cushion. Something like that. . . . Who told you? Who could possibly *know*?"

Better not bring George into this.

"When you walk in your sleep, you talk, too. I am sure it must have been a very painful experience for you. And I am sure it would be better to talk about it—when you are awake. Come along, tell me everything."

"Mamma, you cannot imagine and I cannot possibly describe the utter humiliation. Taking money from Deb was bad enough, but I did it. I was so sure that once Everard was started on his own, I could repay. And in the meantime—it takes so long—I thought I should *do* something. So I tried, and I failed. Even Mr Burton said he'd never seen embroidery like mine. But there is no longer a demand for it. . . . And since we are having such a frank talk, I may as well tell you. . . . I very much doubt whether Everard's fine friends have stood by him as they should. He does not discuss business with me, but I should have known. If any one of them had entrusted him with a real piece of legal work he'd have come home so uplifted. He never has. They're all false, but he can't see it. I knew from the start. Hateful people. And there is poor Everard, so deluded. He considers it a privilege to belong to Brinkley's Club; at ten guineas a year! Sometimes I *despair*."

"That is the one thing you must never do, Diana. I can't remember who said it, or if I read it, but it is true. Despair is the ultimate sin. And I don't mean that in a religious way; I mean that once you despair you're done for. And your situation is not so hopeless, my dear." She had been in worse herself, but harking back was a futile exercise. "We must take a good cool look and consider what we can do. Anything but despair, my dear."

Yes; take a drink, take to chicanery, tell lies, cheat—all active, living things, whereas despair was dead. The thought of death linked with what George had said about poisoning. Self-inflicted? In a moment of despair? Ignore that for the moment; concentrate upon the general situation. Take marriage first. Diana had certainly made a love-match, but Mrs Thorley knew from her own experience that that was no guarantee of a happy marriage. Avoiding the use of the word love, she said,

"You and Everard get along well together, do you not?"

With some fervour in her voice, and deliberately ignoring that part of marriage which she did not find enjoyable, Diana said,

"Oh yes! We never quarrel. Of course I see less of him now and he is often preoccupied. But as you know it was his idea that I should take my holiday early—and indeed it was he who suggested prolonging it. As I was only too glad to do."

So far, so good.

"And you have two adorable children."

Perhaps a slight exaggeration; Belle was extremely pretty and could be engaging when she chose, but she had a wilful, spiteful streak and Mel was querulous, inclined to start every sentence with "I want," or "I don't want," and roaring loudly if his will were crossed.

"Yes. But to be honest, London is not a good place for children. I wish with all my heart that we had stayed in Baildon. That move was a mistake, I knew it at the time; and every subsequent one has been worse."

That was an extreme statement, coming from Diana, never a girl to face unpleasant truths; the girl who had prepared herself for marriage by making dainty tablecloths. But then Deborah, so far more sensible, who had set about learning to cook, had fared worse. And look at Caroline!

Still it seemed to Mrs Thorley's practical mind that there was nothing much about Diana's dilemma that a steady two pounds a week couldn't alleviate. About that she must talk to George, for although she had been left in complete control until George attained the age of eighteen—still a year to go, she had never regarded herself as more than a trustee.

"We'll see what can be done," she said. Then she remembered that one thing had not been mentioned. "Diana.

when you feel out of sorts and depressed, do you buy any patent medicines?"

Could that horrible, but effective brew be called by that name? And how did Mamma know? When I wander in my mind how *much* do I say?

"What makes you ask that?"

"In one of your somnambulist states you used the word poison."

"No more than that?" All Diana's defences were up; for if Mamma *knew* about that there would be certain disapproval. Mamma might in many ways be unconventional but she was a monument of moral rectitude.

"Just the one word," said Mrs Thorley, who in fact had not heard it.

"Then perhaps I was talking about some fish. Bessie goes some distance to shop because ours is an expensive area. In the hot weather... Nobody else was affected, I was poisoned. Hideously indisposed for two days...."

"Why, of course we can manage it," George said. "What's two pounds a week?"

About what most working men earned in a fortnight; exactly the amount that Diana had earned, sewing herself blind during a period of employment which, fortunately for her, had been brief. Almost three times as much as Mrs Thorley had managed to scratch together in Leicester, piano lessons at sixpence a time, designs for dresses, designs for china, letting the spare room

"I can make that much any afternoon at the races, or in an evening with cards," George said.

"It would be most unwise to look upon such entertainments as a source of income, George," Mrs Thorley said, not too sternly, for George's generosity and good will were disarming. And in fact George was anxious to help Diana, poor girl, and to please Mamma because he wanted Mamma's approval for what he meant to undertake in the coming autumn—amateur steeplechasing. It was not in her power to stop him taking up this pursuit, but if she protested and grumbled life at Gad's would not be very happy, and misery anywhere, but particularly at home, was one thing that George wished to avoid. Mrs Thorley recognised in her son many of the qualities of his father, the open-handedness, the generosity of spirit which had made him accept Diana and Lavinia as his own—an action which she had reciprocated by accepting Deborah and Caroline as her own. Then there was George, their own. She'd often said in the early days that if she had only one apple she would divide it fairly amongst the girls. Quartering a thing was dead-easy; once George was born such strict material impartiality had failed her. If she had but one apple, half would be George's, the other half fairly quartered.

"It may not be for long, George. Just until Everard finds his feet."

Everard was about to find his feet in a most unexpected way.

It was August, Brinkley's and indeed all the fashionable part of London was deserted. But Everard had worked out the economics of belonging to a club; a glass of sherry—really good sherry—was threepence a glass cheaper there than in any ordinary public drinking place and twopence a glass cheaper than a much inferior beverage at home. That was one slight bonus which the ten-guinea subscription conferred.

Di was back home, seemingly fully restored in health and saying rather smugly that Mamma had promised her two pounds a week to help out for a time. Alison was lost to him—that was nothing new; every one of their encounters had left him with the feeling of never more, a feeling which had served to keep a sharp edge on appetite, since every parting seemed to be the last, every reunion seemed to be the first. But now she had gone forever, married to a self-exiled Hungarian, Prince Rakoczy, who had chosen to live in the South of France, where he had built himself a kind of fairy-tale palace overlooking the Mediterranean midway between Nice and Monaco. She'd had her fling, Everard Spicer only one of her many lovers, and the idea of being a Princess appealed to her. Also, as she explained to Everard, even the will which he had so fortunately *discovered* amongst Mr MacFarlane's muddled papers did not make *her* very rich. That grim, uncomfortable castle at Lumsleydale, with its eight hundred unprofitable acres, all entailed, must be kept up, out of the rents derived from the other Lumsley property. Lumsley House in Piccadilly was also very expensive to maintain. "But, darling, I shall miss you, quite terribly."

"I shall miss you, too," Everard said, with great truth.

But it was not of Alison nor of Diana that he was thinking as he sat, drinking his subsidised sherry on that August evening. He was thinking, very glumly, about his failure in life. Frustrated in Baildon, frustrated with Binder, Upton and Smith, and now frustrated when out on his own. *Why?* He knew that he was a very good lawyer, but Goddamn it, how could you be a good lawyer with no practice? It was like asking a chef to show his skill with nothing to cook.

The stranger approached with the curiously light and quiet step that went, incongruously, with bulk and weight. Making straight for him. That was the worst of the Club in the off season; only the dregs remained, lonely men who just wanted somebody to talk to.

Like me? No! I don't want anybody to talk to, or anybody to talk to me.

"Mr Spicer?"

"Yes," Everard said in the manner which so many people found discouraging. There was less than half an inch of sherry left in his glass. One gulp and then he could say he must be going.

"Lord Westward said I might find you here."

Instantly Everard was all attention and he said, "Yes" again, but with a different intonation.

"My name's Crawford. Not that that'll mean anything to you."

"That rather depends." Everard produced his most charming smile and manner. "Mr Ralph Crawford? Then of course I have heard of you. How do you do. May I offer you a drink?" Everard wondered about saying *sir*; a term of courtesy used by any man to any other man obviously his superior in rank, or his senior in age. Oddly enough, between equals it was used as a challenge: Sir, you are a liar! Mr Crawford was perhaps a trifle young to relish being called sir by Everard.

"Thank you. Not sherry," Mr Crawford said. "Livery stuff. I'll have whisky."

Mr Crawford was not exactly a gentleman; he was a very astute businessman. Everard recognised his name because he had figured largely in some of the many inquiries which had taken place following the Mutiny in India. The East India Company, which had begun just over two hundred and fifty years earlier as a mere combination of merchants for purposes of trade, had grown into a powerful oligarchy which ruled all but the few remaining native states of India, raising its own army, waging its own wars, and employing a vast number of administrators. It had, in its time, been self-critical, Robert Clive and Warren Hastings, both servants of the Company, had been obliged to defend themselves against charges of misrule and extortion. Now the whole future of India, how and by whom it should be ruled, was under discussion. Ralph Crawford, who had gone out as a servant of the Company when he was sixteen, had spent twenty-four years in India, built up his own business and prospered by *strictly legitimate means*, which could not always be said of similarly successful men, had attained some fame as a kind of specialist on the subject. He was knowledgeable, honest, seemed to be open-minded, and was capable of making a pithy retort to criticism. Amongst other things he owned jute mills near Calcutta, and when a member of the House of Lords, noted for his humanitarian leanings, made a remark, well-intentioned, but ill-informed about wages and conditions in such places, Mr Crawford had said, "My Lord, I'll make you a fair offer. Let you and me go and work, as ordinary workmen in a Manchester cotton mill, and then go alongside and work the same way in any one of my jute mills and then you decide which you like best." The challenge, though not accepted, gained him the nickname of Honest Offer Crawford.

And it was an honest offer which on this glowering August evening he made to Everard. There was, he said, "a lot of reshuffling to be done in India, and that means a lot of legal business. There'll be a need for well-qualified, honest men. And they're scarce." He gave Everard one of his straight honest-offer looks and said, "Let's admit it—apart from the Army, the best in the world, they proved that in the Crimea, India has been ill-served on the professional side. All too often, and I speak from experience, we've had lawyers and doctors who'd failed in some way, or done something they'd be unfrocked for if they'd stayed in England. But there you are, in areas as big as England and Wales put together, a bad doctor is better than no doctor, a bad lawyer better than none. That's got to be altered."

He talked and Everard listened. Cautious, as was his way.

"Yes," Honest Offer Crawford said, "you have a wife and two children. You must talk it over. Bear in mind that India is safe now. The Mutiny was just a boil that was bound to burst. It burst and it's over and done with. Maybe the climate isn't healthy for the young. Personally, I think a bit too much has been made of that. People who can't afford to send their children home as they call it, keep them there and a surprising number survive. In any case, if you decide to accept, you could well afford to send your wife into the hills during the hot weather, and your children home to be educated. Give it a week," Mr Crawford said. In his opinion that was a fair offer; caution, up to a point, was a virtue, but any man who needed more than a week in order to decide a vital issue wasn't worth bothering about.

Diana recoiled from the idea of going to India, just as she had recoiled from coming to London, and from the idea of Everard setting up on his own. One couldn't possibly say it, but the fact was that every move that so far Everard had made had been in the wrong direction.

"It needs thinking over," she said. Everard agreed, but she knew, just by the look of him, that the offer had restored his self-esteem and that he would take it. She also knew that if she could produce any good argument against going herself, with Belle and Melville, she would use it.

Only two doors away was Mrs Pembroke, who had spent many years in India and had painted the bungalow in Simla, where she had spent the hot weather. Mrs Pembroke was dead against it.

"There were certain advantages," she admitted, "but they were dearly bought. I do not wish to discourage you, but the filth . . . I soon learned not to go near my kitchen. This you may find hard to believe, but it is the truth. Before I had learned better, I did visit my kitchen—they're set slightly apart—and there was my cook boy straining soup through one of Algie's old socks! That and a few other things with which I will not disgust you taught me to avoid the kitchen. In order to eat enough to keep oneself alive it was necessary to turn a blind eye. That I eventually managed. One can shut one's mind, to a certain extent . . ."

"My chief concern is the children," Diana said, using her old trick of ignoring the unpleasant.

"I had three," Mrs Pembroke said. "They all died."

She could have been speaking about plants which had failed to take root and flourish. It was an old grief, healed over, but under the scar enough feeling was left to make her advise very strongly that even if Mrs Spicer felt impelled to accompany her husband, she should not take the children with her. "It is a matter of hygiene," she said. She had often wondered how it was that people thought and spoke nostalgically of the scent of the East, meaning spices and jasmin; the scent she remembered most clearly was that of human ordure. But naturally she would not say that to young Mrs Spicer.

Mr Crawford had said that it was a thing to talk over, yet after the first opening of the subject, four days passed without further mention. Diana said it was something that must be thought over, and both she and Everard were thinking. Everard had in fact gone rather farther and talked to Mr Hammond of Hammond and Curtis and learned with delight and relief that the publisher was not only willing but eager to take over his lease. Hammond and Curtis needed more office space, for just as there was the law of diminishing returns, so there was what could only be called the snowballing effect. Several writers with well-known names had noted what Hammond and Curtis had done for D. Willoughby, an absolute newcomer; what might not so progressive a firm do for them?

There was a curious superstition about pork: it was supposed to be more liable than any other meat to go off in hot weather, so there was a rough-and-ready rule about not buying it when there was not an R in the month. What was regarded as uneatable during the last week of August was perfectly all right during the first week of September, and Bessie was glad, for pork was the cheapest of meats.

The dish was presented attractively; a mound of well-mashed potatoes, with the three chops—one for the mistress, two for the master, propped against it and the whole edifice surrounded by apple sauce. Everard helped Diana, then himself. He'd taken and enjoyed several mouthfuls before he realised that she had not lifted knife or fork and was just sitting there, stiff and staring.

"Di."

"I didn't know," she said. "Everything has been so different. So wrong! What seest thou in the dark backward and abysm of time? I always thought that such a silly question. Now I know. You do not, of course, and everybody will say—Another broken marriage! What a doomed family. Quite untrue. And if you are so very deaf you should get an ear trumpet! I was brought up not to shout. But I can. Listen then. Mine is not a broken marriage. We just did not have enough money. That is the nub of the matter. In ordinary circumstances I should have welcomed another baby, but that was impossible. And it is quite possible—as I have proved—to love somebody without all this bed and baby business. And scrubbing steps! What I am trying to say is that I cannot think. Think! Think! As though I hadn't enough to think about with my eyesight failing and my memory going? Yes, I suppose I shall end, blind and idiotic, in some place that Deb said Lavinia should go to. All a very great pity."

There was nothing that Everard could do except coax her upstairs and into bed. Out of the jumble one thing had been made absolutely plain to him: she was not a woman who could be safely taken to India—and he was now absolutely determined to go there; to cast off all the failures and begin again.

"Not here," George said. "I mean not in this house, as a permanency. The children would drive us all mad; and Di is so fussy, always plumping up cushions and emptying ash-trays. Besides, did you know—I only heard the other day—the Chinese write in pictures and their picture-word for unhappiness is two women under the same roof? It wouldn't work, Mamma. And, if as she says she is sure of six pounds a week, she is no longer in *need*. Baildon would be ideal for her. That little . . ." Mind your language! ". . . Belle is just about ready for Miss Hardwicke's, and Mel . . . well, if Everard fails again, Mel can go to the Grammar School—or share lessons with Caro's Noel, or something. Yes, Baildon would be best. Of course she's welcome to come here, but not to stay forever. It wouldn't suit anybody."

"I think you are right. I must go house-hunting again."

"Why you? Di can do her own house-hunting, I should think."

"Of course. I shall just make a few preliminary inquiries. I suppose it is too much to hope that there would again be a house vacant in Friars' Lane. It would be so nice for the girls to be next door to each other again. Poor Di seemed so out of touch with everybody else when last she stayed here."

"It'll be different now that she has a steady income." George's view of money was very variable; he always exaggerated his gains and minimised his losses; if a bet or a game won him six pounds he felt rich and justified in spending ten; the loss of the same amount was a mere flea-bite.

203

Still . . . "Everard must have got himself a substantial job at last, to be able to spare her so much."

"I believe all posts in India are highly paid because of the unhealthy climate. Everard should insure his life."

George took the chance to twist the conversation.

"I'll insure mine, Mamma, before I start riding point-to-points. I'll do it for some fantastic sum, so that if I break my neck you'll never have to lift a finger again."

Her head jerked several times in rapid succession. "Don't joke about such things, George, please."

"Don't count on, though. My neck's good for another sixty years. Old van Haagen made me a cast-iron promise."

For some time after her return to Baildon—and by some stupendous coincidence to Friars' Lane, in the house immediately opposite the one she had formerly occupied—Diana suffered recurrent pangs of guilt because she felt so extremely happy. Without Everard! Anybody would think she hadn't loved him! Sometimes she would deliberately induce a feeling of the kind of melancholy which she *ought* to be feeling, by standing at the window of her present house and looking across at the one in which she had begun her married life; sometimes the feeling would take her unawares, generally at the sight of something associated with Everard; the shabby old chair which he bought cheaply when they moved to Somerton Road and he had room for a study; the few clothes which he had left behind and of which she could not bring herself to dispose. At such moments she felt genuinely bereft. The rest of the time she felt happy and free and secure and would salve the guilt by saying how much she missed him, how she felt always widowed, how worried she was about him.

In fact it was far easier now to be in love with Everard, almost in the old way, when they were just engaged, than it had been to love him when he was present, needing to be fed, inclined to be glum, and sharing her bed.

The house she now occupied, though at the front the mirror-image of its neighbours, had been enlarged by an extension on the garden side, a ground-floor room that could have been designed for children, and a bathroom above it. And for all the sentiment that Diana might feel about Everard's old chair it had no place in her dainty drawing room, it was relegated to the children's room.

Bessie, who naturally had come with her adored mistress, made no secret of her happiness. Far less work in this more manageable house, the High Street barely round the corner and the wonderful market, better even than Soho, twice a week. The prices never ceased to astonish Bessie; nor did the placid, law-abiding atmosphere. No need here to walk warily, or carry your money in a purse on a string around your neck. And here, in this happy place, a lot of things were free; Madam and her sister, Mrs Taylor, often drove out to their old home and came back laden with vegetables, with eggs and cream. And Madam's brother, quite the most beautiful young man Bessie had ever seen, looked in from time to time, always with gifts; two pheasants, their heads tied together; partridges; a hare. Bessie, though inexperienced in such matters, never faltered. If indeed somebody had come to Friars' Lane with a dead lion and said it was edible meat, Bessie would have dealt with it.

With Diana so happily settled, and Caroline settled, if not quite so happily, and George, so far from breaking his neck riding triumphantly and winning several prizes, Mrs Thorley, rather like a clucking old hen rounding up her chicks, often thought of Deborah, not her daughter. But, after George, the son who must take precedence in her affection, the best beloved.

She wrote: "Deb dear, if ever you have the slightest need of money, do let me know. I was prepared to help Diana, but she is well-placed now and needs no assistance. . . ."

Deb wrote back a very grateful letter, but denied that she needed help. "In fact, dearest Mamma, I seem to have hit upon a curious way of making money. If ever you or

George or anybody should need some, just let me know."

It was probably, Mrs Thorley thought, something to do with horses.

There were times, well-known to Mr Hammond, when a new book by the same author knocked the former one into oblivion. It was not so with D. Willoughby. Everybody who read A HOUSE DIVIDED—and that meant everybody who could read, wanted to read, or reread SECRET. Both books were selling in America—not in pirated editions; and there were translations. A good story, as Mr Hammond had always known, was a good story the world over. And of all the authors he had ever dealt with D. Willoughby was the least troublesome. She never came to London, demanding to be entertained or feted; she never interfered; once the manuscript was in his hands, it was his. In return he respected her privacy and hoped with great fervour that the two books might not prove to be just a flash in the pan. Oh no. Almost as soon as A HOUSE DIVIDED was under way, D. Willoughby wrote that she was busy with A WOMAN ALONE. To a large extent this was Mrs Thorley's story, suitably disguised; the woman in the story had not been left alone to deal with a cattle herd in Suffolk, but with a sheep range in the Cotswolds, and with a family far more bothersome than that at Gad's had ever been.

Because she could lose herself so thoroughly in the book she was writing or reading Deborah was seldom aware of being lonely. She shied away from what social contact was offered by the few people who from a sense of duty or from curiosity did call upon her. The standards of social behaviour in the little town were not high and nobody was particularly eager to cultivate the acquaintance of a woman so poor that she had not even the pretence of a parlour and who wore a print dress like a servant's, attended neither church nor chapel, was in fact rather queer.

Presently there was one person in Abbey Norton who could have told people—except for a code of behaviour every whit as strict as a priest's, that Mrs Willoughby was not at all poor, and that was the manager of the bank. He had a sincere regard for money in a curiously abstract way, he liked it to be used to advantage, deployed, used to make more money, and when Mrs Willoughby's account stood at just under two thousand pounds, dead money, idle money, to an extent wasted money, he became quite perturbed. Face to face—at his own request, with this queer client who had once had so little and then suddenly had so much, he adopted a benevolent, fatherly attitude, directed, not at the young woman herself, but at that accumulating money.

"Forgive me for speaking personally, Mrs Willoughby, but I understand that you are a widow? Then you have no husband to advise you."

"I understand about money. At least—what did Mr Micawber say? 'Annual income twenty pounds, expenditure nineteen six, result happiness. Annual income twenty pounds, expenditure twenty pounds and sixpence, result misery.'"

"Mr Micawber is your financial adviser?"

His queer customer disconcerted him by bursting into hearty laughter.

"No, a man in a book, who did not take his own advice. I did, it was so sound."

But already her mind was fitting this delicious conversation into A WOMAN ALONE. What a lovely bit of light relief. She was so preoccupied that she gave the earnest man the minimum of attention as he talked about the virtue of investment, the magic of five per cent. At the end of it she said, "Well, thank you. It was kind of you to bother. But I think I'll leave it. It's safe where it is. And I may have more." She gave him her sudden, entrancing smile and hurried home to incorporate this nugget of real life into her story.

What she missed most of all were horses. Never mind. In her imagination she owned them, rode them, went hunting, enjoyed that intoxicating moment when the horse, trained over false fences, rising inch by inch, gathered itself

207

together and took a real fence, a real ditch. In each of her books she managed to introduce a number of horses and at least one hunting scene.

Sam did not lack for company; he made friends easily, and even when she was obliged to be parsimonious in other ways Deborah provided lavish teas. The empty rooms at Stone House were also an attraction, lending themselves to a number of games impracticable in a well-furnished home. Sam's choice of a favourite friend, a real bosom pal, was surprising, unless one took seriously the attraction of opposites. Sam was big for his age, inclined to be noisy, intelligent enough but far from studious; Robbie Duff was small, frail-looking, bespectacled and very studious indeed. His father had a small-holding—Deb judged it not to be very prosperous—rather more than a mile further out from Abbey Norton than Stone House was, and he had no pony. He had little spare time either, for his father shared Tim Bridges' belief that the young should make themselves useful. It was a red-letter day in Sam's life when Duff could be spared to spend a Saturday afternoon with him and partake of one of Deborah's substantial teas. And yet those visits were very quiet and dull, with no wild romps in the empty part of the house. After tea, out came the homework, followed, if time allowed, by some kind of paper game, or dominoes. It was a curious friendship, but Deborah approved of it. Duff—the use of Christian names was discouraged at the Grammar School—had. Deborah thought, good influence on Sam, bringing out his better side, a kind of paternalism that had no smack of patronage about it.

Like most Thorleys, Sam grew fast and as he outgrew his clothes he invariably suggested handing them on to Duff. "They're very poor, you know."

Duff fell into the habit of calling for Sam on the way into school, and Deborah fell into the habit of giving Duff a supplementary breakfast.

"Plenty of time," Sam said, "if we ride and tie." That meant that Duff rode the pony most of the time and Sam ran alongside.

When Deborah began to earn money and was almost

certain of earning more, she wanted Sam to have some better mount than the one only just saved from the knacker's yard and she suggested buying Sam a new, bigger, more lively pony and giving the old one to Duff. Then all Sam's mixed heritage came together for once and he said,

"I don't think it would do. Mr Duff wouldn't feed him properly, unless he could drag a plough. No, let poor old Merry live his last days in peace in the paddock."

It could have been Tim speaking; or herself.

Is this real, or am I dreaming again? Diana asked herself when Mrs Gordon, invited to a dainty tea, broke down and wept. Diana had always suspected Mrs Gordon as the power behind the scenes which had prevented Everard being taken into partnership with Gordon and Son and thus being the cause of the London exile and all the misery. Mrs Gordon had always been jealous on her son's behalf, thinking the world of James, and she had looked forward to telling Mrs Gordon that at last Everard had attained his proper level. But before she could bring the conversation round in a proper polite fashion, Mrs Gordon, that iron woman, was crying.

"When I think of all the opportunities . . . and then to decide on that *dreadful* girl. I suppose you knew. Everybody knew except me."

Diana remembered an evening, years and years before, when, in the house just across the way, she had tried to please Mr and Mrs Gordon by inviting them and James and Phoebe Mayhew, a most suitable match, and Caro had said that nothing would result because James was infatuated with a girl in a tobacconist's shop. The evening had, in fact, been a disaster. And it was so long ago that Diana could truthfully say,

"At least James has not made a *hasty* decision."

"He was waiting for me to die," Mrs Gordon said. "James knew I should *never* agree. Never accept her, and he knew that my husband has always been guided by me. Now, because I didn't die, even pneumonia couldn't kill me. But

209

I think this will! All that dreadful red hair—dyed, of course. And seeing one's son make such a fool of himself, picking up other men's leavings! Forgive me, such a coarse thing to say, but it is true!"

Mrs Gordon had chosen the wrong confidante. By breaking down and behaving in such an extraordinary way she had robbed Diana of her triumph, which would have been to tell Mrs Gordon how extremely well Everard was doing in India, where, in his own words, a really qualified lawyer was as important, and perhaps slightly more powerful, than a judge was in England. Diana felt no pity; in fact during the whole of life the only person for whom she had felt pity was herself. Naturally she behaved correctly, fetched a clean dry handkerchief when Mrs Gordon's had reached saturation point, emptied the neglected cup of tea into the slop basin and poured a fresh one and made all the correct little remarks—Don't fret too much; Things may turn out better than you think. . . .

As Noel grew out of little babyhood to toddler, it sometimes seemed extraordinary to Caroline that his likeness to Freddy should pass unnoticed. It showed particularly when he was pleased or displeased. When he smiled—and he was a ready smiler—his upper lip lifted so that there was a crease, like a half-moon under his nose; when he was displeased and had what Nurse Rose called a fit of the sulks, his lower lip protruded. Nurse Rose warned him about making ugly faces. "One day when you have an ugly face on you, the wind will change and you'll have that ugly face forever."

Caroline discounted the fact that Freddy had made a far less deep impression upon other people than he had upon her. To most people he was now only a name. And the terrible thing—or perhaps the happy thing—was that even in her memory he was fading, might have faded altogether except for Noel.

Nobody brought up by Mrs Thorley was likely to become a religious maniac. But there was in Caroline the kind of impulsiveness which in other circumstances might have

210

made her when Freddy married Poor Susan fling herself into a convent, and regret the action immediately.

Every decent person attended Morning Service on Sunday morning, and the Taylors were no exception. In the rather clinical, middle-of-the-road church of St Mary's, Caroline's petition was fervent enough to stand out.

"Oh God. I owe Edward a baby. Please give me a baby. I don't deserve anything, but Edward does."

Whatever the power was that ordered such things was kind, and when Noel was two and a half, Caroline was pregnant again.

"I do hope it will be a girl," Caro said to Diana. "Edward would absolutely dote on a girl."

"He dotes on Noel," Diana said.

"I know. But this would be different."

What there had once been of jealousy between them, Caroline envying Diana because she had married for love, Diana envying Caroline because she was comparatively rich, had died down. A small spark shot up at that moment, as Diana remembered how Everard had never doted on Belle or on Melville; never greeted either pregnancy of hers with any positive joy. Considerate, of course. . . . But he would certainly not have welcomed a third child; that little lost one, thing, thing. So one must think. Even now.

George reached his eighteenth birthday and now was, since the will of a dead man could override the ordinary law, master of Gad's and Park, and the herd and all the business that went with it. Mrs Thorley had attained her aim, that when she handed over to George everything should be more prosperous and more promising than it had been when she took charge. There it all lay, in the neat handwriting which had so much impressed George's father: pedigrees, accounts, bank statements, and milk yields and stud fees and a list of business contacts; the summing up in labelled files and notebooks of twelve years' hard labour.

On the eve of his birthday she said, "Well, my dear, here it all is. From tomorrow all responsibility will be yours."

Blank dismay showed on George's face. The notebooks, the files—worse than being back having lessons from old Spicer.

"Mamma, what *do* you mean?"

"It was your father's express wish that I should have full charge until you were eighteen and then hand over to you."

"I can't do it. I just can't do it, Mamma."

She knew that as well as he did, had thought about it a great deal and planned this move in order to shock him into a realisation of his responsibility.

"Then who will?"

"Well, I thought . . . I mean I hoped . . . You. I mean you do it so well. . . . So much experience. Everybody says you're the most knowledgeable. . . ."

"When your father died," Mrs Thorley said, "I barely knew a cow from a bull. I was obliged to learn, by trial and error. And I had no one to whom to turn—if one excepts Joe Snell. *I* shall always be available should *you* need help or advice."

God! She sounded serious.

"I know," he said miserably, "that perhaps I haven't been as much help in some ways as I should have been. . . . But you said yourself that we're only young once."

"That is true. But nobody can stay young forever."

"Eighteen isn't all that old."

"It is the age at which your father, presumably, considered that you would be old enough to be responsible."

He'd never before known her to sound so cold and remote. On very rare occasions—such as that affair over that wretched girl—she'd been angry, but never distant. George's comfortable little world rocked on its foundations.

He had a certain talent for diplomacy.

"You wouldn't know what to do with yourself, Mamma. This whole thing has been your life for so long. And you're far too young to think of retiring."

Nobody, in fact, knew exactly how old Mamma was. Her hair was quite white—but it had been so for a long time; her general appearance was frail and she sometimes—not always—had a tremour, but she was extremely active, both physically and mentally, and by the rough-and-ready reckoning that a woman's childbearing years were over at forty she couldn't be more than fifty-eight—allow for gestation—nearly fifty-nine.

"I think I could contrive to amuse myself, my dear." She was determined to make him *see*. "I should like to visit Deb, for one thing."

Thwarted, George fell back on the rocky obstinacy which he had inherited from both his parents.

"Then I shall have to hire a bookkeeper," and to give emphasis to the statement pushed all the notebooks and files into a clutter at the end of the table.

Mrs Thorley said, "An *honest* fellow would cost you twenty-five shillings a week. And even then you would have to exercise supervision. And since we are now talking frankly, I may as well say that you could not afford it—if I cared to exercise *my* legal rights. Your father, when he made his will, enormously overestimated his resources. At the end of my stewardship, I was to retire with five hundred pounds a year."

She had not the slightest intention of claiming it, but it was her intention to bring home to George—before she died—that his present way of life was untenable. Hunting twice a week during the season, riding in point-to-point races, some of them at a fair distance away, playing golf, playing cricket. Nothing reprehensible, but nothing conducive to good business. He simply had to be brought to his senses, and she was doing it—as she had always done everything—in the way that seemed to her best.

When, just before the nightly whisky served her—and for a long time now she had attempted to ration herself, just enough to stay steady, just enough to provoke sleep—she blamed, in her mind, that chance encounter with Johnny Faulkner for George's failure to attend to business as he should. Johnny Faulkner and many of his friends, God knew, were poor enough, but very few of them had ever done a day's honest work. They shuffled, much as Mrs Thorley's first husband had shuffled, on the wavering border line between affluence and indigence. There were overdrafts, mortgages, expectations. Mrs Thorley knew it all. She also knew that George had no part in that kind of life; George's inheritance, built up by her, a new bee working inside an old almost ruined hive, cell by cell, had solid worth, but definite limitations. Which George *must* realise.

However, her perhaps belated attempt to make him realise was not outstandingly successful. George had other weapons in his armoury.

"This has spoiled my birthday. And I was so looking forward to it."

It was to be one of those purely male gatherings, not dissimilar from those from which Mrs Thorley had successfully weaned George's father during the first year of their marriage, except that dinner was a properly served meal and the card-playing and the horse-play came later, and the noise—plenty of it—had a different quality, since none of George's friends had rustic voices, or became unduly aggressive even when slightly drunk. Most of them were young men whom George had met through Johnny, but there were others, any kind of sport was a great lower of barriers between classes—after all, good old George himself was not County by a long chalk, but he was a damned good sport! A similar tolerance was extended to James Gordon and Richard Walford and Simon Catchpole and a few others who, in addition to being non-County, were getting rather old, being in their late twenties, but James Gordon was still the best golfer in three counties, Richard Walford beside being a brewer had a wonderful wine cellar, and Simon Catchpole, having taking to training racehorses, was a useful man to know. In fact it was only when it came to the question—Would you like him to marry your sister? that the question of family and background obtruded much.

Mrs Thorley, when George gave his own parties, merely received them in the drawing room and made cordial conversation while the sherry was drunk. They were all extremely polite to her; she had acquired quite a formidable reputation, and newcomers to Gad's were invariably surprised by her appearance and her manner. So dignified, so feminine, so utterly different from what one would expect

214

of a she-cattle-breeder and a hard bargainer.

When on the eve of his birthday, George said plaintively that Mamma had spoiled his birthday, she relented inwardly but said briskly.

"Nonsense! I was merely trying to draw your attention to the fact that you must now assume some responsibility. After all I am not going to live forever. Nobody does!"

George looked even more appalled than he had done when faced with the notebooks and the files.

"Mamma, what should I do?"

He was her son, her well-beloved, her justification for making a marriage of convenience, and it hurt her to strike him another blow.

"It is to be hoped," she said, "that you will marry. Not yet of course. And that is another thing I must speak to you about—and then we will have done with this dismal conversation. You must set your sights on a target within reach. You understand me? If you give your attention to business, there will be no need to marry for money, but, my dearest, there are certain rules in this harsh world, and we must learn to live with them."

When, as a child, he had fallen and bumped his head or grazed his knee she'd said: There, a kiss will make it better. Now she had dealt him two blows which no motherly kiss could ease.

"I know that," George said. He gave her a rather wry, half-conspiratorial smile. "No need to worry about *that!* As for these," he indicated the books and files, "I promise you, I will pay all that side more attention. But you must help. Eh?"

"Of course."

"Then we're friends again. Good."

She knew again that little sense of failure. And for a second a flash of resentment against George's father for having made his will as he had. No doubt, she thought, he believed that a half-baked boy could run the business as well as *he* had done; sliding downhill fast when I took it in hand, the herd an expensive hobby and no proper accounts kept. Gross overoptimism was his trouble; five hundred pounds' dowry for each of the girls, five hundred pounds a year allowance for me when George came of age. *Where* did he think it was all coming from?

God send that George would develop more sense. God send she could keep going until he did.

And now, despite the fact that she had braced herself for this little confrontation with a good dose of the eau-de-Cologne-tinctured whisky, she was all of a shake once more and needed another.

"I'll drink to your birthday now, George. Give me a very unladylike whisky."

The adjective was one of their private little jokes. Once George had told her—having surprised her, glass in hand—that whisky was no drink for ladies and she had retorted that old age must have its privileges.

Pouring for them both, George thought what an excellent thing it was—and how rare—to have a mother with whom one could drink companionably; a mother who could deal with all the dull part of earning a living, a mother whom one could so easily coerce. As he had coerced Mamma into agreeing to the form his birthday party should take; she had made a tentative suggestion that it should be a small, family affair, with Diana and Caro and Everard and an old friend or two. Easily argued down; too old . . . after all, it was *his* party, wasn't it?

So tomorrow evening she would stand, looking singularly like a Dresden figurine with her piled-up white hair and delicate features, and she would be gracious to his guests and then disappear.

"You know, you are my ideal woman, Mamma." There was some truth in it, but not the whole. He had another ideal, made in the image of Chloe Faulkner, for whom he had once—when young and silly—gathered a bunch of pink roses and who probably could not add two to two and make four. This clash of idealism, combined with the limitation of choice which George had understood after one rebuff, was to keep him single for thirty years.

Letters from and to India were usually carried by the shorter, overland route, as it was called, though it involved a journey across the Indian Ocean, up the Gulf of Suez to Suez itself; then overland, by swift camels, to Port Said; ship again to Marseilles, by train across France, by packet boat across the Channel and so to England. It was a long process, but if correspondents were determined to keep in touch with each other—as Diana was, as Everard was, and wrote and despatched a letter faithfully once a week, contact was regular and the exchange, though stale, was welcome. Not a broken marriage, Diana told herself, sealing up her letters, all faithful accounts of the children's progress, the weather in England, little bits of news like James Gordon marrying such an unsuitable person; Caroline having another baby—a girl, which was just right. Parish pump news. In return Everard sent her rather carefully edited accounts of his experiences, his progress and above all, his health.

Caro once said, cruelly, "Di, by this time he's either cured or dead." And Edward said, "Warburg's Drops! Do tell him, Diana, that unadulterated quinine would be better. And however hot the weather he must wear flannel next to his skin."

Diana was always careful to mention each of Everard's letters and to make great display of everything he sent in the way of presents: a necklace of moonstones for Belle, some carved animals—really far too good to be used as toys for Melville, a silk shawl for herself, and for the house an exquisite Indian rug which warranted a special tea-party. To talk about money outside the family would have been extremely vulgar, but to Mamma to Caro she could confide that Everard's salary had been increased and the allowance he made her with it. To outsiders she merely said that Everard had gained promotion.

She was not fully aware of the fact that she was following a deliberate policy of giving evidence that hers was not a broken marriage, but as happy, comfortable day, followed happy comfortable day, Everard as a person receded in her mind, became my husband who is in India. "Our Father which art in Heaven," as Caro remarked irreverently to Edward, adding that there had always been a good deal of the spinster in Di and that it showed now in her house. Too finicketty, too many little lace mats and antimacassars and knickknacks. And Edward admitted that Di's house contained only one comfortable chair, and that was in the children's play room, and that to smoke a pipe, or even a cigarette in such surroundings would be unthinkable.

Naturally Everard had holidays, long week-ends, sick leave, but home leave was due only every five years; necessarily a long leave because so much of it must be spent in travelling. The possibility of cutting a canal through the Suez isthmus was being discussed, but not yet as more than a project. Since letters were so slow, mention of this long leave which would bring Everard home was made early and immediately Diana fell to worrying. Five years was five years. They'd meet as strangers, and what would he find? Her looking glass gave her one answer. The happy, comfortable years, with ease of mind after so much anxiety, had made her fat, at least—as usual her mind sidled around any disagreeable fact—plump, and that made her look middle-aged. Worse still, just at the temples some white hairs showed amongst the glossy black. Nothing to be surprised about. Mamma's hair had turned white; not quite so soon, but surely prematurely.

Diana had not changed in appearance overnight, nor had she in any sense, since that frightful time when she'd taken Bessie's dose and been so ill, let herself go, and indeed even now her thickening figure was well corsetted, her hair given an egg shampoo and vinegar rinse once every two weeks, her skin creamed nightly and her hands well-tended. She was vain—always had been. As a girl, amongst girls, she had been considered a model of what a girl should be, in order to secure a husband. But she had never been, like Caroline, a flirt. She'd fallen in love, married, disliked some aspects of married life, but borne up, doing her best. For the last five years she had regained her position among her contemporaries, or women slightly older; a woman with a dainty, well-kept house, pleasant little tea-parties, pleasant afternoons at whist. In five years not the slightest breath of scandal had ever blown upon her.

The notion that five years in a hostile climate might have affected Everard, too, and that he might not be as she when she chose to remember him, did remember him, never once occurred to her. In her mind she had idealised the absent Everard, and she imagined that he had done the same; so she must slim down, apply a little dye to those white hairs—and get that ruined chair upholstered; and find—where was it—the solid ash-tray into which Everard knocked the ashes of his pipe. She made other preparations, Belle and Melville must recognise their father, photographs were a help. And deep, deep down, below all other thoughts was the memory of the bed thing which had so disgusted her fastidious nature, and the possibility of its resulting in something even worse. She was a very good, very devoted mother, but as she had once said to Caro, "We have retrogressed since hens."

And then it all came to nothing. Everard wrote, abjectly apologetic; he'd had another attack of malaria and his doctor had advised him not to make the journey, even by the sea route, around the Cape, which could be rough, and a constitution already debilitated by fever should not be exposed to sea-sickness. The overland route was at the moment even more dangerous, there was plague rampant in Suez; so Everard's doctor had advised a three months' convalescence in the hills and then a kind of working holiday, a combination of business and pleasure in Killapore, where there was still a chance of shooting a tiger. Everard's doctor, not a very good physician, had long ago learned the trick of telling patients what they wished to hear.

Without any conscious intention of being a humbug, Diana behaved as convention demanded: Isn't it terrible? So disappointing. I am thoroughly miserable—who wouldn't be? But in her heart she was relieved, a little ashamed of being relieved, and as over Lady Lumsley completely unsuspicious.

"I want Deb," Mrs Thorley said, and that was the first thing, coherent and clearly enunciated, that she had said since she had what Edward—hastily summoned—called a stroke. Stroke was the right word, one fell stroke.

Friday had seemed the best time for George to do, as

he said, better at all that side of the business, and for almost five years Friday night had been devoted to the record-keeping and to future plans. George was shaping up wonderfully—as she had always known he would, given time, and it was with a feeling of satisfaction that she said, "You finish off, George, I feel rather tired." Violet, whose duty it was to present early morning tea, came down and said that Ma'am was asleep still. "Let her sleep," George commanded, "but tiptoe up and peep in now and again." He tiptoed along himself and peeped in before riding off to the races at Newmarket. Mamma was still asleep, actually snoring slightly. Well, a good sleep never did anyone any harm.

George was back at nine o'clock—early for him, and although he had had a few drinks he was quite sober, and once he was over the first shock he thought that Edward's manner had been unnecessarily reproachful—as though George had deliberately absented himself, out. roistering while his mother was dying.

"There's nothing that I, or anyone else, can do," Edward said. "But I didn't like to leave her alone with servants."

It was a plain statement of fact but Edward's manner made it sound like a rebuke.

Violet had obediently tiptoed and peeped until four o'clock in the afternoon, then Jenny decided to make one more tray of tea.

"Take it up and this time go a bit noisy. *Wake* her up. It ain't natural to sleep all day like that."

Violet made noise enough. In fact when closer inspection showed her that something was badly wrong, she dropped the whole tea-tray, backed away from the wreckage and galloped downstairs.

"Jenny, oh, Jenny! She ain't alseep. Her eye's open. But she ain't awake neither. She didn't know me."

"I'll see for myself."

Jenny's legs, which for twenty years had served as an excuse for not doing anything she did not wish to do, while conveniently allowing her to do what she did wish to do, had been less accommodating of late. She no longer went down to the village on Sunday afternoons and she faced the painful task of descending, and the even more painful one of ascending, stairs only once a day. Now she hauled herself up, took one look at Mrs Thorley and knew the worst. Apopletic stroke, similar to the one that had carried off her own grandfather, and a number of other people. All men, curiously enough. In all her years, and although they could not be exactly reckoned, they covered a considerable period of time, Jenny had never known, or heard of a woman having apopletic stroke.

She did not go down again, but shouted to Violet to send Willy for the doctor and mind he got Doctor Edward, nobody else.

Then Jenny remembered that her grandfather, though paralysed down one side and speechless, could hear and with his one good hand would lash about with his stick if what he heard displeased him, went close to Mrs Thorley and said,

"You've had a slight turn, ma'am, but you're all right. I'm here and Doctor Edward is coming. Could you drink a cup of tea if I held it for you?"

Edward came and confirmed Jenny's diagnosis; and he, too, seemed to understand that people struck down in this way were not so insensible as they might appear to be. He spoke cheerfully.

"You've had a slight stroke. Just take things quietly. We'll have you all right in no time." She mouthed at him. God forgive him for using the word slight; it was a massive stroke. Everybody knew the cause now, but nobody knew a cure.

Then Edward deeply offended Jenny. Outside out of Mrs Thorley's hearing, he said, "She'll need a nurse. I'll send one."

"What for? What could a nurse do that I couldn't do as well or better?"

"I was thinking of your lameness, Jenny."

There again was a recognised ailment, a wearing away of the smooth tissue which made joints move, smoothly, like well-oiled wheels; but nobody knew how to prevent the erosion, or how to restore the worn tissue.

"I'm lame, I know," Jenny said, "but if it come to looking after Ma'am I'll do it, if I hev to go on my hands and knees. We don't want no nurse."

Now, after two days of incomprehensible mumblings, Mamma said, quite clearly, "I want Deb."

"Where, Mamma? Tell me where to find her."

"Secret, darling. Secret."

"I know. I promise, I won't say a word. Just tell me where."

She had moments of clarity, and then everything would blur. In a clear moment she wanted Deb, because Deb, in another crisis, had been her strength and stay. Diana and Caroline, both good girls, but Diana couldn't face—in fact broke down when faced with—anything distasteful; and Caroline cried and cried.

In this, her final extremity, for some reason which she knew was no reason, she wanted Deb. If only to say good-bye. Frantically she tried to tell George where Deb was living and the name she had taken, but the effort defeated its own purpose; nothing but mumbling and moaning emerged.

George, subscribing to the general pretence that this was just a passing affliction, said gently,

"Never mind, Mamma. You can tell me when you are better and I'll have her here the same day." A curious expression, fond yet mocking, almost teasing, lighted and for a second rejuvenated her sunken face; it was as though she saw through the game, knew that she would never be better. Would see no tomorrow.

No clue to Deb's whereabouts could be found amongst Mrs Thorley's personal papers. After Deb had communicated her fixed address and her new name, she had always sent unheaded letters, and Mamma, with perhaps excessive caution, had always destroyed the post-marked envelopes. Her own letters to Deb she always posted herself.

Anything left behind by the dead has a pathos of its own, and George, grown man as he was now, wept unashamedly when he opened a drawer and found what Mamma had saved for sentiment's sake, all the letters he had sent when he was abroad, a few from Diana, a few from Deb. Caro, living so near, had had no need to write. There were photographs, too, one of Sam misled him for a second, the pictured face so closely resembled his own. Mamma had not kept all the girls' letters and from those of Deb's which she had chosen to preserve no useful information could be gained. They sounded lively and happy, but were just the sort of chit-chat about domestic affairs—I have just made fourteen pounds of plum jam. Sam actually won a prize this year; it was for Scripture, and no wonder, though at his school they call it divinity—not unconnected, I feel, with the divine right of headmasters!

On the very morning of the funeral a letter arrived addressed to Mrs Thorley and George very nearly didn't open it, for Deb too was being very cautious, as though suspecting the possible existence of an enemy in the camp, and addressed her letters to Mamma in the characterless block capitals much in use by half-educated people or by those who distrusted the legibility of their own scribble. However, he did open it, mainly because, in his sorrow, he had promised himself to attend more closely to business than ever before—a kind of tribute to Mamma's memory. And there was a letter from Deb. Her real hand-writing was unmistakable. And so was the post mark. Abbey Norton.

He still had time before all the melancholy pageantry of a proper funeral began to sit down at the pretty little desk in the bow window and write to Deb.

In Abbey Norton there were two families bearing the name of Bridges. The postman, a sensible man, took the letter to the respectable family first. Mrs Bridges, the cornchandler's wife, opened it and was bewildered. Her mother had been dead for fifteen years and she had no loving brother called George. So she resealed the letter with a brush of white of egg and next day handed it back to the postman who, conscientious and indefatigable, carried it on to the house of an ignorant family, to which, so far as he could remember, he had never before delivered a letter. Abbey Norton, like every other place, had its rough quarter—to do the distasteful, but necessary work in the shambles, men had to be rough. To the slaughterman's wife a letter meant nothing, except as some paper useful for kindling a fire.

Dearest Mamma, Deb wrote; No letter from you this week. I do most sincerely hope that you are well. If not do tell George to let me know. I would come at once, despite the risk, not that there would be much for me. T certainly wouldn't want me back and Sam is safe. I must tell you about Sam. . . .

As Caroline had once realised, Deborah was interested in abstract generalisations. So her letter went on to mention heredity and to say that Sam's farming blood had triumphed and that he had chosen to spend his holiday helping his best friend on the best friend's father's rather miserable little farm. "Really no more than a small-holding, but for Sam it will be a useful experience . . . if after all he takes to farming."

"But I *did* write," George protested. "On the very morning of the funeral. And the letter did not come back."

Diana said, "Of course there is a possibility that Deb may not be using her right name." Touting for work, she had not used hers; it was Mrs Osborne, not Mrs Spicer, who had haunted Hawksley's, and made that seemingly fatal suggestion to Mrs Preston in Oxford Street. She had reverted to her maiden name and Deborah might well have done the same.

"Try Thorley," Di said.

There was no Thorley at all in Abbey Norton nor indeed any name remotely resembling it.

Another week and no letter from Gad's. Mamma must be ill. That she should be dead was inconceivable; indeed even to those who had seen the coffin lowered the fact still seemed inconceivable; Mamma had always been there, never interfering, but always ready to help, to listen and advise. There'd been no lingering illness to prepare them for the loss; Mamma was a bit shaky at times, that was all.

Dear George—Deb wrote—Is Mamma ill? I said I would come and I will. I could leave Sam easily and I'm better at that kind of thing that Di and Caro. Please let me know, if only a line. In case she hasn't told you and is still preserving my secret, here I am known as Mrs Willoughby, and I live in Stone House.

George was still in that state when seeing something funny or interesting he'd think, I must tell Mamma that and then remember! He derived a certain comfort from sitting down and writing to Deb, telling her what had happened and how he felt about it. Some innate delicacy forbade that he should tell Deb that Mamma's last words concerned her. He could, however, write with truth that Mamma had suffered no pain, had simply had a stroke on Saturday and died on Sunday without ever regaining full consciousness. He also gave details of how he had tried to reach Deb.

Deb, not a facile crier, cried when she read George's letter. There was a tinge of remorse in her grief. If she had been a bit more compliant, a little less concerned for Sam, rather less—let's face it—anxious to get away from Tim and Foxton, she would have been within reach, visiting regularly, enjoying the company of the woman she loved and admired. She'd always intended to go back—one day; acting as though time were inexhaustible, and now it was too late.

Sam came in. Ostensibly he was spending his midsummer holiday with Duff and he usually slept there, but he came back, hungry, to be fed now and again, and to pick up a clean shirt. This happened to be one of those days, and Sam, who had never seen his mother cry, asked what was the matter.

"My mother died. You remember Grandmamma, Sam?"

He didn't really. Multitudinous new experiences had overlain childish memories. But he must not lie. So he compromised.

"Not very well. She was rather old, wasn't she?"

"Not old enough to die."

Sam considered that. Quite young people died. A master at school, a kind man with a terrible cough; and a boy, younger than Sam who had fallen down, with an injured knee during a football game. He'd been taken to Shrewsbury Hospital, had his leg off, since it wouldn't heal, and died.

"All the dead," Sam said, "are safe in the arms of Jesus."

There was really nothing very extraordinary about that simple, well-meant statement. The vast majority of decent people believed in a life beyond the grave, in rewards in Heaven, punishment in Hell. They truly believed that a dead child had been called away, untimely, to join a choir of angels.

It was, Deb supposed, a simple and beautiful faith, one that poor human people clutched to themselves for comfort in moments like these. But it had ugly offshoots; look at the Inquisition! Look at extreme Puritanism.

Now, too sad to put up any argument, she said, "It would be nice to think so. I expect you are hungry."

She produced a large meat patty and Sam said,

"Would you mind if I took it along with me? There's enough for four. Mrs Duff hasn't much time to cook—or much to cook with, to be honest."

To Sam, who had fallen so entirely under Robbie Duff's influence, honesty in minor matters was very important. Sam knew that every time he answered to the name of Willoughby, or wrote it on an exercise, he was living a lie, and Duff had once told him that every lie any man told was an extra nail on Christ's Cross.

Deb said, "Oh, take it and welcome. There's a fruit cake, too."

Wrapping them, and the clean shirt, she looked at her son and recognised once again the force of heredity. Sam's extreme resemblance to George had faded away and now, deeply tanned by work out-of-doors, he was very plainly Tim's son.

Tim's son. Capable of saying safe in the arms of Jesus,

thus disposing of a dead woman, and then walking off, leaving a living one alone with her grief.

Well, there had been some warning signs which she had ignored.

Once she had said—"Come along, boys, surely you have done enough homework now. Knock off and have supper."

Duff said, "I must work hard, Mrs Willoughby. My mother has set her heart on my becoming a minister."

She'd missed that. She had regarded Duff as a good influence. She had hardly noticed the dropping away of Sam's other friends, the noisy, hearty ones who regarded homework as an imposition. Nor had she been disturbed when Sam said, "We can put Duff up for the night, can't we? There's a meeting he wants to go to. And he wants me to go with him." She'd been completely confident that any meeting patronised by Duff wouldn't be cockfighting, or dog-fighting, both sports which though coming under general disapprobation in the wider world were still rampant in places like this. Far more likely a lantern lecture, a missionary meeting, something to do with school.

She'd been very careless and she could not offer, to herself, the excuse that she had also been busy, though that would have been true enough. A book a year for Mr Hammond and some exercises known as keeping in the public eye, which, since she refused to do it in person, she must do in print; stories and articles for magazines and for the annual, beautifully produced Albums which made such excellent Christmas presents. Then there were alterations and additions. Libraries liked long books, reading matter for ten days or a fortnight; foreign publishers who had translation charges to meet suggested cuts. Magazines which published serialisations demanded rearrangements, so that each instalment ended with a crisis or a situation which left the reader avid for the next. With her inborn thoroughness and her grafted-on desire to please, Deborah had complied.

But she had neglected Sam, thinking it enough that he should be well-fed, well-clothed, healthy and happy and, under Duff's influence, getting on well at school. It was not enough. Man did not live on bread alone; he needed some

227

spiritual compass, and having none herself she had none to offer; merely a few rules of behaviour, chaff when compared with genuine religious belief, the sort of thing that could dismiss death—Safe in the arms of Jesus.

Sam, like many new converts, was full of proselyting zeal.

"If you'd just *come*, Mother, with an open mind, I'm sure that Mr Sturgiss would convince you and bring you to the mercy seat."

Trying to conceal the revulsion that this kind of talk roused in her, Deb said,

"My dear boy, I've been to many Revivalist meetings."

This was the time of year for them; those who had harvests to gather had gathered them in, yet the weather was still mild and the roads open. People faced long dull evenings and a rousing Revivalist meeting was a form of entertainment.

One must not decry, of course. At any Revivalist meeting some good was undoubtedly done, and as Goldsmith had said, long ago—Fools who came to scoff remained to pray. Were they fools, or were they fooled? Victims of the mass hysteria which men with the gift of gab and complete conviction could whip up. . . .

It was the language, particularly the phrase "washed in the blood of the lamb," which Deb had found hard to swallow. Just as she had found, at the other end of the religious spectrum, the concentration upon the Crucifixion revolting. It had all happened a long time ago, but there was something in her which, had she been present, would have made her say to the Roman with the lash: Hit me!

Blood, sacrifices; the theme ran straight from the children who were given by their parents to the fires of Moloch to Tim, who couldn't drink a glass of wine at his own wedding, nor allow his wife to wear a rose-trimmed hat when she went to chapel.

The chapel at Abbey Norton was slightly larger than the one Tim's mother had built at Foxton, but it was crowded out. And hot. The packed bodies and the oil-lamps and presently the mounting excitement made the atmosphere almost intolerable; in fact not so unlike the Hell which Mr Sturgiss described so vividly. He was indeed a very powerful speaker, a born orator; he believed in what he was saying; he gestured, his eyes flashed. He would, Deborah thought, have made a splendid actor or a real Radical rabble-rouser.

She was here, just to prove to Sam that she wasn't prejudiced or against him in any way. That was necessary, because the future was concerned. She sat there, obliging, willing as always to do her best, but critical, but sceptical. And she saw a miracle happen.

By this time, although she had avoided as far as possible all social contacts, had lived almost a hermit's life, she knew, by sight, some of the familiar characters in the little town. One was known as Cripply Charlie; born so, a heavy broad torso poised upon useless legs, a freak. He could not use crutches because even crutches needed some propelling from legs; so Cripply Charlie got about on his hands, protected by stout leather pads. Sometimes he begged outright, sometimes he sold matches.

"Come," Mr Sturgiss shouted. "Come to the mercy seat and though your sins be as scarlet they shall be white as snow. Come, just throw yourselves into the loving arms, anxious, longing to receive you." Then suddenly his all-embracing gaze focussed. "You can walk, Brother. Trust in the Lord. Get up and walk."

There was no denying it. Everybody saw it happen. Cripply Charlie did get up and he did walk on legs no bigger than those of a new-born baby's. There were shouts of "Hallelujah" and "Praise the Lord."

"It *was* a miracle, wasn't it?" Sam demanded.

"It seemed so. But, my dear, it raises as many problems as it solves. Why should the poor man have been born so and been obliged to wait forty years? And suppose Mr Sturgiss had decided to end his mission in Shrewsbuy? What then? To be quite honest, Sam, I think the whole thing is beyond our understanding. We just don't know."

"Those who believe, know. We *know* that our Redeemer liveth."

It could have been Tim speaking; in those early days of their marriage, when they could allow themselves the luxury of argument because in bed all was made right.

In a flash of irritation, she said,

"Oh, Sam, *must* you talk like a tract?"

He gave her a glance of deep reproach. And she reproached herself. It was a phase, he'd grow out of it. It was born in him, it was bound to come out. It should not be allowed to come between them.

Until Duff had become the centre of his life, Deb and Sam had lived in exceptional accord, both refugees, both enjoying their new freedom, living in happy-go-lucky fashion. She had eventually been obliged to take him into her confidence about the books—one could not go on vaguely writing "something else" forever, but she had made him promise not to tell—again using Tim as the bogey-man. To speak about her book, Deb said, might lead to their whereabouts being discovered.

Sam's memory of his father had blurred over with the years; he recalled certain incidents—the slapping of the face outside the chapel—somehow connected with the present of a wonderful new pony. A general atmosphere of strictness; a boxing of the ears across the breakfast table. And then the running away, which had fooled Father and seemed, at the time, like a game. Now it assumed a different appearance. To Sam's newly awakened conscience it seemed that possibly Father could have been right, and that, by inference, meant that Mother was wrong. And that thought opened a little gulf, a chilling, too; that atmosphere of disapproval in which Deb had once said she could not live.

It was all the more baffling for Sam in that there was so little to attack. In almost every sense Mother was irreproachable. She worked hard, in the house, in the garden, in her writing; she did not drink, have anything to do with men, use bad language, dress gaudily; her faults were all negative: she refused to attend chapel, or any meeting connected with it, and she had a curious, disconcerting attitude. Towards Cripply Charlie, for instance.

Cripply Charlie was back where he had been before the miracle, heaving himself about on his padded hands, his undeveloped legs again useless.

Deb had an explanation.

"Once, years ago, I saw a hypnotist at the theatre. He had positively staid old gentlemen turning cartwheels, or barking like dogs."

Sam had an explanation.

"While he had faith, he could walk. He lost it and reverted to being a cripple."

Both mild statements; but poles apart.

In Baildon Miss Hardwicke's Academy for Young Ladies was still in existence, though Miss Hardwicke had died, as she had often expressed a wish to do, in harness. The numbers of pupils, both boarders and day girls, had been declining steadily for a decade. There were a number of reasons, mainly the lessening of prosperity in agriculture and all the trades dependent upon it; but, in a sense, the Academy had been self-defeating, in that it had produced a generation of young women who considered themselves capable of instructing their daughters if not their sons. Miss Hardwicke's successor saw a method of survival—take little boys up to the age, say, of eight. Until then they were relatively harmless, practically sexless, though they could only be accepted as day boys.

Both Diana and Caroline were, in theory, qualified to give such elementary lessons as Deb had given Sam, but they'd both been rather poor scholars and shrank from the task. Besides they could both afford to pay somebody else to perform it.

Noel Taylor, escorted by his cousin Belle, began to trot round to the Academy—the word Female had been discreetly dropped when he was five. And he made singularly little progress. He knew his letters, parrot fashion, but had difficulty in assembling them, even on his illustrated bricks, into such simple words as DOG, CAT, HAT, BUN, BAT. He eventually mastered his tables, but the simplest multiplication or addition seemed to be beyond him. Edward tried, with matches, with marbles, even with sweets.

231

"Now look, Noel, here are six aniseed balls. If you take two away, how many are left?"

"One; two; three; four."

"Quite right! Now try to do it in your head. I mean without looking. There are six and I take three away. How many left?"

"I don't know. I can't see."

Apart from this—even Edward hesitated to call it stupidity—Noel was altogether satisfactory and delightful; good-looking, gay-tempered, kind, rather tough. One of his baby teeth failed to fall out on time and developed a small abscess which gave him toothache. And while Edward was deciding between a proper extraction with forceps and that age-old trick of tying a piece of cotton around the offending tooth, attaching it to a doorknob, holding the end and saying, Shut the door, Noel removed the offending molar himself, using a pair of scissors.

"I just dug it out. It was hurting me."

A surgeon in the making.

The little girl, rather more than two years younger than Noel, had been christened Daphne, because just at the time flower names for girls had become fashionable: Rose; Lily; Daisy; Marguerite, even Pansy.

When Caroline saw her two children together she thought how unfortunate it was—even allowing for everything—that Daphne should be so much the less attractive. Caroline knew that she had never been pretty in the approved way, but she had always had *something*. What she had had, and what Freddy had had, had combined to make Noel something quite exceptional. Daphne, oh, poor little girl, was dead-plain. She had straight brown hair which defied all Nurse Rose's attempts with alum water, curl-papers, and finally hot tongs to make it conform. Put a curl into it and within an hour there it was, like a sweep's brush, straight and intractable. Unlike the child herself; even Nurse Rose, whose standards were high, said that Daphne was a very good little girl.

Most fathers were inclined to dote upon their daughters, at least for a time, treating them more or less as dolls; but

Edward tended to concentrate upon his son, who *must* learn; who must carry on the family tradition. Edward was a just man and kind but what energy, and what time he had left, after a full working day, tended to channel towards Noel. Until one evening when Daphne said,

"I know, Papa. Eight. Take twelve from twenty and it is eight."

"How did you know?"

"I have been looking and listening, Papa. I can do it. *I did it*."

The three little words rang out in the comfortable, lamp-lit, firelit gloom and nobody recognised their doomful quality.

Edward said, "That's a clever girl! What else can you do?" A single correct subtraction could have been a mere shot in the dark.

"Everything Noel can." Caro noted that a smug expression did not improve a plain face. But Edward's attention had been arrested. Over supper that evening he said that he thought Daphne should go to school.

"I don't think they take them until they are five."

"Miss Pakefield would take a baboon if *I* asked her," Edward said. It was probably true, for Edward, guessing her financial difficulties, was moderate in his charges and had once given her some splendid, if stringent advice about drains.

Miss Lark, who taught the under-sevens, gave a secret groan when informed that Noel Taylor's little sister would be joining her class. If a boy could be so backward and dull, how much worse would the girl be? Discovering that Daphne was not at all dull, Miss Lark tried to use the fact to her own advantage.

"Unless you make more effort, Noel, Daphne will pass you."

It worked the other way. When Noel was tired of this mild threat, he thought, Let her! and ceased to make any effort at all. Yet one could not really be angry with him; everybody was agreed on that; he was so beautiful, so like a young fawn and he had such an unusual smile.

Imperceptibly Edward's concentration passed to his daughter. Caro hardly noticed the change, partly because it was so gradual, and partly because she was so engrossed in appearing to do good works while avoiding anything unpleasant.

"I think," she said, trying the idea out on Edward, "that the Hospital Ball this year should be a Fancy Dress Ball."

Edward knew, everybody knew, that Caro's ideas were not to be lightly dismissed. Years ago she had suggested, it seemed frivolously, that the sedate Garden Party in aid of Friends of the Hospital funds should include swings and roundabouts and coconuts shies, and the Friends' income had quadrupled.

"It'd be so cheap, for one thing," Caroline explained. "Anybody can rig up a fancy costume out of a little muslin or sateen. And it would help to break down, well the stuffiness; the who can dance with whom. You know what I mean."

Edward knew. All people of good will, County or otherwise, felt bound to patronise the Hospital Ball, but there were the invisible barriers.

"What is more," Caroline said, pursuing her unconsciously egalitarian course, "we could alter the supper arrangements. Pair people off. Lady Norton is certain to come as Britannia and it would do her good to take supper with a Jolly Jack Tar."

"It might work. In fact with you behind it, darling, it can hardly fail to. What role would you assume?"

After the slightest pause Caroline said,

"I think Old Mother Hubbard."

Old Mother Hubbard went to her cupboard, to get her poor dog a bone; When she got there, the cupboard was bare, and so the poor dog had none.

In a crude way it described her own plight. She had everything: a kind, loving, indulgent husband who had never for a second doubted her fidelity; a most comfortable home; a secure place in the social hierarchy; two children, one beautiful and charming, one apparently very clever. But her emotional cupboard was empty and the poor dog—

her one overriding passion—though often apparently dead of inanition, still showed sporadic signs of life, a gnawing at her vitals. The poor dog, denied the bone, would turn and rend other things.

At Foxton, Tim Bridges had suffered a deprivation, dissimilar in kind, but not so different in effect. Caroline, in weak moments, grieved over Freddy Ingram, her own lack of strength of character which had made her choose the easy way. Tim grieved only over the loss of his son. And over the scandal which attached itself to a broken marriage—however innocent one partner might be.

He'd decided early that after the way Deb had behaved, he did not want her back. She'd been, after those first blissful two months, argumentative, sarcastic and—strange thing to think—too capable. He would have been resigned to the dirty trick she had played him, but for the fact that she had taken Sam. If he had succeeded in tracing her he would have said, bluntly, Give me the boy and go your own way. As it was, she had vanished entirely, and the boy with her, and after a while when he ran about like a headless chicken, he settled down to wait. The mills of God ground slowly, but they ground extremely small, and Tim had complete belief in his God who dealt justly in the end, after subjecting true believers to tests and trials such as this— Look at the story of Job.

Everybody said that Mr Bridges had held up wonderfully.

He would, of course, have been justified in divorcing her, but the thing was unthinkable. Whom God hath joined, let no man put asunder. And twenty divorces, in the circumstances, would not give what he wanted—his son back, and all his, with no subversive influence at work, pulling the other way.

There was the Book of Job. There were other encouraging bits of the Bible. I have been young and now I am old, but I have never seen the righteous forsaken. . . .

Gradually, over the years, Tim Bridges, a most practical man, built up a fantasy, based on some extent upon the

Parable of the Prodigal Son. Deb's little dowry could not support two people for long, the way prices were rising and her only other source of income—breaking in horses by kindness, not violence and then training some of them to jump, was obviously lost to her: he'd have heard.

So he waited.

Now and again he woke in the night. (For some reason which he did not examine, the fantasy dealt with night, with Deb and Sam, in rags, footsore and hungry, coming to seek his charity.) The noise, whatever it was, a bough creaking, a window rattling, always woke him to hope, which, disappointed, never ran downwards into despair. He had faith. He could wait. It was all in God's hands. By some quirk of the mind, although he *knew* otherwise, he still thought of Sam as a child.

When the mills of God began to grind their first produce was a letter. It bore a London post mark and was not addressed in Deborah's clear neat hand. Inside, however, was an enclosure. A bit brusque, but not unfriendly.

Dear Tim: I think the time has come to consider Sam's future. I have come, reluctantly, to the conclusion that he would, after all, be happier with you. Some time ago he became an ardent Methodist and we no longer live in accord. He is fifteen and seems to know his own mind. He would like to return to Foxton, and since that is the most *sensible* of his several plans, I felt bound to agree. I do *not* propose to accompany him. Any letter addressed to me, c/o Hammond and Curtis, Exeter Square, will be forwarded, but we are not living there.

She had not been reduced to rags or hunger; she had been driven to appeal. Her intention had been to allow Sam to grow up, to the age of sixteen, and then let him choose. She had then not reckoned with all that fairy gold mounting up in the bank. And certainly she had not reckoned on Robbie Duff's influence; or of a headstrong boy, completely out of hand, proposing the most outrageous plans for his own future.

"It is called united Missions, Mother. It works among

the poor in London. And they welcome young recruits because the young appeal to the young.

"Now I am exercised in my mind, Mother. Duff's mother is absolutely set on his being a minister, so he must have more education and his parents will miss his help. Ought I to go and work there?"

There were organisations for providing sailors with something other than drinking places and brothels when they were ashore; and for offering non-alcoholic refreshments at railway stations. There were, in fact, innumerable good causes. All admirable; that was part of the trouble; nothing Deb could really oppose. She had in the end been driven to say: Look Sam, it's time for us to sit down and have a serious talk.

The letter to Tim was the result of that talk; and proof of her failure. All the subterfuge and the effort, quite wasted. Sam for his own sake must go home.

Nemesis!

But now she could go home too. She had in writing, Tim's writing: I want nothing to do with you; I never want to see you again; but I shall welcome the boy home.

And that left her free to go back to her own country; back to Gad's.

Sam said, "Ever since I saw the light this living under a false name has worried me."

"You were in no way to blame, Sam. It was my idea and it did not work. I tried and I failed. But that does not matter. If you are *quite* sure. All I ever wanted was your happiness."

"I know; and I appreciate it," Sam said gently. Then with a change of voice and manner, "But you know, Mother, happiness must not be the sole object of one's life."

She did not wish to provoke another pious lecture, so she did not say that she intended to be as happy as she could. Returning to Gad's would not be unmitigated happiness, she knew; it would not be the same without Mamma; but there would be Di and Caro and George, friends, the familiar countryside, the well-known streets in Baildon—and of course, horses.

Stone House had never really been much more than a camping place; all she had done was to keep it in decent repair and buy more comfortable beds and chairs, better lamps than those she had started with. These she did not propose to cart half across England, and Sam had often spoken of the Duff's poverty. At the moment she did not feel very warmly towards that family, but common justice made her see that Sam had an inborn fanatic streak and if he had not taken to Methodism he might have chosen something worse, so she sent a tactfully worded message to Mrs Duff, saying that there were certain things she must leave behind and it would spare her a great deal of trouble if Mrs Duff would take any or all of them off her hands.

George had extended the heartiest of welcomes; she could come when she liked, stay as long as she wished. Gad's needed a woman about the place. He added, for kindliness came easily to him and despite the passage of years his memory of Foxton and its master were still vivid, "Make sure the boys knows what he's letting himself in for."

Deb had made sure; it seemed to her that Sam would slide back into his natural environment as a fish, momentarily stranded, would slip back into water.

Sam's first pony, Merry, had finally succumbed to old age, his second, Benjy, made the journey to Gad's in comfortable fashion, in a horse box, specially chartered. The Railway did transport animals of every kind, but trains moved quickly, and since cattle trucks were always attached to the rear end of trains where every movement was exaggerated, casualties were frequent.

"It would seem silly to send Benjy to Foxton where there are so many horses," Deborah said in her sensible way. "And probably one of your cousins can ride him."

Sense indeed rather than sentiment was the keynote of their final arrangements. Sam had an adequate wardrobe which needed a proper trunk, shaped not unlike a Noah's Ark. Rather ostentatiously, he printed labels for it, his correct name: S. Bridges. Deborah had only hand luggage. She had sent a box of books on the footboard on the horse box, and she owned few clothes. There had seemed to be no call for them. But it would be different in future; she must not be a disgrace to her family or her friends; and by ordinary standards she was now quite rich.

Robbie Duff was the only person in or around Abbey Norton who had been told the truth and his lips were sealed because his parents would have been horrified to learn that all these years he had been friendly with the son of a woman, had enjoyed vast hospitality from a woman who was living apart from her husband. It was unheard of.

"I shall miss you, Sam." Was it true, or just a trick of Duff's glasses, that Duff's eyes had tears in them?

"You need not," Sam said. "There'll always be a warm welcome for you at Foxton—I gave you the address. And if you *do* go to work at the United Missions, let me know and I'll take the first train. . . ."

Deborah said, at the moment of parting, "You know, my dear, where to find me, if ever you want me."

"We're not saying goodbye, Mother. Foxton is less than twenty miles from Gad's."

She'd thought the very same thing, on her wedding day; she'd said to Mamma, left in the most awful predicament, "I shall come every week." And that, because of Tim, had not been possible.

"You may not find it possible, Sam. Above all, don't insist. Don't quarrel." Almost as an afterthought, she added, "Don't forget me."

"As though I could," Sam said. But already he had done with the past; was pressing eagerly towards the future. Lost to her; the product, after all of a broken marriage; a boy who, for the time being, had had enough of Mother and was looking forward eagerly to reunion with his father.

George met the train and advancing along the platform thought, with pity and admiration, Poor Deb! She has been putting a brave face on it all this time, pretending she'd found some way of earning money.

The grey broadcloth dress and jacket in which Deb had

239

run away had served her well, perhaps a little too well, for it had made it seem silly to replace it; it was so good and so seldom worn. But it had aged. George couldn't have said, exactly, what changes fashion had undergone in the last few years, but he could distinguish between a well-dressed woman and a shabby one, and Deb, in the late sunshine of a June afternoon, looked shabby. Never mind, he'd soon put that right! His financial position at the moment was a bit tricky for bad luck, both in business and pleasure, had dogged him since Mamma's death, but something would turn up.

He greeted her with enthusiasm, dodging under the brim of the rather battered-looking old hat to kiss her cheek, which was hard and thin. Funny! Both Diana, who was not a Thorley, and Caroline, who was, were exchanging their youtful curves for others, more pronounced.

His conviction that she was poor was confirmed when she said that this one valise was all her luggage.

"I sent my box ahead, with the pony. Did they arrive?"

"Yesterday. All safe and well."

Light as the small valise was, it must be handed to a porter. Porters were very poorly paid and depended largely upon their tips. Twopence would have been adequate, sixpence generous; failing to find a sixpence amongst the small change in his pocket, George bestowed a shilling, which evoked not only thanks, automatic, but blessings.

"Oh, George, let me drive, please. It's so long. . . ."

"He's new, and a bit of a handful; but all right. But make it lively. I've got a bit of a party waiting."

"Di and Caro?"

"No. You can see them tomorrow. Just a few fellows, back from the races. It was fixed, Deb, before you settled your day."

"Oh dear. Have I spoiled something for you? George, you shouldn't have missed anything on my account. I could have hired . . . And I'm not dressed for a party. I'll just slip in and go to bed."

"It isn't that kind of a party. Just men. At least . . . Do you remember Chloe Faulkner?"

240

"Vaguely. Years ago. Wasn't it the year Poor Susan died? And then she married; was it . . .? Yes, Lord Mildenhall. And then, wasn't there a divorce?"

"That bit of information seems to have spread to every corner of the globe." George's voice was bitter. "Nobody knows how that old brute behaved to her—and to Johnny."

"Oh. In what way?"

"Jealous! They're twins. There was always a close bond between them, and the cure for that was that they mustn't meet, weren't supposed even to write to each other. They did, of course, meet on the sly. London mostly, Oxford sometimes. So then he had her *watched*. Can you imagine anything more despicable?"

"Is seeing one's own brother, in defiance of one's husband's orders, grounds for divorce?"

"Of course not. But given a judge who didn't understand the situation, an old, powerful man absolutely set on divorce, and a few bribes . . . They made it look as though Chloe had gone completely off the rails. Meeting Johnny was believed to be a cover for . . . for other activities. Connived at by Johnny, of course."

"How grossly unfair!"

"I hoped you'd think so. Nobody else does. In fact you'd think from the way people have behaved that the poor girl had smallpox *and* leprosy and . . . anything else you care to name. Simply unbelievable."

The whole thing was unbelievable. Sir John and Lady Faulkner could not, of course, refuse to give a destitute and disgraced daughter a home; but when they went out they did not take her with them, and when they entertained, which was rarely, she was banished. In common with most other people they believed that if Johnny had not actually connived, he had encouraged Chloe in her wild career; parents and son were hardly on speaking terms, and old Lord Norton, who had willed three thousand pounds to each of his godsons, disinherited Johnny and let the fact be known. Lady Faulkner wailed, "Now look what you have done between you!"

George was not really surprised that Di should be cen-

241

sorious; she'd always been what he called stuffy; he was surprised and disappointed when Caro took upon herself to point out that running around with a divorcée did his own matrimonial prospects no good.

"God help us, Caro. I am not running round with her! She never comes to Gad's or the races or anywhere else without Johnny."

"You must have been reading the papers!"

That was just another case of speaking-without-thinking, of letting the ready tongue, grown sharper over the years, run away with her. But when George took in the implication of the quip, he was deeply offended. Caro ceased to be his favourite sister.

"So *you* won't feel everlastingly contaminated by sharing a meal with somebody who's been divorced?"

"It'd be a bit idiotic of me, wouldn't it? Tim could have divorced me had he felt so inclined."

There was sense in that statement; Deb had always been the sensible one. Not perhaps as amusing, or as easily indulgent as Caro; but sensible. The one Mamma had asked for on her deathbed.

"One thing," George said, with warmth, "nobody is going to treat you like that, Deb. And while I have a roof and a crust, we'll share it."

Turning skillfully into the lane that led to Gad's, Deb said,

"As a matter of fact, George, I'm rather rich. I seem to have earned a great deal of money and spent very little."

And the manager of the bank at Abbey Norton had at last had his way and persuaded his eccentric client, Mrs Willoughby, that money in a deposit account, upon which interest was paid, was every bit as safe and readily available as money lying, doing nothing, in a current account.

It isn't that kind of party, George had said. And it was not. It could not exactly be called rowdy, George apparently had enough sense not to go in for roughs and toughs; but the only two women present were Chloe Faulkner, still called Lady Mildenhall, whose reputation was irretrievably

242

lost, and James Gordon's wife, who had never had a reputation to lose. It was less the company than the state of the house which gave Deb a mild shock. She'd never been as pernicketty as Diana, but . . . To see Mamma's beloved piano all rings where wet glasses had been set down . . . the chintz covers soiled and rumpled, the velvet ones greasy, a curtain hanging lopsidedly, and dust everywhere.

The meal was bad, too. Not perhaps to men who had spent the afternoon at the races and had drunk well; not perhaps to Chloe, who had never in her life set a table and was thankful to be accepted at any table, not to Millicent Gordon, who had probably never before her marriage seen a properly set table, but to Deb, reared by Mamma . . . Oh dear! Plenty of food, but ill-prepared and slapped down just anyhow. Oh dear! George certainly did need a woman about his house. Now and again, with this thought in mind, Deb glanced at Chloe, upon whom neither years nor tribulations seemed to have made any visible effect; she was as pretty, in a pink-and-white, doll-like, vapid way, as ever. Deb could remember her, very virginal in white muslin at George's doomed party, and now, though dressed for the races in russet bombazine, she looked just as virginal. Every boy's ideal—and every old man's! The contrast between her and Millicent Gordon seemed almost contrived. Mrs Gordon had commented upon her future daughter-in-law's red hair. It was very red, and there was a lot of it, puffed and piled high. Not unattractive—but purple was not her colour. Still, she was animated and friendly and completely unpretentious. "Any of you boys," she said in one of the silences that occur at any party, "want a decent Havana without going broke, me Dad's just had delivery and tomorrow's my day at the shop."

"Milly," James said—and he said it with pride, "only married me on condition that every Saturday should be Dad's day."

"Thass true. But what else could I do? He's such a helpless old b . . . bumbler." Plainly a word substitution! Deb was capable of liking Milly and at the same time wondering about Mrs Gordon's feelings and at the same time thinking about how the housekeeping standards had declined, what could be done about *that?* And how were Sam and his father getting along?

Tim's sense recognised that Sam was now fifteen, yet, because he had not seen him grow from stage to stage, he still thought of him as a child—the young boy whom Deb had stolen from him. Or, conversely, bred of the Prodigal Son fantasy, he'd thought of him as lean and hungry, in rags, glad of a welcome and a meal. Neither mental picture had prepared him for Sam. Nor, though she had tried, had Deborah fully prepared Sam for Tim. She had said that Sam's father was rich, bred horses, lived very comfortably, but such facts had glanced off Sam's awareness. He'd never known a Methodist who was not poor. And rightly so; nobody with any conscience at all had any right to be rich in a world where so many good causes were in desperate straits. Sam knew—through Robbie Duff—of a woman who took in washing and who regularly gave the pay for one household's wash to help missionaries. And the Duffs themselves, very poor, put pennies into boxes with various labels.

Under the text which still declared that Christ was the Head of This House—a sentiment of which Sam fully approved—arguments, quite as bitter and all the worse for being well-founded, were presently to break out. And Tim, who had done his best to convert Deborah and train up his son in the way he should go, found himself subjected to a conversion campaign, against which he had no defence except sense. Sam, who had cut his proselyting teeth on Mother—and failed, was now prepared to tackle Father. . . .

Deb tackled Gad's. It was nobody's fault; Jenny had simply taken to her bed and Violet said,

"She still eat hearty. I spend half my time going up and down with trays and such. I had to let the house go a bit. Master didn't mind. 'S'matter of fact when Jenny took to her bed—it was Ma'am's death *and* the funeral, she would go, that finished her off—I did say to the Master I'd need a bit more help. But he said all right for a bit. *He* been satisfied."

Violet gave Deb an antagonistic look and that part of Deb which was still oversensitive to disapproval hastened to apologise.

"I am not criticising, Violet. Just feeling my way about. I didn't know that you were single-handed with Jenny to care for."

Well, you know now! So don't talk to me about spring-cleaning; I only got one pair of hands.

So much could be said without words.

"I'll get Willy to help, with the curtain's at least."

"And Willy ain't as spry as he was," Violet said ominously.

"Why? What has happened to Willy?"

"Got older. We all do. And some get cantankerous, too. Thass Jenny, knocking now. Got a clock in her head, she hev. 'Leven o'clock and she's wanting her broth. Minute late and bang, bang, bang. Excuse me, ma'am."

Willy—older, of course—silly of her not to have expected that, proved to be spry enough when called once again into service for his idol. His lack of spryness had been defensive; if Violet had had her way she'd have had him in the house all day, even washing up most likely. He was only too happy to help Deb to spring-clean the drawing room, and as he worked he talked. Everything, he said, had started to fall to pieces when Mrs Thorley died.

"And no blame to the Master. He did try. He steadied down considerable; didn't seem like the same man. He just lost heart what with one thing and another. First the foot-and-mouth, then cows slipping calves all over the place. Apart from the loss, that sorta thing get a herd a bad name. Ask me, he went back to the giddy life to stop hisself from brooding." Willy had the feeling, which he could not explain, leave alone justify, that things would look up now that Miss Deb was back. He repeated that he was glad to see her back; and volunteered to polish the piano. "Man's hands stronger'n a lady's," he said. In fact his sharp, loving eye noted that Miss Deb's hands didn't look as though they'd been cossetted much. And her old print dress was no better than a servant's. Whatever had happened to her—

and it was all a bit of a mystery, things hadn't gone easy for her. Once again Willy thought: Oh if only he'd had five acres and a cow and she hadn't been the Old Masters daughter. For *her* he would have washed dishes at a sink.

"I have no doubt at all," Di said, "that George will twist *this* to his advantage and say that if we can be friendly to Deb we could ask Chloe Faulkner to tea. I for one do not intend to." In effect she was warning Caro, who was inclined to be, despite her sharp tongue, rather too easy-going.

"Even George can hardly think the two cases the same. Deb isn't divorced."

"She could have been. If Tim Bridges had been as spiteful as Lord Mildenhall. Hers is, after all, a broken marriage."

Di's was not. She was in fact enjoying all the benefits without any of the drawbacks of the matrimonial state. She was Mrs Spicer, she had two adorable children, she had a comfortable allowance. In a prominent position in her pretty drawing room stood a silver-framed photograph of Everard, standing by the body of a huge tiger which he had shot. She drew everybody's attention to it as diligently as she had once drawn attention to poor Lavinia's painting of Gad's Hall. And her attitude was not false. Everard in this guise *was* admirable, and preferable. . . . He wrote regularly, sent presents. Di was capable of ignoring the fact that the regular letters became shorter and less informative, degenerating into the I-hope-you-are-all-well,-I-am category. Now and again he referred to his health, and then she would worry, too, and invite everybody to worry with her. By no means a broken marriage!

Mrs Thorley had achieved her aim of imposing solidarity upon her girls and both Di and Caro were unfeignedly glad to see Deb and sorry to see her looking thin and shabby. But that could soon be remedied. A little money from both of them, and Diana's skill with the needle . . . And then, in a short time Deb made these kindly thoughts sound ridiculous by saying that she had a pony to give away. Belle and Noel already shared one, and Daphne, who must do everything that Noel did—and do it rather better—was clamouring for one of her own.

"It's a very nice pony, called Benjy. It seemed silly to send it to Foxton. And I couldn't put it on the market."

They both thought, How typical of Deb!

Then she said, "Has either of you been to Gad's lately?"

"I simply couldn't bear it, after Mamma . . ." Caro had not lost her gift for crying easily. "It didn't seem the same."

"And besides, one never knew lately whom one might meet there," Di said.

"It was in a fine mess, I assure you. Violet has been working under difficulties, I admit; but she's just taken soiled table linen and crammed it into a drawer. There are wine stains which I doubt whether even the Hand Laundry can remove."

All the young women, reared by Mamma, knew what a heinous thing Violet had done. They were drawn together by a memory of Mamma putting salt on any stain, then stretching the soiled piece of cloth over a basin and pouring a kettleful of hot water through it.

"Do you intend to stay with George?" Di asked, thinking what a good thing it would be.

"Until I get the place straightened out. After that, I don't know. I did wonder, this morning, about taking Park."

"It would cost a small fortune to make it habitable," Di said.

"I have some money. And it would be an unobtrusive way of helping George."

"But, my dear girl, I shouldn't dream of selling Park. Or anything else—except livestock. I shall pull round. Of course you can *have* Park; do what you like with it. And if you are so flush of money, you can lend me a bit—at five per cent."

"I'll do that. And set the five per cent against rent." She laughed suddenly. "Isn't it an odd world? Do you realise, George, that if Tim cared to exercise his legal rights, he could claim every penny I've earned? I don't think he *would*; but he *could*."

"Damned unfair! How much could you lend me?"

"How much do you need?" Some deep instinct warned her to be cautious. Better not let George have too much, too easily. On the other hand the thought of using some of the money which had never seemed quite real to her on bolstering up Gad's was curiously satisfying.

"What could you spare? Without robbing yourself? I'm not trying to sponge, Deb. I had bad luck with the herd."

"I know. Willy told me."

"And I have a few debts."

"Would a thousand help?"

"God! It'd be a life-raft. But could you lend that and still mend up Park? Deb, I don't want to sound nosy, but how did you come by so much money?"

"Quite honestly." Well, sooner or later, she supposed, people would have to know. And why not? Why this curious reluctance to come into the open? It was nothing to be ashamed of, was it? "I wrote some books," she said in a gruff, offhand way.

"God! Did you really? Well, I always knew you were clever." Silent, upon the air, hung the words: But not as clever as that!

George was all in favour of Deb setting up her own home—though naturally, had her circumstances been otherwise, she would have been welcome at Gad's. He appreciated the better order of the household, he liked a clean tablecloth. But in a way Deb's coming had interrupted a regime which had been jogging along quite comfortably. George knew that Violet was a bit of a slut, making Jenny an excuse for things left undone, or done badly, but it had been only a temporary arrangement. Once he'd pulled round he intended to make better provision for poor old Jenny, hire more help, get things cleared up.

And marry Chloe?

Upon this subject his mind, his whole nature suffered such savage divisions that he underwent the mental equivalent of being torn apart by wild horses. He had fallen in love with her romantically and wholeheartedly, and the thing should have ended there. But she'd come back, just as pretty, so that every time he saw her the old dream woke and walked in beauty; and she was now within his reach.

Sir John and Lady Faulkner would be only too glad to get her, disgraced and discarded, off their hands.

But what sort of wife would she make? A girl in love with her twin brother, whose first marriage had wrecked on that rock. George knew that Johnny's attitude towards Chloe was purely protective, because she was only half-witted; the subtle, mischievous hints about an unnatural relationship, which had been the inevitable result of the divorce court proceedings, carried no weight with George Thorley. He knew Johnny too well. Johnny said,

"That old devil had two things against her, poor child. She was fond of me, and she didn't give him the baby he expected."

Would she do better with George Thorley? There was Gad's to think of. A boy could fall in love without regard to such practicalities and what remained of the boy might be moved now and again, but the man who had grown up around the boy must think.

So George thought and wavered and time moved on. Deb left off fussing about Gad's renovated Park, madly excited to find that several miserable little rooms, their lath and plaster walls demolished, revealed beams as old as and similar to those in the barn at Gad's.

"Honestly, George, I believe the Vikings came ashore and built their houses as they built their ships, but upside down as it were."

At a time when everybody was boarding over, papering over any old beam, Deb was exposing hers and glorying in them. She had also bought two Thoroughgood hunters, a spanking gig and a horse to draw it; two riding habits, two silk dresses and four hats.

Now she said, "I think it would be nice, George, to have a family Christmas party here—if the girls agree; and make it my housewarming, too."

"I'm fully in favour." There had been no purely family party at Gad's since Mamma died. Her memory was too closely associated with the place and everybody would have felt that it was not the same. Nor, try as she might, could Deb build up, in Park, quite the right atmosphere. The family entity had broken, and although the four children enjoyed themselves unreservedly, the grown-ups were aware of change and loss and absences. As Caroline said later to Edward, "I think *all* anniversaries are a mistake."

Still, there was the Meet on Boxing Day to look forward to. Whatever the weather the South Suffolk met at Baildon, outside the *Hawk in Hand*, on Boxing Day. The hounds ran about and were petted by onlookers, especially by children, enjoying for a brief hour the domestic, human contact which all foxhounds secretly craved. And the landlord of the inn, with his henchmen, dispensed punch, steaming-hot and very faintly flavoured with rum. There was always a cap-round, and this year, due to Caroline's mechanisations, it was to be in aid of the Friends of the Hospital. Also, this year, Noel would be there, mounted on his pony, and Melville on the one that had been Sam's. Just part of the parade.

All I wanted for Sam that day; had Tim only been a little less stubborn . . .

"See you tomorrow," everybody said. Though the sky threatened snow and George said, casting an inherited weatherwise eye at the sky, "It won't be much of a turnout tomorrow, Deb, if there's a fall."

"We must go, for Caro's sake. Call for me, eh?"

A few flakes fell indecisively as George walked home. It was still early, Deb's party had died under its own in-anition and the threat of the weather. Was there anything more depressing than the tag end of Christmas Day? He was not going home to an empty house; Jenny's room was lighted and from it came the sounds of seasonable revelry; since Jenny could no longer get to the village, half the village, it seemed, must come to her.

George was closing his front door when he heard the thud of hoofs. One of his bachelor friends come over to share a Christmas evening drink. Happily, he pulled the door wide. A thicker flurry of snow momentarily obscured his view. The rider came on, reined in at the very doorstep in a most unhorsemanlike way, and Johnny Faulkner fell, rather than dismounted, from the saddle.

Johnny Faulkner; about the last person George expected to see; there was always a big family gathering at Stratton Strawless for Christmas.

"George! Had to come, George."

George's first thought was: Drunk. Johnny did sometimes take the glass too many; but in the light of the hall lamp, George saw that Johnny looked more upset than drunk. He was not dressed for riding, wore no overcoat or hat. And he was crying! George had never before seen a man cry and had not, since childhood, cried himself. He was appalled.

It was likely that Johnny had had another blazing row with his parents—probably about whether Chloe should be admitted to the family circle. But there had been blazing rows before and Johnny had been hotly angry, not tearful.

Violet had her faults, but her good points, too; she had remembered to mend the fire and to light the lamps, so that the living room was welcoming. George pushed Johnny on to the settle, poured some brandy and said, "Here, drink this. That'll pull you together."

Johnny's teeth chattered on the glass; tears and drips of water from his soaked hair dripped into it, on to it.

First things first.

"Shan't be a second," George said. He galloped upstairs, two at a time, snatched his warm woollen dressing-gown and a towel. He even spared a thought for the horse, ridden hard for quite a distance and then left out in the snow. He ran along to the door of Jenny's room and shouted,

"Is there a man in there? Go round to the front, take Mr Faulkner's horse to the stable and chuck a rug over it." Then because it was quicker he thundered down the back stairs, through the kitchen littered with the debris of the hospitality that Violet had extended to all-comers, and so into the living room by the rear door.

"Shuck those wet clothes," he said. On the side nearer the fire Johnny's clothes were already beginning to steam. George had a sharp, sudden memory of another time, a long time ago, when he'd been concerned about Johnny's being soaked. That had really been the start of it all, a sincere, happy friendship with Johnny, and for Chloe a love which was more imaginative than real.

Johnny had managed to empty his glass and the brandy had helped. He was no longer crying and the violent shuddering was easing. George replenished Johnny's glass and poured a measure for himself. He was to need it!

"Chloe's dead," Johnny said.

"Dead! Good God! What happened?"

"I knew you'd understand. I had to come, George. I knew at least you wouldn't say, Oh what a pity, oh what a dreadful accident, and we mustn't spoil the children's Christmas. When they know as well as I do she killed herself and they drove her to it. I just couldn't bear. The humbug. I just couldn't stand it. I'll tell you. . . . It was like this. They've been putting out their tentacles, trying to get the poor darling decently disposed of, and somewhere in the wilds of Yorkshire there's an old great-aunt by marriage or some such, going blind; she wanted somebody to lead her about and read to her. I did protest. George, I made a stand. I pointed out—poor darling, she could just read, about like a child of four. No use. They wanted Chloe out before Christmas. All those prim-faced, snotty-nosed little brats might be contaminated! And my sisters and their husbands, all so smug and noble, acting as though she was an open sewer. Anyhow, she said she'd rather go than stay, and can you wonder? So I took her as far as York and saw her safely on to the little branch-line train. . . . I swear, George, she seemed all right then. But she opened the door and stepped out, down a fifty-foot embankment." Johnny's composure broke. "She must have looked like a broken doll. . . . And *they* call it an accident! They're delighted."

George felt a flick of remorse. If he'd been a shade less cautious, followed his heart and let his head have no say, this might not have happened. He would have known that in Chloe's life he would never be first, he could have arranged for her to see Johnny as often as she wanted to.

But that was no way to think! George had never found it easy to accept blame, even from himself.

"I am damned sorry, Johnny."

"I knew you would be. You liked her, too."

"Yes, I—liked her."

"I blame myself entirely. If I hadn't worked like a slave and just for pocket-money, I could have set her up, somewhere snug and away from them all. Waiting for dead men's shoes, George, my boy; very unprofitous occupation!"

When Johnny began to jumble his words, sometimes most amusingly, it was a sign of imminent intoxication. Well, why not? What other comfort could he offer?

"I'm not going back," Johnny said. "That'll give 'em something to think about. Let 'em explain that away. What a pity! What a sad accident!!"

"You mustn't talk like that, Johnny. What'd happen to Stratton Strawless?"

"Rosa's boy can have it and I wish him joy with it. I'm off to Canada."

"That's nonsense, Johnny."

"I'd like to see somebody try to stop me. . . ."

Deb did a bit of desultory clearing up in the big room, went into the kitchen and made a pot of tea and carried it into the little room where she worked. All in all the family party had not been a good idea. Sam was missing. She had not abandoned him, he had abandoned her and no doubt he was happy, in his own way at Foxton. One could only hope so. But there had been, in addition to the general, rather sad feeling of change, a few of those—well, you could only call them unfortunate remarks which could only be made in close family circles. The worst of all perhaps, Edward's earnest, and professional opinion that the best cure for Everard's multifarious small ailments would be a real holiday in England.

"He goes up into the hills," Diana said. She sounded defensive.

"I know. But it is not the same. If it were why should there be the more or less general rule of home leave after five years? You should insist, Di."

Caro said, "How would you like it if I insisted that you came home punctually for supper?" Caro asked.

"I do try," Edward said, humbly.

"Papa always does his best," Daphne said. "Miss Pakefield says my papa is the best man she knows."

"Well, Honey, perhaps she doesn't know very many."

"Miss Pakefield says it's a pity Noel isn't more like Papa."

"And that is enough of the Gospel according to Miss Pakefield for one day," Caroline said, with quite an edge to her voice. She found it extraordinarily easy to be irritated by her daughter, the child she had actually *prayed* for. Plain, solid, stolid and boring, altogether too much like Edward.

Well, it was over now. Deb dipped her pen, wrote *Chapter Five* and underlined it, and was soon lost to the world. She was brought back by a growl from her great dog, a present from George when she moved into her own house. "He's a proper guard dog—Walker still breeds a few. And he'll be company for you."

"It's all right, Walker. It's only Sally."

Sally was Joe Snell's youngest daughter; delighted to find a place within a few yards of her own home. She'd had permission to sleep out on Christmas night, but probably the snow had prevented some other members of the family from getting home, so Sally had come back.

Walker did not believe that. He put up his hackles and moved to the door.

"All right then. Go see for yourself," Deb said. She opened the door of the little room and Walker went bounding across the now dimly lighted space to guard, if necessary to defend the front door, which opened directly into the big room. When the door opened and his sense of smell caught up with his sense of hearing, Walker was all fawning apology. Deb said,

"George! Come back for a nightcap?" But before he spoke she knew that something was wrong.

"Deb, it's too awful. I don't know what to do."

Old Mr Gordon had been Coroner for many years but he had at last handed over the thankless job, and James had, naturally, been appointed to succeed him. So to the horror of it all was added a touch of absolute unreality; James was sir; George was Mr Thorley; Johnny was the deceased.

"Mr Thorley, can you tell us exactly what happened?"

"No, sir. It was too sudden. I was showing him—the deceased—my new gun. It was a Christmas present. It is a new model, one with which neither of us was familiar, but I had tried it out, earlier in the day, so I knew more about it. . . . So I said: No, not that way. Here give it to me. And as it changed hands, it went off and . . ."

The story was a concocted one—never had Deborah's skill been better employed; but the emotion was genuine. Everybody recognised that. And that a loaded shot-gun should be thus casually handled struck nobody as strange. Similarly lethal weapons stood about in almost every farmhouse kitchen, and the first thing a country child learned was not to touch.

As Deborah had said, a story to be acceptable must be simple and plausible, with a grain of truth in it.

What had actually happened was far more dramatic. Johnny, mad with grief and bit drunk, bent on going to Canada, had spotted the gun, snatched it up and threatened George with it. And one grappling hand must have moved the safety catch, another touched the trigger. "Deb, it took him under the chin. But it could have been me. And I wish to God it had been."

Death by misadventure sounded a bit better than plain accidental death, though they both meant much the same thing. The foreman of the jury gave that as his verdict, and said, "Sir, if allowable, we'd like to say two things. Loaded guns shouldn't be played about with. And we all felt for Mr Thorley." They all felt—but in a remote way, for the dead man's parents. But they came from the other side of Southbury; they weren't local as Mr Thorley was, well-known and well-liked, popular as he was to be to the end.

The earth kept on turning on its axis, night and day, day and night, Spring, Summer, Autumn, Winter; Spring again. The peripheral elements of the once close-knit family over which Mrs Thorley had once brooded so carefully spun off

255

and were absorbed into the wider world and were by the years engulfed. Only George left any kind of memory behind him—and that a bitter one.

Sam left no trace. He stayed at Foxton for three years arguing with Tim. Sam said, "The truth is, you care more about horses than you do about people. Think about all the poor people in London. Think of the lepers in Africa."

"I do. I subscribe. I can't save them all. Nobody could. Nobody ever will. And let me tell you, all this Radical talk is damaging the Methodist cause."

"Not as much as apathy. You think your duty's done if you live a sober life and support the chapel."

"So it is."

"Didn't Christ say—sell all that thou hast and give to the poor? And you won't even give fifty pounds to Duff's soup kitchens! All right, I shall ask my Uncle George."

"You'll need to pick your moment, son; from what I hear most of the time he hasn't got fifty pence." Sam thought, but did not say, that he would ask Mother. By common consent, Deborah was never mentioned in house. Some perverse streak in Tim made him more resentful against her now than ever before—she'd taken away a good sensible boy, promising Methodist material, and sent back a daft tub-thumper.

Deb gave Sam what he asked for without a quibble and George, flush at the moment, donated two pounds. Sam thought he might as well take the money to Duff personally, fell under Duff's spell again and stayed, busy and happy in the slums of Bethnal Green until he died of typhus.

Deborah left no trace, except insofar as her constant loans to George kept Gad's intact, and that Melville Spicer owed his education—Eton and Trinity—to her. Her career as a writer proved to be meteoric; as suddenly as everyone had wanted to read D. Willoughby, they ceased to do so; for no specific reason that Mr Hammond could name, except mounting competition; a new meteor every six months. He remained kindly, and aware of the debt he owed her, but his terms dwindled to twenty pounds down and ten for any subsequent impression. A sum he knew he would never have to pay.

Everybody had always regarded Deborah as the eldest of the Gad's Hall girls, so it seemed fitting that she should die first. She died as unobtrusively as she had lived—all things considered. "Just a simple cold, Sally. I'll have a day in bed. And a boiled onion." Three days and several boiled onions later, Sally suggested sending for the doctor.

"He couldn't do anything. I would like to see Willy, though." Her voice was now a croak and a full breath was hard and painful to draw.

Willy came, just as he was, smelling of stables and horses, and almost speechless with distress.

"Willy, if I don't get the better of this, you'll find my will in my writing table, the long drawer in the middle." She had made her will as soon as she received Robbie Duff's letter informing her of Sam's death. She'd thought then— The trouble is, George can't be entirely trusted; he *means* well, but he'd sell my horses, if he found himself in a tight corner. And he had a fatal way of getting into tight corners.

". . . so, if it isn't too much to ask, Willy, look after them all, and pay yourself for the work. When the money runs out, or you get past it, send for the knacker and have them killed *here*. I don't want them sold. I don't want them to go to the yard."

She was not without assets, even now. George had borrowed, paid back, borrowed again. He was honest, after his fashion, and would realise that Park and its meadow were rightly hers until he had repaid every loan, and although both Caro and Diana thought her home bleakly furnished, she had a few valuable things. A pair of superb Chinese lacquer cabinets, several Persian rugs, her writing table, some silver.

It was torture for her to speak, torture for Willy to listen. When he spoke he sounded just as hoarse and choked up as she did.

"You know me. You can trust me, Miss Deb."

"I always did, Willy."

"Yes. We allus . . . got along all right."

He tried—and failed—to reckon the span of years.

"But you'll get the better of this . . ."

"Perhaps. If not, well, you know, Willy."

"I'll see to it."

She said, "Thank you, Willy," and held out her hand. Afterwards when he could think better, Willy reckoned that he'd loved her for thirty years; and they parted with the kind of handshake that men use to seal a bargain.

"Forty-four does seem so young to die," Caroline said, weeping bitterly.

Diana agreed, but felt bound to add dutifully that Everard had died at an even younger age. She had taken so easily to widowhood that convention demanded some extra show of grief as a form of appeasement to some undefined kind of guilt. Even the silver frame around the picture of Everard and his tiger was replaced by a black velvet one. After a time Caro, who was fundamentally kind, said, "Really, Di does carry this to extremes; you can't even mention the weather but she'll drag Everard into it and say that he liked or loathed this kind of day. It's morbid."

The only aspect of her widowed state about which Diana was reticent was the financial one. In India Everard had been successful, earned, by English standards, large sums of money; made her a useful allowance. But his provisions for the future were completely inadequate; hardly anything saved and only a miserably small life-insurance. But for Deb's generosity Melville could not have continued at Eton or hoped to go to Cambridge. But, of course, one could always say that Everard had been cut off in his prime. One could always say that one could just manage, and proceed to do, remembering that odious Mr van Haagen who, years ago, had read in her cards that she would never have much money. One curious quirk of fortune befell her which Mr van Haagen had not foreseen and that was the marriage of Belle to Richard Walford. Old enough to be her father, everybody said with truth. Indeed, except for the arrival of Everard Spicer in Baildon, and Diana's falling in love with him, Richard might well have been the father of Diana's children. As it was, middle-aged, well-to-do, a confirmed bachelor, Richard, across a crowded concert room, had seen Diana's daughter, so like her mother, and felt his blood run hot again. And this time nobody should be given time to intervene. "Pressing his suit with a red-hot iron," was Caro's comment on that whirlwind courtship.

Edward continued to enjoy, in a way, the company of the butterfly he had caged, but by stages too small to be measured he had transferred his attention and his hopes to Daphne, his daughter. All hope of making anything out of Noel had faded. He was idle, just about literate and no more; at the Academy Miss Pakefield had regretted that he was not more like his father; at the Grammar School to which he was presently transferred, he was frequently subject to the cane—not as often, however, as his behaviour warranted. He had such charm, such an engaging manner. Really, the exasperated and conscientious Headmaster thought; it is like beating a roe deer because it is not an ox.

Edward was even more realistic. Bitterly disappointed in his son, he said, "The only future I can see for him is a salesman. He could sell hot soup in Hell." Eventually, using his influence, Edward found a place for his son, selling medical supplies and equipment; quite respectable, and in a way worthy. Edward himself had always tried to keep up to date, but there were, he knew, doctors in outlying places who still used wooden stethoscopes, and if they had ever used chloroform had splashed it on lumps of cotton wadding in an uncontrolled, dangerous way.

Cheerfully, jauntily, Noel set out on his rounds. He wasn't selling hot soup in Hell. He was selling, not only new instruments, new ways of packaging pills and potions, but himself, Noel Taylor. In almost no time at all he had his own business. Doing well.

For Daphne the path was far less easy. She had always been clever; she had always known what she wanted to do. "I want to be a doctor like you, Papa."

"Honey, you can't."

"Why not?"

Why not? Could you say to an earnest, studious girl, fired by a worthy ambition—Because you are a girl? Such an answer, unfair in any case, was rendered more so when Edward thought of his stepmother-in-law who had defied all the rules about what a woman could or could not do, braved the Corn Exchange and cattle markets and Cattle Shows, made a success, without—and this was a vital point—without ever sacrificing her femininity. Even when she drank whisky.

"I see no reason why not," Edward said. "But a lot of other people will. However, we can but try."

So he committed himself to the long, uphill, discouraging struggle. But a well-rewarded one.

When George Thorley was forty he married, because after all a man must have a son to succeed him. He chose well, a pretty, plump girl, one of the many who had been trotted out for his approval. Her father was a hearty, coarse cattle dealer who had prospered and could afford, without robbing his son, to dower his daughter with two thousand pounds, upon which he was determined George should never lay a finger. He liked him, most people did, but he did not regard him as financially sound; too many ups and downs had occurred since that game old girl, Mrs Thorley, died. So Amelia was to have the interest on the money, which should ensure her of moderate comfort whatever happened.

Since Amelia was eighteen and George over forty—and living a remarkably dangerous life, hunting and steeple-chasing, always, however, getting off lightly, his nose broken once and his collar bone twice, it was odds on that Amelia would live longer. So when she was a widow the whole sum was to be hers. In the unlikely, unthinkable event of her dying first, the money was to revert to her father, or her brother. Amelia's mother, with whom every major action was discussed, ventured a protest.

"What about 'Melia's children?"

"They'll be his. He can do the providing. Steady him down a bit to be responsible."

Nothing steadied down George Thorley, least of all his devoted, admiring wife, who thought—as her father did—

that George had shown her great honour in choosing her.

The marriage was happy enough. Amelia had none of the out-of-this-world fairy quality of his first lost love, none of the style or wit of his mother, but she was a good audience, and a good housekeeper. She would probably have proved to be a good mother too, but she died in childbed.

George's son did not admire, emulate, or even like his father, and George found it hard to be fond of the stolid, solemn boy, so plodding, so penny-pinching, so *dull*.

Many people—growing fewer as the years went on, did remember George Thorley for his generosity, his lavish hospitality, his infectious high spirits, above all for his sportsmanship; he rode—and won—his last race when he was seventy-one and hunted until he broke his neck, surely the most suitable death and the one he would have chosen. But to his son he was an extravagant, irresponsible show-off who had damned near ruined Gad's and left behind a pile of debts, all of which were paid. By the son who never had a good word to say about him.

Part
2

Bob and I and our two boys, John and Tony, lived happily enough through our first dark winter at Gad's. I say happily enough, which is a qualified statement, because the family never seemed complete without Alice. Heap the fire, draw the curtains, set the table and listen to the wind howling and think—They're all in, thank God, and immediately I remembered that Alice was not with us. She was safe enough, happy enough and in good health; but she was with her grandmother, in Baildon, not here, part of the family, as she should have been.

Bob, busy with the perfecting of his design for his sugar-lifting machine, thought, or chose to think, that Alice was with his mother to be company for her, and I did not dream of telling him the truth. Poor man, he had enough to contend with, the flaccid left arm and leg, the still unreliable speech that his accident had inflicted upon him. It would have been cruel as well as ridiculous to say Alice was scared to death of something in this house.

John had known—actually before I did—that Alice was

scared to go upstairs alone, even in broad daylight; but he was only eleven and completely engrossed in school and what were called extra-mural activities. He'd probably forgotten. I remembered; and I knew, because I had experienced it, that something *was* slightly wrong with the attic floor. I'd felt it in October when I was storing apples; something that I can only describe as despair, ultimate hopelessness. Not fear. Alice, not yet nine, could hardly have felt despair, that feeling of the utter futility of everything, so in her case it had been fear. She had confided in her grandmother, who from the first had sensed something wrong in the apparently ideal, welcoming, and extremely cheap house. Ella, my mother-in-law, had called it Evil, had understood Alice better than I did, and whisked her away.

I would have avoided, had it been possible, that attic floor, but it was impossible. I was trying to make—making—a precarious living for us all, by selling what Gad's produced, and the stored apples and pears were an asset. I had to mount that last, twisting stairway, brace myself, shut my mind, concentrate upon what I was doing. Is this apple spotted? Has this pear rotted inwardly? Quick, be quick; put anything however defective into one basket, the sound, saleable fruit into the other and hurry down, for this is dangerous ground.

Who coined the phrase, Something nasty in the woodshed? It had passed into common usage; a kind of joke. Well, with me it was something wrong with the attic floor in the house that had been our life-raft.

Whatever it was seemed to be contained there, that is for me; the rest of the house was all right.

It was coming round to Christmas again and I began to wonder whether Ella and Alice could be coaxed into spending it with us. Ella was always such a stickler for family get-togethers at Christmas—it was in fact her insistence that I and the children should spend Christmas with her in Baildon instead of, as I had planned, with Bob in Santa Barbara which had saved us from being involved in the bomb outrage which had crippled Bob.

266

Ella's response to my suggestion was an unequivocal No.

"I'm sorry, Jill. Naturally I want us to be together at Christmas, but not in that house! Quite apart from my own feelings, it would be most unwise for Alice ever to enter it again. It would revive all her fears and set her back. You must come here."

I said—and I knew that it sounded fatuous,

"But Mr Thorley has promised me a turkey."

"And what is to prevent your bringing it here?"

Nothing that I could think of on the spur of the moment. John would grouse, I knew; he'd never really fitted into Ella's small elegant house. In order to help to pay for Bob's expensive treatment at a place called Everton, Ella had gallantly sold her valuable china, but a great deal remained, the worthless things, but pretty and cherished. A growing boy, all feet and elbows, was not at ease in such surroundings and sometimes the very effort to be careful made him seem clumsier than usual. And Tony, emerging from the toddler stage, was just naturally clumsy.

I had no choice, however.

Ella said, when I had conceded,

"I don't think you realised how near Alice was to a complete nervous breakdown. As I have said before, Bob is incapable of believing anything that can't be measured on a slide rule. And you—frankly I don't think you are very different in some respects. Had you been you would never have gone to live in that horrible house."

I remembered how, after one visit of inspection, on a summer afternoon she had denounced it; and then confounded me by offering to sell her pretty doll's house, add her resources to our meagre ones and set up house with us somewhere else.

"It hasn't served us too badly," I said. I thought of all I wrenched out of Gad's garden, of the infinite kindness shown us by the former owner, George Thorley. I also thought about Ella, so staunch in our time of trouble, and how curious it was to be able to admire, esteem, like, even love a person, and yet find hardly an inch of common ground.

Ella said, "Did you ever see the drawings which Alice

produced when she was living at Gad's?"

"Her Art Teacher once told me that her style had changed. And then recovered. But, no, I never saw any that could be called—peculiar."

"Well, I did. Towards the end of each term, drawings not wanted for the Open Day are brought home. Alice brought some of hers. I burned them. They were *so* horrible."

"In what way?"

As so often happened in my mother-in-law's presence, I felt rebuked, without any words. No doubt during that brief period when Alice lived at Gad's she had made drawings under my very eye, but God! I'd had other things to think of at the time. And when her Art Teacher had used the word *macabre* and spoken of imps and hobgoblins, I'd called it a phase. And after Alice had gone to stay with Ella, I'd had a message, saying that I had been right, the phase had ended and Alice was now drawing in her old, promising way. End-of-term, Open Day, exhibitions had confirmed this.

Now I felt that I had been very much remiss, having to ask Ella in what way my own daughter's drawings had been, for a short time, so horrible, so macabre.

"It is very difficult to explain," Ella said. "As you know she paints flowers quite beautifully, but many of those she did at that time had horrid, leering faces in their centres. There were other things, too; distortions—a goat with four horns, for example. . . . Very *nasty!*"

There again one could not quite dismiss Ella's judgement, for she had once told me that she was sure of Elsie, her maid, because she gave her her twice-daily insulin injection, a task I should have shrunk from. There was more in Ella than met the eye. Behind the prettiness—which lasted to the end—the devotion to Bridge, to the Ladies' Luncheon Club and the Flower arrangers, there was rock. I knew. I had now and again butted my silly head against it, and I had leaned against it when the rest of the world rocked under me.

It is strange to think that in a way the Baildon Ladies' Luncheon Club should ever have affected me. I never joined it; I had no time, I had no hat—they still wore hats on occasion! And, on the whole, I dislike being talked to. If somebody has written a book called TWENTY YEARS IN TIMBUCTOO, and one can buy it in paperback, does it further inform one to listen to a repetition?

However, one evening in May—another five months of Alice lost to us—the telephone rang. The telephone was really a luxury which we could not afford, but it suited my customers to be able to ring up and know what I had to offer this week, and Bob's invention involved many calls, too. The telephone stood on his worktable and it was rather clever of Ella to have chosen supper time, when he would not be near it, and I, being more agile, would reach it first. She sounded excited, but of course in a controlled way; except when she cried, which she did easily, Ella was always controlled.

"Jill! Our lecturer at luncheon today was a medium. Mrs Catherwood. Have you ever heard of her?"

"No. Should I have done?"

"Perhaps not. But she is very famous. And I think *completely* sincere. As you know, we cannot afford high fees." Some of Ella's talk was like that; there was a certain logic, but you had to work it out. In this case it meant that she considered Mrs Catherwood sincere because she was unmercenary enough to come and lecture Baildon Ladies' Luncheon Club for five guineas, plus expenses.

I said, "Yes?"

"Well, as you know, dear, I am inclined to be sceptical in these matters, but she was very convincing. *And* since she is staying with Mrs Gordon overnight and a few of us went on to tea there, I seized the opportunity of talking to her about your house. She was immensely interested and would like to see it."

"You mean in a professional capacity?"

"Yes. But, dear, Bob must not know that. You know how he would jeer. You must just say that she is a person who is interested in old houses."

"He might believe that—though there are quite a number about. But what does she intend to *do*, Ella? Hold a séance? Go into a trance? I mean even Bob might notice if she did."

"Dear, you are completely out of date. Nothing like that. Mrs Catherwood is extra-sensitive, but unlike most of us she can *interpret* what she feels."

I thought of what I had felt that October afternoon outside the attic, which had been locked for so many years and which George Thorley had broken open at my request. Let her interpret *that*, I thought.

"All right. When?"

"Well, if entirely convenient to you, tomorrow morning. She has another speaking engagement in Bywater in the afternoon. She drives herself. May I tell her, then, about half-past ten?"

Little knowing what I was letting myself in for, I said yes. I then offered Ella's explanation of Mrs Catherwood to Bob, who accepted it placidly.

Maybe I was out of date. To me the word "medium" called up a woman, fairly old, rather fat and dressed in black, so Mrs Catherwood was a surprise to me. At most thirty-five, very slim, almost, not quite pretty. She wore a very smart trouser suit of a pleasing shade of green, just right with her hair, auburn and close-cropped. You had to be very close to her to see what was different: her eyes. They were greenish and the pupils were mere pinpoints. I thought instantly: Drugs! Not that I knew all that much about them either.

Drugged or not, she drove well; and she had a good car to drive. A Jansen, very enviable!

I had been looking out for her, and though I did not say, Mrs Catherwood, I presume, I did understand in a flash how Stanley felt when he made that famous remark to Livingstone.

"It was very good of you to let me come, Mrs Spender," she said, as soon as we had greeted each other. "I'm always anxious to learn."

Learn what, I wondered.

She entered the house briskly; she might have been come to read a meter. Halfway across the hall she paused and seemed to sniff the air, as I had done when I first entered this house. But I was sniffing for evidence of damp and decay. What was her quarry? She gave a tiny nod of satisfaction, looked at the stairs, hesitated and asked,

"You have another stairway?"

I led her into the kitchen and indicated the back stairs.

"Thank you. Do you mind if I go alone? Some concentration is demanded."

"Help yourself," I said. "Would you like coffee—afterwards?"

She said rather cryptically, "Thanks. I may need it."

She was gone a long time. The coffee was ready, and when the clock on the landing struck eleven I poured a cup and took it through to Bob, who came out of his trance—work-induced—just long enough to thank me. I then went back and began making preparations for lunch, peeling potatoes and mincing cold meat for a shepherd's pie.

When she did appear, Mrs Catherwood looked paler and was wiping her palms on her handkerchief.

Tony had come in for milk and biscuits and was still there. He was now so fully mobile, able to open doors and mount stairs, that I was used to his appearances and disappearances, and to his presence. I lifted the coffee pot and ushered Mrs Catherwood into the living room, where I had the cups and the biscuits ready. She'd lost all her briskness and sat down on the sunny window seat as though exhausted. I thought I saw her shiver.

She said, "*Pas devant l'enfant.*"

Tony said, loud and clear, "Isn't she *ugly*?"

She said, "It *is* contagious!" and I said,

"Have another biscuit, Tony, and then go and feed the hens. The crusts are on the dresser."

"You must be careful of *him*, too, Mrs Spencer. He may be sensitive, too. Your daughter certainly is; and your mother-in-law." She drank some coffee and shivered. This time I was sure.

"Would you like a whisky?" I recalled how I had felt after my experience on the attic floor, and how I had thought about how helpful a good whisky would be. I had not taken it, and so far as I knew the half bottle most carefully and tactfully brought by Ella on the day when she came to lunch—and took Alice away—was still there on the top shelf of the larder.

"No, thank you. That is another thing I must warn you of. Amongst all the many impressions, there is a distinct tang of alcoholism. Compulsive drinking. Until this place is purged, nobody should drink in this house."

That, at least, was original, something Ella could hardly have primed her with. I must admit that in my mind I still half suspected some kind of collusion; Ella saying that she sensed something dreadful and that Alice was afraid, and Mrs Catherwood latching on to it; something else to write about, something else to go hawking round to Ladies' Luncheons.

"Alcoholism is not much of a risk here," I said. "My husband's condition allows him to drink hardly at all. And I'm hardly likely . . . if only because of the cost."

"I know. But circumstances change." From one of her jacket pockets she produced one of those very expensive cigarette cases with a lighter in the lid.

"I'm sorry," I said. "I have some, somewhere."

"Never mind. Have one of these. . . . Now, I have no wish to alarm you, only to help, if I can. And you must not dismiss this as nonsense, Mrs Spender. I am not a novice. I have on more than one occasion helped in police investigations—some of a grisly nature, but physical. This is different, more elemental. I fully realise that what I am about to say may sound ridiculous, but it is there in that attic; devil worship, demoniac possession, ritual slaughter and suicide, that final act of despair. An elemental took over and is still there, evil and unappeased. Hungering for new victims."

She smoked, frowning, for several seconds. Then, in a more composed manner she went on,

"I have a feeling that you think that I am merely repeating—with some elaboration—what your mother-in-law told me. That is not so. She told me that she had felt something evil, she used the expression, "almost overcome," so that she hurried away. She also said that your daughter was always afraid in this house, and began to draw in a style different from her own. I was interested and decided to expose myself. I am not a crank. After all, people vary in their ability to bear pain; hearing varies, so does sight. I just happen to be super-sensitive to something, call it atmosphere if you like; and I assure you I know more about that attic, indeed about the whole house, than your mother-in-law could possibly know. I very much doubt if what I know can ever be checked; it all happened a long time ago. But the subject, the victim, was young—and a creative artist. Such people are extremely vulnerable. I don't suppose that it has ever occurred to you, but think how many creative people go mad, commit suicide or become debauched in some way. The old adage said that Satan found work for idle hands to do. He may. I don't know. I do know that he prefers to use busy ones, creative ones. Who wants to recruit a lot of layabouts? I see that my use of the word Satan embarrasses you, Mrs Spender. Why?"

"I wasn't aware that I was embarrassed. If I seem so, it may be because, well, I think it too personal. Like . . . like calling a destructive hurricane Emily."

For the first time she looked at me with something approaching approval.

"We'll stick to abstractions then. Evil came into this house, innocently invited, by a young girl, an artist. It affected what I gather was a hitherto happy family. It destroyed her. It could destroy again. That is why I say that your daughter should not come home—and that the little boy is at risk—until the place is exorcised."

"Oh, come! That is too mediaeval."

"Evil—and Good are timeless, Mrs Spender."

"Besides, if one can believe all one hears, exorcism can do more harm than good."

"True. The ritual may be improperly performed. Or again it may be performed by somebody who is not strong enough to bear the confrontation. Remember, your mother-in-law spoke of being almost overcome. And even for me, veteran that I am, it was a disagreeable experience. As, I think, it once was for you."

Now how could she know that? I had never breathed a word to anyone about that October afternoon.

I suppose I gaped. Then I hastened to defend myself—not always a wise thing to do.

"I happened to be feeling low, both in mind and body. My back was aching, I'd been overworking; prospects were not too good. And I had a very personal problem."

"I know. *You* left an imprint there, too. But consider; suppose at that moment the Dev . . . the Force of Evil, I mean . . . had presented itself, wearing a very attractive disguise, offering comfort and security, and you had been a weak character. What then?"

"Complete chaos."

"There you are. You were strong enough to resist. I would hazard a guess that you had a strongly religious background, as a child."

"You would be right."

"Well." She looked at her watch. "I have an engagement. I've done what I could, and I do beg you to think seriously about it."

"I will."

She gave me a kind of grin. "Your mother-in-law, who, incidentally, is extremely fond of you said you were incorrigibly stubborn. Try not to be for the sake of the children."

We went out together to the front of the house, where her car stood. A race horse of a car. I thought of my poor, ailing old station wagon.

She caught that in a flash and said, "Window-dressing! I'm most anxious that people shouldn't think I'm *selling* whatever gift I have. Why should I? My father left me a fortune. Easily disposed of with things as they are. But window-dressing comes naturally to me. I was born a Hawksley!"

I knew the world-famous store; I had even been inside it, once. In the good days when Bob was managing a beet-sugar factory at Scunwick, and doing well. But with his ambitions unsatisfied, so he'd joined the brain-drain, and come back a wreck.

Mrs Catherwood stuck out her hand.

"I don't need to tell you to be brave—you are that. Be sensible, though, and hopeful. Much awaits you!"

This was one of the moments when I was aware of a lack. In the old days Bob and I could discuss anything; we often argued—no holds barred. Now I had to be very careful. One of the many doctors who had helped to put him together again had warned me that he must not be subject to any kind of stress. Not that Bob, even now, would worry about living in a haunted house; as his mother said, he would jeer; but he would be annoyed with her and with me, and with Mrs Catherwood. He'd call us a gaggle of silly, superstitious old women. And anger, after all, is a form of stress. Also he was quite capable of saying that if Alice had gone to Baildon because of such rank tomfoolery, she'd better come home at once and learn some sense. That just would not do. Offhand as I may have seemed to Mrs Catherwood, incorrigibly stubborn as I might appear to my mother-in-law, I knew that there was something wrong on that attic floor. I wanted to talk about it. I may give the impression of being strong and brave, etc, etc, but I am not. Actually I'm weak-minded; on almost every subject under the sun I dwell in a halfway house. Even when I appear to be brave it is often because I'm scared not to be.

I said, "Tony, you were very rude to that visitor." He was only three, but manners must be inculcated early. And perhaps . . . Oh, let's swallow the whole dose, I thought; believe that she had actually met Evil head on, believe that it was, as she called it, contagious, and the child had seen more than I had. "It is rude to call people ugly."

"But she was. Just like Mr Thorley's dog. The cross one."

I knew which one he meant. The Thorleys had no children. I think that if they had had, George with his strong sense of tradition would have put up more of a fight against his wife's dislike of Gad's and her determination to have a modern house. But they had no children, so they lavished a lot of affection on their dogs. By that I do not mean that people who have children and love them cannot love their dogs, too. But there was something a little extravagant about Mrs Thorley's poodle, which had bows on its head, and regular beauty-parlour appointments, and could distinguish between plaice and haddock. George's cross dog was the most unfriendly, unrewarding animal I ever met. A real rogue with far more than the first allowed bite on his scoreboard. He tolerated his master, bullied two amiable spaniels and snarled at everybody.

I said, "Darling, how could that nice lady look like Mr Thorley's cross dog?"

"She did. She looked like Mr Thorley's cross dog. Like this."

My three-year-old wrinkled his little snub nose, drew back his upper lip, snarled. And then laughed.

"So I said she was ugly. And she was."

"But it was rude to say so."

"Must I say I'm sorry?"

"You can't. She's gone away."

"I'm glad. She looked just like Mr Thorley's cross dog. . . ."

Ella rang that evening, again as we were just sitting down to supper.

"Well?"

"She came," I said. "And she agrees with you."

There was a small silence, and then Ella said,

"Then, my dear, something must be done about it."

"What?"

"My offer still stands. You know, I was so against that house from the first. Sell it. I'll sell mine and we'll find somewhere where we can all live together. Not in each other's pockets, but together. I believe the Old Rectory at Muchanger is for sale."

I could hear my own weak voice.

"But, Ella, it is such a good garden. And I've worked so hard."

So I had; I'd weathered the winter with cabbages in the open, lettuces under cloches. I'd grown new potatoes in the mended-up greenhouse and had them for sale at Easter. And now, at the end of almost of a year at Gad's, I should have within a month all the produce of the old asparagus bed, and, if bloom promised anything, masses of strawberries.

Must I forgo it all? Move away? Begin all over again. Just because of something, still not truly defined, in one small part of this house.

And there were other things to think of. George Thorley had only sold Gad's to us because he feared compulsory purchase, or squatters. Most of the furniture in the place belonged there; stuff he'd taken away and stored in the loft down at Park, and so gladly given—or lent us—on permanent loan, as with museums. We couldn't take that away with us.

"And besides," I said, "Bob is so happy here. No, Ella. It is most kind, and I do appreciate it. But I think we must stick it out."

"You're being unfair to Alice."

"I know." And probably to Tony too. There must be some reason why a perfectly normal young woman, not pretty, but far from ugly, should seem to him to resemble a snarling dog. God! What a muddle.

My first-born appeared in the doorway carrying a bowl of soup with exaggerated care. He said in what he considered a tactfully low voice,

"I thought you'd better have this before it was cold."

I managed a smile of thanks as Ella said,

"Jill, *do* think about it."

"I will. I'm grateful, Ella. Good night."

John said, "I knew it was a female. How they do natter! Now Terry and I can say all we have to say in half a minute flat."

"That's sex discrimination, dear boy. You'll end in jail!"

I'd seldom felt less like cracking a joke, however mild.

I'd washed up and was just putting things back on the dresser when George Thorley walked in. He often did. The machine upon whose design Bob was working owed a great deal to George's practical suggestions and they enjoyed talking about it. Often, too often, he'd bring gifts, stuff from his dairy, toys for Tony—that I found pathetic in a man who should have had children of his own, some contribution towards whatever John's latest hobby was. There never was a more generous man.

"It's such a nice evening," he said, "and this brute needed a walk." The cross dog, inaptly named in puppyhood, Chum, had defeated his own purpose in life; he'd been bred as a guard dog, but a dog so congenitally ferocious as to attack everybody, postmen, legitimate callers, regular workpeople, is no guard at all, and Chum spent most of his time in a wire enclosure, big enough for an elephant. Even on his walks he had to be on a lead, the end of which George now attached to the dresser leg, as usual. As usual I offered a bowl of water, ungraciously received.

"Nobody ever got himself lumbered with such a beast," George said. "I ought to have him put down, but I can't bring myself to it."

I said, "I think Bob went back to his workroom. Do go through."

I believe Catholics, absolved, are exhorted to avoid the occasion for sin, and George Thorley and I, without a word spoken, had done just that. There'd been just that one flash between us, a communication between eyes, no more, and after that absolute caution.

This evening he said, "It's you I want to have a word with."

My heart gave a painful little jump and I thought—He's heard from that engineering firm in Peterborough. They're not going to take Bob's machine after all, and I shall have to break the news, which will just about finish him. It had been the idea that despite his handicaps, he could still be useful, productive—and eventually earning—that had kept Bob going. It had allowed him to ignore the fact that physically he had not improved quite as much as the optimists had predicted.

It was not that at all.

When we were seated, opposite each other by the kitchen table, George said,

"I've been a bit worried about you. Doris went to her

Ladies' Luncheon thing, yesterday, and then on to tea with the chosen few and then to Bridge somewhere. So I didn't hear until breakfast time this morning, and then it was market day. I came as soon as I could. . . . Did that bloody-daft woman come here and bother you?"

"Mrs Catherwood came this morning."

"And scared you? I was afraid of that. Look, you mustn't take any notice. Doris never liked Gad's; she'd say anything to decry it—it was too inconvenient to run without more help than was available; it was isolated, it was draughty. I don't have to be mealy-mouthed with you, do I? It's a well-known fact, no animal breeds in an unfavourable environment. . . . So I gave in; moved down to Park, built her that pink boot-box and hoped—with what result, you know." I knew; at our first meeting he had mentioned his childlessness in a surprisingly resigned way. "I suppose we all have to justify ourselves, and of course Doris joined in that gabble, saying the place was haunted and all that rot. I don't often allow myself to get irked by Doris's goings on, but this morning I was damned annoyed. She shouldn't have done that. . . . There's some excuse for your mother-in-law, she's old and entitled to her fancies, and the daft creature, I suppose, makes a living out of quackery. Doris shouldn't have joined in."

Bob once said of me that in conservative company I turned bright red, in the company of those with socialist views, dark blue; he said I had an anti-chameleon complex. It went to work now.

"I'm not so sure," I said. And suddenly there I was, pouring it all out: Ella's experience, my own, all about Alice and Mrs Catherwood, who certainly was not a quack out to make a living. I cracked up entirely. I actually cried. George got up and came round the table and held me and made soothing sounds. Just what I needed, of course, strong supporting arms and a solid shoulder to cry on.

Absolutely disgusting!

Finally I pulled myself together sufficiently to say, "Go and talk to Bob. I'm all right. I shall manage. It was just . . . everything piled up."

"I know."

He did understand; he went to see Bob, having given me a final assurance that everything would be all right.

I was too utterly exhausted even to wonder how.

My grandmother—Mrs Catherwood had guessed, or sensed, rightly, about my childhood background—had often said that self-pity was the most destructive emotion. All afflictions, she held, were put upon us either by God, and therefore to be accepted with patience and humility, or brought upon us by our own foolishness, and therefore to be accepted with patience and humility and a determination to do better in future. So self-pity was despicable. I knew that and was indulging in it nonetheless. It seemed to me that from the moment Bob had decided to take that very inviting post in Santa Barbara, I'd been forced to pretend. I was against his going, but must pretend to be agreeable; pretend I didn't mind our separation; and when we were reunited, thanks to America, I had to pretend that he was getting better every day, pretend that I believed him capable of earning a living. . . . Finding Gad's had seemed such a stroke of luck, a roomy, solid, watertight house, a garden that could be made productive. And look how that had turned out—the biggest fraud of all. Now I didn't know what to do, or what to think.

I said to myself: Snap out of it! Go tend your garden!

It was still light; the lingering end of a hot dry day. A good many things needed water. And water was handy. I had only to open the movable part of the chestnut fencing—Ella's gift to prevent Tony falling into the moat—and dip up bucketsful. Bob said that once he had his present job off his hands he'd rig up some less primitive way of irrigation.

I dipped water and sloshed and my back began to ache; a reminder of my moment of despair outside that attic door when I'd seen myself hopelessly disabled . . . That was back in October, and this was May, and here I was, still going strong, except for moments like this. I tried to cheer myself up; strawberries already formed; little pods on the peas, an abundance of asparagus, potatoes doing well. . . .

I closed the gateway in the fencing and turned and there

was George Thorley, huge in the glimmering dusk.

He said, "If I've told you once I've told you a dozen times . . . You have only to say and I'll send a man up. But that's not what I came to say. I've been raking in my mind. I was so inattentive, your husband thought I had market-day hangover. But I was putting bits and pieces together in my mind and I'm certain—so far as anybody can be about the long ago, that your Mrs Cather-whoever had it wrong. You remember, I told you once that Gad's had gone straight from father to son? It was a byword. Thorleys didn't breed girls—except once. I never knew my rascally old grandfather, and my father hated him because he damned near ruined the place, but he talked about him sometimes. *He* did have some sisters, at least two sisters and two half sisters—my great-grandmother had two of her own, so that makes four, and then, years younger, my grandfather. And adding this and that, all the girls are accounted for. So far as I can put it together there never was a girl here who fits in with that load of rubbish. According to my father, all his aunts made decent marriages. . . . My father never knew them; my grandfather lived to a good age, and my father couldn't marry till he was out of the way. But one of them lived down at Park—the old house—for a bit. I believe she wrote a few books. One of them married the doctor at Baildon. Another married a solicitor. And the other, the youngest, I think, went to India and died young. So you see there couldn't have been anything like the goings-on that crank described, could there?"

I could see that he was desperately anxious to reassure me, so did not say what I thought, which was the goings-on might have occurred at some much earlier time, before the byword of Thorleys only breeding boys had become established.

I said, "Yes. That sounds reasonable. And of course Mrs Catherwood's story was rather extreme. I was silly to let it upset me."

"If you ask me, you're in state where you could get upset over a broken plate. I've been thinking about that, too. In future I'm going send a man up every day for a couple of hours, whether you like it or not."

The gable end which contained the attics jutted out over the garden. Without thinking I looked out and saw something move behind the bars of the window. Vague, pale grey, a face, but not human. So now, I thought, you're beginning to *see* things. I looked away, screwed my eyes shut, then looked back. It was still there.

"Look!"

"My damned dog!" George said. "He must have chewed through his lead."

He was right. Chum, having freed himself and found no other exit open to him, had galloped upstairs, and up and up. And Mrs Catherwood must have left *that* door open.

On Saturday I went into Baildon, taking some of cloche-grown stuff, and some flowering sprays from the shrubs which grew under the walnut tree, and some eggs. I did some shopping and then went to Ella's, with a dozen of the eggs and the very choicest of the sprays. Alice greeted me with the news that Gran was having a day in bed, but would like to see me.

Ella, though not far short of seventy—she was cagey about her age—had, for as long I had known her, enjoyed very good health, despite, or perhaps because of her fragile, Dresden china appearance. Nobody expected her to make any physical exertion or venture forth in bad weather.

Her bedroom—and never forget that when we were homeless, she had given it over to Bob and me because it was the largest in the house—was all pink and white and blue, except for a great bunch of dark red carnations, sent, I knew, by Ella's long-standing, absolutely platonic Boy Friend, Colonel Murray-Smith. Ella looked very pretty, but pale.

"It's nothing," she said. "I think I overdid things. Tuesday was a very busy day—as you know. On Wednesday I went to a Coffee Morning in aid of Oxfam. On Thursday there was a meeting of the Flower Club about the June display in St Mary's. Yesterday I felt quite exhausted. So today I thought I'd be lazy."

"Have you had the doctor?"

"My dear, what could he do? I'm beginning to suffer

from a very common complaint. Anno Domini. For which, so far, nobody has found a cure. I must resign myself."

Something inside me fell away as I imagined Anno Domini catching up and devouring Ella. I admired her. I was grateful to her, I loved without liking her, which sounds a contradiction of terms, but can be fact.

Almost instantly there was an example of what annoyed me about her. I'd given my flowering boughs to Alice and said, "Put them in water," and now Alice came in with the vase, carrying it with that same care as John had shown, bringing me my cooling soup.

Ella said, "Thank you, darling. Is the vase quite dry?"

"Yes, Gran. I wiped it. Shall I put it on the dressing-table?"

To this trivial problem Ella gave concentrated attention and then said,

"I think not. On the chest-of-drawers."

It was probably this meticulous attention to detail which had transmitted itself to Bob and made him such a good engineer. It should not have grated on my nerves, but it did.

When Alice had gone, Ella said,

"Well, have you thought about it?"

"I have indeed. All the time."

"So has Mrs Catherwood. In fact I had a letter from her this morning."

Ella's mail, brought to her bedside, was not just scattered, helter-skelter; it was in a neat pile, under a very pretty paperweight, on her bedside table. Before I could move to reach it, Ella leaned over, slid the wanted letter out neatly. It had been neatly opened, too. None of this hasty ripping-open-with-the-thumb.

"She says that she was extremely perturbed, and having thought it over, sees the only solution in exorcism. Of course you know what that is."

"In a vague way. I mean I've read about it."

"Well, I intend to consult Canon Lauder—with your permission, of course."

"Oh, I'd agree to anything, so long as it didn't make things worse . . . Or upset Bob. I managed to pass Mrs Catherwood over as a woman interested in old houses. Bob didn't even see her. But a religious ritual . . . that might be more difficult. Bob would get angry, and anger is bad for him."

"I think we may rely upon Canon Lauder to be tactful. The point is, my dear . . . I cannot be expected to last forever. When I go, sooner or later, Elsie will be obliged to go into a geriatric place where she can be given her injections. And where would that leave Alice? With no home but that horrible house to which you are so stubbornly attached and in which she lived in complete terror."

That was indeed a cogent question, but I let it go. I was overcome for a moment, by the prospect of life without Ella. In my limited firmament she had been a fixed star for so long. She remembered birthdays and any other kind of anniversary. . . . She was brave and she was good. Pernicketty, conventional, a bit snobbish, she could be exasperating, particularly to anyone like me, but she'd leave a terrible gap. So of course I said, in the wrong tone of voice.

"Oh, for Heaven's sake, Ella, don't talk about dying."

One's perspective changes with age; when I was eighteen and my grandmother nearing eighty, I was sad, I felt bereaved, but she seemed—and had seemed to me for a long time—so old. It had seemed natural that she should die. And of course, while I haunted that hospital in Miami where Bob lay in a deathlike coma, I'd been prepared for the worst every moment. This was somehow different.

"I merely mentioned the fact that I am only mortal, dear, and that we have Alice's future to consider."

"I know. I promise you, I will. And I'll come in tomorrow and bring Bob."

"That would be very nice."

Downstairs I said to Elsie that I thought a visit from Doctor Taylor might do no harm. Elsie's face set like concrete.

"Mrs Spender want the doctor she'll say so. Mrs Spender say she don't want him, I go by what she say."

"Of course." But outside I looked at my watch. Just on eleven. I might catch him. His house, with surgery attached, was only on the other side of the square. Going towards it, needing to distract my mind, I thought what a triumph of mind over matter, his being called Doctor Taylor represented. His grandmother had run Elizabeth Garrett Anderson pretty close in the race to force the recognition of women as doctors. She had qualified; then she married, a man named Bennett, and was known, during her lifetime, as Doctor Taylor Bennett. But the people of Baildon didn't take kindly to the name. They'd known her father, possibly even her grandfather. To them the name Taylor was practically synonymous with the word doctor; so her son was Doctor Taylor, the Bennett dropped into obscurity.

Her grandson, the current Doctor Taylor, was a thin, rather harrassed-looking man who I had met briefly as a fellow member of the Parent-Teacher Association. Doubting whether he would remember me, I said,

"I'm Mrs Spender."

"I know. What is it?" What did I want, bursting in on him, just as he was arranging papers and preparing to close his surgery and start a round of urgent house calls?

"My mother-in-law, Mrs Spender," I pointed towards Ella's house, "doesn't seem well. But she didn't want to bother you, so I thought . . ."

"You'd do the bothering?" For a second his worried face changed contour and took on a mischievous monkeyish look, almost immediately banished. "I didn't mean that, Mrs Spender. It's no bother. Is she in pain?"

"I don't think so. No. At least she didn't say. She said she was tired and having a day in bed. But I thought she looked pale. So I wondered . . ."

"There is nothing I can do. Except of course relieve pain, should it occur. She has a valvular lesion, of long standing. She has lived with it for years and been very sensible; and if she is now resting and not in pain . . . There is nothing I can do. But . . ." He scribbled a note on one of his papers. "I'll try to look in, later in the day. . . ."

He was a busy, an overworked man; hurried meals and disturbed nights showed in his face and his manner. I was not old yet, but I could just remember more leisurely days. On his paper-cluttered desk the telephone gave its raucous call. He snatched the receiver up and said, "Speaking!... Yes!... Yes!... No! On no account! I'll come right away."

Next morning I drove Bob in to see his mother. John, who had always been a sensible, reliable boy, was now quite capable of seeing that Tony came to no damage; and of switching on the oven at a given time.

Ella was up and dressed, and looked pink and white again. Perhaps, I thought, she was always pale behind the discreet make-up and her appearance had alarmed me yesterday because I was seeing her with a bare clean face.

"A most curious thing happened yesterday evening," she said. "Doctor Taylor dropped in for a glass of sherry. Most unusual for him; he is such an unsocial man. Very different from his father."

I was glad that he had been discreet enough to make his visit seem casual. He may have been a trifle out of line in telling me what ailed her, but perhaps he was issuing a warning.

Was Canon Lauder's visit that morning similarly contrived? He'd never seen Bob or me, for he'd come to St Mary's after we moved to Gad's. I knew that Ella liked him and did not deplore, as some people did, his mild attempt to shift St Mary's towards a higher form of Anglicanism. Ella said she thought Matins and Evensong sounded nicer than Morning and Evening Service and she approved of the proliferation of candles. Also, of course, he played Bridge.

I suspected that she had talked to him on the telephone the previous evening, for he subjected Bob and me—especially me—to very close scrutiny. His rosy, well-fleshed face gave him an appearance of benevolence contradicted by his eyes, a cold grey in colour, rather small, very shrewd. Did he see in me a rather hysterical woman who had been listening to some old wives' tales? And worrying her mother-in-law.

Alice came back just in time to say Goodbye to us. She had attended Matins, but had stayed to help arrange the Lady Chapel for some meeting to be held in the afternoon.

"Gran, your flowers looked lovely."

Ella said, rather hastily, to me, "I sent the carnations, dear. They were so very *red!*"

The year moved on, into a hay-scented June. A busy season for most people. George Thorley had been as good as his word and every morning a very amiable, very idle young man whom at first sight I had mistaken for a girl— not only on account of the long beautiful hair, but with beads, with several bracelets—came up, dipped some buckets of water, planted main-crop potatoes, runner beans, tomatoes. I gathered strawberries and cut asparagus, and lettuces and radishes, and rushed them down to the Women's Institute shop and the private customers I had acquired. I was glad of the help, limited as it was, and thoroughly grateful to George Thorley, who was very busy too, with haymaking and with Agricultural Shows.

I tried to see Ella every day instead of two or three times a week, and just at this season I could do so without seeming to be watching over her; there was always something I could take from the garden. I noticed that she was cutting down on her activities slightly; playing Bridge less often in the evening, handing over some of her little offices.

"I feel, dear, that it is time for younger people to take over. I don't mean you, of course, you have your hands full, but your Mrs Thorley, for example, no children and every labour-saving device known to man. I've suggested that she should take my place in the Flower Club."

"That should please her."

All the same it was sad. Flower arranging may sound trivial, but it gave the arrangers aesthetic satisfaction, and their exhibits, as well as raising money for many a good cause, had brought beauty into a world from which it seemed to be receding every day.

"I refused another job, too," Ella said with a little laugh. "Canon Lauder asked me to organise the provision of new kneelers for St Mary's. Various designs, but all on blue grounds to give a look of uniformity. Guess whom I foisted that on to?"

"I have no idea."

"Fred Murray-Smith! I don't expect you knew that he is a devoted embroiderer."

"Wonders will never cease." Hard-bitten old ex-Indian Army officer, living in a strictly run buff and brown house, kept in meticulous condition by his ex-batman, even more hard-bitten. Towards the end of our stay with Ella—just before we found Gad's—Bob and I had dined and eaten curry so hot that it almost blew our heads off.

For at least a month, even between ourselves, Ella and I did not mention Gad's. There were times, during that busy season, when I forgot for hours on end that I lived in a haunted house. Such work-induced amnesia never lasted long, however. I would become aware of Alice's absence; I'd look at Tony and wonder.

It was Ella who broke the silence. I remember the rich ripe scent of the basket of strawberries I had brought her and which stood between us as she said,

"This business of *exorcism* is very complicated, Jill. Canon Lauder has been *most* kind, *most* sympathetic, but there are difficulties. Apparently the Anglican Church has abandoned the ritual and even the Roman Catholics have become very wary. I suppose rightly so. With them it seems, it is no longer sufficient to ask permission from a Bishop—a priest must be specialist... Not unlike getting a driving licence. But I *think* we may now be on the right track at last."

She reached out and took from her pretty little davenport, a letter. Holding it well away—most people, normally sighted all their lives, become long-sighted as age creeps on—she read it again and said,

"It all sounds very pompous and legal. First you must be investigated to make sure that there is nothing frivolous or anything pertaining to undesirable publicity. I am fully prepared to say what I know. I shall shield Alice, of course, though it will be necessary to refer to her. And I took the precaution of getting a written statement from Mrs Catherwood. That was *totally* disregarded. However, I shall bring it up again when Father... really, how badly people write! It could be Jessop or Joseph, Jessop, I think. When

288

he comes to make his preliminary investigations. And you will co-operate?"

"Of course. But it is going to be difficult with Bob." *He* mustn't be upset; *she* mustn't be upset, *thou, we, they* mustn't be upset; only *I*. I could be upset. And was.

Ella said, "I am not altogether sure whether this policy of concealment is wise. I know he would jeer, but we could bear that."

"He would get angry, Ella. There's that place on the side of his head where the exposed vein shows; it swells when he is angry."

And he was so often angered now.

"My God," he said, "if only I could get about, I'd ginger them up. Lot of lazy slobs. Here we are, June! They were interested last October; they wanted modifications, I made them. They deferred, they discussed, they keep me informed. I've worked like a slave, and what have they done? Sweet . . . damn all! June . . . and they haven't . . . even made a proto . . . type. I'll sell it . . . to the . . . Germans."

The vein swelled, and as always when he was angry his speech deteriorated. I hastened to soothe.

"Would it hasten matters if you went to Peterborough?"

"No! Fine impression . . . I should make. Shambling, stuttering. . . . They'd think . . . I couldn't design . . . a corkscrew."

Poor Bob. He'd been so marvellously confident and optimistic; hardened doctors had remarked upon what an asset his attitude was. Now because he was progressing more slowly—or not at all, and his brain-child had been, not rejected, but subject to delays, probably inevitable ones, something seemed to have seeped away. Apart from lightning flashes of temper, he'd had such a sunny nature; now it was souring. Not towards me, however. After that outburst he said,

"My poor girl. I've mucked up your life. And . . . I meant . . . so well."

I said, "Don't talk rot, darling. I'm fine. So are you. This hitch is probably due to a little jam in, I quote—Those devious and uncertain waterways known as the usual channels. It'll get unjammed and you'll make a million."

But that night, in the big old four-poster, on permanent loan from George Thorley, I woke, as though somebody had shaken me by the shoulder. And something inside my head said: *It could be that the house is having an effect on him!* The grandfather clock, also a loan, struck three.

Beside me Bob stirred and turned clumsily; with one side weak the movement was difficult.

I asked, softly, "Are you awake?"

"Yes. For a long time. Thinking. Darling... you should... quit. Divorce me. You'd... be all right then. One-parent family. Everybody'd be... bending over ... backwards to help you. And me... home for derelicts."

Pretend again! I said,

"If that's the best thought you can come up with in the middle of the night I don't think you're very inventive."

"Maybe I'm not. . . . Been thinking that... too. Maybe they've... detected... some flaw that had... escaped me."

That, coming from Bob Spender who *always* knew best, was a shattering statement. The idea that the house was affecting him lodged more firmly in my mind. It was despair, rather than terror, that I had felt outside that attic door. I longed at that moment to talk to Bob about it, tell him everything—except of course about my feeling for George Thorley, and offer Gad's as an explanation for his despondency; but somehow I couldn't do it. All I could do was give him a near-maternal kiss and assure him that everything would be all right.

However, in the morning I rang up George.

"I know you're busy with hay and the Shows, but if you could spare half an hour. Bob is getting a bit downhearted."

"Funnily enough, I was coming up this evening. I wondered if he'd like to come to the South Suffolk next Thursday. It's at Southbury this year, so he wouldn't have a tiring drive. I suppose you wouldn't care to come too?"

I excused myself.

And then, by one of those curious chances which Life does occasionally throw up, Father Jessop chose that very day to make his preliminary visit of investigation.

So far everything to do with this side of the affair had been conducted by Ella, who had also, incidentally, begun to correspond regularly with Mrs Catherwood.

"He will drive himself," Ella said. "It is no great distance. His headquarters are in Essex. I shall give him coffee—or sherry—and tell him all I know, and I shall try again to draw his attention to Mrs Catherwood's statement. He will then visit you. And, my dear, I shall *pray* for a happy outcome."

I should have to give him lunch, but at this time of year it was easy; salad stuff with hard-boiled eggs.

In appearance Father Jessop was exactly what I had expected, priestly garb, thin ascetic face; but his manner was disconcerting. A bit like a police officer sent to question someone of whom the authorities entertained the deepest suspicion—tax evasion, drug smuggling, murder. This impression was emphasised by the fact that, having shot questions at me, he wrote—in shorthand—my answers in a little book. And by another thing: he never permitted me to say much; he always cut me short, quite courteously, but firmly. "Yes, we shall come to that later." Or "If you would just answer the question, Mrs Spender."

One of the questions was: Had there been any sign of poltergeistic activity? I could only say, No. So far as I could tell nothing had been moved by any supernatural agency; nobody had been hit on the head by a flying saucepan.

Any visible or aural manifestations? I could only say that Alice had heard bumps, that I had asked her, when next she heard a bump, to call me. She never had.

Patiently and meticulously he discounted this, eliminated that, and reduced the whole thing to what Ella had felt, what I had felt, what Alice had felt—and to him feelings were not evidence.

He then came up with an ingenious explanation.

"Prior to your coming here, Mrs Spender, you lived with your mother-in-law. Did it ever occur to you that she was opposed to your move?"

"No. I should have said that exact opposite. She had

291

been obliged to give up her bedroom. . . . And three children, however well-behaved, were a disruption in that neat house. I think she welcomed the move, until she came to see this house and felt . . ."

"Yes. I know." He flipped some pages of the little book backwards.

"You saw no significance in the alternatives which she suggested?"

"You mean . . . Buying another house which we could share. Certainly, since that would have entailed great sacrifice on her part, I considered it evidence of her sincerity of feeling concerning this house."

"Which she was not invited to share?"

"Good . . . Heavens, no! Why should she be? She has a perfectly good house of her own. Near the shops, near all her friends. . . ." My voice tailed off. Now he seemed not to be suspecting, but accusing me.

"Friends grow fewer with the years, Mrs Spender; and can never be a full substitute for family."

I said, "Are you trying to tell me . . ." My voice sounded too loud, angry almost. "I mean you are implying that my mother-in-law *wished* to share a house with us?"

"It would be a natural desire. And a feasible explanation."

"That I *cannot* accept. The consequent implication is quite unthinkable. I've known my mother-in-law for a long time. She is *absolutely* honest. I've never known her to tell a lie; she's far too . . . honourable."

"I am not suggesting otherwise. But we must allow for the subconscious, which often dictates in an extraordinary fashion."

"Then we'll allow for it. Let us postulate," good word, I thought, "that Ella—my mother-in-law, wished to share a roof—but not a kitchen with me, and came and saw that Gad's was not suitable; so she went upstairs and her subconscious took over and translated her dislike of the house into a conviction that it was evil."

"Stranger things have been known."

"But that does not account for *me,* Father Jessop. Or for Alice. Or Mrs Catherwood."

292

"The subconscious is an area peculiarly susceptible to autosuggestion."

We were reaching that point of abstract discussion in which some priests were trained. How many angels could sit on the point of a needle?

I said, "Would you like to go up to the attic floor?"

"There is no necessity. But if it would help in any way, of course."

"Then may I offer you lunch?"

"That would be very kind. I do not eat meat in any form."

I was gently fatiguing as the French say, the salad, when Tony came in. He had been, for the last five or six days, the proud owner of a rather battered, third-hand tricycle which *his* subconscious mind was busy translating into a car. He made all the appropriate noises, low gear, middle gear, top gear, hooter. A stick tied to the handlebar was the gear lever. It kept him happy for hours on end. But he had an in-built clock of appetite and came in saying he was hungry. I gve him a quick wash—he had an infinite capacity for getting dirty. Then Father Jessop came down, having experienced—I could tell at a glance—absolutely nothing.

But—and it is a fact, I think, nobody brought up on the Bible ever gets completely away. "Out of the mouths of babes and sucklings," it says.

Tony said to me, "Mummy, may I whisper?"

Manners had been drilled into me so thoroughly that I said to Father Jessop, "Do excuse us."

"Mr Thorley's cross dog," Tony said in a whisper calculated to split an ear-drum. He gave me a conniving look, wrinkling his nose and his upper lip; a joke. Shared. "Don't let him kiss me, will you?"

I said, "Of course not. Would you like to take your plate and make a picnic?" He scuttled away. Father Jessop, eating salad with the impersonal air of a car taking in fuel, seemed not to notice this small exchange of words which to me were meaningful. Finally I said, "That *was* relevant, you know. Tony is too young to pretend. Even *you* can hardly regard *him* as the victim of mass hysteria."

"Is there, in fact, an ill-natured dog?"

"Yes." I told him about it.

"And your little boy sees few strangers? Then the association is obvious. Any person unfamiliar to him takes on the semblance of hostility."

"Casuistry," I said, "is an art."

"You intend that as a reproach? Or are you using the word loosely? It means concerning one's conscience. To the best of my ability I have conducted this inquiry in a conscientious manner. The outcome, of course, is not for me to decide—that will be for my superiors. Believe me, that you dislike me, and all that I represent, has no bearing on the matter. None at all. I shall report, impartially."

Yes, go away; dismiss Ella as a cunning old woman telling lies; me as a dupe; Mrs Catherwood as a fraud, Alice as a silly little girl. . . . Tony as a child living too insulated a life.

"You are wrong in imagining that I dislike you—or what you represent. It is simply that I cannot share your clinical approach."

"No. I fully understand. You need sympathy. I will risk a very personal remark, Mrs Spender. I think you may *require* sympathy with problems quite disconnected with your attic floor."

Nudging middle age, mother of three, I blushed as though I were twelve.

We took leave of one another civilly, he assuring me that I should be hearing from his superior, and I thanking him—for what? He was an appalling driver; his mini stalled twice and then went off down the drive in a series of bucking leaps. I telephoned Ella.

"He's gone. I don't think he's going to *do* anything."

"Nor do I. I thought his manner very casual and very inquisitive. I fail to see how my age, or whether I have ten children or one had any bearing on the point in question. . . ." She still sounded ruffled. "Never mind, dear. I still have another string to my bow. I'll tell you about it when I see you. When will that be?"

"Tomorrow." Ever since I had learned that she was, i

ot actually ailing, in rather a frail state of health, I'd tried
o look in, if only for a moment, every time I went into
3aildon. On this Friday morning I was keyed up to note
ny sign of that loneliness which Father Jessop had appar-
ntly detected in one short visit. And naturally, I found
hem. Tiny things.

"When I relinquished my active part in the Flower
Club," Ella said, "I said that of course, all the committee
neetings could be held here, as in the past. This is so
entral. But your Mrs Thorley thinks otherwise. For those
vho drive—and the majority do—her house is more cen-
ral. Or so she says."

"I suppose Mrs Gordon will give you a blow-by-blow
ccount of all the meetings." Mrs Gordon, a friend of long
tanding and not long widowed, could always be relied
pon to make up a four for Bridge, or share a little outing.

"Oh, didn't I tell you? She's gone to visit her daughter
vho married an American. If she likes California, she may
tay there. I told her it was insane at her age, but it was
ike talking to that chair."

Even the Boy Friend, dear old Fred Murray-Smith, did
ot escape criticism.

"He has those kneelers for St Mary's on the brain. He
as a team of embroideresses—some living at quite a dis-
ance—and he regiments them like soldiers. Last time I
aw him he told me how many miles he had driven in one
veek, delivering materials, collecting finished pieces and
ncouraging laggards."

I thought: Yes; Father Jessop was perceptive, though
erhaps wrong in his conclusions.

Ella then abruptly changed the subject.

"If, as we both think, Father Jessop proves to be un-
elpful, I shall appeal to Mrs Catherwood. Not only is she
nore sympathetic, but she has infinitely more experience."

There was no real reason why I should feel dismayed.
Ars Catherwood had herself spoken of the necessity of the
itual of exorcism being *properly* conducted. I could rely
pon her to be careful. Would she be orthodox? And that
vas a strange question for me to put to myself; I had as a
ule so little use for orthodoxy. Still, I did hope at that

moment that Father Jessop's superior would take Gad'
seriously and send a priest—or two; I had a vague idea tha
where some things were concerned they were coupled—
like old-world hunting hounds.

Nothing happened for an extraordinarily long time. I
made some futile, forlorn little attempts to alleviate Ella's
loneliness. The tropical weather continued, and for Bob's
birthday I suggested having a party in the garden. John
said he could rig up all that was needed for a barbecue.
He'd seen one at some Youth Club outing and was sure he
could improve upon it. I was reasonably certain that even
Fred Murray-Smith would approve of an impromptu, out
in-the-open meal; I'd ask the Thorleys, too, and maybe
drop a little hint about Ella and the Flower Club; I'd tell
John to invite, not only Terry but any other friend who had
a bicycle, and Alice could do the same.

Ella said, "It is very kind of you, dear, but I hardly think
I should fit in."

"I thought of it because, this way, you need not come
into the house." By this time we had been there more than
a year and she had come only twice; on her first visit of
inspection when she talked of evil and haunting, and begged
me not to go there, and later, one brief luncheon, after
which she had taken Alice away. Never again; and not now,
even in the garden. "I think I am getting a little old for
such things, dear."

"What about you, Alice? It is Daddy's birthday."

"I might," Alice said, but as I left she came with me to
the door.

"Mum. I can't. You see Elsie keeps going off."

"What do you mean?"

"Funny turns. Only two nights ago she had one. I
thought I could smell gas, so I went along. One jet was full
on, but either she hadn't lighted it or it had blown out, the
kitchen door was open. And there was Elsie, absolutely
purple—and unconscious. Like being asleep. You know."

"And what did you do?"

"I turned the gas off. And telephoned Doctor Taylor."

"Good girl! And then what?"

"Elsie had to have some sugar, at least glucose. You see, if you're diabetic you either have too much or too little. Elsie knows and keeps some sugar lumps handy, but sometimes she isn't quick enough. Then she goes off. And it upsets Gran. So I don't think I ought to leave them, even for Daddy's birthday."

Alice was right; but the whole setup was wrong. Too much responsibility, too soon.

In the end Bob's birthday was celebrated in two places and in very different ways. I could not deny John his barbecue nor let Ella and Alice be left out. I took Bob and Tony and a fully prepared meal along to St Giles' Square and John and twenty of his friends had a barbecue you could smell a mile off.

On the way home, Tony asleep on the back seat, Bob said,

"Jill, we have to face facts. You may not have noticed, but Elsie has got to the end of the road. I've been working it out; she must be eighty. And I doubt whether Mother could boil an egg—and she's too old to learn now. It may . . . sound . . . silly, but she . . . never had to, so she never did. It would be like . . . you or me . . . in old age . . . having to learn . . . to play the piano. God knows . . . you have enough to carry and I shouldn't say this . . . but I must. . . . She'll never find another Elsie. I think . . . we should . . . offer her a home. I know . . . I'm a bloody nuisance. . . . But she is my mother . . . and so fussy. She'd be . . . happier with us . . . if you . . . could bear it."

"Look, darling . . . To begin with you are *no* nuisance. Let's get that straight to start with. There isn't a more independent man in the world. And I would most gladly offer Ella a home and I'd cook. But she wouldn't come. For a reason you would never understand—not in a million years."

"Tell me. At least give me a chance to understand."

"All right. But not just now. Never the time and the place, as somebody said. By the smell of it the boys have set the whole house on fire."

Two corners to negotiate and both leading to inclines.

Unless I were careful with the worn gears on the old car, I'd be bucking along or stalled, as bad as Father Jessop. And in the lane I had to be careful, so many boys on bicycles . . . Some of them shouted, "Good night." They had not set the house on fire. John and Terry, who was staying the night, hauled Tony off to bed. He was more than my ricketty back could manage at the end of a long day.

I went into the kitchen and made a pot of tea. Then in the living room, I said,

"Now I will tell you all, and please, Bob, don't interrupt me. Above all, don't laugh."

I had—as usual—been wrong. Bob listened as it all came pouring out and he did not even *look* mocking. Just profoundly concerned and pitying. I didn't cry, as I had done when telling the same tale to George Thorley. I did my best to sound phlegmatic. At the end I said,

"So you see, darling, the position I'm in."

Bob heaved himself up and stumbled over to where I sat on the settle. He sat down beside me and put his good arm, his right, around me, holding me close.

"You poor, silly girl. Keeping it all to yourself. Why didn't you tell me? Don't you know that bottling things up is bad for you?"

"We, Ella and I, thought you'd jibe. Ella said you couldn't believe anything you couldn't measure with a slide rule."

Then he did laugh. "Just because I don't go to church! In any case my belief or lack of it doesn't affect the existence of anything. I might not believe that this is Saturday—but it'd still be Saturday for most people."

Once he had commiserated with me on being left with only half a man, which was true, in a physical sense. He had a flaccid leg and arm, his speech was sometimes hesitant but what was left of Bob Spender was worth half a dozen other men.

"Something must be done about this. To start with I'm going up to that attic myself, first thing tomorrow morning."

"The stairs are very difficult."

"I'll go up on my hands and knees and come down on what I was once chided for calling my bum."

He was up there for a long time. I interrupted my baking three times to go to the foot of the attic stairs and shout, "Are you all right?" His third answer was irritable. "Of course I am."

Tony was with me in the kitchen, diligently clearing out the bowl in which I'd mixed the ingredients for a chocolate sponge. When, at last, Bob came through from the living room, Tony dropped the spoon and bolted. Mr Thorley's cross dog again?

Bob, tired by the unusual exertion, dropped down on a chair. I produced coffee and the mid-morning cigarettes.

"I've been flaking off whitewash.... Somebody ... to say the least ... highly peculiar ... painted a wall up there. Then somebody smeared black paint, or ... tar, and ... then ... somebody whitewashed. The face I managed to uncover was ... devilish. I think perhaps your Mrs Catherwood had something there."

"Did you *feel* anything?"

"Curiosity. A kind of disgust."

"No despondency?"

"No more than usual. But that's not to say that other people didn't. Even *I* admit that feelings are things that can't be measured on a slide rule."

It was wonderful to be able to talk about it.

Father Jessop wrote me a letter which could have come from a lawyer; rejecting a dubious case. He did indeed use the word. The case had been subjected to the most careful consideration and was not deemed suitable for such extreme measures as exorcism. So that was that.

During that week another letter came, too; from the Peterborough firm who had been interested in Bob's invention; they finally surfaced with the news that they had been in negotiation with their German counterparts who were willing to make it a joint production. They were now anxious to take an option, £2,000 down (non-returnable). Patent rights must be established, prototypes made, etc. etc.

"There you are, darling," I said. "I told you you'd make a million."

"Well, at least it is launched. But before I dance in the street I shall need to know that some ironmonger in Wuppentaal or a blacksmith in Hockwold hasn't forestalled us. . . . Still, even now, two thousand is not to be sneezed at. I must sound out George Thorley. The original idea was his. I only put it on paper."

Orthodox approaches having failed us, Ella appealed to Mrs Catherwood, who responded gallantly. Yes, she did know a priest, Father Lomax, who was extremely interested in the occult. She would get in touch with him on our behalf before she herself went off to America on a prolonged lecture tour. Father Lomax was currently without a parish, being one of those who could not accept the change from Latin to English Mass.

"All the better," Ella said, surprising me again, for she had always seemed to me a very middle-of-the-road Anglican who had accepted Canon Lauder's small changes on purely aesthetic grounds. And she was totally ignorant of Latin.

But in fact, Ella was changing, even in looks. Maybe that pretty beige-blonde hair had always been the result of regular visits to the hairdresser's; it was now fading, growing duller and greyer, and no longer cut and curled, let to grow and turned up at the back of her head into a surprisingly tiny bun. Oddly, her eyes had faded, too, from bright cornflower to periwinkle blue. Age and circumstance were catching up on her at last. The cherished look had vanished.

Changes in the house, too. Less clutter, and more dust. "I have put my few silver ornaments away, dear. Elsie has all she can manage now with the cooking. And even so I am worried about her. I feel that she needs more *expert* care than I can give. The injections are no longer *entirely* effective. But I simply cannot consign her to Sunset Court, can I? Not after sixty years."

Paternalism had become, within my time, a dirty word, but the thing itself was not without virtue.

Mrs Catherwood wrote to me, a hurried cryptic scribble. "Sure you're doing the right thing. Hope all goes well.

Have alternative host ready. See Mark 12:5."

Father Lomax might have no parish, but he seemed to be extremely occupied. It was September before he wrote to say that, if convenient, he would like to come on the 18th—a Saturday—and stay the night. He would take no food until after the ceremony, and anyone intending to participate should abstain from food after Saturday lunch time.

Food had become my bugbear—not the preparing and the cooking, but the organising. I was now trying to feed two separate households, and just at my busiest season. Doctor Taylor had finally insisted upon removing Elsie; not to the Old People's Home, of which both she and Ella had such a dread, but to the Hospital, where she could be observed and tested, and if not cured, at least relieved. That left Ella, genuinely helpless where food was concerned, and Alice, who was at school all day. Alice did at least get a dinner at school, and although she, being faddy, often made derogatory remarks about school food, John spoke well of it. Smashing grub, he called it. There was some wonderful comestible known as Meat Loaf, which I tried—without much success—to produce myself; there were beefburgers and chips; fish fingers and chips. All the same, he was always ready for his supper, and it was my desire, my intention, that Alice should also have some sort of meal in the evening. And what about Ella, during the day?

The answer might appear to be that she should go out for a meal; but that was difficult. Baildon boasted three public eating places. There was the *Hawk in Hand;* "Under New Management," it always was; it served a business man's lunch; a bar snack and a proper luncheon in the newly decorated (it was always being newly decorated) restaurant. There was also a place with a pretty shady reputation, known as *Round the Clock,* and one of those ever-so-dainty tea-shops, tea, coffee, biscuits and scones. A luncheon in the restaurant of the *Hawk in Hand* might have served, but it was terribly expensive. Ella tried it once and said, "It was extremely nice, and of course all the waiters knew me, from the Ladies' Luncheon Club. But I only had one dish, nothing to drink, and it was over two pounds. Two pounds ten, or as you would say two-fifty. I simply cannot afford . . . Not, my dear, that I want to bother you with my financial problems. But since Arden and Somers went into liquidation, my income has been even more reduced. Jill dear, you must *not* worry about me. Whatever Bob says, I *can* boil an egg. And I do. I fully realise that Alice is growing, but they say a boiled egg with whole-meal bread and butter is quite as nourishing as steak."

Outside the boiled egg area she was genuinely incapable. She did not even know that an oven should be hot before meat is put in. Of potatoes—"I just went to answer the phone and they boiled dry, quite ruining my saucepan." Of apples—"There are some apples that simply will not cook. I stewed some for two hours and they just got harder and harder." She'd cooked eating apples, of course.

In September the hot, dry, and but-for-the-moat ruinous summer, ended in torrential rains and days as dark as November. Through the rain and the mire I flogged to and fro, with produce to sell, and food that could either be heated up by Alice, who could at least distinguish between the switches of the oven and the grill, or eaten cold.

Just before Father Lomax's letter came, I said,

"Honestly, Ella, I know how you feel, but apart from that top floor Gad's is all right. If you liked I'd make the drawing room into a bedroom for you. Alice could sleep there with you—or I would. It'd be so much easier—for you," That day she'd washed and ironed some handkerchiefs; they couldn't go to the laundry because she never got the right ones back; she'd left the iron, still switched on, on the ironing board and damned nearly caused a fire.

"Dear, I know. It would easier for all of us. But until something is done, I cannot enter that house. And it is absurd to say that whatever it is is contained on the attic floor. Alice was terrified everywhere—and affected in other ways. As you well know."

I tried an alternative—in my mind. We'd come back to the pretty little house. I'd make everybody a good breakfast; leave something for Ella's lunch; drive Bob back to his worktable, tend my garden, collect my produce, let Tony work off his energies on the tricycle, which was now more like a car than ever since Goerge Thorley had found somewhere one of those old-fashioned horns with a bulb. Then I could do the whole thing in reverse, go back to St Giles' Square, make supper for us all.

Double journeys for my poor old car, already on its last legs, more muddling about for Bob—now busy on a new project which often occupied his after-supper hours. And John would most strenuously object.

For me, Father Lomax's letter came just in time.

He came, on an ink-black evening, though it was barely six o'clock. He was driving Mrs Catherwood's Jansen and emerged from it like a grub from a chrysalis; such a small man and so thin, so frail-looking that when he began to haul a quite oversized bag from the car, I ignored my aching back and said, "I'll take it."

"Thank you."

"Would you like to see your room straightaway?"

"Thank you."

Possibly he weighed seven stones, certainly not more, and his head, almost completely bald, looked too big for his body. His eyes were remarkable; that warm green-brown that for some reason is called hazel, with whites as clear as a child's, though what remained of his hair was quite grey. Eyes any girl might have envied, but their expression was disconcerting; even when he looked straight at me he seemed not to be seeing me.

I'd made Alice's room as nice as I could, even to a bowl of my very best chrysanthemums, the kind that fetched 9p each at the W.I.

I said, "The bathroom is next door." I'd made that nice, too, and threatened John with unspeakable things if he entered it for what he called "a quick swill," which meant that blobs of soapfroth, the size of a 10p piece, bore evidence that he had washed, though the towel said otherwise.

Father Lomax said, "Thank you," again.

"I know you said no food, but I could make tea, or coffee. . . ."

"No, thank you. I shall do very well." Aiming his glance at something deep inside my head, or far behind it, he said, "I understand that neither you nor your husband is a member of *any* religious community."

"That is so."

"Were you baptised?"

"I was born Methodist; they call it christening. My husband was baptised—Church of England." Ella, so very correct, would have seen to that. He should have been confirmed, too, but by the age of seventeen he'd lost faith. Probably I was the only one who knew why, probably I was the only one who knew that Bob, up to age of sixteen, had had faith until he saw his father die of cancer. He'd only spoken to me about it once, saying briefly, "I prayed. Not that he should live, I knew by that time that death was inevitable, but I did pray, with all my heart, that he shouldn't *suffer*. He was the kindest man that ever lived; he just happened to be impervious to morphia. They gave him enough to kill a regiment, but he died in screaming agony. . . . I gave up then and went over to St Augustine; if God is benevolent He is not omnipotent; if He is omnipotent, He is not benevolent. So I quit."

"But not confirmed?"

For the sake of politeness, I said, "I'm afraid not," instead of a plain "No."

"Will there be present any person in a state of grace?"

The only person I had asked to come was George Thorley, who was to bring his dog, and if by being in a state of grace meant coming straight from Holy Communion, the answer must again be: No. George was strictly a Christmas and Easter communicant, Sunday being his busiest day since only one of his workmen would work on Sunday, despite the overtime pay, and cows must be milked and fed as usual. Doris went regularly to church, but she had no part in this. George had decided against telling her— much to my relief. "She does so love to talk," he said, "within two days half Suffolk would have heard a highly coloured tale."

"A pity, but never mind," Father Lomax said.

Since we were now talking about tomorrow, I said ten-

tively, and feeling rather foolish, that Mrs Catherwood
ad suggested an alternative host and that I had asked Mr
horley to bring his very unlovable dog.

I think Father Lomax, as well as abstaining—and asking
s to abstain from food, had imposed, if not silence, at least
e minimum of speech upon himself.

"Not strictly essential; but harmless," he said.

Just then Tony yelled up the back stairs,

"Mummy! Mumm*ee*. I want my supper."

Something within Father Lomax sprang to instant at-
ntion.

"A child?"

"Yes. My youngest."

"How old?"

"Just over three and a half."

"Baptised?"

"I'm afraid not."

"Good. Baptism is a form of exorcism. With your per-
ission I will baptise him before I undertake the other
sk."

With that he turned away, dismissing me. He threw
pen his big suitcase and I caught just a glimpse of a huge
ucifix, silver and ivory, beautiful, if a crucifix can ever be
id to be beautiful; personally I shrink from them, as I
ould shrink from models of the rack, the thumb-screw,
 the Iron Maiden of mediaeval times. Below there were
me folds of gorgeous-coloured stuff.

Both Bob and George, in their differing ways, had been
ery tolerant and indulgent about the whole thing. Bob had
 least admitted that feelings could not be measured on
slide rule; and he had been worried about conditions in
lla's house since Elsie had been taken away. If anything
uld persuade her—and Alice—to come to Gad's and share
mily life, he was, he said, prepared to stand on his head.
eorge was more guarded, partly because it all reflected
pon his beloved Gad's; he called it a lot of mumbo-jumbo;
ut if it would ease my mind he was willing to go along
ith it. As for the dog, he had an inbuilt devil, one more
uldn't hurt him.

Once, in the happy days at Scunwick, I had attended—wishing to be friendly—a Catholic baptism of a child, th daughter of a friend of mine. She and her husband wer absolutely decent characters, and as the ceremony pr ceeded, in essence a purging of a three-week-old child fro original sin, I stood there in my church-going hat an thought: What utter rubbish! What an implied insult to th little baby, who could not yet have entertained even a sinf thought.

And now, there I was, years later, committed.

Bob said, "Well, it can't do Tony any harm. He'll prol ably think it's a game. Having started on this, we might well go the whole thing."

I had taken the precaution of getting John out of th house. He was old enough to be inquisitive, so he'd gon off, happily enough, to spend a week-end with Terry.

Except for the absence of godparents, Tony certainly ha as splendid a christening as any prince. I'd warned hi beforehand to stand still, not to talk, but such behests wer unnecessary. Father Lomax, in full panoply, was awesom even to my eyes. His outer robe was white and stiff wit embroidery in gold and silver thread; his stole was purpl with gold fringe. Everything else was equally sumptuou he had come well-prepared; all he needed from me was small table, he said. I thought wildly—Just the one thir we don't own! Then I remembered that John and Ter had spent a blissful wet Saturday at what they called ca pentry. The result of their work was in John's room.

"Where?" I asked. "Where would you want it?"

"In the infested place."

I hauled it up; it was heavier than it looked, and at th turn in the stairs I was awkward, or it was awkward; n back gave its preliminary protest. Like a voice saying: U less you watch it, I'm going to give you Hell.

And now I had to go into the attic itself, not skirting b as was my habit. The feeling that emanated from the plac utter hopelessness, hit me again—and this time with a sens of inexplicable guilt.

In a flash I saw how wrong I had been. Listening

‌lla; taking notice of Alice's feelings, misconstruing my
‌wn. And being led, simply by being weak, into dabbling
‌ith something better left alone.

Then all that was resistant and sceptical in me asked,
‌Vhy? What would be better left alone—if there is nothing
‌ere, *what is to be left alone?* Argue your way out of that!

It took Father Lomax a very few minutes to transform
‌at clumsy table into an altar; a blue cloth, like his robe
‌eavily and richly embroidered; candles in silver holders,
‌ small, beautifully chased silver bowl; a censer, a bejew-
‌lled bauble, its chains dangling.

I had another thought.

For so many hundreds of years people had complained
‌bout the outward grandeur of the church, asking how it
‌tted in with the teaching of a humble carpenter from Naz-
‌reth. I saw why. The worldly grandeur of princes, kings,
‌mperors had to be matched, outmatched. Authority must
‌e seen to be authoritative. An Emperor must hold the
‌ope's stirrup.

"Send the child to me," Father Lomax said. "I will deal
‌ith the rest later."

I said, humbly, "Do you wish me to be present?"

"Better not."

So I went downstairs and found Tony and said,

"Now remember what I told you. Just stand still and do
‌hatever you're asked to do. And then . . ." I opened the
‌idge and showed him the covered bowl of ice cream,
‌omemade, in the freezing compartment. "You can come
‌own and help yourself."

"Two helps?"

"As much as you like."

Very soon after our coming to Gad's, in fact as soon as
‌lice had mentioned bumps in the night, I had put that
‌rooked flight of stairs out of bounds, saying I doubted its
‌afety. So Tony was entranced to be allowed to scramble
‌p them.

I stayed just long enough to hear that this service was
‌o be in Latin. At the Scunwick baptism we had been given
‌ folder, Latin on one page, English, for the benefit of the
‌gnorant, on the other. So standing on the landing and

listening would not enlighten me much. I went down and found that George Thorley had arrived, very formal-looking in a dark suit.

Since the evening when Chum had bitten through his leather leash he had taken his walks on a chain, no thicker or heavier than a bicycle chain, but very strong. It had a catch which fastened to his collar, and at the end a similar catch; this, passed round the dresser leg and snapped into one link in the chain, bigger than the others, tethered him securely. He greeted me with his usual snarl, though over the months I'd done my best to ingratiate myself with him. I'd even tried bribery with biscuits and bones. All to no avail, and yet, at this moment I felt that my suggestion of *using* him had been callous, a bit too light-heartedly suggested—and as light-heartedly accepted by George; one devil more couldn't hurt him. It was unlikely that a dog would feel what I had felt, despair and the complete futility of everything; but who knew? Also, would what Mrs Catherwood called an elemental be content with a dog as dwelling?

Bob said, "Don't look so worried, darling. If what's going on will just satisfy Mother and get her here, we're doing the right thing."

"I'm thinking about the dog."

"Then don't," George said. "If he hadn't had this appointment with the Devil this morning, I'd damned well have shot him on Friday. He bit *me!*"

The ultimate offence! George had gone through the gamut of excuses. Chum was young, he'd learn; he was too much inbred; he was nervous; somebody had been frightened just by the sight of him, and dogs could smell fear; somebody else had been too bold and tried to stroke him. I'd heard the lot. Now Chum had overstepped the mark.

"Where?"

"I think we won't go into that," he grinned. "He ruined a damn good pair of breeches."

"Did he break the skin?" Bob asked. "If so you should have an injection."

"What for? Rabies? If you ask me, we're all pretty mad as it is."

I said, "No, seriously, George. I think they now give tetanus injections for dog bites."

"Load of old rubbish. If his teeth weren't clean to start with, they were when they'd been through all that good whip-cord."

Before there could be any further argument, Tony clattered down the back stairs.

"The lady says she is ready now. But you must wait outside. *I* can go in. *I* have something to do." He was bursting with self-importance, and his eyes were just like Ella's when she was feeling emotional, wide black pupils with just a rim of blue.

Bob went towards the front stairs with shallower treads and a sturdy banister. I knew he hated to be watched, even making that comparatively easy ascent, the flight to the attic would be more exacting, so George and I waited.

"Is it true about the dog? Or did you say that just to make me feel less guilty?"

"It's true. I can show you my breeches. I'd taken the brute for his run, then I fetched his food, put it down, and was just at the gate of his enclosure. He came at me from *behind*." He sounded genuinely aggrieved. Then with a complete change of manner, he said, "Jill, if this . . performance doesn't satisfy the old lady or make you feel happier, we'll think of something else. Maybe I could get possession of Park Old House again; I did a good job making that into two. In any case, of course you could have your money back."

"That's mighty noble of you, George. But . . . well, I like this house. Apart from that one place."

"I know. Well, let's hope a drop or two of holy water will work."

"You don't believe a word of it, do you?"

"Do *you?*"

"I truly don't know. I'm doing this for Alice—and Ella. . . . I think we could go now."

Sometimes, not always, there'd been a faint foul stench near that attic. I had not been aware of it when I went up earlier with Tony for his lonely baptism; but now it was very strong, indefinable but nauseating. I thought: What ever it is, it *knows* and is mustering its forces.

And Father Lomax was mustering his. Even his voice had changed. What few words he had said to me had been spoken in a low, ordinarily civil voice; and what little I had overheard of the beginning of baptism rite had been gentle. Even an unknown language has its cadences.

He said, in English, "Come no further!" And that was an order. So Bob and George and I halted on the landing. Three people not in a state of grace; mere witnesses. I had cricked my back and knew that I must lean against some body, or something, or drop. On one side of me was Bob leaning on his stick; not to be leaned upon for obvious physical reasons; on the other side stood George, sound as rock, but not to be leaned upon for other reasons. So I leaned against the wall and had but a limited view. I could hear though; and I heard Father Lomax's voice take on, not merely authority but absolute aggression. He held the beautiful crucifix high, and with his free hand scattered water from the beautiful bowl. And my son waved the smouldering censer as though he were sixteen years old and had been doing it since he was ten. . . .

And then there was the most awful noise, a crash, as though the roof had fallen in. I disgraced myself by fainting, a thing I had never done before in my life.

I came to on the settle in the living room. Bob's big chair had been pulled close and he sat in it. He was rubbing my hands. George Thorley was on his knees, propping up my head with one arm and trying to make me drink brandy. They both looked pale and extremely concerned. Father Lomax sat slumped in a chair, completely exhausted. (I discovered later that he had fasted for forty-eight hours.)

Tony wasn't there. Fear seized me.

"Where's Tony?"

"In the kitchen. Eating a chicken drumstick and ice cream simultaneously," George said. "Try a sip of this now."

Bob's sound hand tightened on mine.

"My God," he said, "you gave us a scare."

I whispered, "Offer Father Lomax a drink." I was too

ack-minded to wonder then where the brandy had come
om. Actually I'd been out long enough for George to take
y car and rush down to Park.

Father Lomax accepted, only stipulating that he should
ave a little water with his brandy.

George said, "Well, I must now go hunt my damned
og. He can't have gone far, lumbered as he was."

I understood that when, feeling better, and remember-
g my obligations, I went into the kitchen.

The huge dresser there was, literally, part of the house;
formed the greater part of the wall between the kitchen
d the living room. Its back was the wall, its front sup-
orted on two stout legs, at least four inches in diameter.
he one to which the dog's chain had been attached had
en literally ripped away, so that now the whole thing
gged.

I'd never had anything really worthy of that dresser, just
dinary, utilitarian household crockery, but I'd been fond
the things I had, and now all were smashed. Out of the
sightly mess I salvaged only two things, a saucer and my
ooden pepper mill. If only I'd had sense enough to set
e table beforehand!

Now we had no choice but to follow Tony's example and
t our cold chicken without bothering about plates.

I have never seen a few mouthfuls of food work such a
ansformation on anybody as Father Lomax's few bites did.

"Food tastes much better, eaten like this," he said cheer-
lly, munching away. "Though of course I regret the rea-
n." He eyed the pile of broken shards. "I was negligent.
should have warned Mr Thorley of the force which no
ain can hold. Tennyson was in error in imputing the
rength of ten only to the pure in heart."

"Where *did* the cross dog go?" Tony sounded rather
prehensive.

"Uncle George will take care of him," Bob said. "You
n't have to worry. Nor do you." He shifted his glance to
e. "If Ella now decides that this is a fit place to live in
e shall have china galore."

"She should so decide," Father Lomax said, speaking as

though it were a matter of choice between two colour

"It *was* a very strong infestation, but it is ended now. Ye you may be assured of that."

I said, "Tony, go and see if there are any of the r apples down, you know which ones."

When he had gone I asked what to me seemed a vit question.

"If somebody shoots that dog, what happens then?"

He turned his luminous eyes on me.

"You have an inquiring mind and *some* belief. I cann answer you exactly. Deprived of a habitation, the evil m dissipate itself. It was concentrated here; I gave it a de tination. As you did, just now, to that dear child. It perhaps an oversimplification . . . but if you had said, (away, the response might have been less immediate, le willing, less directed, even, perhaps, negative." He rubb his high, domed forehead. "It is a little difficult to expla without sounding puerile; and there are so many variable Each case is different. This, for instance, would have bee easier for me had I had the support of positive believers even a member of the Salvation Army." That was said ha jocularly, and I managed what I feared was a rather pall smile.

Almost immediately he said he must be going; he h to drive back to London and he was not yet thorough familiar with Mrs Catherwood's car. He parted from us wi solemnity, wishing us better health and more happine and bidding us remember that Tony was now a child God. He said, "Peace be with you, and upon this house.

Tony came in with some of the red apples.

"Oh, has she gone? I wanted to give her some. I rubbe them shiny. She was a very nice lady."

Ella's house, which had once smelt of potpourri an lavender water and other pleasant things, absolutely stan I'd made a beef-steak pie which simply needed to be heate through. She'd put it in a roaring-hot oven before she we to church and left it to burn. Returning to the stench, an some black charcoal in a pyrex, she'd taken it out, put in the sink and turned the cold tap on it. "It made a noise like the shot of a gun," she said, mildly surprised. "I've been hunting around for a replacement. I seem not to have one exactly the right size or shape." She looked quite distraught, wild wisps of hair all adrift, a smear of dust on her forehead and a fair-sized burn on her right hand. I was truly happy to be able to say what I had come to say; but first . . . "Where is Alice?"

"Gone to borrow half a loaf. Since I ruined the lunch we had to eat bread and cheese. There is not enough now for supper and breakfast. I'm afraid I am not a good provider."

I said, "Ella, I want you to come to Gad's and make a test. A very nice old priest called Father Lomax purged the place this morning, and judging by one result, he did it most effectively. If you think it's all right now, I'd like you to stay . . . Apart from everything else," I gave myself high marks for tact, "it'd be such a help to me. Tony is now far too much for Bob to manage, and when I take him around with me, he is a nuisance. I have to lock him in the car at each stop while I unload, and even so he tampers with the dashboard."

Ella began to cry and then Alice came in, carrying what looked like a whole loaf in a plastic bag.

She turned on me like a young tigress.

"Have you made her cry over that pyrex dish? She couldn't help it. It was my fault. And I was going to buy a new one first thing tomorrow."

Ella's tears, as I knew, came and went in unpredictable fashion. They stopped now and she said, "Alice! That is no way to speak to your mother! Apologise immediately!"

Alice said, "Sorry, Mum," but with a glare that was anything but apologetic.

"If you will go upstairs, Alice, and look in the bottom of my wardrobe, you will find a little blue overnight bag which I keep packed ready for emergencies. Pack a similar one for yourself—including whatever you may want for school tomorrow."

"Why? Where are we going?"

"To Gad's."

Alice looked horrified. "Oh no! Gran, please, please, not that. I know it has all been awful since Elsie went, but I have tried. I'll try harder. I won't forget things. I will learn to cook. . . ." Hysteria, threatened.

Ella said—her Rock-of-Gibraltar quality well to the fore, "Alice! Come here, dear. How long have you known me?"

Checked, Alice said, "Why, Gran—well, as long as I can remember. All my life."

"And in that time have I ever done or said anything to make you consider me untrustworthy? No. Then trust me now and go and do what I asked."

When Alice had gone, I said,

"How much does she know?"

"Nothing; except, of course, that she was frightened at home and I said I understood and brought her here, where she ceased to be frightened. We never discussed the matter; she is far too young."

I spared a moment to consider Alice. More guilt.

"She never even *told* me that she was frightened. I think John knew. . . ."

"She knew that you were very busy, dear. She's a considerate child. Or she might have feared that you would laugh—she's very sensitive, too. But if the absolute evil which I sensed on that first day has been . . . overcome and if you really want me . . ."

I said, "Ella, you aren't all I want! Of my pitiable collection of goods, I now have one saucer and a pepper mill."

"Why? What happened?"

"It was part of the procedure. I'll explain, later. In the meantime, if you could lend me a few things, cups, plates . . ."

"But, dear, I told you, when you moved to Gad's and went to buy a teapot, I had at least three unused. I have masses of things, in the cupboard under the stairs. Nothing of value of course or they would not be there. Now, let me think. In the old days the laundry used to come and go in a hamper. I think I could find it."

She found it; she opened the cupboard, Ali Baba's cave.

I took only essentials, aware that I should have to lift the hamper into my car and that I had already broken my back once that day. However, when I lifted it I felt no pain at all.

Alice remained withdrawn—some people would have called it sulky—during the drive. Ella chattered quite gaily, mainly about the beauty of the golden September afternoon. Both she and I addressed Alice occasionally and drew monosyllabic replies. I was anxious to get home and the experiment made.

John was there, with Terry. Terry's mother, though very hospitable, was a haphazard housekeeper and believed that boys could forage for themselves on Sunday evenings, so we often had Terry's company at Sunday supper. The boys, directed by Bob, had already made a good temporary repair to the dresser, and were promising to make a new leg in the woodwork class during the next week. They had also cleared away the mess. They carried the hamper in and would have started redecorating the dresser, but Ella said, with truth, that everything needed to be washed first. "You'll see to that, won't you dear," she said to Alice. "You wash, the boys can dry." The sight of the new—and if worthless, rather beautiful teapot inspired Bob to say he'd make tea. Ella gave me a beckoning glance. In the living room, she said,

"Now. I propose to go up and test the feeling of the place."

I then remembered that she had an unsound heart, so I said I'd go first. Not that I was really a good test subject; I'd never felt what *she* claimed to have felt, and what Mrs Catherwood and Father Lomax had confirmed. I'd simply felt despair, and now and again been conscious of a faint, foul stench.

That, at least, was not there this afternoon; the attic floor smelt of apples, eaten long ago, and the incense. I went right into the attic itself and stood, almost inviting despair and despondency. I could very well have felt, if nothing so extreme, a certain *dismay* at the prospect before me.

There was the question of fitting Ella in, both physically and psychologically; which rooms should be hers, so absolutely hers that she would have her own place, while being one of the family. Alice was hostile to the move—to me? And I'd seen the boys exchange glances, mocking, but not lacking in significance when told to dry crockery. Bossy grandmother!

I knew all these things in my mind, but I did not feel them. What I felt was joy at being all together again, the surety that whatever cropped up, I could cope ... and my back was strong again.

Then I noticed a curious thing. Bob had tried to understand, to investigate, had flaked off some whitewash and found what even he described as a nasty face. All I could see in the space where the whitewash had been removed was a beautiful garden poppy, pink, with black stamens.

I went down and Ella was waiting at the foot of the twisty stairs.

"*I* think, it's all right." I said. I added, sounding very urgent, "If you feel ... anything in the least hostile, call me. I'll wait here."

I watched her as far as the first bend of the stairs; I saw a particular pathos about her ankles and what showed of her calves. They'd always been slender, no doubt, now they looked shrunken, an effect accentuated by the shoes she wore; the type known as court, with high, rather waisted heels.

She was gone rather a long time. I went on to the stairs and called, "Are you all right?" "Yes. Just looking at something." From below there were calls, "Tea's made! Tea up!" I yelled back, "Coming! Just a minute."

Ella came down. She looked radiant.

"Not a flicker," she said. "And I've had such a wonderful idea. I do hope that you and Bob will approve."

Afternoon tea as an institution had ceased to be regarded at Gad's. Bob or I made a pot if we felt like it and drank it in the kitchen. Our real tea was high tea or, as we called it, supper, a solid meal, with tea to drink, taken at six, or thereabouts. Such an arrangement fitted in with working habits—as working people learned long ago. How this would suit Ella was one of things which might have worried me when I stood in the attic. Bob had shown a nice sense of situation by having tea brought into the sitting room, and at the same time murmuring to me that he had switched on the oven. John and Terry accepted a cup of tea and a biscuit as they would have accepted anything for the stomach, and went off. Alice somehow managed to give the impression of a grand lady doing a bit of slumming. Only Tony protested. Brought in from his tricycle by calls about tea, he said, "Is this all?"

"It would make a delightful apartment," Ella said. Two attics thrown into one would be quite a spacious drawing room; the third would be my bedroom, with a part of the landing—all waste space now—made into a bathroom."

"What about those fiendish stairs?" Bob asked, forestalling me.

Once again Ella surprised me.

"I thought about them. Possibly the person who planned them had some reason for giving them a double twist, but a new staircase, rising towards the *other* end of the landing, could be straight and far less steep. If I had a pencil . . ."

I provided a ball-point and some paper and she scribbled. Bob watched and said, "Quite feasible." I don't suppose that even he had guessed that part of his talent was derived from his mother. He sounded surprised.

"Here," Ella said, pointing, "I should have a tiny kitchenette so that I could make tea, or coffee, or boil myself an egg. I have no doubt that it would all be very costly, but I have a house to sell. . . . I think I could afford to instal full central heating, which would be to the advantage of us all, and even, if the planning people agreed, alter those dormer windows into French ones, opening on to a balcony, with a few plants in pots. That is all I need, nowadays, especially as my windows would overlook your garden."

Alice's, the only dissentient voice in the atmosphere that all was for the best, asked, "What about *me?*" Ella and I began to speak simultaneously. A bit of jumble, assurances that Alice was home—would always be welcome in Ella's apartment, should have a bicycle. . . .

The jumble was interrupted and ended by the sound of a shot, very clear in the still afternoon air.

When everybody spoke as Gad's being up and Park being down, they were being literal. Gad's stood higher, surrounded by George Thorley's arable fields; beyond them the ground rose into what, in rather flat East Anglia, was called hill, meaning slight rise. Its summit and its inclines comprised a farm, devoted mainly to sheep. Its owner was a man of marked melancholy nature to whom the long drought had been a great trial. Another few days without rain, he'd frequently said, and he'd shoot himself. He threatened the same thing indirectly when he had his rate demand, his income tax form to fill in, when his car broke down, "Might as well shoot yourself and have done with it." Bob and George Thorley said that potential suicides never made such threats, and were inclined to joke about it, varying the formula sometimes into—I'll shoot *you*.

The drought had broken; it was Sunday when even the tax gatherers cease to trouble and the rate demanders take their rest, and yet somehow that one single shot sounded ominous, coming as it did from that direction. We'd never heard a shot from Top Farm before, and had, indeed, no evidence that Mr Sutton even owned a gun. And what, but himself, could he shoot? On his sheep-nibbled land a rabbit would have found it hard to exist.

I said, "Bob, do you think . . . ?"

The special kind of communication that had enabled us to stay in close touch when Bob was speechless, and when his speech was greatly impaired, worked again.

"He could have, poor bastard, and probably made a balls-up of it. We'd better go see."

Ella's face and Alice's face registered identical expressions. What language! With ladies present, too!

"I'll go," I said.

"You will drive me, Honey; and stop when I tell you to. You've had enough today without a lot of rawhead and bloody bones."

318

I gave a few instructions about beds and sheets and pillows, and going through the kitchen, switched the oven to a lower heat. Then we got into the car and I drove. A short distance, but uphill. Well away from Mr Sutton's house Bob said, "Stop here." It may have been my fancy but he seemed to me to walk better, stumping away with his stick, using it as a motive power rather than a support.

Mr Sutton came out of his house and gesticulated. I relaxed. No need for me to brace up and help to get an ineffectual suicide into Baildon, to the Hospital.

They came towards me. I still thought Bob was walking better, and I remembered the optimistic doctor who had said improvement would come, even if it seemed slow.

I wound down the window and could hear Mr Sutton speaking with more than his usual grievance against life in general.

". . . off the place for weeks on end," he said, "and never at week-ends, people out with their curs. Then today I just go down to Muchanger, sick-visiting. Get asked to stay for dinner and come back to bloody massacre."

"How much damage?"

"Remains to be seen. Had to shoot the thing first, then call the vet. Save what we can, but the damage may not be all on the surface. Fright like that could make ewes abort. Good afternoon, Mrs Spender. Nice of you and your husband to look in, see what happened. No sight for anyone, I can tell you. Dog was mad. Always was. I've said to Mr Thorley twenty times if once—If I couldn't get a better dog than that, I'd shoot myself."

I said, "I'm very sorry indeed." I was sorry. Sheep are such defenceless things. *And the most generally accepted official sacrifices!* Even Christ—the Lamb of God!

"One thing though," Mr Sutton said, "I always insured the flock. Well, must get back and do a bit of first aid till the vet comes."

Bob came round to the driver's side of the car and said, "Move over, Honey. I'd like to *try*."

"Well, if you feel like it." I was pleased; a little dubious.

"I do. And where better than on a road where there's no traffic?"

He was wrong; on that short bit of unfrequented lane we met George Thorley in his Landrover. He had his gun propped beside him.

"Too late," Bob shouted as we drew level. The two vehicles slid past each other, and both drivers backed, very expertly in the narrow lane. Bob explained what had happened and George said,

"Thank God! I was so damned afraid it might be a child. . . . I've been on the hunt ever since. All the villages, Layer Wood. I never thought of poor old Sutton. . . ."

Hooting, the vet came up behind George, who just had time to shout,

"Can you give me some supper? I've had nothing since . . . I'll just see if I can lend a hand. See you!"

Hoping for the company of Ella and Alice, more or less expecting Terry, I'd made a huge casserole, rich with the mushrooms which had just begun to whiten one of George's meadows. I had also a dish of what in high places is called Pommes Lyonnais, simple to make, tasty. Followed by baked apples and cream, this was a good meal, whether one called it supper or high tea. Alice seemed to have resigned herself; Ella was happy, full of talk about her plans. George and Bob had a lively argument about insurance.

That little whining wind which makes indoors on an autumn evening seem to be so extra-valuable sprang up; and now I could look around with satisfaction. All is safely gathered in—at least for the time being. . . .